RUFIUS

Sarah Walton

For Catherine,
Enjoy the Read!
Sarah

BARBICAN PRESS

First published in Great Britain by
Barbican Press in 2016

Barbican Press, Hull and London
Registered office: 1 Ashenden Road, London E5 0DP
www.barbicanpress.com
@barbicanpress1

A CIP catalogue for this book is
available from the British Library

ISBN: 9781909954168

Text designed and typeset by Tetragon, London
Cover by Jason Anscomb of Rawshock Design

Printed and bound by Totem, Poland

for Martin, my mentor

All persons who have the shameful custom of condemning a man's body, acting the part of a woman's, to the sufferance of an alien sex (for they appear not to be different from women), shall expiate a crime of this kind in avenging flames in the sight of the people.

ROMAN LAW, 6 AUGUST, 390 AD

You sleep with big-dicked boys, Phoebus, and what is erect on them is not erect on you ... I used to want to believe you were a soft male, but rumour has it that you are not a *cinaedus*.

MARTIAL, 3.73

The great and holy temples of Serapis will pass into formless darkness

THE PROPHECY OF ANTONINUS,
4TH CENTURY AD

'Aoi aoi aoi'

PISTIS SOPHIA,
4TH CENTURY GNOSTIC CODEX

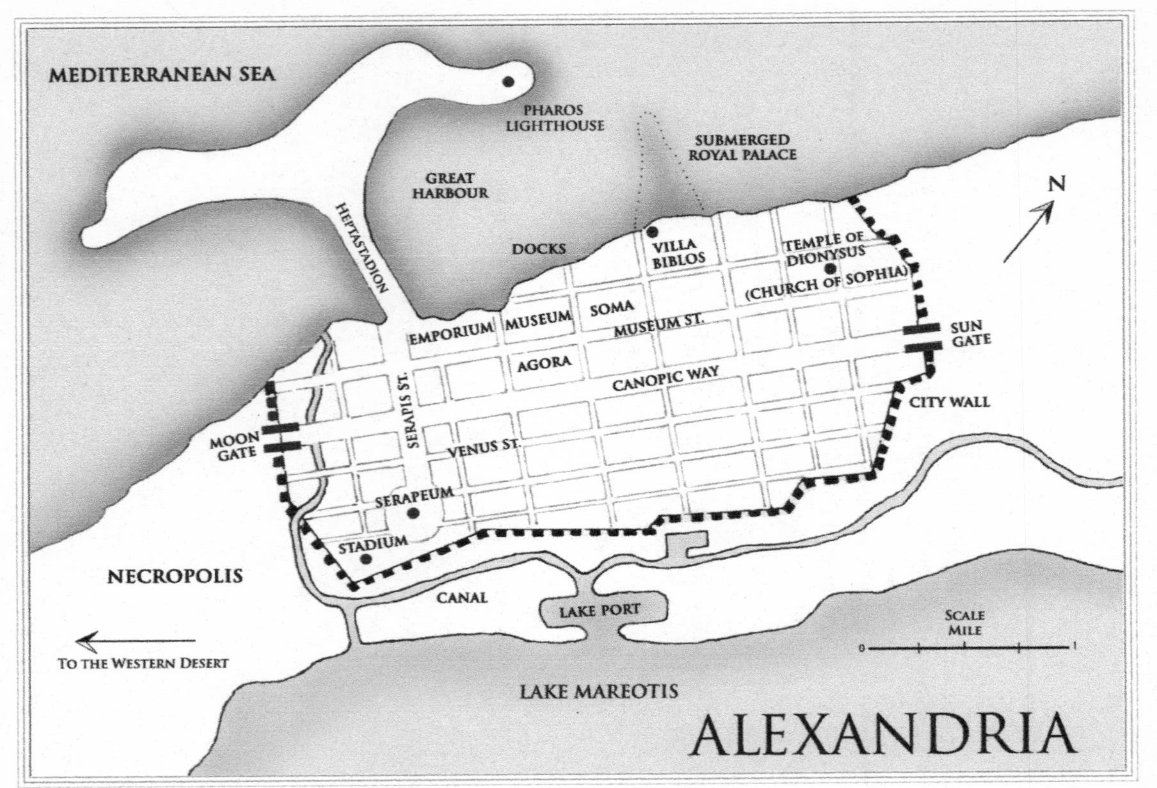

Fourth-century Alexandria after the AD 365 earthquake

PART I

PROLOGUE

366 AD

The scream of a desert cat startles the hermit and his snake hisses in its basket. Wrapped in a blanket on the altar, a baby gurgles. His father stares into the fire in trance. The man is a seeker; he paid in dates for a prophecy for his newborn son. The hermit did not ask what tragedy sent the city man trudging across the Western desert. His job is to find answers.

The hermit's deep chant echoes around the cave and across the rocky canyon. Any words will work, but the sacred vowels usher in the silence quicker and are always the first to come to his lips: 'Aoi-aoi-aoi.'

A vast black night stretches out beyond the entrance. Dera the Hermit imagines the whole world is a peaceful desert, the excesses of Empire a hallucination. The hermit's huge black hand glimmers as the fire throws shadow and light around the small cave. He mutters faster, 'Aoi-aoi-aoi,' and touches *The Book of Wisdom* on the rock-hewn altar.

The seeker's limbs tense. He snorts cold desert air in quick breaths. The signs are always the same. Bile burps onto his chest. It's the sacred plant that makes them puke – the bitter seed the hermit crushes to send the seekers into trance. The seeker's blue eyes flick open, fretful. He wails like a woman stalking a funeral procession and his eyes roll white in their sockets, head stretched back on a vein-tense neck.

'Serapis … my son …'. He stares at the fire in his solitary vision, his voice a torrent of urgency, 'It is time. Return to Alexandria, Dera.'

The hermit's spine stiffens at his name. In the desert the hermit has no name: don't drag me into your vision, city man. Dera the Hermit must remain detached to facilitate the seeker's vision, interpret the hallucinations, remind him of his gibberish when his soul returns to his body.

The seeker's arms stretch out in delirium, hands clench and unclench. His back bolts upright and he stares into the fire like a man possessed. Flames flare and spark.

'The Serapeum will fall.' The seeker's voice has acquired the depth of an oracle.

That is an ancient prophecy, thinks the hermit. A hot fever prickles his body as the shape of Serapis forms in the flames. Dera the Hermit watches the vision in the fire, his gaze unblinking as the god's features sharpen, his beard sprouts, the basket of grain on his head glows gold. Never, in all his years of divination, has Dera the Hermit seen such a clear apparition: polished-bronze with sapphires for eyes like the statue of Serapis in the Serapeum at Alexandria. It keeps growing. The hermit's jaw gapes open as his neck bends backwards to look up at the god's sombre face – the basket of grain's nearly touching the rough rock ceiling.

'Darkness will consume The Temple.' The seeker's words echo round the cave. Dera's snake hisses in its basket.

Serapis blackens and crumbles and smothers the flames. The vision is gone as quickly as it came. Smouldering embers give off an acrid reek of sacrifice and an atmosphere thick with grief fills the cave. To soothe his heart, Dera the Hermit touches the sacred book – a tick to calm his nerves, fetish of the faithful.

The seeker slumps back against the cave wall, eyes wide, rolled back to the whites. 'Protect my son.'

Dera doesn't respond – there's no point: the seeker's not aware of the hermit's presence. 'Aoi-aoi-aoi.' He chants louder to quell his unease.

'PROTECT MY SON.' The seeker shouts the order like a general.

Is that a boy in the flames? The image forms. A child's blue eyes stare out from the fire: a face so lovely, a gaze so clear and innocent it could thaw the most jaded, depraved soul. The boy is writing. Paper blackens, curls and burns; letters unpeel and lift off the page like tiny insects: the black tails of the alphas, the round bellies of the omegas.

Dera the Hermit gasps at the sight of them: the sacred vowels. 'Aoi-aoi-aoi,' he mutters and touches the book again. This is a sign – a sign from Holy Sophia. An omen.

The boy's face cracks and crumbles to ash.

As if the baby senses its own fate, it gives out a shrill cry.

A sob rises in the hermit's throat. The soles of his feet find their balance on the cave floor as he shuffles the short distance to the altar. He picks up the swaddled baby and holds him close to his chest, stares at the embers and chants as if the sacred vowels were a lullaby, 'Aoi-aoi-aoi.'

The seeker is spent, face slack, eyes closed. The plant sucks a man's knowledge then spits him out. The baby's father will sleep until morning.

Sweat cools on the hermit's brow in the night air. The vision has left him with an urgent purpose: he must protect the baby. This boy must never learn the sacred art of writing, or he'll be doomed like the Temple of Serapis to which this child's fate is linked.

'Destinies can be changed,' mutters Dera.

Red paint from the crucifix on the cave wall has peeled and flaked off. Life's impermanence is mirrored in the holy places of the Snake People – they do not build for posterity and their sacred decoration will not be discovered by future generations.

Dera stares at the cross and mutters a prayer: 'Sophia, Holy Spirit of Wisdom, if this is my path guide me.'

* * *

This was a time – or rather, on the cusp of the age – when rational men sought the wisdom of oracles and sacred chants written in ancient languages were firmly believed to hold magical powers. Neither man saw Rufius in their desert vision. But who – with the exception of a horny god with a naughty sense of humour – could predict Rufius?

Σ

RUFIUS

—Thirteen Years Later—

379 AD

'Ouch. Careful. Give me that here.' I snatch the hand mirror from the poor wretch who has the misfortune of being my cabin slave. Let's inspect my shave.

'You've cut me, you little shit.' The dab of bright red on my throat's making me woozy. I detest the sight of blood, especially my own. More importantly what's happened to my eyebrows? 'By Bacchus, I look like I've just witnessed my own death! Off with the kohl. This simply will not do. Quick, quick, wipe it off.' At least he's plucked them clean, but with all this swaying about it's impossible to paint them on with any precision. I'll have to look surprised for the remainder of the voyage.

In the hand-mirror I watch the boy duck behind the chair. Clever lad: put some distance between us. Ha! I don't have the energy to strike you, dear, but it's amusing watching you jump. Lovely-looking boy. Earthy pink-brown skin's rather fetching: rustic, but healthy. His eyes, shadowed by thick lashes, resemble a deer. Apollinos chose well. The boy's been a diversion.

'Where were you born, dear?'

He shrugs his shoulders and laughs at my question – at the idea of having parents perhaps?

'You very handsome, master.'

'Piss off.' He's not admiring me. They once had, when my hair was black, and not creeping away from my brow like a thief in the night.

'Fill my glass, boy.'

What a drag. *Avoid the pirates*, Damasus had said. I could strangle him. Who'd have thought I'd be cast off to the East? I must be the only *cinaedus* exiled in the history of the Roman Empire. Exile's a punishment reserved for senators and poets. Legally it's a valid sentence for my kind, but no judge would bother … unless bribed by Damasus, the Arch-bloody-bishop of Rome. Curse you, Damasus. I'll fleece you for this.

A worthy task, Rufius. Imperial business, Rufius. An honour, Rufius. The thought of Damasus in Rome, and my assets left unguarded, was a concern. He'll be livid when he discovers I paid some of his thugs twice as much as he does to protect my estates, and ensure the wine and olive oil gets to market.

We believe in one God, the Father Almighty. Maker of all things … and here's the bit those crackpot bishops quibble over, whether the son was human or not: *And in one Lord Jesus Christ the Son of God, that is of the substance of the father, bla-bla, true God of true God* …

Damasus' sibilant mutterings of the Nicene Creed's been going round and round in my head the whole way from Rome. The prayer hisses in the night as I lay in my bed. True god indeed! When did Olympus become so bloody exclusive? I should have held my pagan tongue. It's getting mixed up in Damasus' battle for the papal throne that sent me off to Alexandria. And now I'm sucked into his treachery. He murders men and women for being heretics, but he'll gladly sell their sacred books to the highest bidder.

'By Bacchus, the hypocrisy!'

Take that, Damasus! My beaker flies at the cabin wall and bounces onto the floor.

'Sorry, master.' Poor boy, cowering as he crouches to mop up the wine.

'Bah! Curse that Archbishop and his double chins – at least he has a few more than me.' Men are tortured and beheaded without a trial for being in possession of heretical books. Exile and in league with that scoundrel! But what choice did I have when he waved the law at me … and the Emperor Gratian wrapped around his fat finger … *need I remind you of the punishment for being a cinaedus, Rufius?* I recall the smell of the roses in the Lateran Basilica that day. Yellow rose petals, crushed in Damasus' hand, fluttered through his fingers as he spat out the word *cinaedus.* His laughter at having me cornered still makes me shiver with rage. I'll fleece him for this. If he thinks he's getting fifty percent of the profits he's misjudged me. The best way to hurt Damasus is in his precious purse.

'Pharos,' shouts a deck hand. 'Lighthouse. Starboard.'

'Shut him up will you, dear.' I reach out to stroke the slave's hair. 'I can't tip you, but I can give you a kiss.' He lets me pet him, ready to jump away at the slightest angry twitch. He'll receive a decent tip for putting up with my ill temper. Simple joys, like surprising slaves with the odd forbidden possession, are what keep my pulse throbbing these days.

'Wonder of the World. Starboard.'

Footsteps hurry on deck above us: bloody tourists. Such a fuss for a Lighthouse! I blame the artists. There are some fine paintings, but artists are prone to exaggeration. It's bound to be an anti-climax.

The boy's jigging about. He wants to see it. A rare inquisitive notion motivates me to throw myself up the narrow wooden stairs.

'Let's see what all the fuss is about shall we, dear? Lead the way.' I'm more interested in the Serapeum – my new battleground.

The boat dips forward. I lunge with the sudden motion and grab the slave's shoulder for support. Dear Bacchus, these old knees are not seafaring. The boy's skinny legs hold my weight.

My hand clenches the side of the boat. Spray from the waves splashing against the hull will make me stink like a fisherman.

Alexander's city planners were organised, I'll give them that: wide avenues, row upon row of polished marble, some blocks nine stories high. A well-planned city, but boring. Rome's messy streets and alleys disguise hidden thrills to satisfy the most rampant hedonist.

My cabin slave points and grins like an imbecile. 'Look how wide the roads are, and so white, and the towers are so high, and gardens on rooftops, and the Serapeum, master, look …'

The boy's jabbering. That's more than he's said the whole voyage. But why?

Alright, the harbour's large, but 'Great Harbour' is arrogant. The long walkway clad in white marble that joins Pharos Island to the mainland is a tad unusual, granted. True, the gardens, leading up to the island, are immaculate. So Alexandrian gardeners can root out a weed from a rose: big deal!

The colossal pink eyesore at the top of the only hill must be the Temple of Serapis – The Temple, some writers call it. Nothing in Rome, Athens, Carthage or even Constantinople comes close in size. How vulgar!

The Serapeum dominates the skyline, at the top of two hundred steps behind high pink walls. Famous as the most magnificent temple in the Empire and home to half of the Great Library's collection. Part temple, part fortress, part library. Like its god and everything else in Alexandria, the Serapeum is a Greek-Eygptian hybrid.

The Serapeum is the hub of Egypt's wealth. Serapis is responsible for the Nile's annual flood and Egypt's grain keeps the Empire fed on bread, pastries and cakes. But it's the Nilometers, which measure the water levels and enable the gold-diademed Priests of Serapis to set taxes, that give this god his real power. Ha! Money, as ever, is at the root of divinity. Local bishops must be itching to get their greedy paws on it.

'So that will be my new arena,' I mutter.

'Look, master, Lighthouse …'

'As I thought, the Pharos is an anti-climax.'

The Lighthouse dominates Pharos Island – I squint and shield my eyes with my hand – its polished bulk reflects the intense sunlight. The last thing I need is a tan. My crows' feet will grow whiter than they already are. Ghastly! Poseidon stands on top of three hulking sections of white marble. Hoards of tourists hang over balconies eating some rubbish they've bought from the stalls below. The fools must have queued all morning judging by the length of the line waiting to enter.

A mirror winks at its apex. 'That is where they light the fire at night.' I point. That irritating paternal feeling comes over me, as it often does in the presence of a young mind I can feed some worthless fact. The boy's face is a picture. If only I were so easily pleased. 'And those four statues at each corner are Triton.'

He looks at me blankly. Bacchus only knows what minor desert deities he worships.

'Triton, king of the seas. He calms the waves with a blow of his conch-shell.' I wag my finger and bellow above the roar of the waves pelting salt into my clean-shaven face – ouch, my cut's stinging. 'Wretched boats!'

The slave turns and grins at me. No doubt about it, I want to hit him. It's not this gormless boy's fault I'm disappointed. Those hyperbolic artists have ruined it. Oh, is there anything new for me to experience in this world? A sigh farts from my lips. I might as well go back downstairs. The Pharos has failed to charm me – profound reflection is best reserved for boys and wine.

The Alexandrian Library is delighted, Rufius – a great scholar from Rome. Damasus was being sarcastic. But there were those lectures on The Phaedrus in the forties. I must have written something important since then. Oh, the poems of the fifties are still in circulation among the few discerning readers left in the Empire.

I'm going to puke. The land in the distance swerves, tips the white city forty-five degrees south. My stomach churns.

'Slave!'

Here comes the retch. Red wine splats the deck. What was that I ate for lunch? Cod. Its white flesh now pink lumps of vomit.

'Oh, my whole life's a disappointment!' Where's Apollinos when I need him? I've hardly seen him the whole voyage.

The cabin slave scrambles after me. I slam the cabin door behind me loud enough for him to think it is his fault. Let him gawp at the view all he pleases. It will fuel stories for his grandchildren: the day he sailed into Alexandria and beheld the Seventh Wonder of the World.

Who's this ugly fellow? 'Tickets for a tour of the Serapeum, sir?'

How do I say piss-off in Greek? Oh yes, I remember.

'Piss-off!'

The Egyptian looks suitably shocked and scuttles off to find another mug to prey on. Where, in Bacchus' name, is Apollinos? I'll tan his leathery hide for abandoning me here with this rabble.

'Whooa!' I must sit down. It still feels like I'm on that bloody boat the way the ground's swaying about. This bench will do.

Some urchin will fleece me sitting here. We need transport. I've a good mind to sell Apollinos.

'Hello, hello, sir. I help you find chariot? You very proper Roman man. No good you sit here alone.'

Too eager. I hate it when they suck up. His complexion's yellow. I've seen every skin colour imaginable and heard at least twenty different languages – Alexandria's more cosmopolitan than Rome and Constantinople put together.

'Piss off, dear.' No need to look so shocked. 'I said, piss off. Your ugly head's blocking my view.' Just pretend you're sightseeing, Rufius, and this rat of a foreigner will get the hint.

That must be the Museum's gold roof. Its white marble columns stretch high above the surrounding buildings. The ancient institution houses the bulk of the Great Library, the Serapeum has the rest of the books. Why do Alexandrians have to describe everything as great?

At least we're in a Greek city. There are probably more eunuchs in Alexandria than in the whole Empire. No Alexandrian will turn their noses up at kohl eyebrows. Bugger it! That cabin slave let me disembark without my eyebrows. By Rome's standards, I'm practically ordinary. Look at the strange black lines painted on that man's face … or is it a woman? Oh, I feel quite at home!

Let's try walking again.

No good: I'm still swaying … as if the invisible strings that hold us to the surface of the planet have slackened … what did Archimedes call the phenomenon? Oh memory, memory. Who cares? I need a stiff drink, a good scrub and a blowjob.

Where is my welcome party? Surely the Library's sent some skinny Egyptian slaves to distinguish me from the disembarking rabble of Roman tourists and businessmen.

There's Apollinos. His eyesight must be failing him.

'Apollinos.' I wave. The tall Greek rushes over, all fuss and apology.

'I've a good mind to flog you, Apollinos.'

'Yes, master.'

He clicks his fingers. Three slaves run over with a cold cloth, a jug of wine and a glass cup. That's better.

'I trust you had a pleasant voyage, master?'

'Don't be ridiculous, Apollinos. Where's my ride?'

Why's Apollinos trying to direct me towards a row of desks in front of the storehouses that run parallel to the docks? The Greek sign says 'Library Customs'. Am I in charge of that as well as the Scriptorium?

The commotion and crowds, combined with me ignoring him, makes the veins bulge on Apollinos' neck.

'The Museum sent these slaves, master.'

I won't be keeping any of those ugly creatures.

A scrawny-looking slave addresses me. 'Is that your book chest, master?'

'What of it?'

'Every book needs to be registered at the harbour office for copying.'

'Apollinos here will deliver my books and manuscripts to my Museum office tomorrow.' I don't want my library getting mixed up with the thousands of manuscripts taken for copying from every bloody boat docked in the harbour.

'But policy …'

'Bugger policy, dear. I am the new Director of the Scriptorium. Argue with me and you'll be back in the gutter.' Oh, my Greek's all coming back to me. Marvellous.

'Your Greek's fluent, master.'

'Don't sound so surprised, Apollinos. Now toddle off and deal with the harbour officials for me, dear. You have the Archbishop's letters?

'Yes, master, but …'

'Shoo.'

That will tie-up Apollinos for the rest of the day. I'll rescue him later. Let him sweat for a bit as revenge for neglecting me.

'And don't take all day, Apollinos. We have slave shopping to do later … and lighten up, or I'll replace you with a younger version.'

'Yes, master.' He knows I'm just tired and crotchety.

'Now hail me a ride. Those gorgeous boys carrying that sedan chair will do.'

Shopping can wait. First I intend to orientate myself. There is one place I've heard talk of that mildly sparked my interest.

Apollinos frowns but runs over and points in my direction. Here they trot. Lovely movement. Four galloping beauties.

'Where are you going, master?'

'Venus Street.'

The two at the front giggle. How sweet!

AESON

Good, Dera's out. Dad's tool bag's scratched a wiggly line in the dust behind me. Just need to pull it into Dera's room and I'll be off. Tools are no use to me now; Dera can sell them and return to the desert. He never liked the city. Hermits are more at home in caves. A shiver goes through me. Feels like the red cross painted on the wall above the wooden box Dera uses as an altar is watching me. Need to be quiet. I don't want to wake Dera's snake in its basket.

Smells of Dera in here, spicy like his sweat. Apart from the snake basket and sleeping mat, rolled up in a corner of the room, it's empty. Dera was the hermit who gave Dad the prophecy about the fall of the Temple of Serapis, and of my fate. I never understood why Dera and Dad argued so much over what his vision meant. Dera may have come back to the city and got odd jobs as a brickie to pay his way, but he was always hidden away in his room, praying to his Christian god. Have to get out of here … before I lose my courage.

Mustn't look back. Feels like the limestone apartment block behind me, the only home I ever knew is tugging at me to turn around and go back. Familiar smells of the brickie wives' cooking remind me I've not eaten yet today. Just keep on walking. Focus on the wide palm-lined street ahead. Stomp the wobbly feeling out of my legs: that's it, big steps. Don't stop. Nearly at Serapis Street.

Feel crap about not saying goodbye to Dera, but he would have tried to stop me, nagged me about the prophecy. Heard enough of

Dera's and Dad's arguments over the meaning of their drugged-up desert vision to know neither of them knows my fate.

My load's light and lonely without Dad's tools, but a man who's changing his destiny don't need to lug his past with him; he only needs money. That's the most grown up thing I ever thought.

Exotic noises from the Emporium boom outside the copyshop, tucked under the arches of the arcades. Dad said everything the Empire produces is for sale here: colourful silks sold by flat-faced Eastern traders, spices and woody-smelling incense from India. Lions roar in cages, talking parrots call to shoppers in the endless rows of stalls and shops.

'Silika for the cripple.'

Where did that voice come from? It makes me think of milk and honey.

Ouch! What's that? A stick knocks my leg.

'Down here, Aeson.' Big dark eyes stare up at me. A girl cripple. Her gaze is tight on me, like she's looking right into me.

'How do you know my name?'

She's got a huge snake round her neck!

'Dera sent me.'

Dera? She must be one of the Snake People. I want to ask her why he sent her, how he knew where to find me, but I can't take my eyes off the snake. It's huge, much bigger than Dera's. Wrapped round her neck, browns and blacks and green and white lines move in waves as it holds up its head. The skin on both sides of the snake's head fan open.

'Ah! It's a cobra!'

'Don't be afraid, this is Sophia. Say hello, Sophia.'

As if it's doing what it's told, the snake spits out its long tongue. I jump back.

'Give her a stroke. She's friendly.'

'No way! Cobras are poisonous, Serapis knows!'

'She's trying to smell you, silly. Snakes smell with their tongues. Anyway, the Holy Spirit of Wisdom is inside Sophia. She's never bitten anyone.'

'How do you know Dera?' Steady your voice, Aeson. She's just a cripple with a snake.

'Go back home, Aeson.'

'I'm not being told what to do by a crazy cripple.'

The girl just keeps looking up at me with her big, round dark eyes.

'Aoi, aoi, aoi.'

That's the prayer I've heard Dera singing from his room for thirteen years. She's a Snake Girl alright.

The copyist smells of ink. He stares down at the purple marks he's made with his reed pen on a corner of parchment, replaces the cork stopper on Dad's glass ink-bottle, puts it back on the desk and narrows his eyes as if to say, *where did you pinch this from?*

My useless inheritance, ain't it? Dad, a brickie born and bred, left me a bottle of ink, a statue of Serapis and a bag of tools. I can see his feverish face staring up at me, his dying wish: *write, my son. Don't jump ropes like a monkey. Learn to write.* My promise to him was as mad as his dream – that I'd learn to write. Purple ink won't feed me and he never trained me up on the tools. Convinced he was, certain I'd become a scribe. Serapis, curse that prophecy.

'Well, how much will you give me for it?'

We both look at the bottle on the desk. Ink's useless without the skill of the sacred art, so I'll have to sell it to buy some lessons, won't I?

'Five silikas and no more.' The copyist talks like a honey-nose.

Five silver coins sounds like a fortune, but how do I know what ink's worth? Let's try my luck.

'Ten silikas and you got a deal.'

The copyist looks like he's trying not to smile.

'It's your lucky day. I'm feeling generous.'

I hold open Dad's drawstring purse before he changes his mind and watch him count the coins as he drops them in. That's more silver than I ever seen.

The hullabaloo of the Emporium makes me feel dizzy as I step out of the shop.

'Silika for the cripple.'

She's still here, smiling up at me. Pretty for a cripple. Her stick clicks on the ground as she uses it to pull herself up on to her one good leg. The foot of the other one is shrivelled, the size of a baby's foot. She must be about my age. Big, round Egyptian eyes with that far away look Dera has when he's having a vision. Need to keep my focus on the snake.

'Aeson, where are you rushing off to? Wait for me. It's important. You must go home.'

Dad's dead. Ain't got no home. I'm getting out of here. She's doing my head in.

I weave through the crowds, and leave the click of her stick behind me. Can't shake the memory of cementing Dad in that low, dark hole in the tomb wall. Got to perk myself up. Now I have everything I need for my quest.

KIYA

Sweet Sophia, what's Dera got me following prophecy boy for? I expected Aeson to be a bit more unusual. Henite will be wondering where I am. I have to be at the Necropolis before sunset to finish inscribing the tomb. If I nip down this alley, I'll cut him off. Well, I s'pose his beauty is unusual, and those piercing blue eyes, the colour of sapphire … the same colour as the gems in the eyes of Serapis in the Serapeum.

This pillar will do. He won't see me waiting behind here. After chiselling stone, it's good to breathe in fresh air. Dust is caked inside my nostrils; I'll have a good pick later. Sophia's scaly skin undulates around my neck where she's wrapped herself. I like her weight on my shoulders – makes me feel solid and heavy on the earth. Snakes' bodies are all muscle. I wish I could move with their grace, instead of jerking along on my crutch.

Here he comes. Out with the stick.

'Ah! What the …'

He's down in the dust. Go get him, Sophia.

Laughter bubbles up in my chest at the sight of Aeson pinned to the pavement by fear at the sight of Sophia slithering towards him.

'Get that snake away from me.'

'Sorry, Aeson, but I need you to listen to me.'

'Why should I?'

'My name's Kiya. I'm a tomb-inscriber.'

'You're a crazy cripple with a snake. Leave me alone.'

Sophia hisses.

Aeson shuffles back on his arse. People always keep their distance when Sophia's with me. God's Holy Spirit protects me.

'Because you are in danger. You're not safe in Alexandria. Your fate is bound to the fate of the temple and the temple is doomed.'

His blue eyes roll.

'Not you too! I'm sick of hearing about my fate. I'm me own man.' He shakes the leather purse tied to his belt. 'Here, this is my only link to Serapis – have it. Serapis knows, it didn't bring Dad and luck.'

He raises his right arm and throws something at me. 'Take it.'

It lands and spits gravel up at the bare ankle of my good foot.

'I'm sorry, Aeson.' He's an orphan like me. Silently I chant, *Aoi-aoi-aoi-amen.* Dera the Hermit says the words have a healing frequency. I feel Aeson's anger collapse, fall away as I continue to chant, *Aoi-aoi-aoi-amen-aoi.* Let the healing thoughts lap his body like the waves caress the beach. Sweet Sophia, work your magic.

I slip down my crutch and pick up the tiny statue of a household god.

'Serapis.' It's been skilfully chiselled.

'Dad prayed to this stupid chunk of wood all his life and now he's dead.' His voice cracks. 'Maybe he'll bring you better luck. With your leg, or something.'

I prop my crutch under my armpit so I can hold the tiny statue in both hands. It's so light, the wood so smooth. I know as well as any Alexandrian the form of Serapis with his beard and basket of grain on his head.

'Grief makes us do odd things.' I know that well enough in my job. Night after night I watch mourners beat out their grief on their chests, tear the skin on their cheeks with bloody nails … although most women cheat and buy a beaker of blood from the local butcher to paint their faces.

What's this? A faint sound – not audible, but with a quality Dera, Seth, Henite and the other holy Aberamenthos have taught me to hear with my mind – makes me still my breathing. Concentrate on the silence, block out the city noise. There it is: a ring of bright, white energy only years of continual prayer can create buzzes around the statue.

'I can't take your god.'

'Don't blame you. He's useless.'

'You're mistaken. It's too powerful to give away.'

I hold out my arm. 'Sophia, come here.' She slithers up and back around my neck. Released from the snake, Aeson gets up with the grace of a cat.

'Here, take back your god. Keep Serapis safe.'

Aeson looks sad as he takes Serapis. He tucks the god into his purse.

'I'm sorry about your Dad.' Dera called Henite to nurse his dad, but she said he'd given up on life by the time she arrived.

He nods. 'How do you know Dera?'

'Dera's a holy man.'

'That's what Dad used to say. He's clever alright, but I'm not buying into no prophecy.' His eyes roll again. Sunlight makes them even bluer. Celestial, Seth would call them.

'Dera has visions.'

'Having visions don't make you holy.'

My heart's beating so fast. Sweet Sophia, maybe Aeson's an angel … all that energy round the statue of Serapis. I'll know if I touch him.

'Give me your hand.'

'Why?'

'Please.'

His hand is warm. There's definitely divine energy coming off him. Sweet Sophia, it's throbbing all over me!

'Ouch, you're strong for a girl.'

He pulls his hand back and laughs.

'Aeson?' I know that deep, calm voice. That's Dera the Hermit.

We both look back towards the Emporium exit. The hermit's size always surprises me: Dera the Hermit must be the biggest man in the world ... and the gentlest ... funny how people cross the street to avoid him. Strong as the columns of the Temple of Serapis. His skin glistens, tight across muscles like aubergines. He never comes to church. Seth says hermits are loners. But he has that calmness about him all Aberamenthos have. Please, Sophia, help me grow wise like our holy ones.

'Aeson, come with me. It is what your father would have wanted.'

'My father wanted me to be a scribe.'

'You are not safe in Alexandria, Aeson.'

'Dera, I'm not coming with you.' Aeson sounds like he wants to run into Dera's arms, but instead looks up at the tall wall next to us, uncertain. 'Bye, Kiya.'

'Aeson, come with me, please.' Dera stretches out his great sea-monster arms towards Aeson.

With one quick movement, Aeson runs up the side of the wall, pulls himself on to a window ledge and is away. He won't get far – there's a gap in the buildings. Sweet Sophia, he's going to jump it!

'Aeson, don't jump ...' I'm not sure if my voice can reach him.

He's mad if he attempts that jump. He looks back at Dera, then at the gap between him and the next block, takes a few steps back and launches himself at the wall on the opposite side of the street.

The huge African runs along the street adjacent to the wall.

'Aeson, you promised your dad not to climb. I'll find a way to pay for your apprenticeship, put you on the tools like you always wanted. Aeson, come back.'

Aeson stops, turns and yells back, 'I promised Dad I'd learn to write and that's what I'm going to do.'

We watch Aeson disappear over the rooftops.

'Dera, why don't you stop him?'

'Not even I can jump like that, Kiya.'

'Are you sure he's the prophecy boy … I mean he's not taking it very seriously?' And I didn't expect the prophecy boy to be so smelly.

'You know every nook of Alexandria, Kiya.'

Dera's gaze shifts to the desert dunes, beyond the Serapeum on its hill.

'Where are you going?'

'The Necropolis. He might go to his father's grave.'

'And if he's not there? I heard your thoughts. You're leaving us, going back to the desert, aren't you?'

Dera laughs a strong, hearty laugh. 'You're a sharp one, Kiya. Keep listening like that, with the wisdom of Sophia, and you'll make a fine Aberamentho one day.'

My cheeks burn hot at the compliment. Me, an Aberamentho!

'I'm going back to the desert, Kiya.' His aubergine hand looks camouflaged against Sophia's skin as he bends down and strokes her. He looks me straight in the eye. 'Keep close to him, Kiya. Any trouble, tell Henite or Seth. They know how to find me.'

My cheeks blaze hotter at the honour of having a task other than inscribing dead people's tombstones.

AESON

Reckon I lost him. Even Dera can't keep up with me. The Canopic Way that cuts across the city and joins the East and West Necropolis seems bigger than usual. It's so wide I reckon two ships could easy fit side by side across it. Tall marble buildings make me feel small. My bag strap's too long, but not as long as it was last month. How tall will I grow? Tall as Dera? That would be top.

A boy-racer swerves as he charges past in his chariot. Thinks he owns the road, he does. Some honey-nose's son. Dad told me to stick to the main roads. Look where caution got Dad? I'll nip down this side street, away from the traffic.

I swallow the puky feeling that's lodged itself permanently between my belly and throat. If I play at guessing smells that will keep my mind off Dad. Flare my nostrils and inhale. Incense, but which? Amber. No. Patchouli. Horseshit. Shit doesn't count as it hides behind every smell in Alexandria. Rotting vegetables. Cabbage, that is. Fresh baked bread. Grilled meat … and honey … sweet-chicken sticks. Yum! Sweet-chicken brings back happy memories.

What's that noise? I look up the street. The Khamaseen roughs up my hair as it speeds through the alley off the desert. Thousands of voices hurry past on the wild wind: I've sniffed my way to the games.

A cheer goes up from the stadium. Dad bought me sweet-chicken the last time he took me to the games. We'd sat with the other labourers on the marble steps, gawping at the rich on swanky cushioned balconies as exotic as the beasts and gladiators.

The sun's low in the sky over the Western Necropolis. Didn't Dad say something about tickets selling cheap for the last fight of the day?

Umm, sweet-chicken. My stomach groans. Food stalls skirt the huge walls.

'Five chicken sticks please.' Dad would call me greedy, but I'm my own man now.

The face of the chicken man shines with sweat, like he's coated in honey too. He peers at me through the smoke from the grill, hands me the sticks and coughs. For a moment I thought it was Dad's feverish face.

'Sir – what about my change?'

'What change?' He bellows it. People push to be served, laugh and point at me. My cheeks burn. Reckon I've been conned, I do.

Drum rolls signal the last fight of the day. There's the ticket man.

'Lucky you are, lad. The Prefect of Alexandria's got Saracen back on.'

'Saracen!' My gob goes limp like an idiot.

'Chop, chop or you'll miss him. I've got ten on him myself.'

I bite the chicken sticks hard between my teeth, and open my bag to get my purse.

'Don't worry about that, lad. Hurry up those steps or you'll miss him.'

'Thank you!'

The ticket man chuckles as I rush up the stairs to the cheap seats. Ten what? Surely he didn't bet ten silver coins on Saracen. Ten silver coins is what I got for the ink, and now the chicken man done me over, I got nine.

Another drum roll; I'll think about it later. I run through the arch and squeeze onto the back step of the top tier. The cheer of the crowd is one big, throbbing roar. My body thumps with the pulse of the stadium. Can't believe I'm going to see my favourite gladiator in the flesh.

A huge man swaggers, sword and shield in the air, into the arena and stops in front of the Prefect's balcony. He must be Saracen. From up here the gladiators and beasts look tiny, but I know Saracen's shape from the toys in the Emporium. He's not as tall as Dera, not as black either, but he's wider. And his legs are bigger.

Dera don't like the games – *Alexandrians are a mob in the stadium*, he'd nag. I think the games are the best thing ever.

'SaraceEEEEN.' My voice is lost in the wild cheers of the crowd. Hands above my head, I clap in time. The stadium vibrates with the thump of feet on marble. It's like my little cheer is a small part of a huge pounding marble beast with a roar of a voice.

Round, flat pieces of bone are being exchanged for money on all sides of me.

'Saracen. Never lost a match yet. Double or nothing,' shouts the bet-maker next to me when the rush for roundels slows down.

Dad warned me against gambling: *only hard graft brings a man wealth.*

But I've got Serapis with me. I root around in my bag and pull out the little statue and clench it in my palm. Kiya said it's powerful. 'Double my money, Serapis.'

'Last bets,' shouts the bookie.

'Five silver silikas' worth, please.'

Saracen swings his sword around his body. The crowd's cheer sounds like a roll of thunder.

I tug at the bookie's tunic, hold up Dad's old leather purse and shake it so the coins chink.

He gives me the once over. 'Show me your money.'

The silver coins wink pink in the sun streaming through the huge arches of the stadium as I empty them into my palm. The bookie's eyebrows rise and his brow wrinkles like one of the fat elephants parading around the circle below.

'Only five? Saracen's never lost!'

A sweat breaks out on my top lip. He's never lost ... and I've got Serapis.

'Well, what's it to be?'

Make some magic happen, Serapis.

'Nine. Nine silver silikas.'

I drop them in his big open palm. He passes me a large bone disk and laughs. It's got an X on one side and some letters on the reverse. I remember what Dad said they say: *I promise to pay.*

'You'll be a rich young man before the sun sets.'

I clench Serapis in one hand and the roundel tight in the other. Eighteen silikas, I'll win. And I'll spend them all on writing lessons, I promise, Dad.

The Prefect nods to signal the start of the fight.

Saracen's muscle-bound opponent runs across the arena – exotically white, with hair almost as pale as his skin – mouth wide open towards him. They circle each other like animals. I chant with the crowd. The gladiators look like they're shouting at each other, but it's too noisy to hear them.

Saracen throws himself at his opponent.

The audience holds its breath.

He knocks the white man down.

We all gasp.

They're on their feet.

We sigh, a huge, loud sigh.

Again and again they plunge at each other – charging, circling, striking, then falling apart. The audience breathes in time with their moves. It looks like a dance from up here, a violent mime. The crowd's reaction is the only sound.

They throw themselves together again. This time they don't pull back from each other. Saracen's opponent throws him down. The white man holds the black man face-down to the sand, one knee into his back.

'Saraceeenn. Get up. Saraceeeenn,' we cry.

Like he hears us, he throws his opponent off. But the white man's too quick, slicing his sword at Saracen's ankles. Down Saracen goes. Sand sprays up with the impact.

He's up again, with a cheer. He has a loyal following. Every time Saracen throws him off, his opponent throws him again. He's fast and fights in a strange way, less with the sword, more with the body, like he's wrestling. Sometimes Saracen fights from the ground, writhing around like a river crocodile, swinging his sword like the scaly creatures throw their tails. These are not men. They're ferocious like animals, strong as gods. Perhaps they are gods.

Saracen loses his footing again. Are his ankles cut? He's unstable on his feet, lurching like a drunk. I'm too far away to see the damage.

I clench Serapis.

'Boooo!' The crowd is losing patience with their favourite. Not me. I'm behind you, Saracen.

The white man's lost his sword. His right arm's limp, hanging like a dead chicken. Saracen's on his knees, sword still in hand, he sways in the dust. Lifting a leg, he slumps, elbow on knee, head hung over.

His opponent stretches for his sword.

Their movements are slow and heavy.

Saracen collapses onto his hip and elbow.

The roundel is sweaty in my fist, nails pinch it into my palm.

Eighteen silikas. Come on, Saracen. Get up.

'Saracen. Saracen. Saracen,' I chant. My whole body wills him off his elbow and up onto his feet.

Saracen stumbles, but makes it to standing, takes slow swaying steps towards his opponent. The other gladiator desperately reaches for his sword again.

He gets hold of the hilt and sends his sword flying towards Saracen.

The crowd gives out an 'ARHHH.'

My stomach clenches. My nails dig deeper into my palm around the roundel.

Saracen sways, but keeps his footing. He draws back his arm to plunge his sword. My thighs, calves and toes grip as he sways around, disorientating his wounded opponent. My body mimes his movements.

I swing each blow with him. I feel the strength of the Saracen's arms and legs. His huge back is mine. This is how it feels to be strong. My bulrush arms are solid muscle. My body obeys my will. And when Saracen thrusts the fatal stroke, we slay our opponent together.

The relief of survival roars from my lungs. 'Saracen. Saracen,' I chant with the crowd.

Panting, I sit back down on the cool, marble step, grin and look up at the bookie beside me.

He grins back.

I take a second look, although I know it's not the man who I gave my money to.

Where is he?

I scan the crowd. He must be here somewhere.

Maybe he's gone to piss. He'll be back.

I wait.

The crowd starts to spill out of the archways leaving stadium seats empty.

Gone! But he can't have gone!

The puky feeling's back, along with a strange dizziness, like all that wasn't real. I'm not really in the stadium. Didn't really lose my money, did I?

I crouch down to look along the row of steps, past the crowds. Maybe he's sitting down.

'Get up you drunk.' A sandalled foot kicks my arse.

I stand back against the marble columns to avoid the scrum shuffling and elbowing for the exit. My heart pounds. When the crowds are gone, and only a few men and women sit settling bets, I search the rows, running up and down, desperate to find the bookie.

My gut tells me the bookie's shafted me, but I check the exits again to make sure.

Pink light sinks below the arches and I slump on the steps near the arena and sob. I'm broke! Cleaners sweep and pick up rubbish around my feet.

'Stadium shuts soon, lad.' A short Egyptian man looks down at me from the row behind. 'You don't want to be locked in. They say dead gladiators stalk the steps at night looking for their killers.'

Forehead on knees, I stare at my dusty big toes hanging out of my sandals.

'Alright, I'm going.'

I walk down to the front row. Arena's stained with huge patches of blood. Six cleaners drag away the last of the lions by his mane. What had he made of the stadium? His back's singed black, flesh raw and hanging loose, his yellow mane soaked in black oil.

'Why … didn't you … train me up … on the bricks … Dad?' I shout between sobs.

Stupid chunk of wood. 'I hate you Serapis. I don't believe in you.'

I chuck Serapis as hard as I can into the arena. The tiny statue disappears in the huge circle below – too light even to spray sand. Dad would say throwing Serapis is shameful. I slump down on the step and spew. Chicken splats my toes, still smelling like sweet-chicken, not puke.

If the gods exist, they don't give a shit about humans. Greedy gods. You've taken my dad. We're just like that lion to you.

I turn my back on the quiet, bloodstained arena. Still holding the bone roundel, I walk to the exit swaying like I've been mortally wounded.

The sweet smell of honeyed chicken hangs in the air. Got to spit to get rid of the taste on my breath.

Outside the stadium walls I stare into the faces of the stragglers milling around. Give it up. You idiot, Aeson. The only people left are slaves and labourers who pull on ropes to bring down the huge canopy that shielded the stadium from the Sun. The bookie's well gone.

5

AESON

'Oi you! Lazy good-fer-nufink! Get your skinny arse up that rope and make yourself useful.' A big man, whip slung across his broad chest, leers at me.

'Me?' I look around. A dozen or more boys, some men judging by their strong shoulders, pull themselves up the ropes that hang over the stadium wall. A few carry torches in their mouths like dogs with sticks. Nobody behind me. All the stallholders have packed up and gone. He's talking to me.

The rope he's pointing at is the only one without a boy on it. Frayed, it swings in the breeze that creeps off the desert at dusk, the tail end of the Khamaseen. He thinks I'm one of his workers.

'But ...'

'Don't you give me no buts. Do you want to feel this?' He points at the whip coiled round his chest. 'You're lucky to have a job, you lazy good-fer-nufink Greek.'

People always think I'm Greek. It's the colour of my eyes. Most Egyptians want to be Greek.

'Me? I'm Alexandrian.'

'Don't give me no cheek. Up you go or your arse will be so sore you won't sit down for a week.'

Who's sniggering? Snorts and titters come from above. Think I'm funny, do they? Twats!

'You won't climb it by looking at it. Scoot. Up you go. I got dinner waiting for me.'

A boy with a mass of hair messy as a bird's nest swings near the bottom of the wall. He's got a hiccup of a giggle that makes me want to laugh too. He grabs the free rope next to him and shakes it. 'Come on, man. Pretend it takes you to Olympus.'

So hiccup-boy thinks I'm scared, does he?

Climb me, the rope's saying. But I promised Dad. *Don't climb, you monkey*, that's what he said. Promised him, I did.

'You asked fer it.' The boss grabs his whip and lunges towards me. By Serapis, he's going to whip me!

Sorry, Dad! Here I come, rope ... and jump. The burn of the dry, course fibre feels good on my palms.

My feet push against the wall: lean back at an angle and bounce myself up, one hand over the other. That's how it's done. I'm practically running up the stadium wall. This is top – the easy buzz of being good at something. Saracen must feel like this when he swings his sword. My lightness makes me want to laugh like the boy. Where's he gone? Still half-way down the wall. He's not confident on the rope.

Boss's mouth is moving, but I'm too high to hear him. Now I've found my rhythm, the workers have stopped laughing – I'll reach the top before all of them and they know it.

The wall juts out here, where the arches are. It's harder to climb as the rope don't hang flush against the wall. Let's wind the rope round my leg, make a temporary tension to pull myself up. That's it. Now arms pull one after another against the rough jute fibres.

Made it. The wall's so thick I can't dangle a leg either side. If I stand up I'll still have loads of room both sides of me. It's like a circular road. I slowly stand. My gut and arse tighten for balance. I raise my arms over my head like Saracen did when he won and punch the sky. Bet Dad never had a vision I'd stand on top of the stadium wall and look out over Alexandria. Surprises are better than prophecies.

The sky's blue-black except for the pink fuzz that hangs over the sea by the Western Necropolis. Hope Dad can't see me now. Sorry I didn't keep my promise, Dad, but I've got to make difficult choices now I'm a man. The last of the pink sinks into the ocean, and the Necropolis disappears except for the lines of torches on the seawall and down the main street that passes under Moon Gate connecting the City of the Living with the City of the Dead.

Some boys look nervous perched on top of the massive white marble wall, check their footing and peer down. Never rely on my eyes; I trust my body to adjust itself to keep my balance.

A couple of men with long stretched muscles from climbing ropes pour oil from vials hung round their necks onto the Stadium torches, and light them with the small torches carried between their teeth. The metal supports are spaced close together, so the stadium looks like a hovering gold halo at night. Their hair's been shaved like temple slaves. Maybe it's been singed off. Others pull at the knots securing the canopy: that must be my job.

Torch-lighters and canopy-knotters work alone. On site brickies worked as a team. The torch-lighters have the easier job; they don't have to leave their ropes and risk losing their balance on the wall. From this height a fall is certain death. Canopy-knotters struggle; they fear pulling too hard and falling backwards when the knots loosen. I've seen it on site: men so scared of falling they can't work. Teamwork's what we need up here.

Hiccup boy next to me is really screwed, giggles long gone. His eyes are tight shut, his body rigid … maybe it's the torchlight, but his skin looks scaly.

I swing to get close enough to jump on his rope. Dad's voice nags inside me, *don't climb like a monkey.* Reach, and jump.

His rope jerks with the extra weight.

'Fucking nutter! Man, what you doing? You'll kill us both.' Voice a panicked squeak, eyes wide with terror he looks down at me.

What filthy feet he's got.

'Two's better than one. Hold tight. I'll climb up next to you.'

'Steady, man.' His voice trembles and he clings to the rope. I'll have to manoeuvre up and around him.

'Put your right arm round my neck.' He's shaking. 'That's it, hold on to me.'

We're face to face now. His skin's scaly like a desert lizard, rosy for an Egyptian. His smell's musty like street sleepers. Big dark trusting eyes, lips full, mouth wide. I want to kiss him, tell him he's safe. My legs wrap around his and pull close to his hips. He clings tighter round my neck. It makes me feel strong.

'Don't worry, I've got you.' My voice is low, cock hard against his hip.

He blinks, like he's seen me for the first time.

'Breathe.'

He gulps and pulls in closer to me.

A wolf-whistle from one of the boys makes us laugh.

'Let's get this knot undone. I'll hold the rope still while you untie the canopy.' Now twist the rope taut round my legs to steady myself so I can get a strong grip round his waist.

'That's got it.' He wipes the sweat from his palms on ragged trousers. Only barbarians and slitty-eyed traders from the East wear trousers. His chest's bare and hair sprouts where mine's still smooth. He's no older than me though. Serapis, give me chest-hair soon. No point asking Serapis. Left me skint, he has.

'I'm Aeson. Why you wearing trousers?' I hang backwards, hands free, arch my back, and grin up at him. I'm showing–off.

'Careful, man.' The brickies used to give me that look when I did somersaults.

When we're all back on the ground the group of women who've been waiting for the canopy sections get busy folding. The boss swaggers over clapping. Look at that stubble. He's a real man. I need a razor. My wispy down makes me look younger, not older.

'In a line, you monkeys.'

We arrange ourselves in a knotty queue of different heights and ages. The usual colourful mix of faces: hybrid city boys like me.

Boss-man clicks his fingers and points me and hiccup boy to the back. 'You two last.'

We shuffle forward and the boss slaps a coin in each boy's hand.

'Well, well, our Greek monkey.'

'Alexandrian born and bred, I am.'

'I stand corrected!' His mock bow makes the boys laugh as he presses two coppers in the palm of my hand.

'Thank you.'

'Share those between yer both, seeing as you're joined at the hip.'

'But Boss, that ain't right. I never asked him to help me.' Scaly-skin's pissed-off.

'Don't be late tomorrow.'

'Don't call me monkey.'

'I'll have you lighting torches tomorrow, you cocky kid.' He touches his whip. 'Scoot.'

How many of these coppers make a silver silica? I must have lost a lot of money. Bet Dad never knew there was a job for rope-jumpers. But I'll not let him down … learn to write somehow, I will.

'Oi, deffo. Give me that or I'll fight you for it.' Scaly nudges me.

'Here, catch.'

I flick him a coin.

He bites it. Happy it's real, he puts his hand inside his trousers. Something flops out. A purse … it must be tied inside. A narrow line of dark hair between his belt and his bellybutton makes my cock throb. Scaly strokes his flat stomach and shoves the purse back inside. He likes me watching him.

'You an acrobat or what?'

'Used to be a brickie.'

'Man, what you doing odd jobs for then, if you got a trade?'

'Never got trained.'

He's looking at me like he's deciding if I'm worth talking to or not.

'You got a place to sleep?'

'No.'

'Join us?' I follow the nod of his head to the group of youths and boys standing under an old fig tree. Normally I wouldn't talk to street kids. Dad said they'd steal your food from your mouth if you chewed with it open. But if this copper won't buy me a sweet-chicken stick, it won't get me a room for the night.

'Where do you live?'

When he laughs he drops his head back so far and opens his mouth so wide, I can see the dangly thing at the back of his throat through the gap in his two front teeth.

'Croc is my name.' He snatches hold of my wrist to introduce himself. I thought only warriors and gladiators greeted each other like this. His grip's strong – there's something solid about him, now his feet are back on the ground.

'What sort of name's that?'

'Some name's are given. I earned mine.'

Did he earn it because he's got crocodile skin, or because he wrestles like a croc? Better not ask.

He slaps me on the back and heads over to the fig tree, picks a fig, gives it one chew and swallows.

'Patch, where's Turk?'

A boy with a patch over one eye shouts back, 'Venus Street. You coming?'

We head off. The gang arrange themselves in twos and threes, joking and throwing bits of junk around in a game without rules. We're running parallel with Serapis Street towards the docks. Eye-patch boy throws me a hunk of bread. It's stolen, but it feels like a game.

Four boys who disappeared down a side street run back shouting, 'SCARPERRR!' Angry voices shout after them.

We leg it.

'Come on, Aeson. Sounds like Roman soldiers.' Is that their feet pounding, or ours?

Croc shoves his hand in mine and cuts down a narrow alley. He knows the roads. We dart down this one, then the next, kicking up dust as we skid fast round corners. At each one I catch a whiff of the sea. My heart races faster than my legs. Never been in trouble before, I ain't.

Croc skids to a stop on the corner of a street I don't know. There's an arch at the entrance to it.

'Phew, that was a close one. Soldiers don't know their elbows from their armpits, eh, man?' He nudges me, breathing heavily.

A grubby-faced lad about sixteen struts over in a bright yellow toga. It's folded all wrong. 'Catch!' He chucks an apple in my direction.

Curse it, I was too slow. The apple rolls into the gutter.

'So here's the pretty boy everyone's talking about.'

'Turk, this is Aeson. He's good on the ropes. Got nowhere to sleep tonight.'

They all have made up names like gladiators.

'Ain't it a shame, Lanky.' Turk calls to a tall, skinny boy – more man; he must be at least sixteen – I hadn't noticed slumped under the archway. He looks up and down the street, then at me, plucks a streetlamp from its bracket, walks over and holds the torch to my face. His lips don't cover his brown teeth. Even when he closes his mouth they're bare. He looks like a skeleton, like there's not enough skin stretched over his long, bony body. I avoid his eyes: they're scary.

His bony fingers grab my jaw.

'Greek.' His spittle makes me flinch.

I pull away. 'Alexandrian, I am.'

'Don't mind Lanky.' Turk takes the torch from him. 'Let me see. Um, blue eyes, eh. My new client will love you.'

'Pretty's more a *cinaedus* than that fat Roman.' Lanky's still hovering over me.

'Don't you call me a *cinaedus*.'

Croc hiccups, trying not to laugh. What did Lanky have to go and call me a *cinaedus* for? Anything but that.

'Lanky, I beg to differ. A little on the skinny side, but get those arms pumping iron and fattened on chicken … Pretty has potential, eh?'

'My name's Aeson.' I don't like the way Lanky's looking at me.

'Aeson, of course. Now, you two hand over the rent.'

'But man, he only gave us a copper each tonight.'

'No rent, no room.'

That made me shudder. It's the second time someone said that to me today. Can't believe it was just this morning the landlord chucked me out.

Croc flops his purse out of his trousers. I dig in the bag still strapped across my body for mine.

'Come on, you know the rules.'

Our coins chink in Turk's dirty palm. Didn't keep my first wage for long, did I?

'Follow me, Pretty.'

'Aeson. My name's Aeson.'

Lanky scowls and pokes my shoulder to hurry me down the street: a hotchpotch of cheap facades trying to look grand. Oil lamps shine on painted walls and statues of Aphrodite – Venus, the Romans call her – welcome men into taverns. I know what street this is. Alexandrians call it Venus Street.

6

Aeson

If Venus Street ever had an official name, nobody knows it anymore … maybe the Greeks called it Aphrodite Street before the Romans arrived? Latticed shutters open wide where women sit, boobs out, heckling after no one in particular:

'One silika, all night.'

'Make you a happy man.'

I stir beneath my tunic. Venus Street ain't as cheap as it looks. One silver coin! No wonder Dad told me to stay clear of it.

Drunk men loll outside bars under red canopies on oversized cushions, tunics hitched up to their bollocks, and grope women in colourful togas who whoop and shriek.

'Keep up, Aeson!' Croc knocks my elbow and grins.

Music, singing, grunts of pleasure louder than the muffled moans of the brickie-wives come from inside buildings. Is Croc a virgin? Nah, can't be. He's so cocky.

'Man, stop gawping.'

Boys position themselves along the street at intervals and pose like statues of the gods set into the alcoves of the stadium. Turk's talking to a tall, fat man at the other end of the street.

'Man, this is my spot. Turk's waiting for you. By the look of the gold dripping off that old Roman, your ship's come in tonight.' Why's Croc winking at me?

When I'm close enough to hear their conversation, I hover behind Turk.

'New in town, sir?'

'Ha! Some assistance at last! Show me your trade, dear.'

The fat Roman has a *cinaedus'* lisp, but his voice is deep, not high like a woman. Hand on his hip … he must be the *cinaedus* Lanky mentioned. A Latin word, but it's the same in Greek. Romans pinch all our words. Usual curled hair and eyebrows painted on like a eunuch, but there's something different about him …

Turk points at the gang posing along the street.

'That's Patch, the one with the eye-patch.'

'I can work that out for myself, dear.' He adds impatiently, 'Show me a boy in good condition.'

'A man of fine taste. In that case let's start top end, eh?'

'I'll see for myself.' The *cinaedus* sweeps past Turk like a senator; he doesn't flounce like a woman. That's what sets him apart: his walk, his Roman determination. It's the most impatient walk I've ever seen.

'Come on, *cinaedus*, Show us what you've got.' A woman hangs out of a first floor window and heckles like she's at the theatre.

The *cinaedus* pouts his lips, puts his hand on his hip and lisps, 'At least I don't look like Venus after a night on the town with Bacchus, dear.'

She laughs and blows him a kiss. I can never work out if people love or hate the *cinaedi.*

As the fat Roman glides past the row of boys, Croc puts his hand down his trousers, pulls out his empty purse and laughs his hiccup giggle. The Roman laughs too.

'Rubbish! This is the scrawniest, most diseased bunch of street urchins I've ever had the misfortune to lay my eyes on. Most of them are too butch for my liking. I may be a *cinaedus*, dear, but I don't like my boys too old. I like them young, but not too young. On the cusp.'

'On the cusp, eh?' Turk looks at me.

The Roman walks over to Croc.

'This one at the end's passable. Clean set of teeth, but what's wrong with his skin? He might be fun for a night if you can't show me anything better …'

He's spotted me. The Roman gasps like an actor, a kohl eyebrow rises: he's a *cinaedus* alright.

'… and who's this lovely creature …' He trails off when his eyes meet mine. Makes my skin prick like it's alive the way he looks at me, but I'm not being his bit of rough trade.

Turk slings an arm round my shoulder. 'New boy … on the cusp … but Pretty's not trained up yet, sir.'

'I'm a man, I am. Thirteen. Aeson, sir.'

I clasp the man's wrist with the same force Croc clenched mine. His hand's soft as a woman's.

'Oooo, what a manly introduction, dear!' He stares at me like he wants to eat me. 'Olympian eyes … and the grip of a gladiator.'

I'm used to people being put into a kind of trance by my eyes. I like it, makes me feel powerful.

He turns to Turk. 'I'll take him.'

'I'm not his. I'm me own man.' Not going to be pimped by Turk, I'm not.

'Ha! You cheeky Siren, playing with an old man's feelings.'

Turk frowns and points back down Venus Street. 'Pretty, wait at the end of the street, eh.'

'I'm talking to the boy, dear.' The Roman doesn't look at Turk. He's focused on me. 'I do hope you reconsider. My name is Rufius. It's a pleasure to meet you. When we meet again, perhaps I'll have my slave give you a Roman shave.'

Knew I should get rid of this bum fluff.

'All deals go through me,' Turk butts in, and clicks his fingers for Croc who runs straight over. 'Take Crocodile, sir. He'll show you a good time. Pretty can entertain you when he's trained up …'

My face is burning up I'm so angry. He takes my money and now he acts like I'm some slave at the Emporium. My teeth clench.

'Don't … Call … Me … Pretty!'

Rufius' eyelashes flutter as he looks at me, shy like a young girl … like I'm the man.

'It doesn't suit you, dear. Beautiful, a tad androgynous, but not pretty.'

'Like I said, eh, he's not trained up.'

Turk ushers Rufius and Croc to the end of Venus Street, where they get into a sedan carried by four exhausted-looking boys.

Patch looks disappointed as the sedan turns the corner. 'Croc'll get a more comfy sleep than the rest of us.'

7

RUFIUS

How in the name of Bacchus do these sedan curtains open?

'Stop there, dears – at the entrance to the Museum.' The dishevelled trotting boys look relieved.

We fall out the sedan and stagger to the gate. Crocodile's good fun. He dragged me into nearly every seedy bar and whorehouse in Alexandria. Shame the feisty Aeson couldn't join us.

'Why wouldn't your pimp let me take the Greek boy?'

'Cos' he's new. He don't know the rules.'

The Museum guard's nearly as old as me. Who appoints these mongrels?

'All librarians must present their identity cards after hours, sir.'

Insolent slave! Doesn't he know who I am? Well he's about to.

'You are addressing the Director of the Scriptorium, Rufius Biblus Catamitus. I'm here to inspect my office.' My speech is slurred, and I'm swaying about like I'm back on that bloody boat again. Crocodile puts a hand behind my back to steady me. Sweet boy.

'Apologies, sir. We expected you earlier. Your secretary has arranged your rooms.' He bows and eyes Crocodile with suspicion. 'Who is this?'

'Let my guest pass or you'll regret it.'

His gaze drops to the floor as he takes a step back, and waves at the guards to open the gates. Crocodile puffs out his chest and struts through into the gardens after me.

The massive Greek columns would dwarf Damasus' churches back in Rome … and the roof, lit by hundreds of torches, is an eruption of gold. Crocodile isn't impressed. He flicks his hands through the water fountains and splashes me. Playful, but simple.

'So d'ya live 'ere at the Museum then?'

'I have an office here and another at the Serapeum.'

'Where's your house then?'

'Overlooking the harbour I believe.'

'Don't yer know?' He laughs.

'I arrived this morning.'

Suitably disinterested. Good. I dislike whores nosing into matters that don't concern them.

A hinge squeaks. It cuts across the hush of the Museum gardens, and a guard opens the night door at the side of the large main entrance. No doubt grumpy at the gate sent a messenger ahead of us down some hidden pathway.

The entrance hall is enormous. Crocodile stops by the statue of the Muses and looks up. Alabaster glistens in the torchlight … the three colossal women have the fresh faces of young boys.

'Nice tits.'

'I'd prefer them without the udders, dear.'

A slap of sandalled feet makes Crocodile turn. I can guess who that is: Apollinos in his usual flap.

'Master, master.'

'You'll have to excuse the slave, Crocodile, dear.'

'Master.' Apollinos is sweating so much it looks like he's bathed in his tunic.

Crocodile slaps the foot of Memory, throws his head back and hiccups with laughter. His passion gap reminds me why I brought him here.

'Unauthorised guests aren't allowed into the Library after hours, master.'

'Rules are made for breaking. Now, do you have something for me?'

'Rules for breaking. Like it, man. Philosophical.'

Apollinos looks at the boy as if he's a bad smell – Croc's tatty trousers are a tad musty – and passes me a small wooden box. Um, a sniff of those intense earthy tones is enough to relax me. One of the benefits of Alexandria: good quality intoxicants. Perhaps it won't be quite so dull here after all.

'That will do. Where did you get it?'

'The Emporium, master.'

Apollinos swipes Crocodile's dirty fingers off the wall paintings. Trying to scratch off the gold leaf? Ha! The rascal.

'Oi, get off, will ya?' Crocodile shrugs him off.

'Apollinos, lead the way. My guest is hungry, I'm sure.'

'Starving, man.'

'You just can't get the slaves these days. I do apologise.'

'Man, I can see that.' He's still laughing away. It amazes me how jolly street urchins can be.

Not a bad sized room, generous terrace … the frescos will need modernising.

'It's a bit on the poky side, wouldn't you say so, Crocodile?'

'Can't swing a cat in 'ere.'

'This office has a splendid view of the Great Harbour, master.' Apollinos holds back the curtains for me to see. The Lighthouse casts a yellow glow over the water.

'If I want your opinion, I'll ask for it.'

The cushioned seating built into the terrace is ideal for entertaining.

'Wine and music for our guest, Apollinos.'

'But, master, there's a letter, from Archbishop Damasus of Rome.'

'Hand it over.'

The snap of the seal sends a pinch to my heart. Curse Damasus! I'm like a slave to him now. He's not written this – cautious as ever. If we get caught, it won't be Damasus' neck under the executioner's sword. His first order: *The Gospel of Philip* and *The Book of Wisdom.*

'Here, Apollinos, check these books are in the Library catalogue.'

I exaggerate a sigh. Crocodile sighs too, then hiccups. Ha!

Apollinos frowns as he reads.

'The Archbishop requests the delivery is made in two weeks … a Constantinople address. Master, that's a tight deadline … and who will deliver the books? I've already acquainted myself with the catalogues: the Library has *The Gospel of Philip* stored in one of the warehouses on the docks, but *The Book of Wisdom* is not in the catalogues … '

'Oh do stop panicking, Apollinos. Damasus wants us to sweat and I refuse to get my toga in a twist for a jumped up bishop. Do I have to do all the thinking around here? It's quite simple. We borrow *The Gospel of Philip* and have it copied. Then we find the church, or whatever hovel the Ophites are hiding in, and …'

'Ophites haven't been heard of for at least a century, master. What if the Ophites are extinct and their books buried with them?'

'Then loot their tombs, dear. You know as well as Damasus why that book is in demand. Ophites taught that Jesus was a mere man, that any man can attain divinity. At the rate the bishops are condemning heretics, there won't be any books left that teach anything other than the Nicene Creed soon. Basic economics of demand and supply, Apollinos. That book is valuable.'

Apollinos nods towards Crocodile who is leaning forward, elbows on knees, listening with keen interest.

'Perhaps I should fetch the guest some food, master … and we continue in private?'

'Maybe Crocodile can help us?'

'That depends, man.'

'Well, of course, Crocodile, I can see you are a man of business. I'll make it worth your while. We're looking for a group of Christians.'

'Man, give me more to go on than that. Alexandria's full of 'em.'

What was it Hippolytus wrote about them in his *Syntagma*? Ah, yes … 'They wear the mark of a serpent on their earlobes.'

'You mean the Snake People. They keep to the desert, but you sometimes see 'em in the Agora on market day.'

'Where do they live?'

He shrugs and plucks a fig from one of the two trees potted in large urns either side of the terrace. 'Where's the grub?'

'On its way.' Apollinos' tone is curt. Ha! How he despises my taste for rough trade: a delicacy suited only to the discerning palate.

'Send a slave to fan the boy. He's sweating nearly as much as you.'

Apollinos opens the door, mutters an order to the slave outside who pads over to the terrace with a peacock feather fan.

Crocodile lounges back on the cushions, one hand thrown over his crotch.

'Dunno where the Snake People live, but it's easy enough to find out.'

Street urchins are so resourceful.

'How?'

'Follow them. The women come to the Saturday night-market to sell baskets. Me and the boys don't bovver with 'em. They got nothing to pinch.'

He picks up the fruit knife and tests the blade, cuts his palm and squeezes it to stop the bleeding.

'Saturday is tomorrow, master. You have a welcome dinner with the Head Librarian.'

Apollinos snatches the gold knife from Crocodile's hand before he can slip it under his belt. 'That's Library property. You can't trust these street kids. They're all thieves.'

'Ha! Takes one to know one, doesn't it, Apollinos. We're little more than thieves now Damasus has us under his fat thumb. Off you trot.'

Two slaves enter as soon as he's gone. I recline and pretend not to notice Crocodile slip a knife under his trousers as a slave kneels to remove my sandals.

'Crocodile, come and sit here and tell me all about your little friend.' I pat the couch.

'Which little friend?' He strokes his groin. 'You mean Aeson?'

'Both, dear.' I've drunk too much to cause a stir, but as long as he's hard, we'll have some fun tonight.

'Man, give us some of that.' He nods at my wooden box. 'And I'll tell ya all about him.'

Two slaves enter with washing bowls for our feet.

'Watch it! That tickles.' He laughs like he's choking.

'My dear, if they weren't so filthy you wouldn't need them scrubbed so hard.' I'm laughing too, but at the look of disgust on the slave's face.

'What's that on your arms and legs?' His limbs are scaly like he has some sort of skin disease. As the slave scrubs they turn red and blotchy.

'That's why they call me Croc.' He grins.

'After your scaly skin. Why don't we all have names which mean something … what would you call me?'

He rubs his hand on his fine stubble. 'Peacock, is what I'd call yer.'

'Why Peacock?'

'Cos you dress like an old Pharaoh, and you got a low hanging belly and a skinny neck.'

'You might want to work on your seduction technique, dear.'

The slave at my feet is smirking. He deserves the bowl kicked in his face … drenched the little shit. Serves him right.

'Bring beeswax and a pipe. Let's smoke Dionysus' health, dear.'

'What's the beeswax for?'

'Your flaky skin. It must itch terribly.'

He stares at me with surprise. He's probably never had a tender thing done for him in his life.

'We don't want you shedding your skin over my cushions like a snake.' I don't want to spoil the atmosphere and get too paternal. He's the entertainment after all. 'Well take off your trousers so the slaves can wash you down, dear.' I like them cheeky, but clean.

His name does suit him. He's scaly all over.

'What do you want me to do when I get to where the Snake Women live?'

'Apollinos will fill you in on the details.'

'What you after? I wanna know what I'm getting into here.'

Perhaps there's more he can do for me. To borrow all the books Damasus demands will eventually raise suspicions.

'Crocodile, how good are you at climbing?'

He looks nervous all of a sudden. 'Like climbing walls, you mean?'

'Yes, walls, terraces, roofs.'

'You want Aeson. Climbs like a monkey, he does.'

'Interesting. And would you and Aeson be available to do a job – for me, not Turk?'

'Sounds like you need a librarian, not a thief.'

'Out, slaves. That's quite sufficient.' I must keep a muzzle on my mouth. Damasus is shrewd. I must be careful too. As Apollinos keeps reminding me, in the East they gladly administer the death penalty just for handling heretical books if there's so much as a hint of magic in them.

Croc gets up, slides his cock back and forth in his hand and waits for me to turn my arse to face him. They've covered his skin in so much wax we'll slip all over each other … beeswax might make a better lubricant than olive oil.

'Slave, leave the beeswax.'

'Good idea, man.' He sticks his hand in the pot, rubs the wax between his palms and coats his cock. By Bacchus, my sphincter's gasping for him – I'm in the hands of an expert!

'You see, dear, it mustn't look like an inside operation.' What's he waiting for back there?

'Let me get this straight – the Director of the Scriptorium, who has access to every book in the city, wants to steal his own books?'

He's laughing so much, his cock's bouncing.

'Well when you put it like that it doesn't sound like theft at all, dear.'

He throws his head back, pumps his arm fast and laughs. Delightful!

'Man, I'm blasted. The moon, the stars, they're all spinning.'

'Pop him in, dear.'

Kiya

Looks like us Snake People aren't the only ones using the old Egyptian tombs. Belly flat to the edge, Sophia curled up next to me, we watch.

Aeson's curly hair looks neat compared to the wild manes of the boys playing dice in a circle near him. Legs hugged up to his chest, he's not moved from the spot where the man in the yellow toga ordered him to sit.

Finally we found prophecy boy, Sophia. Henite said he's fated. If I save him, maybe I'll get my Aberamentho robes …

Boys perch on ledges and dangle dirty feet over the funerary area, lit up by torches like an atrium in a grand villa. The gang must have lived here for ages by the look of all the furniture: chairs of all shapes and sizes, tables, cooking pots and jugs of wine.

He must be the ringleader, the one in the yellow toga, lounging on a mattress plonked on top of the sacrificial stone table. Who does he think he is, the Emperor? On the ground in front of him, the group of seven, no eight boys argue over who's winning at dice.

'Patch, throw Pretty the dice. Make him feel welcome.'

Aeson gives the leader a look, shifts closer to the circle, and takes the dice from the boy with an eye-patch.

'We don't want Pretty to think we're not friendly, do we, eh? No wonder he did a runner on Venus Street. Show him we're all one big happy family, eh, lads?'

The ringleader leans on one elbow and swigs from a beaker. Why's he calling him Pretty?

'Pretty needs a copper to join the game.' A tall, skinny man tightens his scabbard round his waist and jumps down from the ledge. I hadn't seen him there. My heart-spasms flutter like flamingos fleeing from a lion. He has the dark energy of a demon. Long in the tooth, that grin is fiendish. Sophia juts her head forward and hisses. She needs a stroke. There, there, Sophia. Snakes are nervy creatures.

'I don't know how to play.' Aeson looks up at the ringleader. Who in Hades does he think he is anyway, dressed up like a grand Roman in that toga? I don't like the look of him either, but he's no demon. He's just full of himself.

'He don't know how to play, you hear that lads?'

They all laugh, dirty laughs like drunk old men.

'About time you learnt then, eh? Lanky will teach you.' The ringleader downs the rest of his drink and holds out his beaker. A young boy, no more than six, crawls onto the mattress and fills the beaker from a wine jug that's nearly as big as him.

The demon slaps Aeson on the back. That was too hard; it hurt him. Swine.

'You can't play without money.' The demon's toothy sneer shows both sets of long teeth, upper and lower. He's horrible. Aeson looks like he wants to punch him.

'I gave you all my money.' Aeson's voice sizzles with rage.

The ringleader laughs, props himself upright, pulls a coin from his purse and flicks it into the middle of the circle. 'That's a loan, Pretty.'

The boy with the eye-patch throws Aeson a playful grin. 'I'll have your copper before you realise what's hit ya.'

'Just try, cockeye.' Aeson has a tongue on him. That's good, these sort of boys respect rude talk.

'Nothing wrong with my eye. This patch is protection against spells.'

The demon, all long-limbed, knees bony and jutting out, sits cross-legged in the circle and leers at little Patch. 'I can put a charm on the other one for you.'

Patch drops his head and rattles the dice in the box. For no reason at all, the demon slaps him round the head. Nasty demon.

'What you do that for?' Aeson, keep your mouth shut. He'll hit you too.

The demon turns his toothy sneer on Aeson. 'You want an eye-patch too, Pretty?'

The slap of the demon's long, bony hand against Aeson's face stings my own. Sophia, what can we do?

Aeson's on his feet. 'Don't call me Pretty.'

Sweet Sophia, he punched the demon in the face!

Boys shift closer and chant encouragement, 'fight, fight, fight, fight.'

Sophia's tucked her head under my armpit. She hates commotion.

Aeson runs at the demon's ribs, but the demon grabs him by the waist and pins him down. Aeson swings and kicks for all he's worth, but the demon's too strong. His fist thuds down on Aeson's cheek, sending his head swinging like a ball on a string. Aeson's dazed. Oh, Sophia. What can we do to help?

The demon raises his fist again. Aeson just looks at it. Hit him back. Hit him.

'Eh, eh, Lanky, that's enough. We don't want Pretty losing his looks before his first night on Venus Street.'

Lanky the Demon is poised, arm back, fist clenched ready to throw another right hook. He loosens his hold on Aeson's tunic. Aeson slumps to the gravel with a crunch, rolls on to his side, hands over his face.

Sweet Sophia, is he hurt? We should fetch Seth … but what can he do? The gang's armed with knives and judging by the scars and bruises, this lot won't hesitate to use them.

The demon laughs and whips off Patch's eye-patch. There's just skin where his eye used to be, a permanent wink.

'Look, Pretty. Ain't much profit in one-eyed trade is there, Patch?

Lanky grins. 'You won't have those looks long, Pretty.'

'I, Turk, will decide Pretty's fate. Now settle down and throw in your bets, men.'

Turk talks like he's delivering a line he's memorised from a play.

Directly below me and Sophia, Aeson and Patch lean against the wall and watch the three players left in the game. Aeson's rubbish at dice – lost his coin on the first throw.

'The object is to finish as low as you can with all five dice you started with,' Patch leans over and tells Aeson.

Aeson nods. 'I worked that out too late.'

'Quiet!' The demon shrieks in his shrill evil voice, moves his focus from the dice on the ground in front of him to Aeson and back. Sweet Sophia, he's a vile, evil creature. Aeson keeps glancing over to the entrance, but there's no way he'll escape with the demon leering at him.

Patch pokes his tongue out behind Lanky's back, then looks at Aeson and grins. Aeson gives him a half smile, but looks tired. Don't trust any of them, Aeson, not even little Patch.

Turk yawns, pushes himself off the mattress and walks over to the entrance. He slaps one of the skulls hanging over the archway. It swings and clatters against the bones strung next to it. My heart flips – they're human bones.

'Lanky, anyone for debt-watch? Otherwise it's your turn.'

'I'm in the middle of a game, Julius Caesar.' Lanky's tone is a lash of evil.

'We all do our share here, Lanky.' Turk clenches his fist and smashes a skull square in the jaw. It's bottom set of teeth come lose and clatter to the ground. The boys' murmurs stop. All eyes dart from Lanky to Turk and back again.

Lanky continues to stare at the dice.

'Pretty owes me a copper. He's skint, so he can pay it off on watch.'

Turk clicks his fingers at Aeson, and points up to ground level.

'Don't owe no one nothing, I don't,' Aeson shouts as he walks past Lanky.

Aeson, don't argue with him.

'You little shit.' Lanky looks shocked, gets up, and stomps over to Aeson. Aeson's fists are up, his stance grounded.

'Lanky, sit down. Pretty, follow me. It'll do you good to learn the ropes.'

Right Sophia, round my neck, and keep quiet. We can follow them if they walk slow enough.

The tomb Turk's taken Aeson to near the seawall must be their lookout. There's a limestone staircase cut into the rock that leads to a high roof terrace. Let's squat behind this bush, Sophia, see if we can catch any of their conversation. It's hard to hear with the sea sloshing against the wall.

'First time you played dice?'

'I play by different rules.'

'Best to let Lanky win …'

The thud of a wave against the wall drowns out Turk's voice. Be quiet, sea.

'… you'll get a good view up there. If you're taken by surprise, yell. Got it?'

Turk gives Aeson a friendly slap on the back and walks off.

Aeson climbs the steps to the roof terrace then shouts, 'When shall I come back?' His voice is shaky – he's scared of the hungry ghosts, Sophia.

'Sunrise. No yelling unless there's danger. I don't want to come and rescue you from a fox!' Turk takes a few steps, then turns and shouts back, 'The Necropolis is the safest place in Alexandria.'

Turk holds up his filthy yellow toga like a young girl, and disappears into the shadows as soon as he's out of range of the torches lining the seawall. His silhouette appears against the faint glow at the entrance to the gang's hideout, then disappears below ground.

Up the steps we go, Sophia. My crutch scrapes the crumbly old limestone.

'Who's there?' Aeson's voice trembles.

'It's only Kiya.'

He stands at the top, fists clenched, jaw tight, feet set ready to attack. I can't see his eyes or his face. In the thin white blade of light thrown off from the Pharos behind him he's just a black outline.

'It's just Kiya and Sophia the snake.'

'You again! What are you doing here? You have to go. If Turk finds you, or worse Lanky, Serapis only knows what they'll do to you.'

'That demon doesn't scare me. You need saving and I'm here to rescue you.'

'Keep that snake away from me. Hooded snakes are deadly.'

'Sophia protects me. Look, stroke her like this. Feel her soft scales on your fingers? She's friendly.'

'Her skin's dry … and so warm …'

'That's because she's full of the Holy Spirit of Sophia.'

Good, Aeson's asleep at last, curled up, knees tucked to chest, head resting on his arm.

'Aoi, aoi, aoi.' The sacred vowels sung to the melody mothers use to lull babies to sleep has calmed the night. Even the sea is silent.

We must be quiet as we leave, Sophia. We need to get back to the church before sunrise or Henite will worry.

AESON

What's poking my leg? 'Ouch!' Hey, where am I? What's tickling my arm? I rub my eyes. Am I dreaming? Who's that standing above me? Why's the sea behind him? It all comes back at once, the stadium, losing my money, the gang. And crazy Kiya with her snake …

'Hey, dozy. Some watchman you are!' Croc stands over me tickling my legs with a stick, laughing. The hilts of two knives shoved in his belt catch the light from low morning sun. This tomb's roof terrace is higher than it seemed last night.

'Croc. You just got back?' I push the stick away and scratch my legs. Is that dirt, or are they getting hairier?

'I'll tell you about it later. Let's get some grub, man.'

'I told Turk I'd go back at sunrise.'

'Man, you're about three hours late then. Come on, I'm starving.' He grabs my wrist and pulls me to my feet. Does Croc ever stop laughing?

'Just gonna stash this lot.' There's a clatter as he picks up four silver cups by the piece of string he's tied around their stems. It's not string. It's a shiny cord that looks like it's come from some grand house. One of the knives slips free from his belt and falls on the dusty terrace.

Let's have a look at that. 'By Serapis! This is gold!' The hilt's studded in turquoise and coral.

Croc's foot kicks it out my hand. The pain makes my eyes water.

'Ask before you touch.' He's still laughing his hiccup laugh. I bet he giggled as he pinched this lot. He passes me the other knife. Smaller and plain, more of a food knife than a honey-nose's dagger. I bounce it in my hand – the handle's well-weighted. I know when a tool feels right in my hand.

'Keep it. You'll need it tonight.'

'Why?'

'Man, where can I stash this so Turk and his skinny side-kick don't find it?'

We look around. The Necropolis looks harmless in the blue morning sky. I was glad to have Kiya with me. When she left, I whispered her chant to block out the noise of rats scurrying through bushes. Won't tell Croc about that.

'I know, downstairs in one of the rooms. No one will snoop in the lookout – too obvious. Aeson, let's go before we're spotted up here.' Croc never calls me Pretty. Respect.

'Croc, what's happening tonight?'

'Meet me at the Agora at sunset.'

The Agora's massive. 'Where?'

'Temple of Antinous. We gotta job, man.'

'Who says?'

'D'ya want the knife or not?'

I shrug. 'Just wanna know the details is all.'

'Need to know basis.' He taps his finger on his nose, and runs down the steps, his stash clattering.

That rustle from the bushes at the bottom of the steps – that's no rat. The whole bush is moving.

'Croc, wait.' I catch hold of his arm to stop him going any further down the steps. 'There's something in that bush.'

'Just a bird. Man, you're jumpy.'

We stare at the bush.

'There's someone in there, Croc, watching us.'

'Man, I was the same after my first night on watch. You'll get used to it.'

Croc's probably right. We walk down the rest of the steps, silver cups clanking together as we go.

'You'll never guess where the old *cinaedus* took me last night.'

I'd heard some of the lads talking round the fire about their nights in the great villas with sea views and swimming pools and hundreds of slaves waiting on them like they was the Prefect of Alexandria.

'Honey-nosed was he?'

'Man, was he? Crazy too. Go on. Guess.'

'The Serapeum.'

He rolls his eyes and laughs. 'You're not far off.'

'Dunno – where?'

'Only the frigging Museum!' He looks at me, eyes wide. He gets the reaction he was after. My eyes widen too.

'No way you liar!'

'Un-bloody-believable, man! Pigged-out on meat and fish and cakes and pastries and quail and nuts all covered in honey and crunchy white flakes that tasted better than anyfink they sells in the Agora. Covered in coconut they was.'

'Coco-wot?'

'Coco nut. It's imported from the East. Brown hairy balls with a white centre. They shave out the white flesh and drink the milk.'

'Yuk! Is that where you nicked the knives?'

He winks at me and launches into another long description about the Museum's treasures. I touch the hilt tucked into my belt: can't believe I own something from the Library. It's worth a year of night-watches. I'm getting closer, Dad.

' … hundreds of slaves walk through the corridors all night long checking for fire. They can't be too careful since Julius Caesar burnt all those books down in the warehouses on the docks.' These are the Roman's words, not Croc's. 'Talking of warehouses, that's where our job is … Man, he's gonna pays us loads.'

'How much?'

'Handsomely, he said. How much d'ya reckon that is?'

I think about the ten silicas I lost and the copper I earned at the Stadium. 'Dunno. Is he paying us coppers or silver coins?'

'Handsomely's gotta be gold in my book, man.'

Gold! I've never even seen a gold coin. I touch the hilt of my new knife. I need a scabbard for this or it'll cut me when I sit down.

'I s'pose everything in the Library's made of gold.'

'The Library? Well I didn't rightly see the book rooms, but the Museum …'

'What was it like, Croc?'

'Man, ain't you bin listening?'

I hadn't meant the Library, but I don't want to ask what the sex was like directly.

'The work was over pretty quick.' Croc knew what I'd meant. 'Old guys are the best. Easy money. Grateful. I even got a massage from the slaves. Covered all over in beeswax. Look how shiny my skin is!'

It doesn't look flaky and dry anymore, but it's redder, and he's not itching today. Thought he had lice.

'I touched the Muses. Man, the marble must be polished everyday it was so clean.'

Imagine getting a private tour of the Museum!

'Mind your head.' We bend our knees as we go into a small damp room that smells of the sea. Croc kicks a loose brick from the wall, turns, laughs, and throws me the brick.

'Come on, give me a hand.'

'This is the best bit: Rufius – that's the Roman's name – he likes being shafted by boys.'

'No way!'

'No joke.' Croc bends over, slaps his arse and pouts his lips. 'Oooo, Croc, give it to me, Croc. Begged me for it, he did.' Croc's impression of a *cinaedus* is so funny.

'Man, can you believe it? A Roman acting like a woman! I mean

I'd heard about it, knew it happened, but you never fink you'll end up on a job with one of 'em, do yer?'

'I thought all *cinaedi* took it up the arse.'

'Course, man, but you don't get many *cinaedi* after young ones like us, do yer? They usually go for big, hard hairy men.'

'Like me, d'ya mean?' I pump the muscles on my arms like I'm lifting iron weights above my head and shake like it's too heavy for me to lift.

Croc looks at me serious all of a sudden. 'I reckon you'll be hard as iron one day, Aeson, no matter what Turk calls you.' The gap in his front teeth shows when he laughs. 'Not as strong as me though.'

I elbow him in the ribs and remember the hardness of my cock against him on the stadium wall. He takes a step closer. His lips on my lips surprise me. I can't remember being kissed since I was tiny. The sensation is foreign, my lips hot. I want him to do it again, but he just laughs and carries on digging out the hole in the wall for his stash.

'He's the sort of bloke you could make a killing with: old, no kids, lonely as Hades. Just off the boat from Rome.'

'How much is a killing?'

'Set you up for life if one of those old fellows takes a liking to yer. Not many years left on him the way he swigs back the grog.'

There's loads of ways to earn a living in the city, but how many can set a boy up for life … and get you a ticket into the Library?

'Not my type; I couldn't stand the chat. Hard work in other ways too, being tied down to one fella. But if you can stand all the bullshit…' Croc glances up at me from where he's squatting. Cups clatter as he pushes them in the hole.

'He asked about you. Wanted to know if you was Greek. Like the idea of having a Greek those old Romans do …' Has Turk put Croc up to sussing me out? No, he won't have gone near Turk with those cups. I trust him.

I give him a shove. He wobbles, but keeps his footing and laughs. Croc's stable as a goat at ground level.

'Don't mention anything to Turk about the job. This is our own little earner, got it?'

'But what about the rules?'

'Since when has Turk kept to the rules? But he mustn't find out. Don't want my bones dangling over the entrance to the Necropalace.'

I thought they were old Egyptian bones. A shiver runs through me. I want to get out of here and into the sunshine. I squat down and help Croc push a large limestone block in front of the hole.

'That should do it. Let's go.'

It's good to feel the sun warm on my face. Croc points with his knife towards the Agora and nods. 'The Agora at sunset, Rufius said.'

'But won't the old *cinaedus* tell Turk?' Saying the word feels bad. Dad used to clip me round the ear if he heard me say it. *That's a serious insult. Don't let me hear that word pass from your lips again.* I got the same when I called widow Leila a cunt; she'd hit me so hard I was bruised for days after. Never thought I'd miss being told-off.

A rustle from a bush makes us turn.

'Tell Turk what?' That's Lanky's voice, thick with menace.

The hard blade of a knife's at my throat.

Croc's eyes are wide with surprise. He's not laughing. I knew there was someone in that bush.

'Lanky, man!'

It's hopeless struggling; he's stronger than me. Lanky tightens his grip and presses the blade against my throat. Must stay still as I can. All my focus is on the knife.

'Get off him, Lanky. This is my gig.'

He's a demon, the lanky one. Kiya's words float back like from a dream. Dunno about demon, but he's a thief and he has my copper I earned fair and square last night. I'm not paying rent for sleeping rough on night-watch.

Lanky yanks my arm higher up my back. 'Ah! You're gonna break my arm. Let me go.'

'I'm in, or I tell Turk and slit Pretty's throat.'

Croc's shoulders slump. 'Man, let him go. You'll get a cut of the gold.'

Lanky lowers the blade and shoves me away.

'You don't have any choice you little shits. A whiff of this and Turk will hang your bones above the entrance to the Necropalace.'

Now I'm free, the anger heats up my face. I want to hit him.

'So, what's the deal?'

'Meet me at the Library warehouses on the docks tonight, after yer done the rounds down Venus Street.'

'What you got there, Pretty?' Lanky whips the knife out of my belt.

'Give it back.' I jump on his back, and scratch his face. Croc snatches the knife from his hand.

Lanky lunges forward, head to the ground and shakes me off his back. Can't keep hold of his neck. Gravel scratches my face. Mouth's full of sand, need to spit.

Lanky's like a wild animal. He kicks me hard in the shin. He's going for Croc – the force of his punch makes Croc fall backwards. Croc kicks and tries to reach his knife, but Lanky's on top of him. Punch, slap. Punch, scratch. One more of those and Croc'll lose his senses.

I scramble over to where my knife's fallen, grab Lanky's matted hair and pull his head back, knife to his neck like he did to me.

'Let him go.'

Croc gives him a kick. It lands full on Lanky's chest with a thud. The force of it sends Lanky falling backwards. Shit, I'm going down with him ... turn to keep my footing. My knife catches Lanky's mouth and slides through his cheek like slicing meat.

'Arghhhh!' Lanky reaches for his mouth.

Shit, I didn't mean to cut him.

Croc pushes himself up from the ground, his mouth wide open in shock that I've hurt Lanky.

Lanky faces me; his hands tight over the right hand side of his face are covered with blood.

'You'll be worthless on Venus Street once I've finished with you, Pretty.' Blood splutters from him mouth, hate in his mad, wild eyes. He stands, spits, then takes his hands away from his face and looks at them.

Croc shakes his head, dust flying from his hair, and jumps to his feet.

'Lanky, man, it's just a flesh wound. It'll heal. Go and bathe it in the sea.'

Lanky looks at his hands covered in blood, then at me.

'Come on, man; it's just a scratch – there'll be loads of gold knives you can pinch at the warehouse. No harm done.'

Lanky scowls at me. He's in pain and I'm the cause of it, but I didn't mean to cut him. 'There'd better be treasure or you two will pay. I'll start by cutting off your fingers and toes and make you watch as I feed them to the seagulls.'

My toes scrunch up at the thought of it. He means it.

'Man, there'll be so much treasure you'll be ringleader after tonight; you'll be richer than Turk.'

Lanky's face changes at that, the idea of being the ringleader. 'You two are fucked if there's no treasure.'

We watch him walk off to the seawall, holding his face.

'Man, there better be treasure in that warehouse.' Croc's not laughing.

10

RUFIUS

'Apollinos?' Through half-opened eyes I can see his long face furrowed in distress. How was he ever my body slave? My throat's scratchy and my voice cracks, mouth parched and rancid. Hangovers are more torturous every year.

'Master, wake up, master.'

Even squinting's painful. I close my eyes against the rude sunlight from the balcony.

'Go and bully some slaves. Let me sleep.' The throb in my head is making my ears ring. I blame Apollinos for not watering my wine.

He props my head on a cushion and offers me a glass of water.

'Mind the hair, dear.' I swill and spit.

He clicks his fingers and a slave runs over with a mop.

'You don't know what's happened, master.'

It sounds like I'm about to find out from the flap in his voice. 'Unless it's a fire or a Persian raid I'm not interested.'

Even sips of water hurt my throat. I smoked too much. Bah!

'The Museum's been robbed. That boy, he stole knives – your favourite, with the coral hilt, and …'

'Get a good eyeful did you, dear? Have a wank too while you were spying?' Jealous of my rough trade, Apollinos? Or relieved you're too old for me now?

'Master, we must inform the Museum Guard.'

'We! Since when are you and I a *we*? Impudent slave.'

My bones creak as I lever my torso up on my elbow – if only it were possible to have one's joints oiled like a squeaky hinge. I must have passed out on this couch. Memory scrambles after flickers of debauched scenes from last night. Blue eyes. Beautiful sapphire eyes as inaccessible as Sappho's apple out of reach of the pickers.

'Ah, but I didn't take him home.'

'But the street urchin. Master, he robbed you.'

'Ah, yes, I took the one with the scaly skin.' I remember now. The pimp was dangling the blue-eyed Greek like an apple. 'The low hanging fruit was fun.'

My temples ache under the strain of a smile. Never mind, I do recall Scaly and I made a deal of our own. What was his name? Fish? No, Crocodile, that was it. So, Crocodile fleeced us, did he? The rascal. 'No need to inform the Library Guard, Apollinos.'

'But, master …'

'Enough, Apollinos! Bring me wine. My mouth's as dry as the Nubian desert and you stand there bothering me with trifles. Ready the morning ritual.'

'It's past noon, master.'

'What of it?'

'Theon will be expecting you in his office, to discuss the arrangements for the welcome dinner he's holding in your honour tonight, master.'

Theon, Theon. Name rings a bell.

'The Head Librarian. And perhaps he should know about the theft … to avoid suspicion.'

'I know who Theon is for Bacchus' sake. And I decide what's urgent, Apollinos. Things disappear all the time. There is no need for the Head Librarian to be informed.' No doubt the boy has more need of silver than us.

'Yes, master.' The veins in Apollinos' neck are bulging again. I've an urge to wring it.

'Disturbs your sensibility, does it, Apollinos? I'll replace the cursed cups, along with the rest of this ugly old furniture.' The couch bleats out a long creak as I move my bare feet one at a time onto the floor. I don't want anything that reminds me of my age. 'But first there's important shopping to do. I can't be expected to make do with a secretary and these skinny Museum wretches, and you need some minions to bash about, Apollinos, if only to satisfy that pulsating neck of yours.'

Oh, I have to lie back down – let him stoop to shave me – I can't manage an upright position with this stinking hangover. Apollinos arranges the blades, scrapers and tweezers in a neat row on the marble-topped table with the oils and kohl.

'Please, master, stay still.'

He's a bit rough as he wipes the smudged kohl from my brow and reapplies it. I hold my breath: for my eyebrows precision is essential.

'Do you really mean to go through with your plan, master?'

Plan? What plan? He pronounced the word with disapproval. Come on, brain. 'Plan, dear?'

Apollinos shoos the slaves from my office, cautious as ever.

'Oh, yes! The plan.' Now I'm sober, I'm not sure it's such a brilliant idea after all … was it mine, or that scaly rascal's?

Apollinos' teeth grind with stress. Ha!

'Shall I inform Theon you will meet with him?'

'Bugger Theon! Bugger formalities!'

He clamps his jaw shut and looks straight ahead at the terrace. That's it, Apollinos, dear: bite your tongue.

'Ready my ride. We have shopping to do.'

'Yes, master. I'll inform Theon you have a headache – from the voyage.'

He slams the door in a strop. Moody slave.

'Think yourself lucky you're too old for me.' The heavy silence of a well-practised sulk hangs in the air to irritate me.

The thought of shopping motivates me to stand and take a leak. By Bacchus, my piss sprinkles bright yellow over the balcony.

'There is a toilet, master.' Apollinos didn't sulk for long.

'Can't I even piss in peace?'

What else do I need for my new entourage? It's hopeless trying to concentrate with this raging hangover: each thought intensifies the painful throb at my temples. The only thing that gives me any relief is the memory of those sapphire eyes. Crocodile had better bring the Greek along with him tonight as we agreed.

'I'll ensure Theon's slaves stock up on plenty of water for your wine at tonight's dinner.'

You're asking for it, boy. Take that! The spoon flies at him. Apollinos yelps and pushes his pelvis forward like a belly-dancer to avoid being hit. Ha!

Bah! So this is the famed Agora. The usual contest of trade, politics and religion: temple priests in jewelled diadems and flower-sellers croon, treasurers hurry slaves with scroll bags and scales, politicians spout monotonous rhetoric from their plinths. Prostitutes hug the corners of the arcades, boys lift their tunics and girls with acorns for tits arch their backs in contorted poses, as Christians toot apocalyptic crap to any mug morose enough to listen to how the world's about to end. Why's it so popular? The audience looks ready to slit their wrists after the sermon of doom.

'Impressed, master?'

'Alexandria's Agora must house more temples than the Roman Forum, Apollinos. Grander, in a brash, modern way.'

'Alexandria has 2,478 temples, 6,152 law courts, 1,561 baths, 456 …'

'Oh do shut up, Apollinos. If I want a tour guide, I'll hire one.'

Alexandrians build high. Huge sphinxes stand at the entrance to Greek temples like sentries. The Roman buildings are newer. Bizarre: the Temple of Priapus is surrounded by a row of baboon statues;

what's the Egyptian god of writing have to do with that horny Roman god? At least they've not been shy about the size of the phalluses lining the walls. My buttocks clench at the sight.

'This way, master, to the Temple of Antinous.'

The sun's descent stains the portico in a pomegranate glow. Dear Bacchus, spare me from this dull huddle of academics, shoulders hunched from too many hours in the library, their jabber lapped up by doting students. The statue of Antinous, Hadrian's deified lover, even looks bored towering above the couches.

So, which one of these windbags did the Archbishop bribe to secure my position? That one with the squint, perhaps? He stopped stuffing his face and pinned me under his gaze as soon as he saw us approach.

'Considering it's my welcome dinner, they could have waited.'

'We're hours late, master.'

He knows full well I had to repaint my eyebrows, curl my hair. Bah!

'What's the latest buzz then, Apollinos?' I lower my voice as we approach.

'Sorry, master?'

'Schools of thought, Apollinos. I thought you were a literate slave?'

'There have been some interesting developments in medicine and technology: the mending of fractured bones and a new version of Hero of Alexandria's water powered engine.'

'And in philosophy?'

'Platonism still holds significant sway here.'

'Perhaps Alexandria has its advantages.' Why's the slave hesitating?

'… the current Archbishop of Alexandria is a Nicene like Damasus.'

'Ha! There's not another living soul on this earth like Damasus!'

Time to make an entrance.

'Well, announce me, Apollinos.'

Apollinos clears his throat. 'Rufius Biblus Catamitus.'

A man with an air of authority looks up, leaves his couch and walks towards me. This bore must be Theon.

'Welcome, Rufius. I'm Theon.' On first name terms are we? He's knocked back a few the way he grabs my shoulders and kisses me on the lips. Two kisses is the custom in much of the Eastern Empire. I rather like it. 'Forgive us, sir – our stomachs could not wait.'

Don't try to impress me with the fluent Latin, dear. He has a gut on him. That's good. And he likes the vine, by the look of the net of red veins over his cheeks. We might just get along.

Smells edible. Slaves carry out plates of steaming game.

'I trust you had a safe journey and are recovered from your illness?'

Greek will do – to cut through this unnecessary linguistic etiquette. 'Apart from the band of Persian pirates, and the crew's mutiny, it was a very pleasant trip.'

Surely he's not credulous enough to believe that? The flicker of disbelief in his bloodshot eyes turns into a hearty laugh. At least he's got a sense of humour.

'Come, Rufius, let me introduce you.'

'Unless I meet some life amongst these dusty fellows, I might have to resort to fiction for the rest of the meal.' At least most of their eyebrows are clipped in the tidy Roman fashion: not as provincial as I'd imagined … By Bacchus! Did Apollinos paint mine on today? Resist rubbing, Rufius: don't smudge the kohl. Apollinos would never allow me to leave the house without my eyebrows. The slave's hide isn't tough enough to endure such a serious error.

'Better get some wine down your gullet, Rufius, before you entertain the old bookworms! It's a shame you missed my daughter. Hypatia will join the academy next year.'

'I've heard your daughter is quite the mathematician.'

'Indeed she is.' He gestures to the statue of Antinous. 'I hope you appreciate the choice of venue, Rufius?'

'If I tire of these ravishing librarians, I can admire Hadrian's boy.'

I chuckle at my mild sacrilege. So does Theon. He's obviously not a Christian: they tend to keep their women ignorant and lack a sense of humour. I'd rather like him if it wasn't for the sickening sense of duty he exudes.

Each man rises in turn and introduces himself. A couple of the young ones make intellectual small talk. If they were more attractive I'd humour them. A grunt will do.

Here's squinty. 'Titus Arius. A pleasure to meet you. I've not long left Rome myself.' He licks his lips with the quickness of a lizard.

'Titus is visiting us on official business from the Library of Constantinople.'

'But a Roman, born and bred.' What's he holding my gaze for? I couldn't care less where his mother spat him out of her womb. And with a face like a raisin, she most definitely did spit him out.

'Well then, Roman, you will know that my stomach needs filling.'

Theon laughs and his minions join in. Thank Bacchus the niceties are out of the way.

Bugger it! Lizard-face has plonked himself on the couch next to me. Titus leans closer, flicks his tongue over his lips and whispers, 'I've heard you've joined the book trade.'

No doubt about it, Titus must be one of Damasus' spies. I dislike being under the Archbishop's evil eye. Before I have a chance to respond, he leans back and says for all to hear, 'Rufius, as the new Director of the Scriptorium perhaps you would be so kind as to give us your opinion on the sharing of books between Libraries? I was just about to suggest to Theon that Constantinople borrow some books for copying from Alexandria's collection, but as you are now here …'

Theon's smiling, but his gaze is nervous. He need not worry. Apollinos has drilled me on policy.

'Borrow? Alexandria has an army of scribes, Titus. We'll gladly have them copied for a reasonable price.'

Theon raises his glass and relaxes. 'He's barely disembarked and Rufius is already filling the Library coffers.'

The old bookworms raise their glasses too. They're so sozzled they'd raise them if I suggested Titus take the collection as a gift. A positive start nevertheless.

Apollinos is still hovering, waiting to be excused. When I'm convinced he thinks I've forgotten about him, I'll wave him away.

Titus leans over and licks his lips. 'We wouldn't want to put you to the bother and expense of copying, Rufius. Constantinople's scribes can do the job if you will send us the originals.'

He discreetly tucks a piece of paper into a lower fold of my toga.

'Who do you work for?'

'My client wants to cut out the middle man.' His lips, stained dark with tannin, try a thin smile.

So he doesn't work for Damasus. Interesting! There's money to be made here, but better still I can smell the sweet prospect of screwing Damasus.

'Tell me more about your client.'

'He is a powerful man. It does not matter who he is. You will only ever do business with me. For a man like yourself willing to take the risk, there's a fortune to be made.'

How to play this without stirring Theon's suspicions? Constantinople might be the new capital of the Empire, but they lag behind in books, and a city's power is in its books.

My hand pulls the parchment from the fold of my toga. It's too dark to read it without a torch. Apollinos tries to whip it from my hand. No you don't; shoo. Interfering slave.

'Come to my house tomorrow. We will talk more then.'

He licks his top lip as he raises his glass. Perhaps this dinner won't have been a complete waste of time after all.

Now where's that little ruffian Crocodile? I'll need his services even more if this deal with Titus comes off. The Agora torches are lit, and a dense mass of people mill around the stalls that have been erected for the night market. Crocodile knows how to make himself blend in with a crowd; I won't see him until he wants me to.

'Rufius?' A broad-shouldered latecomer shouts my name like a general giving orders. Oooo, I don't like him.

'You gave me a fright, dear!'

'I'm Olympus, we were discussing the impact of Platonism on the new wave of Arian Christian thought.' Here we go: bloody bores.

Theon smiles and takes another sip of wine. I get a childish kick that he doesn't have a clue I'm planning to pinch his books.

'It's not exactly new, dear.' Was that vague enough …?

'He's quite right.' A child's voice. I hadn't noticed her arrival with an entourage of slaves. So this must be the famed Hypatia, Theon's daughter. No beauty, but she has an assertive voice.

'They've borrowed the remnants of Egyptian thought from the Greeks – the trinity for example is a regurgitation of the Horus-Isis-Orisis myth. Christianity's a mythical religion.'

It's not often I agree with a woman. Just shows you, if you train them like a man, their brains will develop. No doubt the Museum's laboratories will be after her head for dissection when she's dead. Could one train a street urchin to speak like her …?

Olympus bellows at me. 'And your view, Rufius, on the differentiation between the Nicene and Arian creeds?'

Titus licks his lips and joins in. 'Yes, my Christian colleagues tell me they are quite different, but I struggle to see it.'

I couldn't give a shit about the nuances of Christian doctrine. Best not say that. I need to at least pretend I'm up to date with the latest if I'm going to provide Titus with their books.

'Well, since we stopped feeding the poor buggers to the lions …' Ouch! Apollinos knees me in the back. '… The Arians subordinate Jesus, whereas the Nicenes consider him equal to the father, the creator god. However, there are some minor groups of Christians who do not consider the father the creator of the earth, but a evil impersonator.' I lisp, but it's an assertive lisp. It seems my infamous reputation does not affect my status here. My Roman peers wouldn't bother asking my opinion on Christian doctrine. With all the eunuchs freely sauntering about the Agora, it's no wonder these Easterners are a little more open-minded. But as that's the extent of my knowledge, I'd better draw this to a close. Let's raise my cup. 'A toast to my new colleagues.' Slaves rush to fill everyone's cups.

Theon's being ushered home by his precocious daughter.

'Hen-pecked by my own daughter!'

The conversation slurs into inarticulate drivel. I'll fall asleep with the drone from these bookworms.

Where's that Crocodile? The plan was to meet at the Temple of Antinous at sunset.

What rubbish is Titus spewing to that poor doting student? The way his scrawny neck reaches towards the youth, he looks like a new-born chick hungry for food, one hand high up the student's thigh.

Hold on ... something's not quite right about the student's hand sliding round Titus' midriff. Even if the young lad's arm could reach that far around him, why are his fingernails so dirty?

Let's get up and pour myself some wine to get a better view.

'Shoo slave, I'll help myself.'

Ha! What a pleasing coincidence! My bit of rough trade from last night's fleecing Titus. Oh how funny – the hand that spent the night caressing my genitals gently releases Titus' purse from beneath his tunic.

Where's my blue-eyed Greek from Venus Street hiding?

There, his dark curly head peeps from behind the statue of Antinous. What a joy to see him again. Dear me, even in this light he's a beauty. There's something of Antinous' charm in his features. Aeson ... a hero's name.

He hoots a signal to Crocodile that he's been spotted ... and they're off.

Titus has no idea he's been robbed. What fun! I'm a voyeuristic accomplice to the crime, like I'm one of the boys.

'Thief!' Apollinos points at the two boys running down the steps and darting in between the stalls.

'Apollinos, what are you doing? Come here and shut up.'

'But, master.'

'Apollinos, shush!' I put my finger over my mouth. 'How do you intend to follow them if you get them arrested?'

'But, master!'

'Don't worry, we'll retrieve Titus' purse.' One way or another. Ha! This is turning out to be a very entertaining evening.

'Grab a couple of slaves and follow Crocodile. You know the plan.'

The boys are peering from behind a basket stall, assessing whether they've been spotted. That must be the Ophite's stall, reed baskets strung down the sides and across the top.

I waggle my finger towards the stalls. 'Off you go, Apollinos, before you lose sight of them.'

AESON

'Where'd the Snake Women go? D'ya reckon they magic'd themselves off?' Croc's itching his legs again and looking behind him, down the street.

The old Temple of Dionysus – by Serapis, of course, the Snake People are probably all squatting here. Looks deserted. Street's empty, doors bolted down for the night, but I know they're in there.

'Why are we following them again?' Something feels wrong about this. I don't want to give the Snake People any trouble. Didn't tell Croc that I know some Snake People.

'I told yer – it's all part of old Rufius' plan. Library policy, he said. Now where did they disappear? My guess is they sneaked into that old temple. Come on.'

'Croc! Wait. Are the Library slaves still behind us?'

'They're round the corner up the street.'

'Listen, Croc, you stay here. Tell the slaves to wait. I'm going to check it out, right?'

Croc looks confused.

'... unless you want to climb the wall?'

'Man, be my guest.'

My sandals will have to come off.

Plenty of holes in the temple wall: easy climbing this is. My stomach pinches like it's shrinking. An orange and a half-chewed piece of meat with more gristle on it than scraps thrown to tomb dogs ain't enough to keep my strength up.

There's a gap at the top of this old wooden door. If I can get a hold of the iron bars criss-crossing it, I'll be able to pull myself up and have a look. That's it.

Shit! The door's opening … if I hold on they'll never know I'm up here. My heart thumps in my chest as someone steps out into the shadow of the street.

Now the door's ajar, I can see inside: courtyard's packed with people sitting cross-legged, muttering to themselves.

'Aeson, I've got yer back, man!'

'Croc, stay there.'

Croc's knife's out and he's running across the street.

Who's this? Someone's coming out of the door. That lunge and lurch – it's Kiya. Sophia, curled round her neck, hisses in my direction. Kiya turns and looks up.

'Aeson? Is that you up there?'

So much for not being seen. Time to jump down.

I land next to Kiya. Sophia's hood's open as she hisses at me.

'Oi! Don't you touch him, or I'll stab yer, Snake-girl.'

'Easy, Croc. This is Kiya. She's a friend.'

'Ahh! She's got a snake round her neck.'

Croc raises his knife.

Kiya smiles and ignores Croc.

'Put the knife away, Croc. This is Sophia. Look, she don't bite.' I make myself stroke the snake like Kiya showed me, but my hand goes all shaky.

'Man, don't touch it.' He's jittery; keeps looking behind him.

'Sophia won't bite. She's just smelling you. Snakes smell with their tongues.'

A tall woman with two long grey plaits either side of her head peeks round the door. She's got to be the oldest woman I've ever seen …

'Girlie, what's going on out here. I told ye to keep that door closed.' I know her voice: no-nonsense and deep as a man's. Old women's voices must break like boys' do. Mine's started to. It's the same old woman Dera brought to nurse Dad when the doctors gave up. My eyes sting at the memory of her dressing his wound with her long bony fingers. She made Dad more comfortable at least. She looks like the nomad women who come out of the Nubian desert once a year to trade: tall and thin, long face, long straight nose.

'Come visiting have ye, laddie … and brought a friend wid ye?' She peers up and down the street. 'Get in. Quick, that's it. We don't want no Roman soldiers snooping.' She ushers us in through the door and pulls the iron bolt down after us.

Croc gives me a look as if to say, *how on earth do you know Snake People?*

'I'm Henite. We don't know your name, laddie.' Her face wrinkles like a walnut when she smiles. Almost a full set of teeth.

'Croc.'

Henite squints closer and sniffs him.

'Don't put no snake curse on me, lady.'

'You two need a good scrub. When did ye last go to the baths?'

My cheeks heat up. This is a holy place; it's disrespectful to be dirty.

'We have to warn them, Croc. What do those Museum slaves want with the Snake People?'

Croc shrugs.

'What ye waiting fer, laddies?'

Henite nudges us over to a row of different sized buckets, reaches up and whips a couple of cloths off the hooks on the wall.

'I can wash myself.' Croc looks at the cloth like it's a trick, but he copies me and sloshes water over his face and neck.

'You're a proud one.' She cackles and shuffles off towards the people sitting cross-legged on the floor of the courtyard, mumbling to themselves.

Kiya looks like she's guarding the entrance door, one arm across her chest, the other on her crutch. Why are her earlobes so long and what's drawn on them? A snake? Creepy cripple girl. Croc scans the courtyard walls for an exit, a habit that's fast forming with me too in my new gang-life.

'I'm Kiya. Come in and join us.' Her smile makes Croc force a nervous, clenched-teeth hiccup of a giggle.

'I'll pray to whoever you want if it means I get fed but you're not going to convert us into crazy Christians.'

Kiya laughs too.

The smell of baked bread's making me light-headed with hunger.

'Come and meet Seth. I've told him all about you.'

Croc gives me another quizzing look.

I shrug.

There's nearly as many street kids as adults in the courtyard. Dad used to say Christians will take in any urchin to increase their numbers. But some of them are Snake People – they have a snake inked on their earlobes like Kiya and Henite.

Why's that group of men and women by the table piled high with loaves of bread drawing straws, Henite included? A tall man with pale Greek skin gets the long straw. The prize is a white robe embroidered in ancient Egyptian letters. He puts it on and beams at everyone in the courtyard.

'Welcome to the new faces.' Seth's clothes are made of expensive fabric. Croc showed me how to pick out a rich man in a crowd by his dress and the confident way they walk in the Agora, and Seth's honey-nose way of pronouncing every vowel is a dead giveaway. He scans the group, his deep voice drawing everyone's attention away from the food … except for me and Croc.

'This is where we get put under a spell or eaten, man.'

'Croc, we've got to warn them.'

Croc's gob has dropped open at the table piled with food.

'I'm bloody starving, man. We stay until they let us eat, then we tell them.'

Kiya leans on her crutch and points at the priest.

'Shush! Sit down and listen to Seth.'

'I'll stay for the prayers, but I don't believe in no gods.' I see it like payment for the food. *Nothing's free, Pretty.* Turk told me that.

Seth flicks his long hair with a sharp neck movement. The way it falls back to frame his face makes him look like Alexander the Great. He's gotta be Greek.

Croc's eyes are shut tight. He whispers, 'Man, we need to avoid eye contact to protect us from Christian spells.'

'We thank God the Holy Father and Sophia the Holy Spirit for this food.' Seth sounds like he's gearing up for a sermon. They're going to make us sit and look at the food while Longhair drones on.

Kiya nudges me and whispers, 'Those are magic letters.'

'What?'

'On Seth's robe.' She's nodding at Longhair.

Copying the letters in the dust with my finger will keep my mind off the food. Wavy lines like the Egyptian symbol for life are at the bottom of the robe. A snake, neck up like it's dancing for a charmer's pipe, a cup, a cross and lots of letters. What does it all mean? Who cares … when do we get to eat?

'The knowledge of the snake lives in all of us; we can all transform into the divine.'

'Like Achilles?' asks a young boy at the front.

'Yes, we can all achieve divine powers like Achilles, Horus, Alexander, Jesus – they are all examples for us to follow.'

'How, man? Tell us.' Croc's eyes are open again.

Why couldn't Croc keep his gob shut? I'm starving.

Seth smiles. 'Today we will focus on the power letters: A-O-I. The sacred vowels help us pass through the Gate of Fear. Repeat the mantra often, whenever you need to. At night, after a bad dream, if you are beaten, ridiculed, hungry. It overcomes all fears in this life and the next. Let us repeat together: 'Aoi, Aoi, Aoi …'

The group chant with him. I move my lips, but don't make a sound, in case I'm being cursed. Seth flicks his hair … does he ever stop grinning?

'Jesus was a man, just like you and me, who spent many years repeating the magic words and eventually transformed into an angel of light, a perfect man, an Aberamentho. If anyone has any questions, just shout.' He pauses for a hair-flick. 'Jesus was crucified by the Romans.'

A boo goes up from the street kids. It's like a puppet show in the Agora.

'But the Holy Spirit of Sophia entered Jesus' dead body.'

'Yayyyy,' cheer the street kids. A hand goes up.

'How d'ya know?'

'I saw it in a vision.'

Another hand shoots up. 'What's a vision?'

'Good question. It's like a dream, but when you're awake.'

The same hand: 'But dreams ain't real.'

'How many times have you woken from a dream in fright?'

'Man, if you slept in the Necropolis you'd know how often.'

Croc's mouthy. What's Henite passing Seth?

'Snake alert! Shit man, they're gonna feed us to the snakes.'

Those baskets against the courtyard wall – they must all be full of snakes. Makes me shiver.

Croc leans over. 'This is where it gets weird.'

We keep our eyes on the roof, ready to make a run for it. Seth moves the snake from hand to hand as it wiggles. It's just a grass snake.

'The snake is the great teacher. As we pray I want you all to imagine a snake unravelling from the base of your spines, uncurling and reaching up to the crown of your head. This is the route to salvation, the road Jesus took: the Path of the Snake. We will now pray together.'

Seth hands the snake to Henite. Shit – she's putting it in the basket of bread on the table.

Seth gives his hair a flick, pulls his robes around him, and sits down on the ground cross-legged. 'Repeat after me: *Sophia, send your light to awaken us from our sleep. So-phi-aaa, So-phi-aaa, OIA, OIA, OIA, OIA, OIA, OIA.*'

The courtyard starts to hum. Street kids giggle. They're just here for the grub.

Kiya whispers in my ear, 'Focus on the snake. Makes it easier.'

The snake Henite put into the bread-basket is rising, upright, slowly moving from side to side, like they do from the charmers' baskets in the Agora. Better to keep my eyes on the roof. Definite crazies, these Christians are.

'Can you feel your spine tingling? This is my favourite bit – when I leave my body.'

Crazy Snake Girl. The chant takes on a life of its own: AOI-AOI-AOI. The atmosphere in the courtyard changes. It reminds me of the stadium, like the courtyard has a pulse, and we are all part of it. I'm not joining in … could be a spell.

Longhair raises his arms and brings a halt to the chanting with a hair-flick. 'Sophia bless this food.' Seth's a bit funny. A giggle bubbles in my chest. Just in time, before the laughter reaches my mouth, he adds, 'Let's eat!'

'Yay!' Street kids run at the table like it's a race. My stomach's begging me to join them, but I'm not a child anymore. I'll queue with the adults.

Here comes Longhair.

'Don't worry, we won't put any spells on you, lads.' He's joking. Seth sits down and talks to us while we scoff the food. He's pretty relaxed. I'll tell him not to open the doors to anyone when I've finished my chicken leg.

Seth looks at the symbols I've made in the sand.

'You write well.'

In case he's taking the piss, I roll my eyes and rub out the letters.

What's that banging?

'Open up for the Library Guard.'

The street kids are on their feet – the voice of authority's made them nervous.

Croc and me look at each other.

'Shit, man!'

Croc looks at the roof. I shake my head.

Seth stares at the door, gets up and walks past everyone – robe fluttering behind him – to lift the door bolt. Five Library guards in white tunics follow Seth across the courtyard and go into a room. Street kids scoot for the door, frightened of anyone in uniform.

'No need to run, children. The librarians will not be staying long,' Henite says for the benefit of two armed guards who've remained at the entrance, hands on scabbards. Henite follows Seth inside the temple.

What's she screaming?

'Not the book!'

One of the Library slaves steps back into the courtyard with a scroll of papyrus in his hand.

Croc looks confused. 'That's Rufius' slave.'

'They'll return it,' Seth tries to calm her as they follow the Library slave.

There's panic in Henite's voice. 'We'll never see it again.'

'Lady, I can assure you, the Library has a policy of returning manuscripts.' The slave talks like Seth. Two educated Greeks. Funny the slave's in charge.

Kiya stands at the entrance with a group of street kids she's rounded up, free arm across her chest.

'What's your crazy cripple mate doing?' Croc's as amazed as me.

'AOI-AOI-AOI,' she chants.

'Aoi-aoi-aoi,' they join in, wary at first and then louder as they see the slave stop.

The guards laugh.

'Putting a spell on us are you, little one?' The tall slave is impatient.

'Aoi-aoi-aoi,' they chant.

Oh Serapis, she's not going to, is she? She wouldn't dare?

'Let us pass and there'll be no blood spilt.'

'Go!' shouts Kiya and children tip over the snake baskets.

'Snake!'

'Snake!'

Library guards yell and jump to avoid hundreds of snakes: browns, oranges, greens and blacks writhe on the floor – not all as harmless as Seth's grass snake. Some have hoods.

The guards jump back, swords drawn. They stamp at the snakes to warn them off and slice down on them with their swords.

'Stop!' Seth's voice projects around the courtyard, 'Let them take *The Book of Wisdom.* We trust you will return our sacred book, sir.'

A Library guard pushes Kiya aside.

'Crazy heretics.'

The snakes hiss. Kiya starts to cry, 'But that's the only copy we have.'

Henite's crying too. 'But Seth, they threatened to arrest us all. You know the penalty for possessing heretic books. They can kill us, torture the children. A boy was executed after a sham of a trial at Antioch just for reciting the sacred vowels at the baths.'

Seth is calm, his arm round Henite's shoulder.

'Sister, they just wanted *The Book of Wisdom.*'

'But, brother, how did they know we were here?'

'I don't know, Henite.'

Seth throws us a flick of a look then smiles. Not his fake wide grin, but a kind smile. He knows it was us, but he's not going to tell Kiya and Henite. That makes me feel well guilty. Seth's sweet, like the rest of them.

Croc looks at me. 'Shit, man!'

'Croc, we've got to get that book back. This is all our fault.'

'We'll think of something, but first we've gotta meet Lanky, or you and me, we're dead meat.'

12

RUFIUS

Apollinos should be back by now. We need to organise a distribution network for Arch-bloody-bishop Damasus' books. Where did that slave put my letter box? Boxes everywhere. I hate mess. This villa needs a complete overhaul: new floors, fresh plaster, walls skimmed and painted. Looks like it's been in this state for a century or more. I can't even decipher the images on the frescos beneath the peeling paint. Is that a bird in a tree? Bah! There's dust everywhere.

Ah, here it is, on my desk. Titus' list rests on top of Damasus' list: now that's justice. What an ugly lizard of a man Titus was. I don't trust him any more than I trust Damasus ... although I do like the crackle of his top quality parchment ... I'll need reliable messengers to deliver all these books. Not my own slaves: nothing can lead back to me. Ha! Satisfaction at last – I'll fiddle Damasus and he won't have a clue. I'll have to make deliveries to his clients too, but from the look of this list, Titus is better connected. That will give my old slave something else to fret about.

Where is Apollinos? I hate pacing, but I can't sit still. On a hot night like this it's good to feel the cool marble of the terrace under my feet. Bah! Cursed yellow silks sway around the terrace doors in the sea breeze; they nearly tripped me up. The stars are bright tonight ... perhaps I'll have a starry sky painted on the bedroom ceilings?

The view over the harbour's not bad. Shocking that only fourteen years ago the Royal Palace, built on its own promontory, would have blocked the horizon. Now a peninsula submerged forever, the coastline gives no hint it ever existed. Theon said this house was built for one of the royals, designed by Greek architects, so it's solid … unless another great wave washes Alexandria clean away from the limestone lip of Egypt. What a terrifying thought!

Humph! Old-fashioned wall paintings will have to go … and this terrace needs enlarging, but the house has potential. I will call it Villa Biblus … no, Biblos, now I'm in a Greek city. Apollinos will like that. Villa Biblos.

Bah! My glass is empty.

'Wine, dear.'

Why can't the slave walk without drawing attention to herself? The girl's an exhibitionist. I can't fault Alexandria for shopping. She's just one of many exquisite finds at the Emporium: expensive, captured in some remote city. The slave trader was vague, but it's evident the girl's not been a slave long enough to become meek. *As useless as a princess in a laundry room, master,* complained Apollinos. He might be right, but I like to watch her. Hair black as a panther: Indian hair they call it; eyes set wide on her flat face, skin the sheen of high-polished ebony, tight as if it's been waxed and stretched for a funeral mask. She'll add a decorative touch to Villa Biblos. She's more of a pet, but I can't expect Apollinos to understand that. He's too practical.

'Were you trained by a herd of hippos?'

Did she tut?

'Tut.'

Ha! A tutting slave, well I never! 'Do you want a whipping, girl?'

Her almond eyes widen in surprise. Sized me up as a soft old fool, have you? She's not wrong: I'll leave the whipping for Apollinos.

'I suppose you've worked out my preference by now, dear?' I hold her chin in my hand. As her skinny black arm offers me the cup, gold bangles I picked out for her livery clink. 'My guests might enjoy you, Cunty, but I'll pretend you're mine to keep their greedy hands off you.'

'It bites!' She looks down at her groin.

'Ha! Feisty.' Usually slaves try to melt into the wall paintings.

I had to dismiss the boys tonight. Dear things, but anything short of that blue-eyed siren only serves to torment me.

A door slams downstairs and Apollinos shouts orders. He'll have his work cut out for him training the new slaves: they all fancy themselves, but they're young enough to be moulded.

Here comes his flat-footed slap up the stairs.

Good, Apollinos has a scroll in his hand. He looks rather dishevelled, and why's he panting like he's run a marathon?

'Did Crocodile give you the run around, Apollinos?'

'The Ophites, master, they set their snakes on us.'

'Ha! So that's snake blood on your sword?'

'Yes, master.' He exhales loudly. Apollinos hates anything that slithers, even worms. The new slaves will have fun with him when I tell them. Ha!

'I hope that's the *Pistis Sophia* you're carrying, Apollinos?'

'Yes, master. Here's *The Book of Wisdom*.'

The papyrus is old, translucent in places. Second century, I'd say. And here are the mysterious, untranslatable words, the vowels that make no sense. Some scholars call it magic – 'aeeiouo iao aoi oia' – I call it Christian jibberish, but it's what it's worth that matters.

'Bugger! This book's on both Damasus and Titus' list. I'll need two copies.'

'Yes, master.'

'Stop panting and have a glass of wine, Apollinos.'

'Master?'

'You've earned it, dear.' He looks at the jug. 'Not my wine, dear.' His neck's red with embarrassment. I shouldn't tease him.

'Thank you, master.'

'One down; a list to go, Apollinos. Is Croc clear on the details of his next job?'

'But, master, I only told them to steal, er, borrow the *Gospel of Philip*.'

'Was the Greek boy with him?'

'We followed two boys.'

'Excellent. We need to get all these books on Titus' list tonight as well.' He squints at the parchment over my shoulder. The girl's dark eyes narrow: she's taking it all in.

'We can't manage all of them, master, not in one night.'

'Why not?'

'It's too many. Someone will notice.'

'Well if they do, it won't lead back to us, but to a gang of thieving street urchins.'

'No, master, not tonight. It's too risky. We don't know the guards' routines …'

'No?' Waiting and pacing has made my nerves ragged. 'NO! How dare you. Cunty, pass me the whip.'

She winks at Apollinos and hands it to me. Ha! She'll fit in at Biblos just fine.

'Kneel down, Apollinos.' I should send the girl out to save his humiliation, but better she sees it than feels it. He pulls his tunic up and lowers his head. It's been years, but he knows the drill.

Apollinos whimpers after the first few thrashes. That's enough. The sight of red lines across his back hurts me more than him. 'Pull down your tunic, for Bacchus' sake.' Apollinos knows better than to defy me … perhaps it was the snakes?

The girl's face is grim as I hand her the whip. Not as soft as you thought, girl?

'The whip is not just for decoration in this house, girl. Do as Apollinos tells you, or it will be the same for you. Apollinos, after you've had a glass of wine – the good stuff – nip down to Venus Street, find that pimp Turk I told you about, and bring him back here.'

'Turk? What shall I tell him, master?'

'Tell the pimp I have a job for him. We need an army to pinch this lot.' I hold out Titus' list to Apollinos.

The tall Greek walks quietly to the door.

'Apollinos!'

'Yes, master?'

'You've forgotten Titus' list.' He pads back over to me. 'Keep your wits about you, dear.' I say it gently.

'Yes, master.' His gaze is on the broken mosaic floor. We'll need a new floor too. Apollinos is good at dealing with builders.

'Girl, I told you to keep my glass filled.'

By Bacchus, she still looks like she has better things to do than pour my wine. Ha!

'You'll keep your looks here, sweetie.' Her skin's soft against my thumb. My perfect boy has the same sharp cheekbones.

She thumps back to her position by the door, next to the ivory bust of me as a boy.

'You walk like a bloody elephant, Cunty.'

Back to pacing. A bird flutters out of the palm fronds hanging over the terrace. How bright the Pharos shines beyond the harbour. Now customs are closed the docks are quiet and tavern lights line the main quay. No ships dock this end of the harbour, just houses for Alexandria's rich. Apart from a drunk singing a sea shanty in the distance, the only sound is the waves lapping against the seawall. Aeson and Croc will be at the other end by now, at the Library warehouses.

'Be careful, my Olympian-eyed boy.'

I'm my own man. His defiant voice echoes in my mind; that crackle of boys' voices as they're breaking never fails to excite me. How I long to watch him grow and harden into a man. My whole being throbs at the thought of it. Hurry up, Apollinos. I must have that boy.

13

AESON

We stop to catch our breath at the corner of Serapis Street, throw a few stones at the wheels of the chariots that speed past.

'What's the deal with the Roman?'

'Tell you when we get there.' He slaps my back and runs off down a long alley that leads to the harbour. The sea breeze don't reach down these back streets Croc takes. I've got a sicky feeling about what happened in the church. Kiya and Henite were so upset … their sobs cut right through me, like the brickie-wives' wailing at Dad's funeral.

'Croc, I feel bad about leading Library slaves to the church.'

'Weren't no church. They're squatters, like the gang in the old Egyptian tomb.' Croc sees I'm serious. 'Me too – those Snake People are more generous than Turk with their hand-outs.'

'I'm going to get their book back.'

'How?'

'Dunno yet.'

'You could smooch up to the old *cinaedus.* He was going on and on about you last night, made me promise I'd bring you with me after we done this job.' Croc purses his lips and makes loud kissing noises.

'Give it a rest, Croc.' I'll get him for that … he darts off down another alley, but I'm faster than him.

* * *

Lanky slouches against the wall of one of the Library warehouses that line the docks. 'You two took yer time.' He spits as he says it. He's still angry.

There's a fat boy with him, blindfolded and trembling with fright. Rich kid from the look of his tunic. Can't tell his age too well with the dirty rag Lanky's tied over his eyes. His cheeks haven't lost their baby chub. Lanky whispers something in his ear. The boy gives out a whine like a small dog. What nasty story is Lanky tormenting him with? Lanky smiles to himself, looks at me and yanks off the kid's blindfold.

The boy blinks, eyes wide in terror. We must look like proper scoundrels to him.

'I got you a rich kid, Croc. Now what's the deal with your honey-daddy?'

Croc straightens and takes charge. 'Right, listen up. The Roman wants us to pinch an old book.'

'We'll never get past the Library Guard.' Pinching apples off carts in the Agora's one thing, break and entry's something else. Men get sent to the quarries for that.

Croc's getting impatient. 'Honey-daddy's taken care of the guard, man. Nobody will come snooping 'til morning.'

Lanky steps out of the shadow of the wall and nods up towards the warehouse, six stories high. 'Ready for some climbing, Pretty?'

My belly tightens at the sight of the cut from the corner of his mouth to his cheekbone. It makes his mouth look painted on like a scary theatre mask. The blood's clotted, but that's going to scar his lip.

'Checking out your handy-work are you, Pretty? Don't worry, I'll repay you for it.' His long-toothed sneer makes me shudder.

'It's just a flesh wound, Lanky, man. And this is my deal I got going with honey-nose, so I'm calling the shots.'

Lanky curls his top lip at Croc. Did he growl? I can see why Kiya called him a demon. He points up at a low doorway near the top for the pulley. 'Pretty's gonna squeeze his tight little arse through that hole at the top.'

I look at Croc. He shrugs.

'What about the kid?'

'He's going up wiv you … unless Pretty can read?'

They both laugh: Croc, head flung back, Lanky, lips peeled back from his teeth. His gums are receding. It's not a piss take. What use are letters to a street kid?

The fat kid looks at me and blinks. You're laughing too, aren't you? I want to slap his fat face.

'That's what our little friend's for.' Croc rolls his eyes with impatience.

'A very learned little shit, ain't ya?' Lanky yanks the boy's tunic, scrunches it up round his neck below his double chins. 'Don't mess with Pretty. I told ya, he's got a nasty temper.' Is that respect in Lanky's voice, or is he just tormenting the boy?

'Pl-please don't h-hurt me. I'll d-do anything.' The petrified kid stammers and shakes. Reckon he's a worse climber than Croc, I do.

'Too right you will. Stop crying, or I'll cut out your tongue.'

The boy clamps his mouth shut. I'm just as scared of Lanky as the kid but I don't show it.

I'm not risking getting caught and being sent to a quarry … or worse, a mine for a few coppers. 'What do I get out of it?'

'We split the fee three ways.' Croc looks at us both.

'Lanky? Deal?'

Lanky grunts.

'Aeson, when you've got the book go down to the ground floor entrance – we'll have it open for you.'

I nod and look around for the Library Guard. The idea of being chained for years, digging roads makes me nervous. Not cut out for gang-life, I'm not.

'Pretty's lost his balls.'

When Lanky calls me Pretty, it makes me want to slash his other cheek, but there's no sense starting a fight now.

'I ain't scared.'

'Aeson, fink of the money, man! … I'll finish your night-watch if you pull this off.' Croc's begging me to do it … otherwise it'll be him up that rope.

'How long have I got?'

'Ages – until the morning shift arrives.'

'Come on. It's a perfect plan. Lanky'll keep watch and I'll pick the lock.'

Lanky shoves Fatty towards me.

My fist clenches the boy's tunic by the shoulder and we edge along close to the wall, Croc in front. Lanky disappears back into the shadow. Hulls creak in the silence as waves slap their great bulks.

Croc holds the pulley steady while I tug the rope: it needs to hold Fatty's weight and mine.

'Move honey-nose.' I give him a shove. Fatty whimpers. 'Done much climbing?'

'S-some … in the g-gym-gymnasium.'

He needs to be calm to concentrate.

'Good. You take the rope in front of me.'

The warehouses aren't lit, and it's unlikely anyone would look up in our direction when they can look out at the Pharos, but I keep checking the docks for people.

The boy's a better climber than I expected. 'Don't look down.'

'I'm not s-scared of h-heights. I just don't want to d-die the horrible d-death the tall man said I would if I didn't help you.'

Better he's scared of me.

'You read?'

'I can read and write Greek, Latin, Coptic, and some Aramaic.'

'And the book we're after. What language is that?'

'Greek.'

'Where did you learn?' I tighten my grip round his hands. He winces from the pain. 'Concentrate. You don't want me doing any of those nasty things to you, do you?' Jealousy is a wicked thing.

'A-at the Library School. C-can I go home after I help you?'

'Just climb.' Ain't fair some kids get an education spooned to 'em.

We're nearly at the sixth floor. Over my right shoulder ship sails flap as they catch the breeze and a sailor sings as he stumbles along the quay like a disorientated ant.

'Mama and Papa buy your place at the Library School?'

'Mother died in the earthquake.'

He must be my age. It's not Fatty's fault I can't write, but I can't help wishing I was him … without the flab. Croc wouldn't fancy me fat … neither would the *cinaedus*.

The window where the pulley's attached is bigger than it looked – more of a small door with a narrow ledge. Fatty will fit.

The *cinaedus* better have paid off the guard. Knife secure in my belt, sandals tied round my neck. Butterflies make my belly churn.

'Not a sound after this.'

Fatty pulls his chubby legs up and over the ledge. I hold his sweaty armpits as his legs hang through the doorway and his feet search for the floor.

Fatty's head disappears inside. I wave down at Croc … can just about make out his shadow under the torches that line the quay. Croc had better have that lock picked in time.

Why, in Serapis' name, would a librarian want to pinch a book when he could walk in here in broad daylight and take it himself? It don't add up.

My toes reach for the floor as I manoeuvre my body through the doorway. That feels like wood beneath my feet. Come on eyes – they stretch to get used to the dark, my hearing alert like I'm on night-watch. The only sounds are Fatty's breathing and the thud of my heartbeat.

So we're on a scaffold at the top of a ladder … more a narrow staircase with a platform at the top, steadier than a scaffold. Small high windows in the huge room throw in grey light, lamps sit in niches on the landing. No lamps in the storeroom with all these books, but at least I can see the exit. Sly slits of grey light creep through gaps in the floorboards so I can just about see my feet. We're at the same level as the tops of the bookshelves. They stack them so high. There must be thousands and thousands of books in here.

'Well?' My voice echoes in the silence.

'I don't know where they keep *The Gospel of Philip.* We'll have to check the tags. Christian manuscripts will be grouped together; their tags usually have a sigma written on them.'

'Sigma?'

He's silent. But I know what he's thinking: I'm just a thick street kid. Whereas Croc and Lanky think I'm thick because I'm not streetwise. Book knowledge is nothing to them.

What's that noise? We stop. Nails scratching wood. I hold my breath and listen. Fatty grabs my arm. Let him hold it if it keeps him quiet.

A scuttle of little feet flee past ours.

'Only a mouse.'

Fatty gives out a squeal and pinches my arm.

'Shush!'

The faint edges of the shelves are only visible when I'm right up close. Tags hang from strings in neat rows. So this is how they stack the scrolls. What about the new books with pages that turn? The landlord used one to keep a note of our rent.

Fatty stops and peers at a tag. He turns it to catch the dim light. 'This way.'

We shuffle along the narrow alleyways of shelves. Impressive, how Fatty navigates his way by reading those tags.

My breath comes in sharp little jabs. The air is thick with dust and as heavy as the Necropolis at night. The thought of sleeping in the Necropolis for the rest of my life makes my gut tighten. This isn't an empty building; it's like a cemetery, a book tomb. It's too hot. Sweat re-forms on my top lip every time I brush it away. Fatty's stalling. Panic jabs my chest: what if I'm caught and sent to the mines?

'Hurry up.'

'It must be here, on the bottom shelf.' He crouches down and leans forward to examine the tags one at a time.

'Well, which one is it?'

'I can't see very well.'

'What does it look like, a sigma?'

'Like a Mu on its side.'

I'll twist his pudgy ear for that.

'S-sorry. I'll draw it on your hand.'

His nail – no brickie has nails – makes the shape of two triangles without their bottoms, two pyramids side by side.

He pulls out a scroll and shows me the tag. The dust makes us sneeze.

Need to turn it at an angle to catch the light. I can just about make out a Σ on the tag, written in black ink … and some other scribble. It's satisfying to read the letter myself.

'All these have a sigma.'

'Each t-tag has a letter on it for its category, then the first letters of the title or the letters of the opening line of the book. Or a th-theme the scribes give it if there's no title. Christian books often lack titles, s-so we'll have to check all these.'

Is Fatty just buying time for the Roman to arrive and catch me in the act with the guard?

'I th-think it must be at the bottom left hand corner of this stack.'

Why don't he get it himself if he knows where it is? What's he playing at? My stomach knots at the thought of being chained in a mine. I've got to get out of here.

My knife's out and at his throat. 'Is he here, the *cinaedus*? Is he here to catch me?' My voice cracks close to his ear.

'W-what *cinaedus*?' Fatty's snivelling.

Cool it, Aeson. Croc wouldn't double-cross me.

'Shush. Pull out the one you think it is.'

He pulls out about twenty scrolls and puts them on the floor.

'It c-could be any of th-these.'

'Get a move on. We can't carry them all.'

Fatty wipes his eyes on his tunic and turns each book tag to catch the light. 'I need to check the first line.' The scroll crackles as he unwinds it and peers at the top. '*The G-Gospel of Philip.*'

Down the front of my tunic it goes.

'Let's get the fuck out of here.'

I'll have to drag Fatty back through the shelves to the stairwell. Thank Serapis there's lamps lit out here. Downstairs we go.

The door's ajar. Good old Croc … but what if it's the guard?

'You go out first.' I push Fatty towards the door. He looks at me like I'm abandoning him. I'll wait here and listen. All I can hear is my heart thumping so loud it makes me ears throb.

'Pretty, out you come.' That's Lanky's voice. Thank Serapis! I wipe the sweat from my face and walk out the door.

Turk! What's he doing here? He's got a knife to Lanky's throat.

'Aeson, leg it!' Another boy has Croc, arms held behind his back.

Where to? The gang's got me surrounded, knives out in a semi-circle.

Turk shoves Lanky over to Druid. The tattooed Briton says something in his own language; from the look on his blue inky face, I reckon he's cussing Turk.

'Bind his hands. Patch, you tie up Pretty.'

There's nowhere to run, but I dart away from Patch. Two boys grab me. Patch pulls my arms behind my back, holds my wrists together and ties the knot.

Turk swaggers over to me like he's the Prefect. 'What do we have here then, a little mutiny, eh?' He juts his chin at me. 'Take Pretty to the Necropalace, Patch. I'll deal with him later.'

'That double-crossing *cinaedus.* He screwed us over.' Croc kicks the boy struggling to lead him away. The boy kicks him back so hard Croc falls to his knees.

'*Cinaedus* yourself.' The boy gives him another kick in the side.

'Trade is trade, Croc,' Turk shouts.

An older boy – I think they call him Fish because of his fat lower lip – yanks Croc up by the rope around his wrists as if it's a handle. That will break the skin. Patch didn't tie mine tight, but the fibres are rough as he leads me away.

What are the boys laughing and jeering at? Patch stops and turns to see. Fatty's wet himself. He stares at his feet, shoulders heaving. Poor kid.

'Shut it!' Turk slaps Fatty round the face so hard his head does a sharp twist. He shakes a piece of paper close to Fatty's face.

'These books, can you find 'em, eh?' Turk thrusts the paper into his hand. Fatty just gawps at him. 'Look at it, boy, or you'll get more than a slap.'

Fatty holds the sheet of paper in both hands to keep it still.

'Well? Can you find them, eh?'

'Y-yes.' Poor Fatty – his teeth are chattering. He looks over to me like I can do something to help him.

'Come on, Pretty.' Patch gives me a little shove to make me walk. 'Why d'ya go and do a thing like that? Turk don't take kindly to betrayal. Lost my eye when I did a runner.'

I swallow. Maybe the mines would have been better.

Aeson

Dead twigs and dust fly down the tomb steps. Weather's wild. Grit stings like mosquito bites as it hits my face. It's like the northeast wind speeding in off the sea is having a fight with the blasts of hot air that roll off the desert. With my hands tied, can't stop my hair whipping in my eyes.

Bones rattle above our heads and Lanky sneers, 'This is where they put traitors, under the old bones.' In the torchlight his bony face and big teeth look like a skull. I shudder.

My tunic's ripped and I lost my sandals, but my knife's still safely tucked in my belt. Patch didn't take that from me. Did he forget to search me? He was gentle with me on the walk back from the docks. They're not all bad.

A cheer above ground from the Necropolis: that'll be the gang.

'Turk's back.' Patch and the boys stop their game of dice, stand and look above our heads, at the entrance. The older ones jump down from the ledges and join them at the bottom of the steps.

Croc tenses, tied up next to me, his hands yank against the rope, bound behind his back and his arse shifts on the step. 'Man, we're in for it.'

Feet pound on the steps above, and the lads run past us. Some carry canvas bags that clatter as they're dropped at the bottom of the steps. Others carry scrolls. Kiya would cry to see books chucked like rubbish on top of the growing pile of loot.

Fat-lipped Fish stands at the bottom of the steps and shouts. 'Oi! Turk said put the books in his room.'

Lanky gives us a toothy sneer. 'That could have been our booty. You two will regret this.'

How did Turk know? Was it like Croc said – did that old Roman grass us up?

The sharp whack of a sandal on my back makes me lurch forward over my knees. To give me more space, Croc shifts along as far as he can without his shoulders touching Lanky's.

The gang's yelps of success sound eerie in the wind. How it howls tonight. They bunch together at the bottom of the steps, and wait. Turk must be up there behind us.

'Knights of the Necropolis.' Turk's voice is muffled as the wind speeds and thrashes through the alleys of tombs above our heads.

'Speak up.' Patch's face is turned upwards. In this light his eye-patch might be the black hole of an empty socket. My eyes scrunch tight at the thought of his punishment. Serapis, if you let me keep my eyes, I'll pray to you every night forever, I promise. How can I keep my word to Dad without both my eyes?

Boys heckle and jostle for the best view.

'Come closer.'

'Can't hear yer.'

The whites of their eyes flicker yellow in the torchlight, faces ghoulish as shadows move across them. There's a hush, like before the start of a fight in the stadium.

Turk's dusty sandalled feet are next to me. Don't look up: might make him mad. He sweeps up the folds of his toga like an orator. Where did he pinch that? He was wearing a tunic at the docks. And what happened to Fatty?

Turk raises his arms and drops the folds of material. They trail down the steps like a carpet laid out for the arrival of an emperor. He's not wearing it right. 'Noblemen, honoured warriors of Alexandria, we are gathered here tonight to celebrate this great victory.'

A cheer goes up from the gang. There's something of Seth in Turk. This skill is why he's the leader, not Lanky. The gang loves a performance. They stamp their feet.

'Quiet. Bring me my wench.' Turk milks it. He intends to drag this out.

'Up you get, Pretty.' Lanky's voice is sharp and full of menace.

My heart judders.

Turk looks down at me, his gaze hot on my neck. Don't look up. As long as I don't look up he'll ignore me.

'The little library boy called for you when we blind-folded him. He likes them soft, does our Pretty – thinks he's a man.'

What did they do to poor Fatty? He was too frightened to snitch. The gang laugh and whistle. My cheeks burn. Serapis, help me.

'Quiet, minions,' Turk orders. 'Come, Cleopatra! Take my hand. Let me show you who's the man.'

More whistling. What do I do now? Am I expected to hold his hand and act like a flipping girl? Lanky's wicked grin turns me hot with anger. I'll get you back, you ugly bastard.

'Come on, Cleo.' The lads egg me on, demanding to be entertained. 'On your feet, Pretty.'

Croc nudges me. 'Aeson, get up, man.' There's panic in his voice. I'll lose the gang's sympathy if I don't play the part. They want a show.

Take a gulp of air, swallow my pride. I know what to do: suck in my cheeks and face the gang.

They whistle encouragement, 'Go on, Pretty!'

'Untie me, Marcus, so I can perform my queenly duties.' My voice quivers, high and nervous. Will Turk untie me?

The gang whistle and cheer. Turk leans over me to slip the hard edge of his knife between my wrists. Thank Serapis, Patch left a little slack in the rope.

Now, how to play a girl? Pinch my cheekbones to blush. My hair keeps blowing back in my face every time I give it a girlie flick … and another flick. The lads laugh. Repetition, that's the key to comedy.

Turk offers his hand. 'My lady.'

Flutter of the eyelashes and look away from Turk, like I'm shy. The lads love it. I catch Croc's eye as I look down. He winks. Lanky sneers. I could slit his skinny throat.

Turk exaggerates his gestures. 'What shapely thighs you have, Cleo, darling.'

Cover my leg, make a big O with my lips and gasp, 'Marcus, dear, where's my queenly robe? My queenly thigh is shy.'

Turk grins, clicks his fingers and a small boy scrambles up the steps with a dress, torn at the neckline. What fat old noblewoman did this belong to?

Swing my hips, take a step up to Turk's height. I know: I'll wrap the robe over my head and under my chin, less Cleopatra, more desert nomad shielding her face from the sand.

The gang whoop and hoot. But as soon as they get bored, I'm done for … like when Saracen fell too many times in the arena. Better keep it going then, raise my voice to a squeal, 'Marcus Antonius, you are the ugliest man I ever seen in my life!'

Patch is the only one not laughing. He stands at the front, arms crossed, and glares at Turk with his one eye. Because he knows what comes next? Think brain, there must be a way out of this. I need my eyes.

'Cleo, my love, you are the most hideous looking woman I have ever seen, but if I make you my queen, I promise you'll be the ugliest woman in the Empire.'

Their bodies are scarred like soldiers' broken from battle. Are those missing fingers and teeth from fights, or punishment? One bad line from me and they'll demand my punishment … concentrate, Aeson.

I know what they want: off with this veil and whimper, 'Oh Marcus! Make me your Queen and givus a kiss, you ugly fucker.'

Now, pucker up, close my eyes and face Turk.

The shrieks are wild.

'KISS, KISS, KISS, KISS.'

Turk has no choice.

The kiss is not what I expect, not just for show; it's tender. He's hot for me. Bet he's hard under that toga.

'Ooooo, Marcus! You have such manly lips!' I squeal with delight.

Turk lunges at me, his tongue searching for mine. This is my chance. One hand round his neck, lift my robe and pull the knife. The blade's at his throat in an instant. He's not afraid like Fatty. He struggles and cries out, 'You little fucker!'

The blade's flat against his throat. He must know I gave Lanky that cut through his lip.

'Patch, free Croc.'

He stands, mouth open with the rest of them for a moment, then darts, knife out towards Croc.

'Patch, I'll have your other eye, you mongrel.' Spittle lands on my arm. I jerk Turk back. 'Don't just stand there, eh, you wretches …' Need to keep a tight grip on my knife to stop Turk writhing free.

The gang looks uncertain. Where does their loyalty lie, with the pretty new boy or Turk?

'Who's with me? You'll all have an equal share of the loot.' My voice sounds feeble compared to Turk's. Push depth into it. 'Who's with us?'

'Me.'

'And me.'

Young ones' voices. We need the older boys.

A fight breaks out at the back. 'Cowards! Are you scared of Pretty and his little friends?'

Fish and another older boy run at the steps.

Lanky stands. 'Untie me, Pretty.'

My stomach lurches at trusting Lanky, but we need an older boy on our side, someone they're afraid of.

'Patch, cut Lanky free.'

Croc throws himself at one of them running up the steps. Fish is coming at me. What can I do?

'One more step and I'll cut him like I did Lanky.'

Fish hesitates, then grins. 'You don't have the balls.'

My fist clenches the knife. I'll just nick under the chin.

'Argh!' Turk swings away from the blade. No you don't. I yank him. Shit, the blade's slicing across his cheek like it's a peach. His hand goes to his face, eyes wide with shock. He didn't think I'd do it. Neither did I.

'You little fucker.' He lunges at me, his fist whacks me so hard I fall back, my head thuds on the step. Everything's gone blurry. Turk yanks me up by the neck of my tunic; his face close, a bloody blur. His breath reeks. 'Your bones are mine, Pretty.'

My knife, I still have it. In it goes. Take that! He lets me go and lunges backwards before I can reach him with the blade. My feet find their footing, blade out and ready in a wide stance like Saracen. No need: Lanky jumps him. Two boys have brought down Fish.

It's difficult to work out who's winning on the steps below me, whose side which boy is on. Looks like young ones against older boys, except for Lanky. He's with us.

A group of boys band together and jump from the sacrifice slab on to Fish's back. They hold him down and grab his mouth. A filthy little boy jumps on his chest and shoves his knife in Fish's mouth, pulling on his tongue. The noise of the wind and the shouts of the gang are loud and confusing. 'It's like an eel,' he squeals as he tries to get a grip on Fish's tongue. His little elbow saws back and forth. Fish screams and writhes on the ground. 'OUT, OUT, OUT,' they chant. A tomb dog barks like he's egging them on. Fish has stopped moving – must have passed out from the pain. The little one sits up on Fish's chest like he's on the back of a horse and raises his bloody arm above this head. The cheer is a battle cry as the boy flings the tongue to the dog like it's a scrap of gristle not worth eating. My stomach lurches. They're animals.

'Man, you alright?' It's Croc. His arm's on my shoulder, but I can't feel it.

'Croc, we're leaving.'

'We can't leave. We're the leaders now.'

'Only if we fight Lanky.'

We both watch as Lanky chops and cuts, a knife in both hands, wiry muscles strong and agile as he stabs one boy after another with stadium bloodlust. Lanky's enjoying it! This is the only time I've ever seen him look happy.

Croc shakes himself like a dog shaking out a fright.

'Lanky wants our eyes, Croc.'

'But we got nowhere to go.'

'Yes we do.'

'I'm not living in that church with all those snakes if that's what yer got planned.'

'Come on.' I run up the steps. Why's Croc just standing there? My heart heaves. He's not coming with me. I run back. 'Don't fight Lanky. Croc, please.'

'Why not? You took on Turk.'

'That's different ...'

'You calling me a *cinaedus*?'

'No, Croc. I ... please come with me.'

He throws his head back and laughs his gappy hiccup. Come here, you crazy Croc: his lips are generous and warm.

'Kissy, kissy, Pretty.' Lanky's voice makes me jump backwards.

Croc's quick with his knife. He waves it at Lanky.

Turk's coming at me; his right eye's closed up, face bloodied. He intends to kill me.

'He's mine.' Lanky grins, cracks his neck both sides and races at Turk, a knife in both hands.

'Run, Aeson, while these two are at each other. Go! I've got your back, man.'

The scroll itches under my tunic. I'd forgotten about that.

'Your old Roman, where did you arrange to meet?'

'One of the posh villas on the Eastern wall, the one furthest from the harbour.'

'Croc, don't stay 'ere.'

We look at Turk and Lanky, tight in a wrestle. The gang has stopped to watch.

'Don't worry about me, man. Get out of here.'

Bones rattle as I dash up the steps. The warring winds smash against me at ground level. As I run jumbled images – a child holding Fish's tongue in the air like a centurion brandishing the Eagle after a victory, the hollow socket beneath Patch's eye-patch – drive my legs faster. Sharp stones cut into my bare feet, but I won't stop until I reach the city. The Pharos glows brighter as I approach the harbour. Need a plan, I do.

RUFIUS

Turk said he'd bring the books and the boy, so where in Bacchus' name is he? City lights draw me back to the terrace ... my blue-eyed boy is out there ... somewhere. This wind's making me more agitated than I already am: palm fronds slap the balcony and silk curtains flap like the ritual dance of the eunuch priests of Cybele. Those blasted wind chimes are tinkling so hard and fast ... my anxiety's at fever pitch.

'Get rid of those chimes.'

'Master, pacing will not bring Turk any quicker. Please, drink a little wine to calm your nerves.'

'Wine, bah! I won't drink anymore of that vinegar Theon served at my welcome dinner. I thought Egypt was the wine capital of the Empire.'

'The best vintages are shipped to Constantinople, master.'

'Vineyards have their price, Apollinos. Only the best for my cellars, do you hear me?'

'Tut.'

Even my Babylonian slavegirl's irritating me tonight. 'Stop that tutting, Cunty.'

Why am I so bent on Aeson? The thought of him makes slush of my brain. Why do those sapphire eyes haunt me when I have a mountain of pressing business – the renovation, my new position at the Library, the satisfaction of swindling Damasus and the prospect of making a fortune? Turning ideas into money usually engrosses me …

'*My purpose is to tell of bodies which have been transformed into shapes of a different kind …*'

'Ovid, master?'

'Humph? Yes, *Metamorphoses.*'

He's ripe. Never have I seen a boy within whom the ripple of potential is so tantalising on the cusp of manhood: arms, shoulders, the line of his jaw. How I quivered under his vigilant gaze on Venus Street … and how disappointed I was not to be the focus of his attention in the Agora this evening. It made me crave my own youth, yearn to feel an admirer's gaze so hot upon me that something of me is stolen – or perhaps invigorated – under its scrutiny.

'Apollinos, when you were a boy did you know I noted every small change: how the muscles in your arms would harden after a day swimming at the gymnasium, only to be soft again a day later? Did you feel my gaze gnaw into you?'

Is that sadness in Apollinos' eyes? I regret the thrashing I gave him earlier, but sulking is banned at Biblos.

'No doubt, master, this boy will disappoint like all the others.'

'None of my boys disappoint. They simply … change … change into something quite gross to me. How odd that the bulk of a man revolts me – me a *cinaedus* – who ever heard such a thing! But then one's sexuality is as individual as a fingerprint.'

I do believe the girl flinched at the word.

'Do not think I insult myself, Cunty – although don't let me catch that word uttered in this house by anyone but me – I wear the label with pride. Is it not better to accept our nature?'

'I'm a princess.'

'Indeed you are, dear …' … although Apollinos will have a thing or two to say about it.

'What about the books, master? What if that ruffian sells them himself?'

'It is more difficult than you think to sell heretic books, Apollinos. Collectors must be careful, and they're not the calibre of client a street urchin like Turkey ...'

'Turk.' Apollinos spits it like a curse. He's such a snob.

'Yes, yes. Turk does not keep company with bishops and politicians and emperors ...' What beautiful eyes the Greek boy had ... once I've had the street urchin my business focus will return.

'Master?'

'Roman pimps would never mess me around like this, Apollinos.'

'The university's teeming with boys, master.'

Get a grip, Rufius. What about the books? Titus has a small fortune in newly minted gold coins waiting for their delivery. Think of what sculptures I can commission, what extravagances I can luxuriate in with all that money.

'I want Carrara marble pleasure-loving gods in each corner of the triclinium, Apollinos.'

'Yes, master.' He's relieved I've changed the subject.

'And here, as you enter, that bust of myself at fourteen we ferried from Rome. Um, frescoes of lush forests, I think for this room, that I can dream about returning to while exiled in this city crushed between the salt of the desert and the salt of the sea.' Curse Damasus!

'Master, what about ochre paint for ...'

'THIEF, THIEF!' A commotion in the gardens draws us to the balcony.

'Thank Bacchus! Some sport.'

Apollinos rushes off downstairs, appears on the terrace below and shouts orders. He used to be bossy in the bedroom too. Slaves hold torches above their heads in the garden and look up at the house. Have they spotted the thief?

A svelte figure jumps from the adjacent balcony – what was he doing in my library? – onto the roof below my balcony, and runs across it fast as an athlete with a swift trot ... or is that a limp? He's hurt. My slaves pull themselves up onto the roof after him. They don't have his agility, or his speed even with that limp. Run, my Olympic champion.

Where's he gone? There, climbing the wallflowers.

'Over here.' I point in the direction of the bougainvillea by the terrace. The dry bract cracks under his weight. Twigs fall away, but he doesn't. His speed saves him as he grabs one branch after another above his head. He needs a hair cut whoever he is. Dark curly hair flaps in the wind, but I can't see his face. Villa Biblos needs better lighting. I'll have nooks cut for wall lamps.

The boldness of it – he's heading for the roof terrace.

'Come on, Cunty! The entertainment's arrived.' I rush past the girl and head for the stairs, thrilled by the chase.

She runs past me up the marble stairs. 'My name's Aphrodite.'

What doting Greek named you? 'You're Biblus in this household, dear.'

The girl's ahead of the game – she waves me over to where she's crouched between a potted olive tree and the cushioned seating that skirts the terrace wall. Good, I'm in time. I crouch beside her. Is that my knees creaking?

We wait, slow our breathing and listen.

Bougainvillea rustles … he's nearly at the top. The girl frowns, puts her finger over her bud of a mouth to hush my wheezing. 'Shush.'

Ha! What fun!

She's alert as Diana ready for the hunt.

Is that a hand on the balcony? Yes, an arm, then a foot follows.

Off she darts.

Wait for me, dear! Curse these knees. My joints need oiling.

It's a boy, not a man. The thief pulls himself on to the ledge and crouches on all fours; still can't see his face. He's looking at my neighbour's villa. The crazy boy's going to jump to the next building. An impossible jump.

'Stop, dear!'

The girl grabs his tunic.

He bats her off, stands and runs along the wall; lean muscles shine in the terrace torches. What perfect proportions.

'Stop. We won't hurt you,'

By Bacchus! He jumped.

We both gasp and run to the ledge.

Blood on the white marble ledge makes me queasy – his foot must be bleeding.

'Have a look, dear. I can't bear to. Did he make it?'

She leans over the balcony on tiptoes, as I hold her waist.

'Yes.' She sounds as relieved as I am.

We both sigh.

Let's see. The thief's hanging from my neighbour's roof terrace; legs dangle as he tries to pull himself up by his arms.

Torches flicker in the gardens below. My neighbour's household is in a noisy commotion. Apollinos' face appears over the ledge of my neighbour's terrace, above the boy's head. The thief looks around like a desperate animal. He sees he's trapped. Below are the street guard. Above, Apollinos and a scrum of unfriendly faces.

'Get him,' Apollinos orders.

Slaves in white and gold Biblos tunics swing their legs over, knives clenched between their teeth.

Apollinos looks over at me. 'We have him, master.'

The thief turns his head to face me.

By Bacchus! My Olympian-eyed boy!

What luck! I feel like I've caught a whale whilst fishing for minnow. Time to reel him in.

'Bring him to me, Apollinos. And dismiss the guard.' My voice is firm, although I am flimsy as a moth fluttering around a lamp.

'Yes, master.' He can wipe that look of smug satisfaction off his face.

'No need to be smug, dear.'

The girl winks at me: she's calculated the household dynamics. I chose well.

'Come on, Diana, we have a guest. Tell the cook to arrange some food.'

'Yes, master.' Off she thuds to put the kitchen staff to work. Halfway down the stairs she pauses and looks back. 'Is that my new name, master: Diana?'

'Yes, Diana, why not? You pounce like the goddess of the hunt. Now off you go, Cunty.'

She skips, two pounces to each marble step, pronouncing her new name to herself.

'The goddess of the hunt does not skip.'

Diana slows her step to a calm, measured patter. I did choose well. Now, let's see if I still have the charm to seduce a beauty.

16

RUFIUS

Where shall I sit? On the wide couch with the crimson cushions … in front of my bust? Yes. Legs up or down? One up, one down: nonchalant. What will he see – an aging effeminate? Will that repulse him … or will he yearn for a taste of the high life?

'You're in for it now, you little tyke.' Apollinos' reprimanding tone jars my nerves as the parlour doors swing open.

Oh, Apollinos! Did he have to tie the poor boy with ropes?

'Master, this is the same thief who led us to the Ophites.' So Apollinos recognised the boy. Who wouldn't with those pale blue eyes, bright in his grimy face?

Apollinos nods at the slaves to bring the boy over to me. Look what a good slave I am, what prize do I get? You fool, Apollinos.

'Welcome to Villa Biblos, dear.'

His defiant blue eyes lock into mine.

'The City Guard is waiting in the atrium, master.'

'Apollinos, I told you to dismiss the guard.'

Apollinos turns a brighter shade of crimson than my new cushions, all the way from his neck to his forehead.

'But …'

Don't you but me. 'What is his crime?'

'Theft, master.'

'What did he steal?'

'We caught him in the library, master.'

'And what did he steal?'

'If you will allow me to search him, master, I will show you the evidence.'

The poor boy has something stuffed down the front of his tunic.

'I don't imagine he can hide much under that skimpy tunic, Apollinos.'

'He was with that rent boy who stole Titus Arrius' purse in the Agora, master.' Apollinos' crimson shine is as bright as if he'd stood all day in the desert. 'Remember, master, …'

'No, Apollinos, I don't remember.' My legs are stiff from crouching with Diana on the roof terrace. One knee clicks. Best stay in the one position to avoid looking like an invalid. 'Now, answer my question, what did he steal?'

'Master, he broke into the house …' Apollinos is pleading, grasping like my blue-eyed boy clutched at the bougainvillea.

'Perhaps he lost his way, perhaps he wanted to borrow a book!'

The boy's furtive gaze darts from Apollinos to me. If he's surprised at my reaction, he doesn't show it. I do believe his expression has assumed my own incredulity. The look of confusion on Apollinos' face is an added bonus to this lucky turn of fate, but I'm tired of playing with him.

'You are dismissed.'

'I think I should remain – in case he tries to escape, master.'

'Tie him to that pillar, boys.' That will prevent him running off.

Diana patters in, not her usual heavy step, with a tray of cold meats, figs and bread.

'Thank you Diana, dear.'

Apollinos' jaw gapes lower still at my calling the new slave by anything other than the family name.

'Drama's over. Off you go. I will decide if a crime's been committed.' The slaves patter off. 'And, Apollinos, dismiss the Guard – do as I say this time. I do not expect my orders to be ignored, boy.' He hates me calling him boy.

Aeson's been assessing the dialogue. It's a skill slaves pick up, the ones who retain their wit, but there's nothing in the boy's countenance that speaks of service.

'Do you have something for me?'

He looks uncertain, but senses he should play along in case there's a way out.

'Like what?' Plebeian accent, but soft, no sharp street edge.

'Has Turk sent you?'

His gaze flicks to the terrace.

'Untie me first.'

'How can I trust you won't be over that balcony like a bird?'

'What you want's under my tunic.'

Cheeky Alexandrian urchin … I do believe I'm blushing!

He sizes me up as I walk over to the wine jug.

'You must be in shock. Drink this.' I hold the cup to his mouth. Whoops, let's wipe that dribble of wine from his chin. A soft down, but no bristles yet. He's almost ready. Let's give his bicep a squeeze like a slave would test the ripeness of a melon in the market. Muscle undulates under smooth honey skin as he tugs at the rope like prize carp gliding through water; the jut of his collar bone, the elegant crusade of his shoulders, stretched back around the pillar. Oh my!

'Answer my question: where's Turk?'

'You had a deal with Croc. I'm delivering for Croc, not Turk.' He pushes depth into his voice like all boys that aspire to be manly, but there's nothing gruff in his tone.

Croc's deal … perhaps Turk isn't the pimp I thought he was.

These ropes are knotted too tight. He smells of the streets, but there's a hint of his own odour. He may be a boy, but his armpits emit the robust scent of a man. My ancient groin stirs. That's got it; the rope falls at my feet.

'Thanks.' He rubs his wrists, loosens his belt and pulls out a crushed papyrus scroll. What a way to carry a book! Is he reading the tag? There's more to this boy. 'Here.' He hands it to me and tightens his belt.

The Gospel of Philip. Good. Crocodile is more reliable than his pimp.

'Indeed, you're quite right. Crocodile and I had an agreement.'

His foot's bleeding; the blood on the roof terrace balcony, the limp …

'Dear boy, my men have hurt you. Diana!'

The girl patters in.

'Fetch balm for our guest's wounds … and fill his cup, dear.'

'Yes, master.'

That's it, dear. Drink up.

He raises his cup. 'To your health, sir.' I do believe he intends to charm me.

We drink, both eyeing each other.

'Sit down, relax.' I pat the cushion next to me. Nope, he wants to sit on the couch nearest the balcony, and look around between sips.

'Croc knows I'm here. You can trust me … with the payment, I mean.'

'You seem a trustworthy sort of man.' He liked that I called him a man. This is progress.

Diana clatters in with a tray of vials and a small bowl of water.

'That will be all, Diana.'

'Let me clean that cut, dear.' I motion for him to come to me.

'It's just a scratch.' He shoots a swift glance at the balcony, and gulps back the rest of the wine. 'Thanks for the wine. You have the book. Now pay up what you agreed with Croc.'

I've scared him off.

'There's no rush, dear. Your boss, Turk and I had a deal too.'

'Bet you did, but I'm not part of the bargain.'

'Turk seemed to think so.'

'Turk ain't my pimp, Rufius.' His gaze is steady, defiant. I like the way he says my name.

'Well then, let's strike a deal of our own, Aeson.' By Bacchus, this is too much fun. 'I'm sure we can come to a mutually beneficial agreement. Please, make yourself comfortable.'

His shoulders relax. He's going to explore the room.

I like to watch him touching my possessions, dragging his fingers across the carved tables, the edge of the gold tray, the vials. He picks one up and wafts it under his nose.

'Frankincense.' He picks up another. 'Um, patchouli, rosemary and this one … myrrh.' He places each one back on the tray with respect. We share that: an appreciation of fine things.

'You have a cultured nose. And you read too? I'm impressed.'

'A student showed me the mark.' Ha! Of course, they must have found some kid who knows the Library. Resourceful, these young Alexandrians. He looks ashamed. How curious.

'You are of Greek descent?'

'Yes, my mother was the daughter of a rich man, but she died. I ran away to make me own fortune.'

The usual lie. The more imaginative rent boys like to create elaborate histories about how they fell into the gutter. I love to watch him talk. I search for subject matter in his repertoire so as to not ruin my adulation. Maturity is an act, and some boys are adept at faking it.

'So, our deal, dear?'

'Clean slate, nothing to do with Turk?'

'Just ours. You have been to the games?'

'Course I have.'

'And your favourite gladiator?'

'Saracen. He's filled me pockets many times.'

'Ah! A virtuous occupation.' Hide your surprise, Rufius, don't arch your eyebrows. 'Perhaps we should wage together?'

He's considering, that frown is serious.

'Are you a winner?'

Most boys would jump at the chance to gamble, no questions asked.

'Well?' Aeson arches an eyebrow.

What fun! Rearrange my face: we are entering negotiation.

'I have the means to play.' I walk over to my chest, pull off my ring key, and take a hand full of coins from my domestic hoard. I'm showing him how to rob me.

'How much?' He's taken the bait.

Let's tempt him with the clatter money.

Grubby hands weigh a gold coin in each.

'Not the first time I've held a gold coin, it ain't.' His wonder proves he's lying. Lamplight catches the gold and throws a yellow glow up into his face. What an unusual boy. His whole being has taken up the room like the best actors fill a stage, like he's part of the household. I want him, but more than that, I don't want him to leave Biblos.

'I will advise you, Rufius – for a fifty percent cut.'

'And if we lose?'

'I never lose.' His skin moves fluidly over his jaw as he talks, pulling in on the Greek ωs and os.

'You never lose?' I can't prevent my eyebrows rising.

'Never.' Did he realise I was hoping he'd say lose again?

'Thirty percent, and the book you stole from my library.'

He looks defiant again.

'Forty. Take it or leave it.' 'He throws one of the coins back on the table. 'And I'll take this one for Croc, as payment for the book.'

Most boys would take both.

'You have a deal on the condition you explain what you were doing in my library.' He looks pained. 'I need to know I can trust you, dear. You can borrow any book from my library whenever you wish. All you need to do is ask.'

'Was just looking for something to pinch, sir.' He's lying. There were gold knives on my desk. He didn't find whatever he was looking for.

What's he picked up my pen for? He holds it the way a labourer holds a hammer. Don't ruin the moment, Aeson. It's always the same with the street kids – such financial sophistication, but no finesse when it comes to the arts.

What's that look for? By Bacchus, I'm soft and malleable as wet papyri pinned beneath his Olympian glare.

'Teach me to write.'

'What?' All the control releases from my face. I want to laugh, but I do believe he's serious.

'You want to learn to write?'

His nod is grave. What a strange aspiration in a street urchin. There again … such beauty must harbour something of the Muses, surely. And it would mean I could hold on to him … but I don't have the patience to teach him. It would kill this glorious Olympian haze I've entered into.

'It takes a long time to learn, unlike the art of gambling. A year, maybe more.'

'Not afraid of hard work, I'm not.'

And there's the grammar … I'm pacing again, hot with excitement for the idea – a future with this boy? What an odd sensation: I do believe I feel positive.

'Forget the money, the games and all that. You teach me to write and I'll be your rent boy for free.'

'You have a deal, dear.'

'Just until I can write that is.'

'Of course, when you have mastered the pen you are free to leave.'

I pace the terrace. Ah! The sweet scent of roses. My garden's taking shape. The lighthouse flickers across the harbour … my word it's an imposing building all lit up. I see for the first time what my cabin slave saw, like I'm viewing the Pharos from another perspective.

'Come here.'

He joins me.

'Aeson, you see there, the Serapeum, and over there, the Museum?'

'Yes.' He looks at the buildings like a beggar lusts for chicken roasting on a spit. I have the upper hand.

'Alexandria's Library still holds the most comprehensive collection in the World.' Although it will have reduced slightly tonight if that pimp Turk ran off with the books. 'Once, the greatest minds gathered here in Alexandria, in Eratosthenes' time.'

His expression is inquisitive, not gormless.

'Eratosthenes calculated the diameter of the Earth.'

'Like the diameter of a weight? Makes sense, that the Earth has a diameter – um, it's round.'

'How do you know what a diameter is?'

'I'm not stupid.' With an accent like that he's not educated, but he's quick. This might not be as tricky as I thought.

'Alexandria still has the best medical school in the Empire.'

Success shines in his blue eyes as he looks out over the city. I don't keep boys for more than a night in my own home – responsibility usually kills my passion. He played me better than Diana and has more power over me than the Archbishop of Rome.

AESON

—Two Weeks Later—

This schoolroom don't get enough sunshine in the afternoon. Palm trees cut up the light into thin shadows, they do. Shit, I did it again … I'm surprised that slave Apollinos has a hand left, he slaps it so hard every time he shouts *superfluous repetition!*

His large desk, directly in front of my smaller one blocks the view beyond the terrace. Apollinos is writing another one of his lists. Diana says the only time he smiles is when he gets to cross a word off. Words. Words are built from the letters of the alphabet. A few gangs of letters all Alexandrians know – fish, cheese, bread, taverna, doctor, lawyer, fight, god – signs we see in the street. But writing them is practice and pain, practice and pain … and boring.

Once a week I get to use ink. Writing's easier with the wax tablet as I can scrub out the mistakes. This page is already smudged with inky fingerprints.

I'd grow to loath you, dear. That's why Rufius sent the slave to teach me; his attention span's shorter than a kid's. *Lessons start sharp after dawn. Break at noon, more lessons. We dine together.* Routine, routine, routine.

Looks like Apollinos' long sucked in face will sink into itself one day. Younger than Rufius, but those hollow cheeks make him look older than he is, whereas Rufius' excess fat makes him look more like a chubby-cheeked baby than a wrinkly.

A whiff of cut grass. Garden smells tug like tarts calling from windows on Venus Street. Fed up being cooped up inside Biblos, I am. I want to run barefoot on the lawn, but Apollinos ain't letting me go nowhere, not until I finish the alphabet – over and over again.

Rufius made such a fuss turning this guestroom – Biblos has rooms just for visitors – into a schoolroom. Made me feel well special, it did. The Muses in one corner: all white and perfect, a bust of Rufius in the other. Can't get away from him, can I? It's like he's watching me in every room. How many of them does he have?

A palm frond sways and chops criss-cross shadows on the walls. Apollinos sighs, puffs at his list and looks up.

'Concentrate. The sooner you finish, the sooner you'll be out there.' By the look on Apollinos' face, he wants to add: *you little tyke.*

I'd better scratch my pen across the page or he'll start slapping his hand on my desk again. He wants to whack me, but I reckon Rufius told him he can't. Biblos is better than my plan: pinch the Snake People's book and bargain with Seth to teach me to write. Who'd want to live in a crusty old temple full of snakes and nutty Christians? Not me!

Apollinos ain't bad. Even when he looks at me odd, he don't hate me. Seen hate in Lanky's face, wicked ideas in his eyes; seen revenge in Turk's. When I think of Turk and Lanky my heart goes bang, bang. They'll come after me – unless they kill each other first. I've been searching for Croc, running the rooftops at night. Looked everywhere. Even went back to the gang's tomb. Deserted, it was. Serapis only knows where he's hiding.

Stop eyeballing me, Apollinos. Here he comes again. Better put my head down. He pads over. His eyes dig into the back of my head. I want out of here, away from his beady glare.

My wrist's killing me. Let's wiggle my fingers, clench and stretch. No difference. Ain't natural, holding a pen for so long. Curse this pen for not doing what I want.

'Unless you relax your grip, you won't achieve a smooth stroke.'

Why, in Hades, do all the alphas have to be exactly the same size, with the same shaped loop and tail? Tyrant slave. At least I'm keeping my promise to Dad. Look at me now, Dad.

'Line them up flush to the edge. Your deltas are going to walk off the page.'

How about I itch my head like I've got lice? That'll scare him off. Ain't no lice left after all the stinky potions I've been scrubbed and dunked in.

Apollinos takes a step back from my desk. It worked.

'Relax your hand. It's not a knife. Hold it gently, like you'd hold a fish you've just caught in Lake Mareotis,' ... *like the street urchin you are,* he wants to add. It's a dig: only the poor fish.

His breath stinks: lunch must be rotting in his belly.

I know that look. Dead jealous of me, ain't yer, Apollinos? But he's more secure as Rufius' slave, than I am as Rufius' lover. Reckon he loves the old *cinaedus.*

'Thumb rests against index finger.'

Nag, nag, nag. Yuk, he's sprayed gob on me again. I wipe my cheek. Why does he have to spit his sibilants? By Serapis, I know what a sibilant is! I'm getting clever. Maybe I should start exaggerating my s's? Nah, makes honey-noses sound like snakes, and Apollinos sound like a hissing snob.

Rufius would say what he thinks. 'This room's hot enough without your smelly breath on my neck.' I mumbled it.

'Did you say something?'

'No.' Head down. I'm trapped too, Apollinos. What other options I got? It's the streets, or that snake pit of a church ... or forget my promise to Dad and become a brickie's apprentice like Dera wanted. The thought of Dera makes me sad. I miss him.

'Concentrate!' Spit sprays the side of my face.

'Curse this pen.' The reed pen jerks from my grip and smacks the floor beside the carved legs of my desk ... the feet are leopard paws.

Apollinos bends to pick it up in the automatic way slaves do. So do I. Sunbeams light up his face: he's cross. I get why. It's up-side-down: a brainbox like Apollinos picking up a street kid's pen.

Let the slaves do the work, dear. Rufius' words nag me from last night when I'd poured his wine. It was my way to thank him for my new tunic and sandals, but there's only one way to thank Rufius. Apollinos didn't like me serving Rufius either.

Better sit up and look at the page. My writing's a right mess.

Take the reins, that's what they respect, dear boy. You steal their purpose in life if you do their work.

'Apollinos, stop puffing.' The snap of my voice surprises both of us. Never spoken to an adult like that before. My thighs and buttocks grip the seat – will he slap me?

We eyeball each other … if it's a staring match you want, take a load of these! Hold it. Stretch my eyelids wider … focus on the black dot of his pupils. His lids are a bit stretched. Not slits like the Eastern traders that arrive on the spice boats, but not round like mine. Steady. That's it. This is more fun than the alphabet.

With a sigh, his face softens. I won! His eyes roll as if to say, *you're just a kid.* That's more annoying than him looking down his long nose at me like I'm an uneducated pleb.

A wipe of the cloth and the nib's clean again. He places the pen in the pot and squeezes it to pull the ink up the shaft. Each movement is exaggerated for my benefit.

'You're pressing too hard with the nib. The shaft is like a fish. Hold it too tight and it will jump from your grasp, too gently and it will slither away. Try again.'

He places the pen on the gold tray along with the neat row of nib knives and offers it to me in the humble way he'd offer it to Rufius. Some battles can be won without drawing blood. That's new to me.

This ink's black. Is purple ink more expensive?

'Try filling it yourself this time.'

Why's nothing happening when I squeeze? Squeeze harder.

'Gentle, but firm. A fish, remember?'

'Apollinos, 'ow much does ink cost?'

His eyes narrow. The ink will be locked away tonight. There's less trust in this house than in the Necropalace.

'Some types cost more than others. The most expensive is Tyrian purple sourced from the purpurea.'

He reads the question on my face.

'It's a shellfish. The veins of its neck and jaws secrete a tiny amount of the royal colour. Rare, and in constant demand. I once saw it used by the Head Librarian.' His eyes are distant as he stares straight ahead of him into his past, as if this was an important moment in his life. 'It resembled the colour of coagulated bullocks' blood.'

'Really?' Is that what you left me, Dad – a bottle of Tyrian ink?

'Really.' He mimics my exclamation and shoots me a warning look. 'This ink here is the common sort, made from a solution of copper, soot and charcoal, and not worth anywhere near as much.'

'What does the purple stuff cost?'

'It can cost as much as three pieces of gold.'

I was conned. That copyist in the Emporium gave me silver.

'How much does three pieces of gold buy?' A boat, a house?

'That was the sum the master paid for me.' His stare fixes on the statue of Memory. So does mine. Yup, Apollinos was Rufius' bum boy. No doubt about it.

'Enough talk. Back to the alphabet. Practise, practise, practise.' He never calls me by my name. Can't bring yourself to call me master either like you were told, can you? That'd be strange for me too.

If I push the side of my hand into the desk it's easier to make the α round.

'That's it. Now try to pick up the pace.'

The faster I go the more the letters lose their roundness. The brickies would laugh at me struggling. Apollinos don't laugh. I like him for that.

'Shit!' The pen's slipped out of my hand again. I'm burning up with the shame of failing.

'If you don't learn to write, he'll tire of you. Learn, and you might hold his interest – the master likes a project.' Is he trying to help me, or himself?

'And you avoid a whipping for failing to teach me, right?'

His sigh's lost its edge of irritation. 'The master intends to present you at the Library. He has a fantasy that you will enter public life.'

My head spins. Public life! That's way beyond Dad's vision. But then what exactly was Dad's vision? What would Dera think? It's a trade. Can't imagine Dera would like the idea of me as a … what?

'What d'you mean, public life?'

'The law, politics.'

A politician? Dera definitely won't rate it.

'I just wanna learn to write.' My voice sounds bewildered.

'There are degrees of writing. Beyond copying there are the arts of transcription, translation, of putting on the page one's private thoughts, the thoughts of a nation, or the words of the gods.'

I can't do all that. The room feels smaller like I'm being sucked into an airless tunnel.

'Little by little. Great books are written word by word.' Apollinos speaks in the low, gentle tone mothers use to trick babies to eat.

Breathe, Aeson, breathe in the roses from the garden. Are those hairs on the back of my hand new? Everything's changing so fast. Must keep up with it. This is the pace of my life now. Money did this; money made my life speed up.

'What does a politician do?'

'Talks.'

'Then why am I learning to write? Anyone can talk.'

'To talk well is the highest art. Oration requires written preparation.' His tone is no nonsense. 'You've missed your first level of schooling. We have a year to bring you up to speed. You'll join the Library school midway through the *Grammatica*, which will polish your writing skills, teach you the basics of oration as well as Latin and Greek.'

'I speak Greek.'

'In a fashion …'

'You taking the piss?' That's another difference between us. You speak like a honey-nose, Apollinos, with your fat vowels.

He ignores me and continues. 'You will learn all you need to know by reading Homer and Virgil. There will be some geometry and astronomy, but you won't have the opportunity to focus on any subject in detail until you finish your *Grammatica.* Then, if the master wishes, you will progress to the *Rhetor.*'

'What's that?'

'You will learn to speak. Not recital, but composition, public speaking. You will acquire style – how you say something is as important as what you say. Listen to the politicians in the Agora …' He's on a roll. I don't think I've ever seen Apollinos so excited. He strides over to the statue of the Muses and rests his long fingers on Memory's marble shoulder. 'Finally, you will learn how to memorise your speeches.' He looks into the eyes of the goddess and caresses the marble like Rufius strokes Diana. 'But first you will master the alphabet.'

I can't be an orator. This pen won't ever feel like ropes do in my hands.

'I'm just a brickie's son.' Shit! That's not what I told Rufius.

'All in good time. The best civil engineers know the perfect mix for mortar.'

It's a good comparison.

'From the bottom up.'

He opens his mouth like he's about to say something then clamps it shut to stifle a laugh. I didn't mean Rufius' bottom, but that's what we're both thinking.

'You have wit beyond your years. We just need to make you sound like it.'

Rufius would snap at you for saying *we*. I like it – makes me feel like we're a team. I like that I know it's the first person plural too, makes me feel well clever.

'Deal. Shake on it?'

He stares at my hand.

'Deal.' He says the word like it's the first time he's ever struck a bargain. That's another difference between us: I can trade. 'We all stumble when we learn something new.'

That made me smile. Everyday you dole out another bit of pride, don't you, Apollinos? But then so does Rufius every time he bends over.

18

KIYA

'Aoi-oia ...' ... what if he's dead, or worse, that lanky demon has him? It's impossible to concentrate on the magic words tonight. Two weeks I've prayed for Aeson, begging he's safe and no sight of him. If I kiss my snake one more time my lips will fall off.

Sophia's awake now the moon's high. Hungry Sophia? I must be careful not to let any dormice escape this time. What a wriggler this one is. I'll have to pinch its tail tighter. That's it. Sophia's mouth opens and closes round the mouse. I don't like to watch Sophia eat: mouse tail hanging out of her mouth, the little body manoeuvred down her endless throat. I have an affinity with mice. They're born spontaneously from the rubbish tips like I was. Henite found me – newborn, wrapped in tax returns, wills and leases.

Let's try again. Eyes closed this time. 'Aoi-aoi-aoi. Ma-ma-amen. Aoi-aoi-Ah! What made the floor vibrate? It was heavy. What if it's a demon? I'm too scared to open my eyes.

'Kiya. It's just me.' A kind, hush of a voice ... 'Aeson!'

Thank Sophia he's alive. What's different? The moonlight from the window lights up his face. He's clean. New tunic.

'Why can't you visit at normal times and come through the door like everyone else? We were worried sick. Where have you been?' I sound like Henite when she nags me. Every nasty death's been through my head.

'This was the quickest I could get away. Got myself a right generous honey-daddy – I mean men-tor.'

'Mentor. Only rich kids have mentors.'

Where's *The Book of Wisdom*? He doesn't have it with him, just his sandals strung around his neck.

'I'm learning to write … but your book, I'm sorry Kiya, I don't have it.'

'It was our only copy.' My eyes burn with tears. It's not his fault, but he looks so ashamed.

'I know where it is. Just can't steal it yet, but I will. I promise.'

'It's not stealing if it's our book.'

We both jump at the grunt of snoring somewhere below in the temple. Sophia hisses.

'It's only your friend Croc – he's sleeping.'

'Croc? Here?' His eyes are wide and urgent.

'Yes. He needs to rest.'

Croc was just as desperate to hear if I had news of Aeson when he turned up at the church yesterday. There's love between them.

'Turk shut him in a loculus. Croc said he escaped somehow. It was all a bit jumbled, then he fainted, from hunger Henite said.'

Aeson crouches down beside my straw sleeping-mat.

'Kiya, take me to him.' His voice in my ear is like seashells stroking the beach.

'He's in the room below this one.' I can't refuse him.

Aeson stares at the floor like he's willing it to open. A lot of tiles are missing: Dionysus is almost erased, only his wild hair remains, but his Maenads still dance around him. This temple must have been beautiful a hundred years ago.

'Man, am I glad to see you!'

How did Croc open that door without it creaking? It always creaks. Gives me the creeps, the way these two just appear without warning.

'Croc!'

The two of them look as different as marble and brick under the moonbeams that fall through the high window. Same height, same age; one clean, dressed like a rich boy, legs and arms gleaming with oil; the other in a threadbare tunic, skin scabby and caked in grime like plaster crumbling from an old tomb.

They hug, push each other on the shoulders and laugh. Left out as usual – I never get a hug and a push.

'Shush! You'll wake Henite and Seth.'

'SHUSHHH!' They both hiss.

'Don't make fun of me.' I swipe my crutch at Aeson's legs. He jumps and grabs the rope hanging from the window. So that's how he got up there, the rope must be attached to the roof terrace … but how did he get on the roof? 'I was in deep meditation before you two interrupted me.'

'Croc, let's climb onto the roof. No one will hear us up there.'

Croc grabs the window frame and pulls himself out onto the rope. He looks nervous hanging there. 'Aeson, man, we need to talk. You're in serious shit.'

What about me? Well, I have my own adventure: I follow the power words and they lead me to the Kingdom of God … but I'd prefer to climb up to the roof terrace.

'Come on, Kiya. Pray later.' Aeson holds out his arms. Is he teasing me?

He grabs me under my armpits … over his shoulder I go. He smells like a honey-nose. His grip's strong like a man. I don't let anyone carry me, but this is the only way up to the roof.

Croc leans over the edge of the roof terrace and clutches my armpits as Aeson raises me up.

'Careful with my crazy priestess, Croc.'

Sweet Sophia, no one ever called me *theirs* before. Henite says nobody can be owned, that even slaves' souls are free, but I'm fine being his.

Croc hauls me up and over. 'Up you come, bossy.' Croc grins as

I shrug out of his grip. Never noticed the gap between his front two teeth until now. Aeson likes you, so I will too.

'I can see the whole city.'

Croc laughs and looks down at the rope to check on Aeson. No need. Aeson swings himself over the ledge with the grace of an angel.

Sweet Sophia, it's like I can reach up and touch the Kingdom of God. We lie on our backs on the limestone, arms outstretched over our heads, fingertips touching fingertips like angels. No, like friends. My cheeks hurt I'm grinning so wide.

I turn my head to the right, and look at Aeson. He smiles back. When I look the other way, Croc laughs his hiccup giggle. I laugh too.

'I'm sorry I couldn't get your book, Kiya.'

'I know.'

'The scribes will copy it. Then I'll get it for you.'

'Seth said they won't. He doesn't trust them.'

'Give me some time to get settled in.'

'U-huh.' How am I going to save Aeson's soul without the book? Only the Aberamenthos know the magic words by heart. How will I get my robes?

Aeson pinches my fingertips. 'Kiya. I promise.'

Something in his voice, the gentle way he has, makes me believe him.

'I believe you.'

'Man, stuff the book. Turk's on a warpath for yer balls. You got no idea what kicked off after you scarpered.'

'I went to the Necropalace looking for you. It was deserted.'

'Keep your voices down.' Why are they getting so wound up?

'Turk won the fight.'

'Lanky's dead?'

Lanky's the tall demon. He's still out there: I can feel his evil spirit.

'He ran off. I ran off too, soon as Turk won. Turk hunted down the ones who took our side. It was out and out war. Made an example of the traitors …'

Croc's talking fast like he's running for his life. '… Turk found me sleeping near the rubbish tips, put me in a tomb and closed the slab. Man, dark as Hades in there it was … had to dig me way out, like a fox – dug right under the limestone. Kept thinking, I'm gonna die down here.'

Croc's fingers let go of mine. He's shivering.

'There's a price on your head, man. I know Turk. He'll come after yer. And yer old honey-nose Roman won't be able to do nuffink to stop him. Nuffink.'

'Where's Turk now?'

'Gone after Lanky, but he'll be back. Some of the boys said he was just making a point. Turk'd calm down after a few weeks and forget about it. I said man, I said, no – Turk don't forget nuffink. He bears grudges, Turk does.'

'And Patch?'

'Patch was so scared he went it alone. I said, Patch, I said, we should stay together. He was having none of it. Druid's gone into hiding too. S'pose he can hide easier than the others with all his body paint.'

Croc doesn't laugh at his joke.

Aeson flicks him a gold coin and winks.

Croc bites it and looks amazed. 'Man, d'ya know where the *cinaedus'* stash is? We can do a job. With you on the inside, it'll be a synch, then scarper, live like emperors. You in?'

'I need Rufius to trust me.'

'Oh Rufius, is it?' Croc looks at Aeson like he's betrayed him. 'So now you're bumming honey-daddy you forget yer mates, is that it?'

'I promised Dad, see, before he died, that I'd learn to write.'

'Man, you and your promises. Aeson, life changes. Sometimes it don't make no sense to keep 'em. Sometimes, it's wrong to keep 'em.'

Arm flung over forehead, Croc stares up at the sky. Aeson looks sad. His fingers are limp. I press my fingertips into his.

'Make him love you then, your mentor.'

'Love!' Croc nearly spits out the word. 'Love don't come into it, Priestess. You gotta keep a honey-nose interested, keep him dangling. Hard work the oldies are.'

'I just want to learn to write, then I can earn my own money.'

'What good's writing?' He doesn't seriously think he can make a living from writing does he?

'She's right. That's what slaves are for and they don't charge for it.'

'Dad told me if I could write, I wouldn't have to work like a donkey.'

Aeson's fingers clench into a tight ball. He pulls his hand away from mine. The world seems smaller all of a sudden, even up here under the stars. I have an idea …

'What if he adopts you, like Seth did with me.'

'Adoption?'

'She's crazy as she looks. Adoption. Don't know any lads who've managed that one.'

Croc's such a know-all. I cross my arms in front of my chest.

'Ouch!'

A kick's more effective than words. 'I have one good leg, remember.'

Croc rubs his shin and winks at me. 'I'd shag yer even with yer gammy leg.'

'Tut.' A click of my tongue is all I can manage. Shag! Sweet Sophia!

'Serious, not a mercy fuck.'

'You'd be lucky.' I've heard girls say that to foul-mouthed boys. 'I'm a bride of Christ.' That bit's my own invention.

'Croc, drop it.'

'You're one of us now, Croc.' I hiss and flick my tongue out like Sophia. That will scare him. Gappy grin gone.

'Kiya, real life just don't work like that. Honey-noses don't fall in love with street kids.'

'Love's not a snob.' Aeson's not listening to me, but I say it anyway. Maybe one day the words will fall in … like the magic words. Seth says if you repeat them enough one day they click open the gate to the Kingdom of God.

'How do I keep a honey-nose who's got everything money can buy sweet for that long, Croc?'

'If you want to be loved, be lovable.'

'She's right. Be a little charmer, you do that natural enough.' Croc pushes himself up onto his elbow and looks across at Aeson to get his full attention. 'But you gotta be sly, play the game. He grassed us up to Turk, remember?'

'I'll play him my way.'

'Your honey-daddy, your game. I'm just saying, don't trust him, man. He's crafty. Let him get one over, and he'll spit yer out like gristle.'

What's Croc looking at me for? What do I know about seduction?

'I still say, make him love you.' If I wasn't a bride of Christ I'd fall in love with Aeson.

We stare up at the stars. It's quiet up here. This high up the city noise is just a murmur.

Aeson's curls fall back and cushion his head. He laces his fingers in mine and pulls my arm up again. He does the same to Croc, but Croc's fingertips get a kiss. Wish he'd kiss mine too.

'Love's like cement: it binds people together.'

'Don't go all mushy on us, man.'

'Cement?'

'Just saying. There's nowhere better in the world to be on a clear night than the rooftops of Alexandria.'

'Too right.'

Up here everything feels possible.

Sophia, make the old Librarian love him.

Their grunts, from the room below are driving me mad. I wish they'd stop it. It's too hot for a blanket but I pull it over my head to block out the sound of their lovemaking. It makes me feel lonely. I reach for Sophia's dry, muscly body … she's no comfort tonight.

19

RUFIUS

Tiptoes, Rufius. This is bloody ridiculous – creeping around like a thief in my own home. Perhaps it's the heat that's woken me. You know full well why you're awake at this time of night, you old fool. I won't disturb him ... I'll just take a peek at my lover's beautiful face in the dawn light.

He's pulled the mosquito netting around his bed together. Ever so slowly, let's peel it back, that's it and lean over him. Head tucked under Egyptian cotton sheets, he's silent. I can't imagine my muse snores. Careful, Rufius, don't wake him. Finger and thumb pull back the sheets at a turtle's pace.

'Bahh!' Just cushions! My boy's gone again! His bed's been empty until dawn every night. No wonder Apollinos complains Aeson yawns through his lessons.

To add insult to injury, he's used the brand new silk cushions we chose together to feign his presence in the bed. Sapphire blue ... to match his eyes. Cursed cushions! The netting rips as I throw cushions across the room. Bah! My patience is frayed ... take that. Another cushion bounces off the ledge of the terrace ... and that ... palm fronds swish as the cushions fall into the gardens below. And that ...

'What ya waiting fer honey-daddy?'

One dirty leg swings over the balcony. The other follows. Torn tunic and it's filthy!

'Aeson! What in bloody Hades are you doing? Is this how you treat your new clothes, you ungrateful ...' those legs are too long and hairy to be Aeson's.

A canvas bag hits the terrace, followed by a grunt.

'Like me new outfit, do yer?'

Turk! What's he doing? Dancing? The pimp swings his hips on the terrace, picks a bougainvillea flower and throws it to me with a kiss.

'You should be on the stage, dear.'

'Missing lover-boy, eh?' His laugh is wicked.

'Where is he?' Disguise your horror Rufius.

'Give yer a fright, did I?'

'Get down off that balcony, or I'll call the guards.'

'Calm down, old man. Looks like yer heart's ready to jump straight into yer tomb.'

He saunters into Aeson's bedroom like he owns the place, drags his dirty fingers along the furniture, makes a show of surveying the floor mosaic, squats and runs his fingers across the newly polished panther, its horned prey in its paws. His hands are black with dirt. Is that blood caked on them?

'Nice job you done 'ere. Gotta floor just like this in me own abode. Get yer little brickie to help yer? Or is he too high 'n' mighty to get his hands dirty nowadays, eh?'

So that's how Aeson knew what a diameter was.

Turk's gained a scar. The deep gash runs across his cheek and ends dangerously close to his right eye, healed but still red and puffy. The way the skin's puckered and creased around it adds ten years to him. He empties the canvas bag full of ancient, high quality papyri into a pile on the bed.

'And what do you propose I do with this lot? I needed these books two weeks ago.'

'Blame Pretty for the delay.'

'I'm not interested in doing business with you, Turk. What sort of service do you call this?'

'That's gratitude fer yer.' He shakes his head. 'You've been well serviced for two weeks, eh?' He jerks his chin upwards on the last word like all street scum. Thank the gods Aeson's stopped that. Next Apollinos must get him to round his vowels, or he'll be bullied by the Library brats.

'Put that down.' He takes Aeson's new silver stylus from its box on the clothes chest and spins it in his fingers.

'How sweet. Pressie for Pretty, eh? Didn't want to disturb you and our Pretty while you got to know each other, did I?'

He's playing the dishonoured pimp. Not a surprise. A boy doesn't just walk out of a street gang.

'I'll pay you off for the boy.'

'A lifetime? Good little shafter is he? Expensive, that is. Anyways, what would a man such as your good self do without a bit of variety, eh?'

'What do you suggest?'

'I'll lease him to yer. Annual lease, say one solidus a year. If you get bored you can trade him in for a new one.'

'A solidus! I doubt you've ever seen a gold coin, you scoundrel.'

'Seen a number of 'em in that casket of yours.'

I've bartered with enough street scum to know he's bluffing.

'Apollinos!'

The ruffian's got me! Turk's dirty arm's around my chest, cold metal at my throat. The hard, flat surface of the blade against my neck draws all my focus. Play the game, Rufius. Aeson's worth more to Turk alive. If Turk has him, it's just to barter with. A bead of sweat drips from my nose onto my lip.

'Get rid of the slave when he arrives or I'll be back to slit your throat, eh, Roman.' He spits out the words. Saliva flicks on the back of my neck.

A clink of bangles and the slap of feet coming down the corridor is welcome. It's only Diana.

Turk disappears swift as a gecko; bare feet spring off the balcony ledge and dart behind the bougainvillea.

'We can have this conversation now or later, old man.' His voice is full of malice from behind the flowers. 'I'll lynch yer when you least expect it.'

The door swings open and Diana's gaze darts around the room. She knows something's wrong but has the sense not to let on.

'I'm in the middle of something. Tell that lazy sod Apollinos I have no need of him.'

'Apollinos not here.'

'Where in Hades is he?'

'You sent him to find pimp, master.'

Curse it, so I did! Oh the irony of it.

She frowns at the pile of papyri on the bed. I dart her a meaningful look.

'Send one of the slaves to find Apollinos. I've no need of more Venus Street ruffians tonight.'

I poke my finger under a page of one of the books: Eusebius' *Commentary on the Nature of the Son of God in the Psalms.* It proves the old Nicene Bishop of Caesarea held heretical views. Titus' purse will spill over for that one – top of his list if I remember rightly. Very timely, you disfigured little pimp. I was just about to give up on you.

'Off you go.'

'Yes, master.'

A shuffle of flowers and Turk jumps back on the terrace as the door closes.

'That's it, Roman, got yer balls in a twist, didn't I? Can't talk with an audience can we, eh?'

Diana's disobedient ear will be back at the door as soon as she's sent one of the boys for Apollinos. Any danger and she'll call the guard. Was I less cowardly in my youth?

'Back to the negotiations, eh? With those looks I could rent Pretty out for one solidus a time. You're getting a good deal at one solidus a year, old man.'

'It's all about ownership, dear boy. Diana would have no value if she had another master. It's a lifetime or nothing.' I usually enjoy the negotiation but there's more at stake than usual. Aeson isn't just another boy. My stomach quivers at the thought of losing him. Exile in Alexandria is only bearable with Aeson.

'Pretty's got a debt that only he can pay. I can't sell you a lifetime.' Turk slashes the bedclothes with his knife.

'Everyone has a price, dear.' He knows what my raised eyebrow means: I'm not buying his threats.

'It's a matter of honour, see? Pretty made me lose face.'

What's he talking about?

The blade of the knife pulls my attention. Turk grins as he strokes it up and down his arm. How dare he threaten me! I could have him and his little band of scum sent to the mines. Cool it, Rufius. He's useful to you remember. And Aeson's safe as long as he can be pimped.

'Three solidi a year. That's my final offer.'

He shakes his head. A stench of fish comes off his matted hair.

'Ain't the point. Gotta reputation to maintain, ain't I, eh? This is what I got fer letting him get away with it.' He touches his scar. 'Uprising. Mutiny in me own camp.'

He can't blame Aeson for some mutinous gang member giving him that scar.

'Five solidi, and that's my final offer.'

'We ain't understanding each other, old man.' His hand strokes up and down the blade to keep my attention on his knife. 'Pretty needs to be made an example of, get me? But I understand he's worthless to you scarred, or blind. So I'll lease him to yer for five solidi a year. When you've finished with him, or when his stubble's too thick to be a lover boy, I'll get me revenge.'

Never have I encountered a boy who can excite such extreme reactions in people. Hide your distress, Rufius. If you can haggle with the Archbishop of Rome, you can match this street scum. I pick up a newish looking book of folded parchment from the bed: another heretic historian. It bounces as I throw it back onto the mattress. I hate treating books like balls.

'You're quite right. The boy's already started to bore me. But boys are not my only interest. I'll settle for an annual rent of the boy, but you will only get my other business if you agree to its annual renewal.'

'And why would I do that, eh?'

'Because I'm looking for a business partner and I think you and your band of boys might have the appropriate … skills. There is a fortune to be made in heretical books like these, my dear Turk. A fortune that makes five solidi seem a paltry sum.'

Turk looks deformed when he grins and his scar creases at the corner of his eye. He looks at the scrolls and rubs his hand over his stubble.

'Partners, eh? These rich clients of yours, they live in grand houses with other fings of value, fings of value to me?'

'My dear Turk, there is no need for you to make a criminal of yourself. The price I will pay you for each delivery will far outweigh the need to fleece my clients.' No need for Turk to know they're not my clients. 'All you need to do is make the deliveries on time.'

Titus is getting impatient; he's dealing with powerful men. If I install my own distribution network, he can charge the same but without the risk. He'll agree to it. The authorities are getting hotter and every week there's a new case of torture. Just being in possession of a book of magic – the judges now lump heresy with magic, no doubt the bishops' doing – can result in execution.

Turk picks up a scroll and looks at it with renewed respect.

'You give me addresses, my gang delivers. That's it?'

'That's all there is to it, dear.'

Turk cackles and slaps me on the shoulder. He really does need a bath.

'Fastest messenger service in the Empire, eh?' As he jerks and juts his chin, the hoodlum bares his teeth. Against his dirty, sun-charred skin they look white, but a build up of yellow scum shows now he's closer to me. The chin gesture, everything about him repulses me. Only a few weeks ago I was delighted to watch him do business on Venus Street.

'Sounds like you're getting a bloody good bargain for five solidi. Unlimited boys for a year and a risk free delivery service. Most educat'd men would spend more on boys than that in a month.'

At least he still has a sharp tongue.

'So we are partners, you and me, eh?' He waits for me to confirm the deal.

'Partners, dear.'

He takes a twirl and a bow, then yanks me forward and kisses me.

'You really should be on the stage, dear.'

My bottom jaw softens slightly. The ingenuity of these boys, surviving on their wits delights me.

We both turn at the knock at the door.

'Master, Apollinos is waiting for you.' My clever little huntress knows not to come in.

Turk's muscular arms swing his body up onto the Bougainvillea.

'I'll return for the dosh and the addresses.'

'Wait! Where's Aeson?'

'Don't get your tunic in a twist. Pretty will be back …' he shouts over his shoulder. When he secures his footing on the branches of the wallflowers, he swings back round. '… unless I change my mind.'

'Remember the fortune, dear.'

Dear Bacchus, let his greed outweigh his lust for revenge.

The Pharos flame is out now the sun's up. The moon's a translucent shaving – almost dissolved into the morning sky. Diana jingles her bangles at the door.

'Come in, Diana.'

'Aeson will be back. That man don't know where Aeson is.'

'Remember what I said, not a word to Aeson about that man, you hear?'

'Tut.'

'Stop that tutting and sing me one of your fanciful Nubian stories, dear.'

Her voice is as exquisite as her face: full and soft, but nothing can calm me with my Aeson out there. Tales of strange desert creatures, half-human, half-animal, only serve to stimulate my imagination about what cruel tortures Turk might have in mind. Egypt may be part of the Roman Empire, but it's another world with its exotic mysticism … like that mad new fad of grown men running into the desert to live like wild animals in caves. Only Egypt could have produced the hermit.

'You sing well, Diana.'

Aeson will send me to an early grave with all this worry.

'*In vino veritas, dear lad, as the saying goes; I am in my cups, you will never love me with all your heart. I know this is true; your beauty will give meaning to my half life, while the other half is nothing* … How does it go? Ah, yes … *When you are good to me I spend all day among the blessed, but when you are not I'm plunged into darkness.*'

'Tut, can't sing with you mutter, mutter to yourself.'

'Sorry, sweetie. Theocritus. Poetry. Just came back to me.'

'Who?'

'A silly old fool like me by the sound of it. Carry on warbling, dear.'

PART II

A YEAR LATER

381 AD

The Western Desert is peaceful and the yellow mountain glows gold in the late afternoon sun. Shadowy entrances to tombs of forgotten Pharaohs chequer the cliff face.

Although the hermit's cave was deserted for many years, a red cross has been repainted above the rock-hewn altar. But Dera the Hermit has returned a broken man. The wilderness has not withered Dera's body; he's far from the punished figure of an aesthetic. Black arms strong as ever, chest hard as marble, his presence is still imposing, but his heart is heavy with failure. He didn't stop Aeson running off to fulfil his promise to his father.

Dera stares at the steep rock face. When the sunlight catches its crystalline underbelly and glitters, it reminds him how he's failed; like gem hunters seek crystals winking under volcanic dust, seekers of Wisdom follow the snake, digging ever deeper into their souls … and his soul is dark with fear that prophecy will have its way.

The suffocating despair that gripped him in the city when Aeson disappeared is tight around his neck. After thirteen years trying to convince the boy's father that Aeson should learn the bricklayer's trade, dissuading him from sending Aeson to writing lessons, destiny finally caught up with them all. Dera searched everywhere for the boy, even slept in the guild tomb of the bricklayers in the hope Aeson might visit it. Dera returned to his desert cave plagued by dark thoughts. Night after night he chews the sacred seeds and stares into the fire. If the seekers stop coming with food in return for prophecy he won't return to the world. Never again. He's resolved to die in his cave: another hermit's corpse for the birds. Let them peck my flesh to the bone, he thinks. I've failed Aeson. What good is the long-sight if I can't change fate? The hiss of his snake in its basket snaps him out of it.

Dera spots the long shadow of a man cast against the yellow mountain. A seeker, thinks Dera. He's in no mood for a soul journey today. After nights haunted by apocalyptic visions, his heart pounds with the conviction that the time is fast approaching when the prophecy he witnessed in this cave fifteen years ago will begin to unfold.

Dera guesses the seeker is in his early twenties. He's made a few enemies by the look of the scar that slices across the right hand side of his face. His eye puckers as he squints at the sunbeams falling through the mouth of the cave.

'Tastes like shit. You trying to poison me, eh?'

The seeker spits the crushed seeds on the floor of the cave. His sharp urban slang's Alexandrian and there's something rough about the way he juts his chin up at the end of his sentences. The seeker is Rufius' pimp-turned-business partner, that scoundrel, Turk. To Dera he's just another seeker; he's not in the mood for cityboys enquiring how they'll make their fortune, but he needs the dates they bring as payment.

'The plant's harmless. Drink this.' After weeks without seeing a soul, Dera's voice jerks.

Turk looks at the goatskin flask Dera hands him with suspicion. City people don't trust anyone, thinks Dera.

'It's just water, brother.'

Turk gulps from the flask.

'You a Christian, eh?' Turk's chin juts towards the red cross on the cave wall. He doesn't trust the hermit, and he doesn't like the way the cross looks like it's pulsating. He's not here for prophecy. Turk's here to trade. S'pose I got to test the stuff if I'm gonna flog it, he thinks.

'Surrender to the plant. Focus on what you want it to show you.'

'How do I do that, eh?'

'Look into the flames.' Dera throws resin crystals into the fire. They sizzle and smoke out the cave with a woody scent.

'I want to be rich – not just a bit – honey-nose rich, eh?'

Another lost soul, thinks Dera.

Logs cracking on the fire startle Turk and he checks for his knife, then his hand goes limp on the hilt.

'Books, I see books and heaps and heaps of gold in the fire …' Turk's voice starts to drift, his eyesight blurs: the red cross, the walls of the cave fade into each other like smoke mingling with smoke. Turk's head slumps forward; bile burps onto his chest. The plant's taken him: he's given up the fight for control.

'Man, oh man! What you doing up 'ere, eh? Out 'ere in the middle of nowhere?' Turk sweeps his arm out towards the desert, stares at the pink ray of light on the back of his hand until it fades, then shivers as the Sun drops behind the mountain.

What a chatterer this one was, thinks Dera. He didn't stop talking.

'The desert's my home, brother.'

'You'd make a mint in Alexandria with this stuff. What a buzz. Needs something to make it less bitter: cinnamon, no, I've got it: honey. That would do it. So what do you say?'

Turk opens his arms wide in front of him. His right eye wrinkles with his grin. 'Come back with me to Alexandria. You can stay at my place – right nice pad I've got – you prepare the plant, I sell it and we split the profit straight down the middle. Like partners, see?'

'I don't like the city.'

'Eh, eh? Now listen to me.'

Dera watches as the seeker – he never asks their names – picks up a handful of the sacred white seeds and opens his palm, like he's the one with the knowledge.

'This is freedom, eh? It's alright for you in your tax-free cave, blissed out and miles from anywhere, but what about all those poor fuckers in the cities, eh? Give 'em wine; let Dionysus feed 'em. Wine muddles your head. This stuff, it gives you insight.'

'The sacred plant is not a city drug, brother.'

'Why not, hermit? Thought your god was into sharing, eh? Can't be no more dangerous than wine. Won't kill you if you guzzle too much, so how can these seeds be more dangerous, eh?'

'In the desert the plant offers clarity. In the city it would create confusion.'

Turk leans back against the slab of rock that serves as an altar. The plant's sucked his energy.

'But you said yourself, eh? It shows you the path of wisdom …'

Dera thinks of Aeson's path and urgency replaces the sense of failure he felt earlier.

'… nuffink dangerous about wisdom, eh?'

'Destiny is best avoided, brother.'

'Eh? Eh, so that's why you're hiding out here in the desert.'

Ash floats up from the embers in a waft of frankincense then hovers like specs of dust in the fading pink haze.

Turk needs another tack. He stares at the embers and thinks. Rufius says everyone has their price. So what does the hermit want? Turk props himself up on his elbow and eyeballs the hermit.

'Eh, listen, I know you're communing with your god and all, so what if you get to stay in your cave? Here's the deal: I send one of my men out here twice a year, maybe more if this stuff takes off, and you supply me with the crushed seed. As long as it sells like I reckon it will, you won't have to worry about food – I'll pay you in dates and salted fish.'

Turk's voice is light and confident like he's landed the solution to a problem. Maybe he has, thinks Dera.

'Think about it: all the food you can eat, just you and your god in the desert, eh?'

Seeker and hermit look out at the sky dusted every shade of pink.

What harm can it do? thinks Dera.

'I will harvest the plant on one condition, brother.'

'Anyfink you want.'

'Create a safe place for people to take it – somewhere people will experience the visions away from the stress of their everyday lives.'

'Eh? … I know just the place, cushions and all.' Turk grins so wide his right eye puckers closed and his scar crinkles round his eyelashes like a raisin.

God has many disguises, thinks Dera. Kiya's convinced her snake is the Holy Spirit. Who am I to judge? Sophia, if this is my path guide me.

Turk's still high on the plant as he climbs back down from the hermit's cave. His vision has convinced him that Rufius and their book business will line his pockets with gold. The guide he hired is waiting with two camels.

'How'd you get that scar then, mister?'

Turk scowls at the guide. He'll get his revenge on Pretty one day, but right now he needs to keep Rufius happy. Can't complain about the old *cinaedus*, he thinks, as the camel lubbers along and throws his body back and forth in a steady rhythm. If it weren't for Rufius, I wouldn't have Turk's Honeypot. Can't believe I got prime position on Venus Street.

Σ

20

Rufius

What a vision! Aeson stands in his tunic as Cassius passes Apollinos the *toga virilis.* He's learnt to let the slaves do their job at last. No one folds a toga so it stays where it should like Apollinos, and I want everything perfect for the ceremony this afternoon. This is an important day. Today my boy becomes a man. Still slender at the waist, he retains the featherweight air of youth … but it won't be long before the heavy bulk of manhood ruins him.

The sweet smell of honey cakes wafts from the kitchen into his bedroom. We flare our nostrils and inhale. Villa Biblos finally feels like home.

Aeson rolls back his shoulders as the folds of white cloth are draped across his body, pride in his face. That's how a boy should look on his *toga virilis.*

'Rufius, what do you think? I'm all wrapped up like a bleeding mummy!'

'*Carpe diem,* Aeson, my boy. If ever there was a day ready to be plucked it's the 17th of March. I remember my coming-of-age, and look at me now, dear!' Let's give him a twirl. 'I'm still in my *toga virilis!*'

Aeson laughs. The slaves look to the floor; they'd get a whipping if they joined in my self-mockery. Regardless of the number of gold rings on my fingers, my toga has no purple edges. Bah! The powers that be may deny a *cinaedus* his stripes, but I prefer my brooches. That will not be Aeson's fate. I do not regret shunning the system, not entering public office, but my boy will be a real man ... in Rome's eyes anyway.

Apollinos is such a fusser. He lifts Aeson's arm. 'Stretch, that's it.' Do I detect new respect in Apollinos' tone?

Aeson's bicep drags under oiled honey-coloured skin, and, by Bacchus, how those shoulders have strengthened. It seems like only yesterday he was soft as a child. Did Hadrian think these thoughts as he watched Antinous grow away from his desire? Was it bitter sweet for him too? Their blossom is short-lived, poised between beauty and death. A tear? I'm a sentimental old fool.

'Turn a fraction to the side. That's it.'

The breadth of his chest, the coy curl of black hair peaking out from the top of his tunic hints at the man he will become. Most Roman boys would not look so grave, but my boy has begun the steep climb toward middle age. What was it Horace called middle age? ... *that privileged ridge from which you see both sides – the one you've slowly climbed and the one you are destined to stumble down all too quickly.* Well, I'm certainly tumbling down, but at Aeson's age I had no idea there was a climb ahead ... Damasus would complain I was carried up in a sedan chair. Ha! That light furrow between his eyebrows ... Aeson's conscious of his upward trudge. Today, I hope, I will release some of his angst. Never have I loved a boy like this: his happiness is as essential to me as my own.

'Look like a right honey-nose, I do, don't I?'

'What is the point of looking that fabulous when you speak like a gutter-kid.'

Apollinos frowns. 'He's just excited, master. His writing's up to Library standard.'

'Apollinos, you know as well as I do he must be able to speak. It's all about appearances. Next week he joins the academy.' He'll be bullied for it. Those Library brats will mock him. A reputation is forged in a day. And don't I know it! My lisp, contrived as it is, sealed my reputation on my first day at university.

Rather than sulk, Aeson lifts his chin.

'Rufius, do you approve of my *toga virilis*?'

'Yes, yes. It suits you, dear. And today is a day to celebrate. Today is the *Liberalia*. And we will celebrate in style with Bacchus.'

'Your favourite god, master.' Apollinos is scolding me again.

'I may worship the vine, dear, but Eros is my favourite god.'

Cassius giggles. Apollinos eyeballs him. I assigned the boy as Aeson's body slave. Aeson deserves some young flesh too, but I won't abide slaves taking the piss.

Apollinos reaches for the whip. The tyrant's had one hung on a hook in every room.

Aeson frowns and touches Apollinos' hand. 'No whipping today, Apollinos.' Punishment alarms him.

Apollinos pulls the folds back into place. He's irritated he didn't get to whip Cassius. 'You must keep your left arm tucked into your side, to hold the folds in place.'

'Aeson will be addressed as master from today, Apollinos.'

'Yes, master.' His neck's red with irritation.

'Aeson, dear, before we leave for the Temple of Ceres, I have a surprise for you.'

'I've never seen that temple.'

'It's a small one, a Roman one. Liber, the god of freedom, is like Bacchus.'

'Cicero rejected the equivalence of Liber to Bacchus, master.' Apollinos is such a know-all.

'Cicero, that old airbag! Aeson, dear, you'll obviously learn Cicero's speeches, but look to Fronto, mentor to Marcus Aurelius – they were lovers you know. Even that old fart Cicero gushed over Fronto's talent. As for Bacchus and Liber, stories of the gods are no more than tales fit for school children. However, I'm always happy to bow my head to any god who likes a drink and a healthy dose of fun. And today we are going to have exactly that.'

'I want to come to the party too.' Diana practically falls through the door in her desperation not to be left out. A girl after my own heart.

'Yes, Diana, women may attend the ceremony, but I think you'll enjoy the party better at Biblos.' She'd only get bored and start jingling her bangles.

She skips over and kisses Aeson's cheek. 'You look like you're wearing a blanket, Aeson.'

'I might have to wrap you up in here with me.'

By Bacchus, Aeson's flirting with the girl! Surely he's not banging Diana! That would be foolish. Screaming babies are not welcome at Biblos. I'll have to have words with him … but not today.

'Come here, my boy. I have a surprise for you.'

Diana skips out. She knows what it is. Cassius opens the door.

As we walk into the garden, slaves' comments about how manly Aeson looks in his *toga virilis* please him. Thank Bacchus he's not humble. One should covet a compliment.

White silk hangs over a statue at the centre of the fountain. Aeson knows who it is. He's posed for it for months. Apollinos has rounded up the whole household for the unveiling.

'Apollinos, unveil the statue.'

Apollinos reaches across the jets of water spurting from the open mouths of fish and pulls away the cloth. The slaves cheer and chatter about its likeness … the body slaves are all thinking the same thing: that cock's way too small for my boy. I had it sculpted in the Greek style and I wasn't going to spoil the tradition by turning Aeson into Priapus.

'Ha! Go and take a look at the inscription, dear.'

Aeson needs practice walking in a toga. It's bloody awkward holding your left arm to your waist. There's a knack to avoid looking deformed. Water splashes the white wool as he leans forward.

'Read it out, dear, so everyone can hear.'

'Aeson Biblus Catamitus.'

There's a whistle from Cassius, and a genuine cheer goes up as the news sinks in.

Aeson's gaze is glued to the pink marble plaque. He must be a little shocked. Turn around, look at me, Aeson, my love.

'We'll have the legal documents drawn up soon, dear.'

Aeson drops his right hand onto the edge of the fountain to support himself.

'My boy, are you well?' Do not cry, Aeson. Keep face. The slaves will talk, and talk travels. On the tongues of Library scribes it will be round the University in no time: the *cinaedus'* boy blubbered on the *Liberalia* – that's not manly.

'Yes, Rufius. It's just the heat.' His face is flushed when he looks at me. Oh no, his lip's trembling.

Hold in your emotion, Aeson.

He stares at the ground like an actor preparing himself. When he looks back up his expression is changed. He grins at the slaves.

'Let's get the ceremony over with so I can get out of this toga and we can party.'

The cheer is raucous.

Apollinos gives his shoulder a gentle grip. 'Congratulations, young master.'

Remarkable. He's even seduced Apollinos. Not literally – the only thing that turns the old slave on is his cursed whip these days, but it was only a year ago he was warning me off the little thief.

'Fifteen it says here. Serapis knows, I'm nearly sixteen!'

'We'll have another done for your sixteenth birthday.' So I can look back and keep a chart of his ripening, for when his beauty is a distant memory.

'Perhaps we should commission a statue in your *toga virilis.* What do you think, dear?'

'How's this?' He lifts his chin high and gazes into the distance, towards the climbing wallflowers, wistful like he wants to climb them and escape over the wall.

'Memorise that pose, dear.'

'What, this one?'

By Bacchus, I'm in my cups!

'Come here, dear boy, and embrace your father.' This is the only way to protect Aeson from Turk. If Aeson's my son, that scoundrel cannot claim him.

We face each other. An embrace is impossible in a toga, so our right arms lift to each other's shoulders. I push his dark curls back from his forehead. Paternity has never appealed to me. I would never have taken a wife just for children as many men do, but I could have adopted. What rich Roman doesn't want to leave a legacy? But domesticity's a passion killer. Bacchus, let my lust survive this legal arrangement.

'Thank you, Rufius. Thank you for trusting me.'

Something in his gaze saddens me. I can adopt him, but I'm still locked out. I'll never access his inner world. I was wrong to think this arrangement might make us friends, stop him treating me like his client, his honey-daddy. His sapphire eyes are glazed – like glass, I can see in, but cannot pass beyond the transparent barrier.

21

AESON

Library brats – now I get why Rufius calls them that – whisper, snigger and point at me, have been since Apollinos left me in the queue for the scriptorium. Just like my first night in the Necropalace, this is.

The sight of a tall man in a toga marching towards us shuts them up. Must be the teacher, but he doesn't look like the other teachers I've seen around the Museum: skinny and hunched or fat and soft. This one's brawny and walks like a general. We follow him into the room in silence.

'SIT.' We sit. Chairs scrape on the marble floor.

He circles us like a lion circling its prey. Not all of the librarians wear togas. Rufius doesn't. It's the strict ones that do, I reckon.

'I'm Master Olympus.' Bellows for lungs, he's got.

'WRITE IT.' We stare. Someone sniggers. There's a clatter of wax tablets. The rolls of parchment in the paper stands must be for the scribes. Write what, his name, or the whole sentence?

'Who was that?' He thwacks his large desk at the front of the room, then turns his back to us and reaches up above the red granite statue of Memory in the corner for the whip.

Let's take a sneaky glance up at the ceiling before Olympus turns around. Never thought I'd see the Library from the inside. I made it, Dad.

The scriptorium's directly under the domed roof Hadrian added. Sunlight streams down on us through high windows. This is where the scribes work. If Rufius is Director of the Scriptorium he must be in charge of this room. The old man seemed to enjoy filling my wardrobe, buying me gifts. Even got an ID card: Aeson Biblus Catamitus. DOB: 365. Honey-coloured skin, blue eyes, black hair, no distinguishing features. Rufius said his lawyer in Rome is drawing up the adoption papers. Not pretending, is he? I mean, here I am … in the scriptorium of the most famous library in the world. What a ceiling painting! The Muses, stark naked, cavort with Egyptian scribes and Greek scholars with long beards; hieroglyphs are written on tall obelisks … and there's the Great Pyramid. Wish I could climb up there on the ladders in the rows of shelves, scroll upon scroll stacked like they were in the Library warehouse. Flat shelves for the new page-turning books piled just as high.

'I SAID WRITE, NOT PRAY.'

The whip thwacks my desk. Shit, my stylus, it's heading for the floor. Caught it! More sniggers from the library brats. Head down. What am I meant to be writing … his name?

Olympus is like Apollinos the way he leers over my wax tablet. Must write something. What are the letters? *One letter at a time,* said Apollinos. *Walk through the alphabet if you're not sure.* α, β, γ, δ, ε, ζ, η, θ, ι, κ, λ, μ, ν, ξ, ο. Omicron, that's it. His name starts with an O.

Must hold the pen how Apollinos taught me. Olympus stares at my hand. Keep it steady, Aeson. That's it. θλψμπυσ. Not bad. The letters are round and clear.

'THIS IS A LATIN CLASS!'

Oh no! I completely forgot. Roman numerals, come on brain, think … a, b, c, d, e, f, g, h …

'A-Aeson can't write L-latin.'

Who said that? Posh honey-nosed accent. My gob won't twist into the right shape to make those long vowels. Nudges travel down the rows of wooden desks. Olympus' attention switches to the fat boy squeezed into his tunic in the front row.

'Yes I can.' I'm not letting some honey-nose show me up.

'SILENCE. NO ONE SPEAKS UNLESS I TELL THEM TO SPEAK. OVER MEMORY'S BENCH, BOTH OF YOU.'

Memory's bench? He must mean the low wooden frame in front of her statue. So it's not gymnasium apparatus.

'B-but ...'

'SILENCE!'

The fat boy gets up from his desk. I knew it – that stutter – it's Fatty! Thank Serapis, Turk didn't kill him. Little shit! Can't blame him for wanting revenge. I must have scared him halfway to Hades when we robbed the warehouse.

We both take the slow walk of shame to the front of the room. Our classmates are in hysterics. They're as nervous as we are.

The whip unravels. Olympus' strike, fast and practised, licks across the front row of desks and catches someone's hand. A stylus flies into the air.

'You are the cream of Alexandria ... so you think. To me you're just a bunch of little ignoramuses. And those of you whose faces I have to see again next year will suffer, so I advise you not to muck about, but to work your itchy balls off. Got it?'

The silence is rigid.

'GOT IT?' he shouts across the room, the veins on his gym-thick neck protrude. He's a bloody nutter. I'm better off in the Necropolis. Lanky's scarred face comes into my head. Maybe not.

'Right then, who's first?' Olympus asks as if we're taking turns at dice. 'Cat got your tongues, boys? You. Name?'

'Aeson Biblus Catamitus, I am.' I say it with pride.

A few splutters but no one dares laugh.

'I am! Who else would you be, you fool? I'll not abide insolence, nor will I allow superfluous, non-grammatical effluent in my class. If you want to imitate gutter-Greek, I suggest you join the theatre.'

He thinks I'm putting it on. *Don't jumble your syntax,* Apollinos would say. I hate elocution: talking right sounds soppy, but I got to do it. Belonging is acting. Gang life taught me that.

'And you?' He turns to Fatty.

'I-I-I- …' Fatty closes his eyes and lowers his head.

Oh no, Fatty's gone and pissed himself. Hot, stinking piss splats my ankles. Poor Fatty. He'll never live this down. Olympus flares his nostrils and huffs like a bull. The class hold their noses to keep their laughter in. We're in for a right hiding now.

If Croc was here, he'd do something to save us. The image of him, clinging to the Stadium wall ready to shit his loincloth makes me miss him. None of this lot will help us. That boy, stubble already black and thick, in the front row's enjoying this. Looks like a spectator at the stadium, he does: impatient for the kill. Stubble grabs his own neck, tongue lolls out of the side of his mouth; he points at me and grins. The longer this lesson goes on the better.

'OVER YOU GO. TUNICS UP.'

The class coughs and splutters to hide their laughter. Must be a sight – Fatty's big white arse next to mine: gym hard and the colour of honey. Clench my bum cheeks tight to keep the muscle solid. The whip will sting Fatty's flabby arse more than mine.

22

AESON

'Right, I suppose you scavengers need to eat.' Why does Olympus have to shout? We're schoolboys, not soldiers.

Chair legs scrape, tablets and pens clatter in our rush to leave the scriptorium.

'WAIT UNTIL YOU ARE DISMISSED.'

Olympus gives us a narrow-eyed look that says you're not trusted.

'This morning's lesson was held in the scriptorium under this 600 year-old fresco for you to absorb the legacy of scholarship that precedes you.' Olympus waves his arm at the ceiling, but his gaze fixes in on Fatty and me.

'It seems some of you lack reverence, even in the presence of the Muses.'

We're in the front row next to each other. My thighs have held me in a hover above the seat of my chair since the whipping. *Nine lashes for the nine Muses*, Olympus said.

'Next week we will meet in the Aristotle Lecture Hall. You will just need your ears. No writing, just listening. Tardiness will be punished. Dismissed.'

Scrum for the door. Fatty and me, we hold back. Fatty waits for me to leave then follows. There's no solidarity between us. It's his fault we got that beating. Only one reason he's cowering behind me: he fears the honey-noses more than he fears me. My bet is that boy with the stubble's waiting for us outside the door with his cronies. My stomach's tight, but I'm not scared, not me. Olympus, he scares the shit out of me, but Stubble, he's a pussy compared to Lanky.

Huddled round the door, Stubble and the others hold their pens like knives. They prod and poke as we hurry past into the corridor.

Now where? Left, or right? Best head back in the direction I came.

'Who's your friend, Fatty?'

Fatty's a few steps behind me. Poor kid. S'pose everyone calls him that.

'L-leave me alone.' That high-pitched stutter would make anyone want to bully him. Thank Serapis my voice broke.

'Leave me alone, leave me alone,' they chant behind us as we walk down the staircase.

I'm not running, I ain't. Fatty copies my slow pace, but he's itching to run.

Two grand doors open onto the Courtyard of the Muses. It's a little oasis with palm trees and flowers and the trickle of water fountains. Scrolls are stacked high on the polished wooden shelves under the arcades. Library slaves pad about in soft-soled sandals to stack and catalogue.

Now where?

The whiff of cooked meat and fish is coming from that door on the other side of the three Muses: that way to lunch. They're going to stalk me the whole way, but they won't do anything. I saw their faces when me and Fatty got a whipping. They were shitting their loincloths it could be them bent over Memory's bench.

Stubble and five or six of his cronies, pens raised like daggers, surround us.

'What's with the street slang, new boy?'

Fatty and me, we back up. Nothing else we can do. Ambushed, aren't we? Maybe I misjudged Stubble. The cool toe of one of the Muses is against my arse. Fatty slumps back on her other foot, hands over his face. He's shaking. Still stinks of piss.

The group of boys in white tunics with the yellow library stripe push and poke. Stubble stabs his pen on my forehead. Bastard! Can't risk cuts on my face, can I, not before Rufius gets those adoption papers signed. Scars don't go down well with Rufius. Perfection, that's what he likes. My face is my ticket. Let's flick his hand away.

'Stop it, that hurts.' Fatty's sobbing.

'I decide who plays the joker, who pisses, and when.' Stubble's staring, but he ain't seeing us: the dead eyes of a bully.

Out-numbered, but the rest will probably just watch if I hit him. My muscles are hard as his. How I'd like to test them on his face. All the paybacks I've imagined giving Lanky, and now this stubbly fucker, swill around in my head, all the dreams where I hunt Lanky down, and the nightmares when he hunts me down. I'm so angry my whole body's a hot throb. My palms clench and unclench.

Stubble prods my gut with his pen. It hunches me over. The whip welts on my arse sting as I bend. If he does that once more, I'll, I'll … *Remember, Rufius is the Director of the Scriptorium. Make him proud* … that's what Apollinos said when he left me at the scriptorium door. Getting into a fight won't make Rufius proud.

'Got it, new boy?' Stubble's fat vowels really piss me off.

They all join in.

'Got it?'

'Got it?'

They're enjoying this like Olympus enjoyed thrashing us.

Not the face. My anger's bigger than me now. It's pushing at the edges of my skin. I'm going to hit him if they don't back off. My fist clenches the Muse's toe. Serapis, let me keep my cool. Me and Croc, we'll get Stubble outside school, give him a scare. Keep cool.

Fatty flays his arms about and scrambles higher up onto the Muse's foot. He's hanging round her ankle. What's he playing at?

'A-Aeson's a murderer. H-he skinned a boy alive.'

'Asin Biblas Ca'amitas, HE IS!' Stubble's doing an impression of my accent. Is that how my vowels sound, chipped and short? Why didn't I pay more attention to Apollinos? I'm found out!

'It's t-true. A street kid t-told me.'

'Shut it, Fatty. Aeson might think it's funny to speak gutter-Greek, but we're not stupid enough to believe he's a pleb. We're going to teach you both a little lesson.'

Thank the Muses they think Fatty's lying! In my new clothes, hair cut neat, skin scrubbed clean except for ink-stained fingers, street kid's a step too far.

'I'm not joking.' Fatty's not giving up. 'A-Aeson's dangerous. He's in a g-gang of nasty street kids!'

Maybe this can work in my favour. Time to front Stubble … right up to his nose, that's it. We're the same height. Grew loads this year, I did. Need to push the threat into my voice. 'Fatty's got it coming to him, but he's mine.'

Stubble laughs, but takes a step away from me. 'He's not yours, new boy. Who do you think you are strutting in here like you own the place?'

'Aeson Biblus Catamitus, I AM.' I hiss it like I've seen Lanky do, into his ear. Stubble shudders. He's wary now. 'I'm not interested in your turf, but Fatty's mine, got it?' Keep my voice low, push the threat into it … Croc and me, we'd have this lot for breakfast, we would. 'Your pens won't protect you when I creep into your bedrooms with my gang.'

Now, let's take Stubble's hand and place it over the hilt of my knife hidden in my new scabbard under my tunic. Don't go anywhere without it, not with Lanky still out there. 'Put your pen away, if I was you.'

Stubble yanks his hand back from the hilt and drops his pen. Eyeball him … that's it. I mean it, and he knows it. His eyes have changed. He's looking at me like I am a real person – someone he's not so cock-sure he can push around.

'Teachers!' warns one of the boys.

Two philosophers, both in Library togas with a yellow stripe, walk towards us through the courtyard.

'Fatty's useless to me. Do what you like with him.' Stubble pushes away from me and looks at the others. They look unsure. He laughs. 'Christ only knows what Aeson wants to do with him!' They laugh too. So Stubble's a Christian.

'Watch your step, Aeson I AM.' Doubt, that is, in Stubble's cold eyes.

They laugh and scamper after him like rabbits through the courtyard.

'Y-you'll miss lunch.' Fatty eyes me like I'm a dangerous animal and hugs the Muse's ankle tighter. Now I understand why Lanky put that fiction in Fatty's head the night we did the warehouse job: fear's a useful weapon. Fatty scans the courtyard – wondering if he was better off taking Stubble's shit than being stuck with me.

'If I was going to skin you I've had plenty of chances.' I can't help laughing. 'Come on.' He looks uncertain, but flops down from the Muse's foot like a clumsy pup.

'Where's lunch then?' I'm starving. Never can work out how just sitting in a classroom makes me as hungry as ten laps round the track at the gymnasium.

Stubble and his cronies keep their distance as I walk out the Museum gates. First day at school was a success: fooled Master Olympus and my classmates that I'm a real honey-nose, I did … and scared the Library brats! Reckon I've got enough time to scoot along to see Kiya and Croc before dinner.

'Coin for the cripple.'

Kiya?

What's she doing here? Sophia's head is tucked into Kiya's dress to hide her sensitive eyes from the light. Why in Serapis' name is she begging outside the Museum? She must be here for the book.

It's not like I forgot my promise. I'll find *The Book of Wisdom.* Just need some time, that's all … and now Rufius trusts me, I must be careful. If it's pinched, he'll suspect me … oh, no, here comes Fatty. He runs like a duck.

'W-wait for me, Aeson.'

'Coin for a cripple, sir?' Kiya raises her voice. She's worried. Something's happened. 'Kiya, what are you doing here?'

'The demon's back and he's looking for you.' Her voice is a fast whisper, dark eyes wide with panic.

'A-aeson, thanks for earlier. I m-mean, do you want to come back to my house … I-I have a new p-pet puppy. You can p-play with him …'

'Kiya, thanks for telling me. I'll be careful.' So she's not come for the book. She reaches up and grabs my leg. Sophia wakes up with the sudden movement, her long neck reaches towards me, tongue flicks and hisses.

'A-Argh, a s-snake! C-Come on A-Aeson, get away from the cripple. She'll put a curse on us.'

'Fatty, go home.'

'Sweet Sophia, Aeson, listen to me. Lanky's got Croc. And he's after you too!'

Serapis, no! 'Where's he taken Croc?' Don't need to ask. I know exactly where to find Lanky.

'Aeson, come back!' Kiya shouts after me. She knows I'm going after him.

RUFIUS

The sooner I get rid of Titus the better. He looks even more scrawny and lizard-like this morning.

'Cassius, tell the guards to open the gates and hail a carriage, dear.'

'Yes, master.'

The gates crunch and squeal as the guards push them open. They look embarrassed like it's them giving off a long fart, not the gate. And so they should. They know full well I like Biblos to run smooth and serene.

'We'll get 'em oiled, master.'

Titus looks like a man who's had his fill. And so he should after guzzling my best wines and monopolising my sexiest slaves, but his lizard-face is as creased in worry as when he arrived, fearful and fretting like an old woman.

'Rufius, so we do understand each other: my clients are important men …' Titus' tongue flicks over his thin lips. You would think a man involved in such a risky business would have a little more gumption. What does he expect me to do, draw up a legal document that guarantees the delivery of illegal books, for Bacchus' sake?

Cassius is trying his hardest not to look round the gate and down the street. So am I. School finished hours ago.

'… Rufius? Rufius, your hospitality is second to none.' Titus winks at Cassius. He would have preferred Diana's company, but I won't use her to oil the wheels of my business transactions.

Curse it, Cassius didn't notice the wink: he's too busy staring at the gate. The slave's as impatient as I am for Aeson's return. Where is that boy? First day at school, and he's late home.

'My dear Titus, it appears you have quite exhausted the lovely Cassius.'

Stepping on Cassius' foot should get his attention. Cassius throws Titus an adoring look. It's taken two days to convince Titus my delivery network is sound. That's better.

Now Cassius, the farewell speech. Come on, boy. 'Cat got your tongue, Cassius?'

Cassius blushes. 'Biblos will miss you, please come again soon.' Word-perfect but unconvincing.

Cassius makes the excuse of helping the guards load Titus' luggage onto the carriage. What's Cassius gawping at?

Titus and me walk out onto the street. Not a soul on the wide palm-lined avenue.

'... Rufius, Rufius, do you comprehend the scale of the risk we're taking?'

'Sorry, my dear Titus, my son's late. You know what boys are like, such a worry.'

Titus nods, but he's flapping again.

'There can't be another no-show. The Antioch failure makes me look unreliable. I lose a client, you lose a client ... '

Titus' voice is hushed, but his words rattle out faster than Aeson charges around in his chariot. Why did I buy him that death trap? Where is that boy? I've had enough of repeating myself. How much reassurance does Titus need?

'My dear Titus, as I have said, I will look into the failed delivery. You have nothing to worry about ...'

'You're certain your people are trustworthy, Rufius?'

'Rest assured, my operation is both reliable and discreet. It won't happen again. You have my word.'

Why didn't that rogue Turk tell me about the no-show? Hoped

I wouldn't find out? I thought he had more brains than that. I'll be paying him a visit on Venus Street tonight.

'Master Titus, your carriage awaits. Biblos wishes you a safe journey.' Cassius' voice is seductive and his provocative pose draws Titus' attention. Clever boy, he knew I was getting an ear-bashing.

A slave clinks a glass as he polishes, another whips up dust from the high shelves above my head. Can't I have silence in my own library? Titus has given me a bloody headache. Turk will answer for the no-show tonight … but more importantly, where in Hades has Aeson got to … ?

'ATCHOW!' Bloody dust.

'OUT!'

The boy on the ladder hurries down, the other replaces the glasses and patters out.

'CLOSE THE DOOR.'

At least my library door doesn't squeak.

What's that rustling on the terrace? It must be Turk. I'm weary of these boys. Turk parts the bougainvillea, jumps over the balcony and sits himself in a chair by the door. What a mess: hair full of dust, face sunburnt, scar tight and dry around his eye. He'll have it for life. Looks like he's been sunbathing in the desert … and he stinks of camel.

'Bit old fer yer, that old Roman. Fancied a bit of variety, eh?'

'You know the method of communication, Turk: you send a message and I come to you. Not the other way round.'

'Special circumstances, special message, old man.'

Has he been spying on my conversations with Titus? He can't have, we conducted them in the privacy of my wine cellar. We were careful.

'One of my boys died this week on the Antioch delivery.'

'I'm sorry to hear that.'

'The stakes have changed so delivery price goes up. The trial was a joke, my boys tell me. They tortured a confession out of him, forced him to admit he was a soothsayer in possession of a magic book, then –' Turk slices the flat of his hand across his neck. De-capitation was it?

I'm not in the mood for greedy street scum trying it on.

'Heretical book trafficker executed by the authorities: hazard of the trade, dear. If it's too hot for you Turk, I'm sure there's plenty of Venus Street pimps with the balls for the job.'

If I pretend to read this pamphlet maybe he'll piss off.

'You still owe me fer the Antioch job. Lost a man, didn't I, eh?'

'Stick to pimping if the book trade doesn't suit you, Turk.' I peer over the pamphlet. 'Now, if you would kindly remove yourself from Biblos. If you come here again the deal's off.'

'You break our deal and the other little arrangement's off too.'

I was waiting for this. Well, I'm ready for him. Let's raise an eyebrow and feign surprise.

'Are you referring to Aeson?' Where – for the love of Bacchus – is Aeson? The boy's always late. I'm probably just being impatient.

'You know exactly what I mean, old man. Pretty's all dressed up, running around town in that fancy chariot. Well he's on lease, and I'm calling it in.'

'You can't. I've adopted him.'

The look on Turk's face is a picture. Ha! His scar puckers as his eyes narrow.

'I'll prove it, dear. Follow me into the garden.'

The scoundrel keeps his hand on the hilt of his knife, shoulders tense, his head darts left and right as we walk out of the library, down the stairs and out towards the fountain in the middle of the garden. He's not used to walking through a house in broad daylight.

'Don't show me no statues of loverboy. I want Pretty. Where is he?'

'Take a look at the inscription, dear.'

Turk leans forward and squints at the plaque. I'd fancied Turk at least knew his alphabet. He's more street than I thought. I'll let him suffer from his ignorance just a moment longer. His jaw goes slack; he's worked out what the inscription must mean.

'That reads Aeson Biblus Catamitus. Aeson is now my property and you're dribbling on it so take your sorry arse out of Biblos and wait until I come to see you tonight. We'll talk then.'

Turk looks at me, surprise on his face. I'm not bluffing, dear. I call the shots, not illiterate street urchins.

'Guard!'

Four burly house guards rush over.

Turk makes a dash for it, jumps onto the ledge of the fountain and springs on to the hedge. The guards grab him by the legs and drag him back over the hedge. That will need trimming now.

Turk yanks about, but he's no match for my guards. The ruffian does look ugly when he loses.

'Not too rough with him, boys. Retired gladiator, that one, an expert with the net and trident, dear.' The hairy guard holds Turk by the wrists and drags him over to me.

'Release him.'

Turk smoothes his tunic and sneers at the guard.

'Escort him off the premises, would you, dears.'

The guard shoves him in the direction of the gates.

'You'll be sorry, old man.'

'Oh, Piss-off!' What's he going to do, throw away a fortune. I don't think so. He'll swallow his pride for money's sake.

24

KIYA

'Aoi-aoi-aoi.' Those old bones rattling over the archway that leads down the steps to the funerary area are giving me the creeps. They're children's bones. The gang's old hideout's been deserted for two years since Aeson and Croc left – mutiny they called it. Sophia hisses and wraps her warm smooth body around my neck. She senses danger too. This tomb's jammed with hungry ghosts, young spirits linger, and the air … it's loaded with pain.

Sweet Sophia, did you hear that yelp of agony, it came from inside the tomb. What's Lanky doing to them?

Stupid crutch, stop slipping or we'll be over the edge. The weight of Sophia round my neck steadies me. I need to get flat on my belly to hide my shadow. Slide down my crutch: that's it. Now, pull myself through the scrub – the soil's dry and stony. Let's shift on to the smooth marble ledge. That's it. Now, brace myself for what's below.

Sweet Sophia! That must be Aeson, with a bag pulled over his head. He's on his knees, arms roped behind his back. Lanky circles him, slices his knife across Aeson's arm. Red cuts criss-cross up his arms, tunic in tatters and stained with blood. Leave him be. He must be petrified, not able to see where the next swipe will come from.

A handful of street kids – underfed waifs – watch in the subterranean tomb. Is this Lanky's gang? Some egg Lanky on, others slouch against marble columns.

Where's Croc? Sophia, please don't let him be dead.

I'm close enough to smell the demon. Lanky stinks, like he's rolled in pig shit. The top of his head's just below me. Lanky lunges and jabs Aeson's shoulder. Aeson jerks away. That's Aeson's dagger, the gold one Croc gave him. He treasures that. My body trembles.

Sophia hisses and stretches forwards, her warm skin heavy on my neck. Shush, Sophia. What can I do?

Lanky drives the blade further into his shoulder. Aeson screams. The skinny brute is enjoying this: he's smiling. Sweet Sophia, how I'd like to punch his long teeth into his evil gob.

'We'll kill you like they killed Caesar. You will feel the knives of every one of us slip into your pretty oiled skin.'

The young ones cheer and stamp their feet. A boy with an eye patch shifts from foot to foot.

'Ransom him. The old *cinaedus* will pay a fortune for him.' That must be the one they call Patch. At least he has balls. 'No need to kill him, Lanky. We can make some coin.'

Lanky points the dagger at Patch. 'I'll take your other eye, you traitor. Take the first slice of flesh.'

Patch stares at Lanky, then looks down at Aeson – they were friends once. I hold my breath.

Patch shakes his head and drops his knife. It clatters on the granite. Bones rattle over the entrance as if they're clapping at his defiance. Lanky looks up.

Head down, flatten myself to the ground in case he sees me.

Lanky spits at Patch. 'Do it.'

With a wild thrust to the hilt Lanky sinks the knife into Aeson's shoulder. Aeson's yell is dreadful. My gut tightens. Lanky's going to lose it. I've seen that vacant glare before: the man is gone. Lanky's possessed by a demon.

Sophia, stay here. I stretch out my arm and she slithers off into the undergrowth.

Let's push myself up on my stick. Courage Kiya … for Aeson's sake. If I save him I'm closer to getting my Aberamentho robes.

The demon will be directly below me soon, a few more paces. Keep walking this way, Lanky. His dark head is under me. Now, don't think. Just jump.

I scream like a Siren. 'AOIIIIIII-AAAAAA.'

Grab his shoulder, his ear: that's it.

Bite his ear.

Lanky flays around with the knife. 'Get it off me. Kill it.'

Pain shoots through my leg. He's stabbed me. Hold on, Kiya. What damage I can do must be done up here, on the demon's back. Once he throws me I'm dead meat. He's lurching like a startled horse. My good leg flings away from his waist.

Need to hold on.

My hand slips through his greasy hair.

A young one takes a step forward. Patch slaps him to the ground. They'll pull me off soon. Think.

The eyes.

My thumb presses into his eye socket. It clicks and sucks. The demon's wail echoes around the tomb. He's dropped his dagger: it glints on the ground. He's going to throw me.

Claw it out.

My fingers cup and hook the soft liquid space. It's a scallop – just think scallop. His hands hook mine. Grip his eye, Kiya. He's going to throw me.

'Back to Hades with you, Demon!'

I clutch at his ear. My hand slips with blood. He's got a grip on my arm …

The thud of the ground, the hard shock of my fall does not release my grip on his eyeball. My hand's red to the wrist.

Lanky shrieks like desert prey. The demon's hands hold his eye, body hunches and shudders in pain.

Shocked faces of the gang spin around me.

My clenched hand held out in front of me looks like it belongs to someone else. I cannot open it, cannot move. I'm going to throw up.

Puke hurls over my hand, splats my dress. That's my puke. I did this. I took out Lanky's eye. My sobs wrench my body. Sophia, forgive me.

The gang glare at me. They will kill me for this.

25

Aeson

What, in the name of Serapis, is Kiya up to? Can't see more than shadows through this sack over my head. Curse these ropes, they're tight round my wrists.

'Kiya! Don't hurt her.' She's howling. She must be hurt.

It's hopeless struggling – pulling against the rope tightens the knot.

'Keep your wrists still. I'll cut you lose.' Patch? That's Patch's voice.

'Patch, thanks, mate.' He pulls the canvas bag off my head.

What the fuck's happened?

'Kiya?' What's Lanky done to her? Why's she bent over, retching? 'Kiya?' What's she looking at, what's that in her hand? … And why's Lanky stumbling about, hands pressed over his eye, blood on his fingers and down his arm.

Fuck! She's gone and ripped his eye out!

It's Lanky's eye in her clenched fist.

Lanky's pitiful looking gang's dumbstruck. All of them gawp at Kiya. Can't believe it either, I can't.

What's that moving by Kiya's feet?

'Snake!' Two scrawny boys nearest Kiya leap away from her and point at the ground.

It's Sophia. She's in attack mode, hood fanned open, she slithers to her mistress, up over Kiya's hunched back and wraps her long body around Kiya's neck.

Kiya stops howling, mumbles something and opens her hand. In her cupped palm is a slop of blood and gore, more like a small red squid than an eye.

Sophia's forked tongue flicks in and out like it does before she eats a mouse. She's smelling it. The skinny boys stare in disbelief as Sophia opens her mouth wide, and swallows Lanky's eye whole. Her neck swells and it's gone, crushed by her muscular body.

All I can do is gawp with the rest of them. Only Lanky doesn't watch. He shuffles, bumps into the sacrifice altar, holds out an arm to feel his way around it, the other hand pressed against his eye. I should stop his escape, put an end to it. If it wasn't for Kiya he'd have killed me, but I can't move. It's like my knees are glued to the dusty marble floor of the tomb. All I can do is watch him stumble towards the steps.

'Th-There, that's the L-Librarian's son, in the middle.'

Fatty? Is that Fatty up there at the entrance, pointing at me from under the old bones?

It is Fatty ... surrounded by a group of men from the City Guard. That's a honey-nose solution, that is: call the guard. I cross the street when I see a uniform.

Boys scarper in different directions.

'Patch, run!' I hiss it under my breath.

He jumps up to the first floor of the tomb and is over the edge. Patch will out run them. He was the only one who used to be able to keep up with me.

A stocky man at the top of the steps draws his sword.

'Catch them, men!' The commander's gruff order sends the guards running off after the boys as they make a dash for it. Where's Croc? My heart squeezes: what's Lanky done with him?

Bones rattle above Lanky's head as he stumbles up the steps. A guard grabs him by the elbow, yanks his hand away from his eye. His horrid long drawn out scream makes me shiver. Even the guard looks away, and most of this lot will have done their time on the battlefield. Lanky's no good for the mines blind in one eye.

'Lanky, where's Croc? LANKY!'

He cackles. Blood trickles into his mouth from his eye and runs down his chin. Evil bastard! My gut tightens. Croc must be in this old tomb somewhere. I heard him shout when Lanky's gang caught me. I'll find him.

'Croc?' Shouting's no good from down here. If he's upstairs, he won't hear me. I need to climb on the altar to project my voice. Ah! Left arm's useless: too painful where Lanky knifed my shoulder to pull me up. Fatty runs down the steps and give me a leg up.

'Thanks, Fatty.'

'CROC!'

'C-Croc.' Fatty joins in.

'Crocodile!' Kiya's screaming too. There's panic in her voice. She's in shock. She crawls about on all fours. Must have lost her crutch.

'Aeson?' Croc's voice is a soft groan.

'Croc, where are you?'

We listen, Fatty, Kiya, and me.

'In here, man.' Croc's voice is muffled. It's coming from the loculus where Turk used to stash his loot.

'Fatty, help Kiya find her crutch will you?'

'Y-yes, certainly. Of course.' Fatty looks dubious, but starts searching behind shrubs and fallen columns.

'I'm coming, Croc.' I jump across from the altar to the first floor ledge. Could have sworn there used to be two columns outside Turk's room.

'A novel choice of p-pet.' Fatty's keeping his distance as he hunts for Sophia on the tomb floor.

'She's not a pet. She's the goddess Sophia.'

'O-Of course, my apologies. I f-failed to recognise her.' Fatty looks up at me as if to say, is she a nutcase? He'll get used to her.

'The snake's harmless,' I shout as I press my good shoulder to the slab that's covering the entrance and push. Lime-dust puffs up as the granite shifts. There was a column on either side, no doubt about it. I remember tracing the hieroglyphs etched in the marble with my finger.

'Hang on, Croc, I'll get you out of there.'

My eyes adjust to the darkness. There he is: wrists tied to ankles, curled up in the corner of the loculus.

'You alright, mate?' I untie him and give him a tender kiss on the lips.

'I am now.' Our mouths want more of each other. He's fine.

Why's Kiya rocking from side to side like she's lost her marbles? 'Aoi-aoi-aoi.'

Croc kicks the sacrifice altar as we head towards the steps. 'Man, that's not a good sign. She only chants when she's upset.'

Fatty's crouched next to her. 'I'll buy you a new crutch. Please don't cry.'

Unbelievable, the way Fatty dismissed the guard. He spoke to the commander like Rufius orders slaves. Turns out Fatty's dad's a magistrate.

Croc and me kneel down either side of Kiya. She stinks of puke. If she stank of shit I'd still hug her. This will haunt her, ripping out Lanky's eye. I was grossed out just watching Sophia eat it.

'Kiya. Did Lanky hurt you?'

She chants louder and stares blankly up at the bones over the entrance.

'Kiya, man?' Croc pulls her into his arms. She doesn't seem to notice. 'Kiya, please stop doing the scary face.'

She focuses. Croc gives her a gappy grin.

I stroke her hair.

'The demon didn't hurt me. Someone broke my crutch.'

We look at the pieces of broken wood Fatty holds in each hand. Who knows what happened to it in the scuffle between the soldiers and Lanky's weedy gang.

'I'll p-purchase you a brand new c-crutch.' Don't know what Fatty's more alarmed at: Sophia or Kiya. He's probably never spoken to a cripple before.

Croc throws his head back in relief and laughs. 'Your stick! Is that what you're so upset about, Ki?'

She nods and starts sobbing again as she knows one of us will have to carry her home.

'You should have heard her, Croc: *Back to Hades with you, Demon!* There was venom in her voice. The gang didn't dare touch her – in case she sent them to Hades too I reckon!'

We laugh. Fatty joins in. Croc slaps his back.

'Quick thinking calling the guard, man.'

Fatty looks so chuffed he's blushing.

'Gotta give it to you, priestess, you got balls.'

'Thanks.'

That's it, Kiya: smile.

'Here. Get on my shoulders.'

'No!'

This is the worst form of humiliation for her, but we've got to get home. The sun will be down soon, Rufius will be impatient and I need to get my wound cleaned up before dinner. Now the shock's eased off it's throbbing. The strip of tunic Croc tied tight round the wound's already soaked in blood.

'We won't mention this to anyone. Pretend I'm a camel, Kiya.'

'You smell like a camel.'

I won't tell her what she smells like.

Sophia pokes her head out, hisses and tucks herself back inside Kiya's dress.

'Kiya, give Sophia to Croc or Fatty, just 'til we get to the church.'

Fatty and Croc both take a step back.

'Come on, Sophia's harmless.'

'I'll take it, man.'

Kiya wraps Sophia round Croc's neck.

Right, let's crouch down. Fatty holds his breath and helps Kiya on.

'Mind the shoulder. Up we go. I'm your chariot, command me, priestess.'

'To the Kingdom of God.'

'Kingdom of God here we come.'

Up the steps, nice and slow. The way the road slopes down towards Moon Gate always makes me want to speed up. Let's make this fun.

'Hold on tight, Ki.'

'Faster!'

She's loving it. It must feel like she's running on her own legs.

'Yay!'

I'll remember this feeling, running through the Necropolis with Kiya on my back and Croc and Fatty galloping along beside me for the rest of my life – the city spread out ahead of us, pink-orange in the sunset. This is happiness.

Dionysus Street's quiet as usual, no one about … then why do I have that creepy feeling we're being watched? Come on, Fatty. He's still shuddering from all the snakes.

'I never knew C-Christians lived in that old r-ruin.' Fatty and me look up at the shabby old Temple of Dionysus. Paint faded, bare marble showing beneath it. Bet it looked grand three hundred years ago when the torches were lit and frankincense wafted from the great iron braziers either side of the huge doors.

Fatty looked worried sick when Henite dressed my shoulder. *Let me take you to the university hospital, Aeson,* Fatty had whispered in my ear. But Henite's balms work – they've healed Croc's and my cuts and grazes faster than anything else.

'Lived here for years, Seth and Henite have. They're Christian, but the Archbishop's lot call them heretics, so don't let on they live here, Fatty. It's really important.'

'Of course not, Aeson. What's the A-archbishop got against them?'

I shrug. 'Beats me! They worship the same god …' I need to get back to Biblos. 'I'm late for dinner. How am I going to explain the shoulder to Rufius?'

'Blame Stubble, say the bullies laid into you. My dad usually gives me a slap round the head for being a wimp. Master Rufius will believe it.'

Poor Fatty. Those bullies won't lay another finger on him, not while I'm at the academy, they won't.

'I'll try it.' Rufius won't be impressed I couldn't stand my ground, but how else do I explain the bandaged shoulder?

'Late fer dinner, Pretty, eh?'

We jump and turn round. Fatty gasps and points at Turk. He's slouched against the wall of the temple. How can I make a run for it with Fatty?

'Nowhere to run this time, Pretty.'

Boys step out of the shadows, daggers raised. Turk's got us surrounded.

Turk grins and saunters up to me. His wound must have healed where I stabbed him in the gut, but his face, it's crumpled on one side. Can't make out what's wrong with it in the shadow of the temple.

'What do you want, Turk?' Croc warned me Turk would blame me for the gang's mutiny. He'll blame me for that scar on his face too, so why wait until now to take his revenge?

'The old *cinaedus*' got the right hump with you.'

How does Turk know? Has he been spying on Biblos?

'Tie him up and gag him, boys.'

A couple of young ones I don't recognise bring ropes. Their hair smells like they've been to the baths … strange for street kids to wash. No point resisting the dirty rag they stuff in my mouth.

'Check him for weapons. I ain't taking any chances this time, eh?' Turk scowls and touches his face. My gut flips: this is his revenge.

Turk grips Fatty's cheeks so hard they wobble. Turk's madder than I ever seen him. He's been watching me, I reckon, but why let me live the high life for two years? Makes no sense … and where's he been living if Lanky took over the old tomb?

'Listen, fat kid. Yer gonna deliver a message for uncle Turk to the *cinaedus*. Know where he lives?'

Fatty nods his head. Everyone who's anyone in Alexandria came to dinner at Biblos last year when the refurb was finished. No doubt that included Fatty's honey-nosed dad. Rufius is such a show-off.

'Run to Biblos, quick as your fat legs will carry you then, and tell Rufius this …' Turk gobs near Fatty's feet. '… tell the old Roman to get his soft arse down to Venus Street if he wants to see his precious Pretty boy alive again. Got it?'

Fatty nods like a pigeon and looks at me. Can't talk with this dirty rag in my mouth, can I?

'Trying to say something are yer, Pretty? Isn't he el-lo-quent, boys?'

The boys snigger. None of them know what eloquent means, but it's obvious he's taking the piss. Serapis, please don't let Kiya and Croc hear us out here.

'Do what uncle Turk says, Fatty, or we'll stick yer on a spit and roast yer. Bet all that fat tastes better than suckling pig, eh boys?'

They laugh harder this time. Fatty's no threat to them, but I reckon they've heard the rumours about me. They know I manned up to Turk. Rufius was right: reputation is everything.

'Off you toddle.'

Where's Fatty going?

'Eh? Villa Biblos is by the Great Harbour. Thought you said you knew Biblos, eh?'

Fatty knows. He's scared is all, surrounded by a gang of feral street kids. This lot make Stubble and the Library brats look like angels.

26

RUFIUS

Venus Street and its catcalling tarts and drunks usually get my old juices flowing, but tonight the hoards of lusty Alexandrians and Roman businessmen gagging for flesh repulse me. That rogue Turk had better not hurt my dear boy.

Apollinos positions the house guard around Turk's Honeypot. Honeypot indeed! The scoundrel must have pinched those two columns either side of the doorway from one of the old Egyptian tombs and had the hieroglyphs repainted: red, yellow and blue glyphs glow in the torchlight.

'W-what if they t-torture him?' The chubby library brat who insists he's Aeson's friend has snivelled the whole way here.

'Turk won't dare touch Aeson, dear.' He's got too much to lose, but I'm not taking any chances. Biblos guards are in position, swords drawn. We brought twelve with us, so some must have gone round the back. Patrons scatter when they see the swords. Oooo! I feel like a general watching Apollinos manoeuvre my slaves.

A boy's head pops out the first floor window, and disappears back inside as soon as he sees us. Shouting follows inside The Honeypot. I can't decipher what with the loud music and drunken mayhem of Venus Street, but it must have been a warning as five or six men have run out – some naked, tunics in one hand, purses in the other. Ha!

Apollinos marches over to give his orders to the Biblos guards standing next to me. 'You two, either side of the door; swords ready.' He's very good at playing the boss.

'Master, wait here until I give the signal.' Off he struts again, my manly Apollinos.

Why's Apollinos flapping his hand about? Is that the signal? Not much of a signal. He went into The Honeypot only moments ago.

'Master, come quick!'

'In we go, dears.' I feel quite butch myself with my burly guard next to me. The podgy Library brat's still sniffling.

'Stop blubbing or wait outside.'

The fat boy – son of the eminent Magistrate Marcus Curius Advocatus – might be useful. I do hope that's Aeson's rationale and he's not fucking the fleshpot. The boy sucks the snot into his throat with a loud sniff, and wipes his face on his tunic. Laundry slaves must love him.

By Bacchus, it looks like Turk's fleeced a temple to deck out the brothel atrium: wall and floor mosaics of gods and humans in omnifarious positions. Lavish!

Apollinos waves us into a side room.

'In here, master.'

My boy! Turk holds a knife to Aeson's throat and pulls back my boy's dark curls so hard it tugs the skin around his temples. The tip of the blade glows orange.

Fatty gasps.

Aeson sits rigid in a chair; Turk stands behind him. Perhaps I miscalculated Turk – that blade's been heated for torture.

Don't show your fear, Rufius. The face of a senator: expressionless.

'Think you're clever, eh, *cinaedus*?' Turk's eyes dart from one Biblos guard to another. The pimp's rent boys are dotted around the room, each with a knife to their throats or a sword at their back. Turk won't leave here alive if he hurts Aeson and he knows it. But I must not do anything to startle him. He's unpredictable; he might lash out. Hide my fear, keep my voice low and calm.

'Turk, let him go. I have papers to prove he's my son.'

'Wot do I care about the law, eh?'

Speak slowly so he takes it in, voice level, don't show my distress.

'I can give you two very good reasons, dear. Firstly, our little business arrangement, from which you have prospered, by the look of the décor in here.' Why he chooses to live where he shits is beyond me. 'Secondly – and far more worrying for you – is that, however much you dress yourself up, you are a thief and a murderer, and I have here the son of one of Alexandria's most respected magistrates to prove it.'

Turk looks at Fatty. He recognises him. Ha! That's tied his tongue, but why's Turk not lowering his dagger? He will. I need to take the weight off my poor feet.

Fatty – he told me that's what his friends call him – blurted out the whole story in the carriage on the way here, between sobs and begging to stop so he could pee. I made him piss from the speeding vehicle. Ha! His father won't be happy to find out Turk had the boy find all the heretical Christian books in the library storehouses before his gang roughed him up. Of course, Turk will say I'm behind the book theft. I'll address that if it comes to it. It's my word against his, so a healthy bribe should smooth things over.

These couches are more comfortable than my own at Biblos! And those glass cups, they must have come from a wealthy household: the glasswork's exquisite.

'Fatty, sit down, dear. You make the place look untidy.'

He sits on the edge of the couch. A click of my fingers and Apollinos fills our glasses. Turk didn't like that.

'Drink up, Fatty dear. You look like you need one.'

I must not look Aeson in the eye, or I'll turn into a blubbering mess.

Turk looks unsure of himself. He pulls Aeson's hair back harder. My boy winces, but does not utter a sound.

'You have until I finish my wine to decide, Turk. What will it be, my men alert the City Guard and drag you off to the Agora prison to await your trial … or you come to your senses and enjoy your good fortune?'

I take a sip, but keep my eyes on Turk's hand, the one holding the red-hot blade.

'Mmm, a good vintage.'

Turk needs to know there's a lucrative way out of this – without him losing face. I've already humiliated him in front of his men. Let's get up. Come on, knees.

'Keep your distance, old man.' Turk yanks Aeson's hair. A drop of sweat rolls down Aeson's forehead. My boy darts me a sapphire look as I lean over slowly to whisper in Turk's ear.

'Turk, don't be a fool and throw away a good partnership. I'm going to sit back down and make you an offer to increase the price a fraction and you are going to agree.' Only Turk can hear me, not Fatty, not the others. No reaction. 'Any silly move on your part and, I assure you, I will do things to your dick with that knife of yours Caligula never even dreamed of.'

Turk's eyes dart around him. He'll give in – if the threat of losing his money didn't work, cock torture will. Why Roman generals move straight for the torture implements, I'll never understand. They would do far better just painting a gory picture in their victims' minds. No sense cutting out a tongue when you want information.

Turk's gaze follows me back to the couch. Fatty holds his wine glass in both hands to stop it shaking.

AESON

So, Rufius is running a book scam with Turk – that explains why Turk didn't come after me sooner. Rufius is the reason Turk's come up in the world. This brothel's just a sexy front for the real money-spinner. Rufius relaxes back on the couch as if he's just popped in for a blowjob. Fatty sits snivelling next to him. He might be a cry-baby but Fatty's got guts.

The blade's getting hotter, tip close to my skin. One slice and I'm scarred for life. My gut, my heart, everything thuds: fear's loud on the inside. Rufius will kill Turk if he cuts me.

And Croc was right about not trusting Rufius. It's one rule for me, and another for him. He tells me not to steal books, but he's got a whole frigging operation going on. If I get out of here alive, I'm bloody well pinching Kiya's book back.

'Turk, my dear, let us put our differences to one side. As my adopted son, Aeson is my property; if you hurt Aeson, you hurt me. And I know you do not wish to hurt me, for that would hurt our business relationship. Let's renegotiate terms that will be mutually beneficial over a glass of wine.'

Rufius sips the wine and raise a kohl-painted eyebrow. He's nervous, but no one except me can see it. What an actor.

Turk lets go of my hair. Thought he was going to have my scalp off before Rufius arrived, I did. He lowers the knife and plunges the hot blade in a jug of wine. It sizzles like fat on a spit. Thank Serapis!

Turk leans over me, and hisses in my ear. 'Honey-daddy won't be around forever, Pretty.' Then slaps my back.

'Druid, pour Aeson Biblus Catamitus 'ere a glass of our finest vintage.'

Druid! His skin's blue there's so much ink on it now. The last time I saw the tattooed Briton was over two years ago, the night we robbed the warehouse. Druid looks sheepish as he passes me the fancy glass. He mutters something in his own language and looks over at Turk, top lip curled into a snarl.

'No hard feelings, Aeson?'

You need the protection of a gang when you're a street kid. I shake my head and gulp the wine. Still in shock, I am.

Turk puts on his most magnanimous smile and sits down next to Rufius. Relaxed, like old friends; they're peas in a pod, those two, the way their minds work, the way they put money first.

Rufius smiles back. 'Lower your weapons, men.'

Biblos slaves replace daggers in scabbards, guards lower their swords, but stay put, hands on hilts. Apollinos won't take any chances.

'Druid, bring Rufius here a taster of our Desert Honey.'

Druid's blue-patterned back disappears behind a wooden screen.

'What strange barbarian religion does he belong to with all that scribble on his back?'

'He's a Druid, from Britain.'

'Oh, I've never seen one. Do they paint their cocks too?'

Druid comes out again with a wooden box. He looks Rufius in the eye. 'The Honeypot caters for all tastes, mister.'

Rufius recoils. Druid's patterned face would give me the creeps if I didn't know him. So Druid is Turk's right hand man now Lanky's gone. Reckon we've all seen the last of Lanky … thanks to Kiya.

Turk takes a couple of small glass pots from the box, mixes a dry, whitish paste from one with what looks like honey from the other with a spoon in a little dish, and passes it to Rufius.

'A symbol of our partnership, eh, Rufius.'

Apollinos steps forward. 'Master, no.'

'Taste it, Apollinos.'

'Master, it might be poison.'

'I doubt it very much. Turk dear, do you have any idea of the value of this hairy Greek slave?'

'More than I can afford.' His chin juts. 'The honey's to sweeten it. Tastes bitter but the effect is mellow. It might even relax those veins on his neck.'

'Ha! Yes, Apollinos gets awfully stressed, don't you, dear?'

Apollinos takes the spoon, looks at it, then at Rufius.

'Go ahead, dear. If it kills you, Turk's not the businessman I thought he was.'

Apollinos sucks the honey off the spoon and swallows. His dark eyes are sad. So this is how Rufius treats his lovers when they're too old. Thank Serapis he signed those adoption papers!

Apollinos plonks himself down on the couch between Fatty and Rufius as if he just fancied sitting down. Rufius laughs as the slave's jaw relaxes. Apollinos laughs too. It's not like he's drunk. He's not swaying or anything. He's forgotten he can't sit until he's ordered to.

Apollinos drops the spoon and stares at it like it's the most fascinating thing he's ever seen.

'Well, what's it like?'

'I've never felt so … so free.'

'He might puke, but the nausea passes.'

Turk mixes himself a spoonful then passes it to Rufius.

'Eh, pass it round, we're celebrating Aeson's new status.' He looks at me as if to say, *I'll have my revenge, but I can wait.* 'Druid, mix up enough Desert Honey for everyone, eh!'

This stuff's good. Every muscle in my body was tense. Now I'm all soft and relaxed. Fatty's giggling away to himself.

Turk plays the host as if it's a normal night on Venus Street and we're customers. 'More wine, Druid, eh, for our guests.'

I should want to kill Turk, but I don't. We're enemies, that's for sure, but right now I couldn't muster a curse let alone punch anyone. It's like the god of war has taken a holiday and Eros took his place.

'Yes, dear, and wrap some of that Desert … what is it you call it?' Rufius has scoffed more than any of us. It doesn't slur your speech like wine, but it makes your memory dark, and now and then I see things, things I know aren't real. Like I thought I saw Dera standing in the doorway, but when I blinked and looked again he was gone.

'Desert Honey.'

'Ingenious! Your descriptive faculties are positively poetic, Turk dear!' Rufius isn't being sarcastic. This stuff makes you positive for no reason at all.

Fatty passes me another spoonful. Apollinos leans over the couch from his position behind me. 'That's enough, Aeson.'

Apollinos doesn't trust Turk. Biblos guards are stationed at the edges of the room. They seem out of place in this happy haze.

'No more for me, Fatty. Thanks for getting Rufius.'

His chubby cheeks blush.

'Turk won't cause you any more trouble now he knows my dad's the magistrate.'

Fatty's stutter's gone. Must be the effect of the Desert Honey.

'Turk's not defeated. He's just biding his time.' Patience, that's what sets Turk apart from the rest of them. Patience and planning.

28

RUFIUS

Frankincense. 'Ah, divine scent!' And do I detect patchouli … with overtones of neroli wafting from the bathroom? Indeed I do. Deific highs balanced with low earthy tones and the zest of summer oranges: finally, these Egyptian slaves have mastered my olfactory preferences. The calming effect the right combination of aromatic oils has on fractured nerves never ceases to amaze me.

Although, life's been unusually peaceful recently. Heretic book market's booming; the scriptorium can barely keep up with demand, and Turk's running a smooth delivery operation. That means Titus is happy. Damasus has no idea I supply anyone else but him, which satisfies my vengeful desires, for now. And Theon doesn't suspect a thing … perhaps I should increase the bribe money for the library scribes to prevent them blabbing? No, Apollinos would sense if they were disgruntled by the extra workload. Aeson's knuckled down at school, although he still slopes off at night. Last week I told him to take the front door instead of climbing out from his terrace. The slaves can at least monitor his comings and goings that way, but my wilful boy seems to enjoy sneaking out of windows.

Fig … but there's something else too … my nose twitches, seduced by the trail of scent I follow into the bathroom … the smell of Aeson's skin, a manly scent.

Lamps make gold veins sparkle in the marble steps that lead down to the steamy bath. Is my muse aware he's inspired the refurbishment of Biblos? This bathroom, decked out like a bloody temple, is a shrine to him.

What thighs! Aeson stands in the sunken bath, steam up to his thighs and obeys as his tall Nubian masseur – an indulgent gift from the Emporium – moves his arms this way and that. How my boy manages to come home from school such a mess everyday, I do not know. Better not pry. He's secretive even now the adoption papers are signed.

He laughs as Diana stands on the ledge of the bath to pour water over his hair. That wound on his shoulder's healed well. The doctor who dressed it did a good job.

Why's Diana giggling? What's this? She titters as she squeezes the cloth and rinses the dirt from his stomach like she's caressing a lover. I've warned him about mucking about with the girls. Biblos is no nursery.

'Shush, you noisy nymph. Take off your bangles. You jingle like a cow with bells on, dear.'

Aeson stops laughing and shifts the weight to one leg, hip thrust forward. I do believe he's posing for me.

Two of my own body slaves stand either side of the shelved-wall, stacked floor to ceiling with fresh white towels.

'Chop chop, dears. You're masseurs, not statues.'

Their movements are languid like all Egyptians, but these two look good.

'Feeling revived now, dear?'

Aeson's preoccupied with the bust I had commissioned back in the Spring – like Narcissus staring at his reflection in an enchanted glade, serviced by my nymphs.

The bust my mentor had commissioned of me in my sixteenth year stands on a plinth in the alcove next to his. That marble cost a fortune to import from Rome, but I like a bathroom to sparkle white like a Greek temple. It was worth every solidus.

'How's your shoulder, dear?'

Aeson looks at me, as if he had been staring at something far away and needs to adjust his focus. Has he been on Turk's Desert Honey again?

'Don't 'urt no more.'

Why, oh why does he still clip his 'aitches like a street kid? Resist correcting his gutter Greek, Rufius. Nagging makes his cock soft. That reminds me – I must get the sculptor in to cast Aeson again, full body this time. The Emperor Hadrian was wise enough to document every alteration of his beloved Antinous' growth: each changed line of the lip, hardened chest muscle, hollow beneath his cheekbones … only weeks ago his cheeks still had a childlike roundness.

Capture beauty while it ripens, my mentor advised me. I laughed at him back then. If only I knew what I possessed before it wizened and drooped. This boy lives each day like an immortal, the way he climbs and jumps without a thought for his safety. Sketch this to memory, Rufius: the way his hair glistens jet, his skin is taut across his athletic chest, and torso tapers to his groin.

'Don't worry, Rufius. The shoulder's fine.'

He senses me watching him.

Diana lifts his foot on to her knee. No tight pout like when she works on my hooves. Fussy wench. The Nubian squeezes a cloth against Aeson's inner thigh. The sight of his hardness sends a faint pulse through my groin. By Bacchus, that's a rare sensation! Perhaps Turk's Desert Honey has aphrodisiac qualities?

'Diana, give me that cloth. His face is filthy, and you tend his feet!'

'Tut. He dirty alright!' Diana's giggle is followed by a snort from the slaves by the towel shelves.

'Quiet slaves!' They lower their heads.

'Rufius, 'ave you been on Turk's Desert Honey again? Diana washed my face.'

Desert Honey usually dulls my temper. Why am I so irritated today?

'Have you. It's *h*ave you. Attic Greek pronounces the 'H', dear. I'll tell Apollinos to increase the elocution.' Aeson's *'aitches* are non-existent.

'But Rufius, I do an hour elocution everyday!' His neck bends backwards for me to wash him.

'Dear boy, your face is filthy.'

'Rufius, if you take too much of the stuff it gives you visions. Go easy on it.'

'You both at it. Aeson's doing big stares for weeks, and you, master, you see things that not there.'

'Diana, you're not part of the conversation. Insolent wench!'

My snap put a shake through her small body.

'Rufius, calm down. Diana's right. Been spooning too much of it, we 'ave.'

'We have been. It's WE HAVE BEEN!'

I stamp my foot, and slip on my heel. The Nubian grabs me before I fall.

Aeson holds his stomach, tries his hardest not to laugh. The Egyptians keep their eyes on the floor, but their shoulders judder. Diana's having a shaking fit. She's not even trying to hold in the hysterics.

'How funny, dears! The master slips and breaks his neck and we all piss ourselves laughing. Ha, bloody ha!'

It's Diana's bloody fault the floor's wet.

'I've had it with your brazenness, girl.'

They're still shaking like a bunch of schoolboys at the theatre. I'll put an end to their collusion once and for all. It's time Aeson learnt to be Roman.

'Whip!' I hold out my hand and the Nubian passes me the coil of leather.

'Kneel, Diana. Dress off. Quickly.'

Without looking at her bare back, I strike. That's better. More effective than aromatic oils to calm the nerves: a just whipping.

Aeson flinches as the lash slaps her back. Can't bear to watch, boy? This will not do. You're a Biblus Catamitus now.

'Your turn.'

I toss the whip at his feet. Aeson stares at it, coiled like a snake over manicured toes.

Time for my massage. Face down on the couch, cheek against soft Egyptian cotton, I motion the slave to start.

'Aeson dear, it's time you learnt to administer punishment.' The ultimatum is clear from my flat tone.

Yes, that's it: pick up the whip. His chest rises, but does not fall. Oh no, don't you dare let that sob out. Aeson, don't you dare!

'We're all waiting.'

The slaves keep their gaze focused on the floor.

Diana whimpers but does not dare turn her head.

The whip, wet now, hisses through the air.

Thwack! Thank Bacchus he kept his nerve.

Aeson passes the whip back to the Nubian and climbs on a massage couch.

'Slave, massage me.' Aeson's voice is muffled by the towel. That's it, wipe those tears away.

The Nubian masseur responds without hesitation: as it should be. Aeson will be treated as the master's son by this household; he's no playmate. His past is irrelevant, as is the cut of our relationship.

Diana doesn't dare move. Good, the skin on her back's not broken.

'Go to your quarters, Diana.' Aeson mimics the flat Stoic tone I use with disobedient slaves. Voice, being the only aspect of the Stoic's dull attitude worth mimicking. Austerity revolts me.

Diana tilts her chin up as she leaves. Cleopatra wouldn't have managed such poise after a whipping. Little minx. She'll be fine by the morning. I might even let her bathe in here.

Has he had her? There's a spark between them.

'Pretty little thing, Diana.'

'S'pose so.' He mumbles into the massage couch.

'I didn't think you were into girls.'

'Depends.'

Don't close down on me, Aeson. A sulk is a bore.

'Screaming brats are not welcome at Biblos.'

'What?' That sullen snap is back in this voice.

'One echo chamber is as good as another, dear, if that's your preference, but some holes have consequences.' No point raising an eyebrow – Apollinos wiped off the kohl before I entered the bathroom. 'Look at me, Aeson.'

Short dark curls edge the nape of his neck – Medusa's masculine counterpart. Those sapphire eyes have the power to turn me cold as stone if they do not look on me kindly. He's not happy. His head's turned from me like a disappointed dog.

'There's no harm shagging the slaves, dear, but I don't want Diana out of work for months.' I'm trying to protect her fate. The dear girl has far too much personality for a slave.

'We 'aven't …'

'Just be careful what street you take, that's all, dear. And it's haven't with an H.'

Wet curls fall forward as he pushes himself up from the couch and turns to face me.

'Ain't shafting Diana, I ain't. Not up the butt, and not …'

'This plebeian talk won't bloody do. Bahh! Where were you last night? In The Honeypot with that street scum?

He eyeballs me. 'You said after dinner is me own time.'

'Wherever you were you're squawking like a street urchin again.'

So what if he's banging Turk's rent boys. He likes to penetrate – and slaves and boys are for penetrating. Aeson's too responsible to get the girl pregnant. So what's irking me?

The constant gurgle from the waterspout makes the bathroom's silence oppressive.

I know what it is. The same vexation I've lived with everyday of my life since acquiring the full beard of manhood: ridicule. Beneath the calm, beyond the aromatic scents the joke loiters in the steam; odourless spite lurks like an ambush. Even if they don't come right out and say it, it's implied. *Cinaedus.* I've never understood what's so bloody amusing about a man who bends over. As long as he holds his own in public – and on that count, no one could suggest otherwise. Julius Caesar had to put up with it. He took the gossip and graffiti on the chin. So do I, but I'll not be ridiculed in my own home.

'Harder slave. Increase the pressure, or you'll be flogged too.' Best toss my head away from Aeson to hide my anger.

'Shafting slaves don't do it for me, Rufius.' The sulk's disappeared from his voice. I turn my head back to face him.

'You'll have to remind me what does, dear.' I try a smile but the golden glow of Desert Honey has worn off.

The masseur adjusts to work on my lower back. Vertebrae click as they're snapped one by one.

Aeson gives me a look. No boy stirs me like he does when all his focus is on me. Looking into those sapphire eyes is like floating into another world, a realm of peace.

'What does it for me is a soft man.'

He can change my mood in an instant. His voice is gentle like the oracles at the temples of Antinous. They always choose boys to utter the prophecies from behind the statue of the god.

I need a bit of herbal assistance. Let's see if Turk's aphrodisiac claims make my erection last longer than the last spoonful.

'Slave, bring the pot of Desert Honey.' The slave standing by the pile of towels is by my side instantly. 'It's in a small glass pot on my writing desk in my library.'

Aeson doesn't need an aphrodisiac. A perpetually prepared cock is another memory that fills me with nostalgia. Stay in the moment, Rufius. Aeson leans up on his elbow, lifts a leg, wiggles his toes over the massage bed and orders, 'Slave, pour the wine.'

He takes another spoonful of Desert Honey and washes it down with a beaker of wine. I do the same. I like this shared ritual of ours.

'Off you go.' I wave away the masseur, pull myself up and sit beside Aeson on the massage couch.

'Sweet boy.' A stray hair on his leg prickles my palm ... he'll be a hairy man. Don't think of what he will become, Rufius.

For the first time an unprompted hand strokes me.

'Not if you don't have the strength, dear boy.' Lately he's complained of tiredness after school.

'Leave us,' he orders the slaves. How assertive his voice can be ... Oh Eros, I am mush!

His hand finds its way without me steering it. That's it, Aeson. Don't stop. Stroke me as I like, just the right pressure around the shaft: perfect grasp, perfect pace. I'd like to believe I'd been his teacher, but Aeson never had a virgin's grip.

Don't stop.

That's it, just like that.

Every inch of my body is a soft shudder ... except the only bloody bit of me that counts! Turk's Desert Honey is no cure for this cursed impotence. Even if I don't need to use it, the way it flops in his hand isn't encouraging – especially when he's doing such a splendid job ... more worrying, Aeson's a touch flaccid.

'Play with yourself.' That will harden him.

His low sighs send my blood rushing to where it should be.

'That's it, dear.' You like an audience, don't you? Apollo having a wank wouldn't look as hot. Droplets of water fall from his curls and trickle down his face as his gaze falls to his work. His eyes close onto a scene I cannot share. Who does he see behind those perfect eyelids?

'Bend over, Rufius.'

Oh, my dear boy! My rectum is a slave to my boy's cock. Let's slip off this couch and turn my arse towards him. Getting in position is so inelegant ... if I lean forward and rest my palms on the cotton sheet covering the massage couch that will support me.

'How may I be of service, dear?' My voice is a croak, the words stilted with lust.

His hands either side of my hips tilt me into position. His scent is like leather and sea salt. No matter how much the slaves scrub him, an undertone lingers. It makes me think of sailor boys and undiscovered horizons.

29

AESON

What's that whiff Rufius gives off when he sweats? That posh oil he rubs into his saggy skin don't hide it. A dusty pong, like old rugs. Like it: reminds me of my old home with Dad and Dera.

His back's fat with flesh, can't even see the knobbly bones of his spine … but there's something hot about having a rich Roman bend over, like he's my body slave.

The masseurs are watching through the gap in the bathroom door. Whatever they call Rufius behind his back, they can't accuse me of not being a man. Never bent over to nobody, I ain't.

Eyes closed. Must keep them closed. Going soft on him ain't an option, not the mood he's in today. Poor Diana.

The towel I chucked on the floor to stop me slipping's soaked. Let's snatch a dry one from the massage couch. That's better. Feet firmly planted; now let's get this over with.

Clap: loose skin slaps against skin. Don't look down at his old rump. Whatever you do, don't touch his flapping skin.

That's it. He's nearly there.

'Master. O, master.'

You're right about one thing, Rufius …

'Ah, don't stop. Master.'

… one echo chamber's as good as another.

'Slowly. Please, master.'

Nice and slow. Ah, yes. Dead right: a hole's a hole. Hot as on a night with Croc on Venus Street, I am. Need to keep a firm grip on his love handles; our skin's slipping. Rufius has every last hair plucked. Makes him as smooth as a baby, but his skin's way too slippery when wet.

'Yes! Master!'

Master! Wait 'til Croc hears about this. He'll die laughing. Don't laugh, Aeson. Whatever you do, don't laugh. Think of something sad: Dad dying. No! Sad will make me soft again. Picture something hot: Venus Street. Tunics pulled up, cheeky voices calling down to me from brothel balconies. Saved. That's better, ain't it, my old honey-nose?

'Oh, mas-ter.' His voice jerks.

My cock jumps at the word. As long as I don't think about Rufius' flabby arse, and the excess space inside his well-used arsehole, there's something hot about being called master. My balls clench and lift, buttocks tighten at the title.

'Master-r-r!' His high-pitched lisp sings his climax.

Hold it, Aeson. He's nearly finished.

His arse muscles spasm, here he goes.

'Master-r-r!'

And there I went.

Would a goat do it for me just the same if I kept my eyes shut?

'Thank you, master.' Pleasure cracks on this voice. Bent over the massage couch his upper arms wobble and strain to hold himself up now passion's left him. White skin flaps under his arms like dove wings.

It's over.

Not sure how much longer I could've kept it up today if he hadn't started that master stuff.

'Scandalous talk from a Roman, Rufius!' He twists round and slumps onto the massage couch. Looks ready to keel over, he does. 'Here.' Can't help grinning as I pass him a towel and over-emphasise the H.

'I've always been this way, dear.' He'll talk with a pant for a bit now. He nods at his glass of wine.

We go back to our roles straight away. I'm only master when he wants some. Better add water to his wine.

'Thank you, dear.' Rufius gulps like it's an effort. Tired him out, I have. 'Perhaps it's having control in every other area of my life that makes me want to submit.'

Bad enough taking it – don't tell me he wants to talk about it too.

'They laughed at you, the street kids, when they found out.'

'Dear boy, the whole Empire laughs at passivity in its thoroughbreds.'

'Don't it bother you?'

'Doesn't …'

'Doesn't it bother you?'

'I couldn't care less, dear.'

Good for you, Rufius. Spunky honey-nose, Rufius is.

He swivels round on his arse and dips his mustard-coloured toes into the bath. The rattle of his breath slows. He's got that free look like a kid left school early. Not 'cos he's dropped his load. It's the satisfaction of having what you want, how you want it that money gives.

'It's about time I had the hard-skin scraped off my hooves. It'll give Diana something tasty to suck on!' He laughs to himself.

We both look at his mustard toes.

Smile, Aeson: corners of mouth up. That's it. I hope he's joking. Poor Diana. I'll go and see her later – check she ain't too sore. Tried my best to be light with the whip … what choice did I have?

I look away from his feet to the marble bust. He's sharp, he is. Need to hide that his toes make me want to throw.

'Is that you, Rufius?'

'Yes … vain little beauty.'

He was. Pay him a compliment, go on: 'You were.'

He raises an eyebrow – a bald brow. No kohl today. It's funny when it runs down his face, like black tears.

'Beautiful, I mean.'

'And vain. Pass me the pot will you dear?' He points at the small glass pot of Desert Honey.

Fingers dip in and he sucks off the pale honeyed paste, looking up at me as if to say: how'd you like me to suck your cock like this? How do I tell the old man that look ain't a turn on? Makes me feel like I do when I look at his toes.

'Want some, dear?'

I suck the mixture off his fingers, and eyeball him back.

'I've met my match in you, dear boy.'

'So Rufius, tell me again, why you won't cut me in on the book deal you got going with Turk?'

'Not that again. Let it go, dear. Do you realise the fortune you are set to inherit now that I've adopted you? Hum? Do you, dear?'

It's not the money. Don't trust Turk, do I. He'll be working up some long-term plan, some clever scheme to get his revenge … I want to keep him close so I know what's going on in his head.

'Don't trust Turk. He'll do you over, Rufius.'

'My dear boy, remember last year – did I not demonstrate I can outwit that ruffian?'

Don't remind me, Rufius. Lost face having my honey-daddy come to rescue me from Venus Street, didn't I.

'He's sly, Turk is.'

'Forget about Turk, dear. Concentrate on your studies.'

Rufius reaches for the honeypot. I'm starting to feel heavy-headed, drowsy. It's not usually like this.

'Maybe Diana had a point, Rufius. Maybe we've been spooning too much Desert Honey.'

'It's fine for me, but you do look a little peakish, dear. I don't want Desert Honey getting in the way of your schoolwork.'

I'm hot all of a sudden. Need water. I glug from the jug, water pours down my face. Don't want to go all loony like he did on me earlier, seeing things that ain't there and talking crazy.

Rufius steps down into the bath. His arse hangs loose over the tops of his legs. Usually Roman men's bodies are still hard at his age. Don't bother me. It's interesting, like watching frogs and lizards go about their business. Rufius ain't like other people. He's who he is, no matter who's watching.

'Come and join me, dear. The water's just the right temperature.' He smiles as he sinks into the steam. Least he's got his teeth.

I ain't telling Croc about Rufius calling me master. There's something about Rufius being so up front about taking it. He's dead honest, don't give a shit what people think of him. I respect that. Wish I was more like that – especially at school when those honey-noses make fun of the way I speak.

Never trust him. Croc's words echo in my dizzy head.

You're right you are, Croc, but I got respect for the old honey-nose. Anyways, Rufius and me, we got a deal, don't we. As long as he keeps up his end of it, I'll keep mine. He's been kind to me. Croc don't know him like I do.

RUFIUS

Apollinos flapping again – what a surprise! He had to paint on my eyebrows twice this morning he was so distracted, and now he's charging about the gardens like a general under attack from barbarian hordes. Why's he shouting at the guards on the gates? I can't hear a thing up here on the balcony.

'Apollinos, what's all the fuss about? I'm up here, dear, on the library balcony. Come here now.' He disappears into the house.

'Diana, do you have any idea what the fuss is about?'

'Tut! Big black giant outside gates.'

'Giant?' The natives do have wild imaginations.

Apollinos barges in, snorting from the stress. 'Master, we must talk about the security. The men are jittery. They say a giant's been hanging around the walls of the house.'

'Ludicrous. Giants only exist in myths.'

Cassius is bothered by the conversation.

'Cassius, stop biting your fingernails and come here. What's all this talk of giants?'

'A huge black giant, big as a Titan is watching us, that's what the guards say, master.'

I won't have fear at Biblos.

'Rubbish! I will not entertain any more talk of giants. The guards are exaggerating. Apollinos, sell them both.' What sort of security scaremongers the household? Biblos is a refuge, and it's their job to maintain that illusion.

'Master …' A finger is all that's needed to silence Apollinos. 'The rest of you: out.'

We wait for Diana, Cassius, and my two Egyptian body slaves to leave the room. Apollinos closes the doors and joins me on the terrace.

'If he comes here again, inform me. Tell no one else, do you hear? In the meantime, increase security. Ex-gladiators, not *cinaedi* this time, dear.'

'You see this as a threat then, master?'

'No, no, no! I see this as a failure in security. Any decent guards would have scared off a spy. Since that unfortunate incident last year when Turk's man was executed by the authorities, there's been a string of sham trials. No witnesses, no evidence, but every month another innocent man or woman is tortured and executed before a Roman magistrate. The bishops are behind it of course. We need to be careful.'

'Possession of heretical books isn't illegal, master.'

'No, but magic is illegal and magistrates can sentence soothsayers to be burnt alive and these Christian books that the bishops have unwittingly …' – consciously in the case of Damasus – '… created a black market for are full of magic miracles. Our book trade is highly political. Do I have to remind you of the reason for our provincial exile, dear?'

'No, master, how can I forget! It looks like Damasus' seal on this letter.'

'A letter from Damasus, what were you waiting for, dear?' The wax cracks as it breaks. The paper is the smoothest quality. The client's in Milan. That's Ambrose's territory. Turk had better be extra vigilant – Ambrose is one of those irritating archbishops too bloody pious for bribes. What's on the list this time? Damasus takes no chances – the cunning archbishop never writes in his own hand. Twenty, no thirty books this time. Demand grows and supply dwindles … no different than any other product.

'Apollinos, we need to make plans to move my collection soon. I'm not taking any more chances. This operation is getting too big … I've got three lists' worth of books from Titus waiting in the scriptorium to be copied, and now Damasus wants to send some ecclesiastical twit from Rome to make a new Latin copy of the Greek version of the Hebrew Bible, whatsit called?'

'The Septuagint, master.'

'What's all that noise outside?'

Apollinos darts to the door.

'Stop right there.' Biblos guards shout at the gate. Feet patter all over the house. Metal clangs against metal as swords are drawn.

'Stop!'

It's Fatty. He's run past the guard on the gate and into the atrium. The poor boy's red-faced and desperate.

'For Bacchus' sake! Those guards can't even stop a boy from breaking an entry.'

'S-sir, y-you must help.'

'Calm down, dear. Cassius, give Fatty a cup of wine.'

Fatty waves the beaker away. 'S-sir, Aeson's been a-a-a…'

'Aeson? What's happened to Aeson?' I knew things were too peaceful. There's always a drama round the corner with that boy.

'Spit it out, dear.'

'A-arrested.'

'Aeson's been arrested?

Fatty grabs the wine, gulps and nods.

'On what charge?'

31

KIYA

Sweet Sophia, this crutch has blistered my armpit with all this rushing. Shoppers dart out of my way as I half-hobble, half-run. I'll whack them with my crutch if they don't budge. They stare as I pass like I'm possessed by a demon. Come on leg. The knee of my good leg keeps giving way, but I'm not slowing down.

Orators on their podiums look at me strange. Usually I skirt the shadows of the Agora arcades, but straight across is quicker. Nearly there! I overheard Henite telling the other Aberamenthos that Aeson and Seth are locked up in the Law Court prison. Henite told me to stay at home. As if!

There's the Law Court, between the Temple of Isis and the Temple of Phallus. And there's Croc, down the alley between the buildings. Why's he outside?

Phew! The alley in the shadow of the Temple of Isis is cooler. The black marble wall's cool too as I lean against it and wipe the sweat off my face with my scarf.

'Henite told you to stay at home, Ki.' Croc's frowning.

'Sweet Sophia, as if! Croc, just tell me what's going on?'

'Aeson and Seth are banged up in a cell, the one at the end back there.' He nods up the alley behind the Law Court. 'There's a tiny window too small even for a kid to squeeze through.'

My ears feel like they're ringing.

'What did they do?'

'Ki, don't you know?' Croc's shoulders slump as he sighs. 'Aeson pinched that book of yours.'

'Aeson has *The Book of Wisdom*?' He kept his promise. I knew he would. Everything will be alright if he has the book.

'Ki, they're in big shit and it's all 'cos of that stupid book.'

Croc blames me.

'Where's Henite?'

'She's inside talking to Rufius.'

'Rufius?'

'You know, the honey-nose *cinaedus* – the Roman who adopted Aeson.'

Henite's talking to a Roman? Things must be bad.

'Firstly, Croc, do not call Aeson's new father a *cinaedus*. Aeson would be insulted. Secondly, what are we out here for? We need to get the book.'

'What about Aeson?'

'That's why we need the book. The magic passwords are in it. If the Aberamenthos work together, they can transport Seth and Aeson directly to the Kingdom of Heaven … or one of the places on the way.' I'm not certain exactly how it all works, but Henite must know.

'Ki, stop! You can't go barging into a court spouting that magic stuff. They'll lock you up for being a magician too.' Croc looks petrified. He was a thief before Sophia saved him. No wonder he looks like he's seen a demon. He's probably still wanted for some crime.

'Croc, you stay here. I'm going in.'

What an atrium! The marble must be polished everyday. The guards on the gate told me no begging. Thank Sophia, they let me pass when I said my family was inside. That statue of Justice is nearly as tall as the atrium. Clerks scribble away at their desks, slaves stack papers and carry scrolls from one shelf to another. Nobody looks up. Where's Henite? She must be in one of the rooms off here. But which one?

'Bah! That's making a fuss over nothing, dear. Aeson is a Roman.' That must be Rufius shouting. Only a *cinaedus* would lisp like that. His voice is coming from that room on the right with the large wooden doors.

As I pull open the door the shouts and appeals blast into the atrium. A clerk closes the door behind me.

A group of people, some I recognise from the church, and others – honey-noses I've never seen before – all shout at a huge round man sitting at a desk. He must be the Magistrate. He's trying to hush everyone and get them to sit back down, but nobody's taking any notice. They're all talking at once.

Nobody turned as I entered … except that monk standing against the wall near the Magistrate's desk – what's a monk doing in here? I can't see his face under the black hood of his cloak, but his head's turned towards me. I don't like the weight of his stare: gives me the creeps. If I sneak along the back row of chairs, behind the Aberamenthos, I'll avoid his gaze … no good: he's so tall he can still see me over their heads. If I sit down he won't be able to see me. Anyway, I've got to rest my leg. That's better.

'Let me speak!' That's the Magistrate. I've heard him before in the Agora. He's not got the best voice for his job. And that scroll on his big cherry-wood desk, it must be *The Book of Wisdom.*

Everyone ignores him and continues to shout over each other. It's impossible to make any sense of the babble. Their arguing won't help Aeson. I wish Seth was out here and not locked up. He'd make everyone listen to each other.

'Hello K-Kiya.' It's Fatty, Aeson's school friend. He looks worried.

'Hello Fatty. What are you doing here?'

The chair creaks as he sits down.

'Dad's the Magistrate.' Why's he blushing?

'Well, tell your dad to let Aeson go then.'

'He won't l-listen to me. That p-priest over there says it's a serious crime and there needs to be a p-public trial.' Fatty nods towards the tall man in the black hooded cloak of a monk. He's no monk … he's a demon!

As if the demon had heard my thoughts, he takes a step away from the Magistrate's desk and stares in our direction at the row of chairs at the back of the room.

Fatty and me, we stare straight ahead until he looks away.

The hooded demon listens to the appeals bombarded at the Magistrate, arms crossed under his cloak.

'One at a time,' orders Fatty's dad.

'They're innocent citizens, your honour. Aeson's only a laddie.' That plea was from Henite.

The demon unfolds his arms, and lifts his hood back. In his thirties, I'd say. There's nothing of the monk in his face. He's clean to start with. Monks are always filthy and this man's not undernourished either. Smooth-shaven, sharp features, he has that hard, grave look that men respect. But I see through him: he's evil like all demons.

'Quiet, all of you.' His smooth voice projects above everyone's.

All heads turn to the left – Rufius' curled hair dyed red, Henite's headscarf, and the backs of the other Aberamenthos' heads – to stare at the demon priest. He crosses his arms again inside his cloak, and steps in front of the Magistrate's desk.

'I should not need to remind you, Magistrate, that it is a crime to be in possession of magical books. And this heretical book …' He points a long, clean finger at the scroll on Fatty's dad's desk, ' … is packed with incantations, heresy and magic words.'

'My dear priest, we understand your concern, but I can assure you my son is innocent in this matter. I am the Director of the Scriptorium and can speak on behalf of the Great Library of Alexandria. The Library took this book from its owner for routine copying last year. The boy was merely returning it.'

Aeson's adopted dad's a quick-thinker. Henite knows it's a lie. So do I. The Library had no intention of giving us our book back, but the Magistrate doesn't know that and neither does the demon priest.

The priest isn't ruffled. He reaches for the scroll. Oh, no you don't. Get your demon hands off our sacred book. I press my lips together as he reads from *The Book of Wisdom.*

'Magistrate, listen to the magic spells in this evil book.'

Old Papyrus crackles as he unrolls the scroll. 'Listen to this blasphemy: *And Jesus stood before the offering and made the invocation, "Hear me, O Father of boundless light: iao iouo iao aoi oia psinother theropsin opsither nephiomaoth marachachtha marmarachtha ieana menaman amanei* ... and the heresy goes on.'

The demon priest slings the scroll onto the Magistrate's desk in such a fury Fatty's dad jumps in his seat. He's as nervous as Fatty.

'Those are the sacred words of Jesus. How dare you.' Henite whispers it. She's as shocked to hear the passwords spoken from the mouth of a heretic priest as I am. Her scarf is wrapped tight round her head, covering her ears. It's hot in here, but I put mine back on too. *Keep your earlobes hidden, girlie, if them Romans are about.* Romans, priests and demons fall into the same group for Henite.

The Aberamenthos start to appeal to the Magistrate again in low voices. They sense there's a demon in the room too.

'Order!' Fatty's dad bangs his hand on the desk.

'Heretics, all of them, Magistrate. The Archbishop sent me here to ensure the law was carried out. Here is your evidence.' The priest points to *The Book of Wisdom.* 'Try those men tonight and torture them for a full confession. They are magicians, diviners, both of them, unholy heretics.' The priest's words are poison, but his tone is level and smooth. My ears feel like they're burning with evil.

'Next you will imply it is illegal for The Great Library to hold books, dear. I remind you that this book is the property of the Library until returned. Aeson was on Library business. I remind you, your honour, of the Library's manifesto: The Great Library of Alexandria aims for a comprehensive collection, regardless of the race, language, religion or politics of its books. The Library is above censorship.'

Rufius turns to the priest. He's not scared of him. 'And I remind you, priest, to keep your nose out of Library business.'

'God will see justice at the trial …'

Rufius sweeps up his toga and marches around the Magistrate's desk, white folds of linen eclipse the demon's black cloak … Rufius looks like a chubby white angel! He clicks his fingers and his slave follows him.

'Magistrate, a word, if I may, in private, in the name of The Library?'

'Yes, of course, Director.'

Rufius' toga has no official red border and he swings his hips like a woman. The priest follows Fatty's dad and Rufius, his gaze on Rufius' hips as they sway in the folds of fabric, murder in his eyes.

Rufius turns, and snaps at the demon. 'This is Library business priest, dear.'

'The Archbishop of Alexandria has given me the authority to act as I see fit to ensure the law is upheld.'

Rufius looks at the Magistrate, who coughs and looks up at the demon.

'I can assure you, Brother Theophilus, the law is the only issue of consequence in this Law Court. If the Director of the Scriptorium, the owner of the book in question, wishes to speak with me in private, the court is obliged to hear him.'

'And I remind you, Magistrate, that an infamous man may not come to the defence of another person in Roman law.'

Rufius raises his painted eyebrows, puts on the face of an actor, eyeballs the demon as if to say, *bring it on,* and sends him a patronising smile. 'Theophilus – a novice, I imagine?' Oh, Rufius is entertaining the way he turns back to face Fatty's dad, lispy and innocent as a girl. 'If the Archbishop wishes to send his minions, I can't imagine this little matter is a priority, can you Magistrate? This is not a trial. I merely wish to talk with you in my capacity as Director of the Scriptorium.'

Fatty's dad doesn't like the priest either. Fatty's got a mini-bronze Phallus hanging round his neck. They're pagans.

'The Director is correct. This is not a trial and I have not decided whether there will be one yet. You can assure his Holiness the Archbishop that the law will be carried out, to the letter, Brother Theophilus. Now, this court is adjourned.'

Rufius and his tall Greek slave follow Fatty's dad through a wooden door behind his desk. Rage simmers in Theophilus' tight-lipped expression as the door closes.

'Fatty, I need to get out of here before Henite spots me.'

'Follow me, K-Kiya.' How sweet – Fatty offers his hand to help me up from my chair.

'I can manage.' Ah, that's sore. The blisters under my armpit burst as my crutch rubs against them.

RUFIUS

I refuse to wait a moment longer for that boy. I'm ravenous. The slaves spent days preparing this dinner.

'Cassius, cut the lamb, dear.'

Flesh falls away from the bone as soon as my knife prods it. That's how lamb should be cooked. The combination of spices surprises my palate: turmeric … and cinnamon. Um, not bad at all.

'Finally you Egyptian skivvies have learnt to cook like Roman slaves.'

The boys keep their eyes on the floor, but a subtle release of the shoulders tells me they were anxious for a positive response. It's taken them longer to produce these dishes than it took Aeson to learn to write. Where is that boy? The food will get cold.

That must be him, running as usual.

'Rufius, sorry I'm late, I … ' Aeson gawps at the feast laid out on the low tables. Dinners have been sour affairs since the scene at the Law Court last week. I'm still furious he stole from my own library shelves, from Biblos. From his home! *Once a thief, always a thief* … Apollinos' words have haunted me all week, but tonight I will put my disappointment aside. At least the Magistrate and Theophilus thought Aeson took the book from the Library.

'This is your leaving dinner, dear. There's stuffed dormouse, lamb, suckling piglet, three types of sea bream, lobster, and your favourite – sweet-chicken wings.' I wave at the trays of dishes filled with sauces and spicy vegetable concoctions. 'Apollinos can tell you what's in those Eastern delicacies.' Aeson will play it safe with the sweet-chicken and fish … he still has the palate of a pleb.

For the love of Bacchus! My darling boy, he's crying. He stares at the low tables crammed with dishes and trays in a desolate silence.

'Shoo, all of you. Out slaves.'

Apollinos, Diana, Cassius and his tiny brother Antinous all slink out. Apollinos slides the door shut.

'I'm sorry to disappoint you, Rufius, but I made a promise to a friend.' His blue eyes are watery.

'My dear boy, do you think I'm disowning you?'

He's staring at the feast as though he's witnessing his life's savings vanish after backing the wrong charioteer. He thinks this is the end of us.

'No, no, no, my dear boy. You're going to the University of Constantinople. And you're enrolled as Aeson Biblus Catamitus.'

My poor boy needs a hug. A plate of stuffed figs clatters to the floor as I walk round the couches and fold him into my arms – he's my height now. He pulls away and stares at me as though I've landed him an even greater blow.

'Rufius, I can't leave Alexandria. I'm Alexandrian. This is home.'

'Of course you can, dear. Did you honestly think I'd allow a son of mine to be educated at a second rate university?' He'll come round, when he's over the initial shock. 'Come, sit down and eat. Apollinos has been fussing over this dinner all week.'

He sits on the couch opposite me staring at a piece of sweet-chicken.

'This is because I stole the book, isn't it, Rufius? I'll pay you back whatever you bribed Fatty's dad to get me and Seth off the hook … once I can earn my own money, I will, I promise.'

My appetite's gone too.

'Do you realise how close you were to being put on trial, Aeson?'

He lowers his head.

'Look at me, dear. This isn't a punishment. But you do realise the grisly fate of people caught in possession of magical books?' Thank Bacchus Fatty's father was open to a bribe.

'I do now.'

'What is it? I want to know you understand.'

'… but Rufius, it was that priest … Fatty's dad was going to confiscate the book and let me and Seth go until the priest turned up.'

'Soothsayers and magicians are burnt alive. That priest was one step away from building a case to imply you and that Ophite were magicians …' He's not touched his chicken. '… Aeson, we live in volatile times. The Archbishop of Alexandria may not be a murderous old battle-axe like the Archbishop of Rome, but they're all bent on rolling magic and heresy into one crime. That priest – what was his name? Theophilus – he might be more than a priest one day, and you, my dear boy, have made an enemy of him.' And so have I.

'But, like you always say, Rufius, money's above the law.'

'Aeson, let me be blunt. You know what I am. I'm a *cinaedus* …'

'No, Rufius …'

'Let me finish, dear. In the eyes of the law, I am classed as infamous. That means I cannot defend you. If your case went to trial I would have had to pay some lawyer, also open to bribes and the pressure of the Archbishop, to defend you. That, my darling boy, I will not risk. Justice takes a hike when it comes to religious squabbles.'

'But Rufius, it won't happen again.'

'You're in with the wrong crowd, Aeson. I had hoped you would make more friends at school.' Rolling around in the gutter's fine, but he treats those Ophites … like family. The way he begged me to extend the bribe to ensure that smooth-talking Ophite didn't go on trial either … what hold do they have over him?

He wipes his eyes. Good, the old defiance is back.

'My friends are good people, Rufius.' His loyalty's unnatural.

'That may be, but Fatty aside, your friends comprise of heretics and street boys. No, no, no, my mind is made up! You are going to

Constantinople. My friend Titus has arranged a place for you. In Constantinople you will make the sort of friends who'll help your career.'

He bites off a chunk of chicken and frowns. What's he thinking? Surely he won't refuse me now I'm his father.

'You wanted to make your fortune. Well you have, in one swoop you landed yourself a goldmine, but fortunes don't maintain themselves. You need friends in the Empire, a wider horizon. I'm only thinking of your future, dear boy.' And I want him far removed from heretics, as well as that vengeful pimp and his rent boys.

'What if I get top grades in my *Grammatica*?'

'You would have had to leave next year anyway, Aeson. Fatty's father has plans to send Fatty to Athens.'

I'll never forgive Olympus for refusing to put Aeson forward for Athens. I had hoped he could pull a few strings, even if it's a year too early. He's so revoltingly upright.

'What if I refuse to go?'

'It is your choice. I will not force you, but if you disobey me, I'll have to revoke the adoption.' My heart skips. I'm bluffing. Concentrate on the food, Rufius. Don't let him see it's a bluff.

He sips his wine the way I've taught him.

'How long before I depart?'

'Two months. Apollinos will make the travel arrangements.'

He lifts his chin and raises his voice. 'Apollinos, come in here.'

The five slaves patter back inside. Apollinos looks like he's been crying too … and Diana. And Cassius. They love him. What's not to love?

'This is delicious. What are the other dishes?'

'Thank you, master. This dish here is an Indian speciality made with crushed coriander seeds and cumin, and this …'

Apollinos continues to describe the dishes, with his usual precision. I've lost my appetite.

'Come and sit next to me, dear.'

Aeson climbs over the couches. It's a comfort to feel the skin of his arm against mine.

'You know I'll miss you, don't you, dear? I wouldn't send you away unless I felt it was in your best interest.' I twist his soft curls through my fingers.

His expression softens. 'Yes, I know that, Rufius.'

'Biblos is your home. When things have died down here you can visit.'

Something tells me Theophilus meant what he said: *Next time, Director. The next wrong move, and I'll be ready for you and your boy.* There's something of Damasus in him, but worse. He lacks Damasus' business sense – Damasus would have had a cut of the Magistrate's bribe. Theophilus isn't the bribing type – too bloody holier-than-thou.

Apollinos will drone on about recipes all night if I don't shut him up. Aeson throws a leg over mine – By Bacchus, I'll miss his thighs! – and plays with my hair. He wants something.

'Rufius, I'll go to Constantinople on one condition.'

'What's that, dear?'

'Return the original copy of *The Book of Wisdom* to Seth.'

Apollinos stops his culinary prattle and looks at me.

That's my boy: the perpetual negotiator. Let's give those sexy thighs a slap. He laughs.

'Apollinos, you've had your orders. Return the original to the Ophites.'

What is Apollinos doing in my bedroom? It must be the middle of the night.

'Master, the giant … I mean, there's a man here to see you. He said he won't leave until he's spoken to you.'

'I thought you bought new guards. Tell them to do their job. What's come over you disturbing my sleep, Apollinos?'

'It was something he said, master, about Aeson.'

Apollinos helps me into my tunic. Oh, my head. This hangover will be a bad one.

'Where is he?'

'At the gate, master. He's unarmed.'

'Alright, tell him I'm coming.'

I can see why they call him a giant. He's the largest man I've ever seen. Through the iron grills of the gate, torches outside the house cast shadows across his body. He's twice the height of the guards, swords raised either side of him. I can smell his body odour from here – animal fur and bitter spice. Head shaved, flat African features. He looks like he lives rough, but there's something majestic about him.

Apollinos looks uneasy.

'What do you want?'

'My name is Dera. I've come for Aeson.' His voice is deep, as one would expect of a man of his stature, but low like a Vestal and his teeth glow white in the lamplight.

'What is Aeson to you?'

'Brother, I was a friend of his father. God rest his soul.' Brother indeed! Another nutty Christian.

'Aeson Biblus Catamitus is my son. What do you want with him?'

'Yes, I watched his *toga virilis*.'

Biblos security's bloody hopeless. No wonder the guards look sheepish.

'Brother, I come to warn you, Alexandria is not safe for Aeson.'

Tell me something I don't know, will you? My head's throbbing from Turk's Desert Honey.

'I can take him somewhere he'll be safe. Evil hunts him in Alexandria. Let me take him, brother.'

'Dera, was it? Are you a monk, Dera?' He certainly smells like one of those fanatics that live like swine off slops in the desert.

'I'm a hermit.'

He's desert-mad, no doubt about it. Best thing to do is to tell him what he wants to hear and send him packing.

'Aeson is safe with me. Look at this house. It's well guarded, and he has the best money can buy.'

The huge hermit leans down towards the grill and whispers.

'Brother, the evil that pursues him will make the walls of the Temple of Serapis crumble. If he remains in Alexandria, neither you, nor I can protect him.'

Apollinos gasps. The hermit's grave tone sends a current of fear through my whole body. His words echo in my brain … keep your head, Rufius. Evil pursues him, bah!

'Do not worry, dear. Aeson is leaving Alexandria. I happen to agree with you: this city is no good for him. He's going to Constantinople to finish his education.'

The smelly hermit's deciding whether to believe me or not.

'When does he leave?'

'This month.'

'Brother, Aeson must never return to Alexandria.'

'Biblos is his home. I cannot prevent him from returning when his studies have finished …'

The man's eyes widen, the whites glow in the torches. They look like they're going to pop out of their sockets.

'No! You will refuse his return – if you love him.' The hermit's voice does not rise, but the force of it is final and hypnotic. 'You will refuse his return.'

I want to tell him not to boss me about at my own gate, but the only words in my head are his. 'Aeson will not return, dear.'

'If Aeson tries to return, you will stop him.'

The whites of his eyes seem to grow. It is as if the grill in the gate has disappeared and this enormous man and me are making some kind of silent agreement, as if he is forcing me to repeat his words.

'If Aeson tries to return, I will stop him.' My voice sounds distant, as if I'm speaking the words in a dream and those words tie me like a promise to a god.

The hermit steps back, out of the light of the torches.

'I believe you.'

I can hear his voice but I can't see him.

'Where'd he go?' One of the guards darts his sword about in front of him.

Apollinos peers out, through the grill, into the night.

'He's gone, master … master?'

My eyes are wide in a stare. I blink and shake my head.

'What an unusual man, Apollinos. Did he say how he knew Aeson?'

'A friend of his father, master.' Apollinos is still frowning at the grill in the gate. He shakes his head, like a dog shakes out a shock, and turns to the guards. 'Check the perimeter. I want the watch tight tonight.'

The guards look as uneasy as Apollinos.

'Apollinos, I want Aeson out of Alexandria within the month.'

'You believe an evil force hunts Aeson?'

'Don't be ridiculous, Apollinos, unless you count street urchins and heretics. Bah! But the sooner Aeson's out of Alexandria, the less likely he'll get into any more trouble. Aeson's fallen in with a bad lot. And now this stinking hermit – who knows when he'll turn up again, spurting that Apocalyptic tripe Christians are so fond of and frightening the household with his ludicrous prophecy.'

ONE YEAR LATER

382 AD
Letter from Rufius to Damasus

My Dear Bishop,

In response to your recent request, the scriptorium of the Alexandrian Library is at the disposal of your secretary Jerome. I can confirm that the Great Library of Alexandria holds the original version of the Hebrew Testament in Greek, and that it is in acceptable condition for copying. I will make the necessary arrangements. Like all books of great value, it is housed in the Daughter Library at the Serapeum. I can also arrange a guest room for your secretary at the temple if that suits his needs.

On another matter, I seek your venerable assistance. My adopted son will visit Rome on his tour of the Empire. He will stay at my house on the Aventine. It is my wish, as his father, for him to be initiated into the Nicene faith. It would be a great honour if he could be baptised at your own bishopric, at the great Lateran Basilica, by your own holy hand.

Your faithful partner in crime,

Rufius

TWO YEARS LATER

384 AD
A letter arrives from Jerome to Rufius

'Do you miss him, Diana dear?' We both look at the statue of Aeson in the fountain, commissioned for his *toga virilis*. She purrs as I stroke her black hair, head in my lap.

'It's quieter without him around.'

'Yes, there was never a dull moment was there, dear.'

We brush the water from our skin as we look at his beautiful face. I should have this bench moved further back to avoid the spray.

'He had bigger cock.'

'Diana dear, the language!' Thank Bacchus he didn't get her pregnant. One Diana is quite enough.

'Is truth.'

'He'll be nineteen this year.'

Here's Apollinos with the post. Perhaps there's one from my boy. He writes regularly enough, but his tone saddens me. More like a letter from a son to his father than a lover. He tells me about his schoolmasters, his studies, his successes – never his screws and hangovers. I should write to him, but of what? A sad old fool who swoons at the sight of his statues all over the house. Hadrian's loss was less bitter than mine. He witnessed the full growth of his Antinous, from ephebe to man. Eros cheated me of Aeson's best years.

'This one came from Constantinople this morning. I imagine it is from Aeson. The other was sent from Antioch.'

'Damasus' sidekick secretary. What's he want? When Damasus said Jerome would be coming with his devotees, I didn't expect an entourage of Roman matrons with their beautiful daughters in tow on hunger strike. Ha! Apollinos, wasn't that the funniest thing you've ever seen, that fool Jerome spying through the keyhole at them!'

'He was pulling on his cock so hard I feared it might fall off, master!'

'And then he thanked you for throwing a bucket of water over him … ha!'

Ripples of laughter convulse up into my throat. I can't speak I'm laughing so much. So is Apollinos. Diana's shoulders shake in hysterics in my lap. I've not seen him laugh since I used to tickle him as a boy. He's trying to say something.

'M-master, did I tell you he begged me to whip him?'

'Ha! Oh Apollinos, tell me you obeyed him, please!'

'Why of course, master! I gave him such a thrashing. And he thanked me again when I had finished. It wasn't the first beating he'd had; Jerome's back was a mesh of healed lash marks.'

We laugh uncontrollably.

'Oh, Diana, you must move your head from my bladder before I piss myself.'

Apollinos yanks Diana off me, shaking like a schoolboy, face wet with tears.

'Sit, sit here next to us, Apollinos.'

We take deep breaths to calm ourselves down. I cough and slap his knee. He knows that means wine and gets up to pour me a cup, still chuckling to himself.

'Thank you, dear.' That's better. 'Oh, Apollinos. That poor wretch Jerome is quite obviously a hedonist at heart. He told me he tried going out into the desert, like they do – lived in a cave, ate scraps pigs would turn their snouts up at. He couldn't hack it. *It wasn't God's calling*, was how he put it. He was quite proud of himself though, like it was a notch on the bedpost.'

'Well he had the ladies in a swoon over him. Pauline's daughter fasted for a week to impress him when all along he was banging her mother.'

'Likes them skinny does he?'

We laugh, but the thought of those dear girls, all bones and elbows, struggling to eat a sprig of asparagus sobers us.

'Apollinos, you don't think Aeson will turn out like them do you? What if Aeson stops eating, or runs off to the desert, or worse still …'

'Master, calm yourself. Aeson has a healthy appetite.'

'Aeson hungry boy.' Diana thrusts her tongue into the side of her cheek several times.

'Vulgarity is not becoming in a lady, Diana dear.'

My boy's no fool, although it is a shame he refused to be baptised. Christianity is the best club to belong to if one wants a career in the Senate these days.

'What does Aeson have to say, Apollinos?'

He breaks the seal and reads, then hands the letter to me.

'The usual: doing well in his studies, his health is good.'

'Aeson not going to write to papa about orgies.' Diana sounds incredulous.

The thought of my boy at an orgy has me in an emotional tangle. How jealous I am of any hand that touches his soft curls, his honey skin when I cannot. Bah! These thoughts merely serve to torture me.

'Amuse us, Apollinos. Let's hear what our hedonist masquerading as a monk has to say.'

Apollinos clears his throat. Aeson may be the love of my life, but Apollinos is my pillar.

'My most esteemed Director.' Apollinos' voice is as level and sober as ever. 'I know, even in exile, that you and my dear departed mentor – might I be so presumptuous as to call him friend, for Damasus was that to me – '

'Departed? Did he say DEPARTED? Diana, stop leaning on my stomach. My bladder's full.'

Apollinos' eyes flick ahead. His wide grin discloses what's coming next.

'Just tell me is he dead, Apollinos?' The loud impatience in my voice brings several slaves padding over.

'Dead, master. Damasus is dead.'

'Apollinos, at last. We can go home to Rome.'

Up we get, on my feet, tunic flung over my head. Oh, I want to kiss everyone, to dance. Apollinos looks shocked as I plant a kiss on his lips. Diana tuts as I slobber over her. Cassius and his brother Antinous stare at me in confusion.

'Cassius, Antinous, fetch the musicians. Biblos is celebrating.'

'Would you really return? I hear Rome is not so accommodating to, to …'

'Say it Apollinos, to *cinaedi*. I've heard the reports … but nobody's ever actually been sentenced under that law.'

'That is true, but how many men have been unofficially exiled, blackmailed, like you?'

I sit back down. Now I have the option, would I take it? I look around me, at the house, the marble, the rose garden, my beautiful family. Alexandria accepts everyone, the more exotic the better.

'Biblos is home for now.'

'And when Aeson has finished his studies?'

'He can't return.' A dark foreboding falls over me, the memory of the huge black hermit, the smell of him still lingers in my memory: animal fur and a bitter body odour. 'Perhaps Constantinople. There are more eunuchs in the Imperial court than courtiers they say.'

'But master, they are slaves. It is your patrician status polite society takes issue with.'

'Enough, Apollinos. I will have my party and we will celebrate. Remember, no invite to that old bully Olympus … and don't tell anyone we're celebrating the death of the Archbishop of Rome. Say it's my birthday or something. My colleagues won't care – any excuse for free wine and food.

Part III

SEVEN YEARS LATER

25 May, 391 AD

Peace is disrupted in the Egyptian deserts. Gates of monasteries are flung open and an exodus of monks abandons caves, hovels and remote oases. They have been summoned by the Archbishop of Alexandria to do God's work. It's against the law for monks to enter the towns and cities: they're outcast, considered filthy fanatics and troublemakers. The Archbishop finds them as repugnant as any other civilised person, but trouble is exactly what he needs to stir up in Alexandria.

The yellow mountain, dotted with Pharaohs' tombs, looks like honeycomb in the dying sun. It will be dark soon. Dera the Hermit is blind to the trouble heading in his direction – he did not see three monks approach in black hooded cloaks. The weight of prophecy has hung in the air for twenty-five years; he's numb to its nagging knowledge. There is nothing he can do to stop the destruction of the Serapeum. Aeson is safe. That is all that matters.

Dera flexes his inky fingers and rubs his palms together to bring back the circulation. How strange and out of place the pen looks on the rock: a tool that belongs in a library, he thinks. His work is done. Seth and Henite will finally have a spare copy of *The Book of Wisdom.* The top page of parchment lifts at one corner. Dera places a rock on the book to keep the pages from flying free in the breeze that wafts into the cave, rolls up the original scroll he used for copying and puts it back in his date bag. He'll return them both soon. It will be my last journey into the city, he thinks.

With a sense of satisfaction he picks up the bowl of paste on the altar, mutters thanks to the Holy Spirit of Sophia and eats the sacred plant. After months of abstinence it tastes more bitter than usual.

A shadow blocks the sun from the cave and casts a chill across Dera's body. He's disappointed his prayer's been interrupted. Dera smells them before his opens his eyes: the stench of human filth. When he sees their black cloaks he knows they are not seekers. Monks.

'In here, brothers.' The spiteful voice of the tallest monk makes Dera's spine stiffen.

'He's on a trip, look at him.' A second voice with a city snigger.

Three monks stare down at him cross-legged in front of the altar. They must be Nicenes – only Nicenes would travel in a group. They're a long way from a monastery, thinks Dera.

The tallest of the three sits down by the fire. There's a hollow black socket where an eye once was and his face is tortured into a frown of perpetual rage.

'He's off his head.' Menace in the one-eyed monk's voice unnerves Dera. He blinks, tries to shake off the effects of the sacred plant. 'Are you with us, brother? We come for a prophecy.' The skinny monk has the mocking tone of a bully.

Dera's not fooled by his request: Nicenes think prophecy's a sin. And these three are the typical, uneducated louts that would be on the streets, scavenging and stealing, if monasteries hadn't recruited them.

'And for some of that.' The third monk swipes the bowl from the altar.

'Be careful, brother. The plant is potent. Sit, we can taste the wisdom of the plant, discover our paths together.' Dera's inky hand beckons them in the hope they will soften to hospitality.

'We don't need yer hermit wisdom,' spits their lanky one-eyed leader.

'There's only one path,' chips in another, breathless and wheezing from the climb. He looks as though he's not fasted a day in his life.

Dera is nervous as the fat monk picks up the stack of parchment. 'What's a book doing up here, brother?'

'Just my scribblings. It is of no importance.'

'Read it.' The monk thrusts the top page in front of Dera's eyes.

'Aoi, aoi, aoi. When Jesus had risen from the dead, he spent eleven years instructing his disciples on the Mysteries of …' Dera's voice is level, but he knows, whether he reads or not, they'll be trouble.

The fat monk looks at the other two. 'Sounds like heresy to me, brothers.'

The tall monk's single eye narrows – yes, it's Lanky. He snatches the wad of parchment. Dera's large hands flex. He wants to snatch it back, but is anxious not to aggravate them. He can feel their rage simmering: they're looking for an excuse for violence.

'Stay where you are, brother.' Lanky's knife's out, his face an evil one-eyed scowl.

'Settle, and chew on the plant a while, brothers. We are all the same in Christ.'

'Have you not heard the laws passed against magic, hermit?' Lanky circles Dera in slow, measured steps. 'Think the law won't catch yer out here, do yer?'

'Please sit, brothers.' Dera beckons them to the fire.

'Shut it, heretic scum.' Lanky kicks Dera hard in the stomach.

The monks look surprised that the hermit did not shift from his spot cross-legged, back straight on the cave floor. His stoicism unnerves them – they want a reaction. Lanky hovers the parchment over the flames. 'We will sit, brother, and watch this heresy burn together.'

'That'll teach yer some wisdom, eh, brother,' wheezes the fat monk.

A charge of anger pulses through Dera's body and before logic can stop him, he shoots up. Even Lanky's shocked by his height.

Three blades are at the hermit's throat, their tips jab up at his neck.

Lanky's single eye locks into Dera's. 'Stay, dog. Watch and suffer.'

Page by page Lanky feeds *The Book of Wisdom* to the fire. Parchment folds in on itself, blackens and burns.

Aoi-aoi-aoi, Dera chants silently to himself.

The monks laugh and jab Dera with their knives making little red cuts on his aubergine skin. They're jubilant when the last page sinks into the embers. Like demons, they jump and leap around the fire in their black hooded cloaks, high on the plant and the glory of their destruction.

'Get up and fight, you heretic scum!' The hard leather of Lanky's sandal breaks the skin of Dera's jaw. Sour and metallic, blood fills his mouth. His other foot presses the hermit's head down against the cave floor. Wicked laughter echoes in the cave.

'Come on. The Archbishop needs us in Alexandria, and I ain't staying up here all night with heretic magic,' wheezes the fat one.

'Finish him off and get a move on.' Lanky stamps down on Dera's skull. The sharp sting of a knife burns in his neck, and his sight fades with the pain.

Sophia, let me die well, he prays. I must follow the snake up my spine and leave my body from the crown of my head. Through my crown, through my crown … *aoi-aoi-aoi* …

Leaving Dera for dead, Lanky and the monks descend the yellow mountain, and cross the Western Desert to the marble city of Alexandria.

The law has kept monks out of the cities – even the pious rich are disgusted by extremists who never bathe and live on slops – but Archbishop Theophilus is a strategist and fanatics are what he needs now. Rioting in Alexandria between the faithful and heretics of all kinds – pagans of the old religions and heretic Christian sects – is out of control.

Archbishop Theophilus, now an imposing man of forty-six with sharp black eyes, nods at the lines of inspectors he's employed to hunt out heretics. Taller than all of them, slender and self-assured he eyes his recruits.

'Today we do God's work.' Theophilus' level, steel voice echoes round the stables.

Horses grunt and clop their hooves as if they too are gearing up for war. Theophilus has the support of the Prefect and the army, but that will not be sufficient to stamp out heresy once and for all. The monks must obey him, they will obey … if he wears their drab hooded cloak, does not flaunt the wealth of the Alexandrian Church, he, Theophilus will win their loyalty.

Theodosius is now Emperor of both the East and the West, and Theophilus intends to take full advantage of the Emperor turning a blind eye to the wave of destruction of pagan temples sweeping the Empire. Every year the Nile must flood. Egypt's grain feeds the Empire and whoever controls the Nilometers wield Egypt's power. As long as the Nilometers are in the hands of the Priests of Serapis, the Church of Alexandria is overshadowed by a bunch of pagans. Only the Priests of Serapis stand in Theophilus' way.

Besides, thinks Theophilus, as he looks out of the window of his carriage on the trot to the Agora, since Emperor Theodosius was excommunicated by Archbishop Ambrose, it's us bishops who must uphold the will of God. This is my chance not only to bring order to the city, but to knock a few bent noses straight. Alexandria will not tolerate the unnatural habits of Rufius' kind. There's no place for a *cinaedus* in a Christian city. His boy may have escaped trial, but Rufius will pay for humiliating me, vows Theophilus.

The Archbishop's face is flushed pink with determination and vengeance as he leans his head out of the window. 'Whip those horses to a gallop. God's work is waiting.'

The slave lashes his whip on the horses' rumps with a lust that matches the Archbishop's thirst to see his plan put into action.

He must be careful – in the eyes of the people the Archbishop must appear innocent. Theophilus has no intention of going down in history like Damasus the Ear-tickler, Damasus the Butcher. Theophilus' eyes do not glaze over like dreamers lost in their visions – he is a realist who never let's go of his focus – but today he allows his imagination to project into the future: I will be remembered as Theophilus Destroyer of Idolatry, or Theophilus the Great … no, too worldly … Theophilus the Virtuous … Theophilus the Pious … or simply Saint Theophilus. Too lofty? If they made Damasus a saint in the West, the Eastern Nicenes will not hesitate to call me a saint, he ponders.

'Yes, I like the sound of that: Saint Theophilus.' He repeats it to himself like a prayer as the white marble buildings of The Canopic Way speed past.

Σ

33

AESON

'Alexandria.' My cabin boy sighs like he's watching the love of his life. So do I. 'It's the shiniest city I ever seen, sir.'

'Yes, Kelso, it is.' The haze is still blurring the view no matter how much I squint to pinpoint the Serapeum in the distance.

We hang over the side of the ship, and let the spray pitter-patter up our arms as sailor boys run about the deck, climb masts and shout above our heads. Nearly home. How could I have stayed away so long?

With a jerk and creak the ship is manoeuvred from the open sea into the less choppy waters of The Great Harbour. I wish this boat would hurry up and dock. My childlike excitement matches Kelso's, but I'm anxious too … how will it be with Rufius … now I'm a man? The saltwater's left little white splashes on my forearms … will my hard muscles repulse him?

'Sir, what's that big gold roof behind the docks?'

'That's the Museum.'

The boy's gaze follows my finger, eager to explore the city skyline. 'Beyond the Library warehouses is the Emporium, and behind that … can you see those two obelisks? That's the Agora.'

'Where's the Temple of Serapis?'

'Hidden under the mist. Look to your right where the land rises upwards.'

'All I see is the city wall … there's a hill in front of it, but it's covered in clouds.'

'Keep your eyes peeled. The mist will rise soon and you'll see the most magnificent temple in the world on top of that hill.'

Passengers jostle for the best position to see the Serapeum; some mumble to Apollo to give them a view from the harbour. Here comes the Captain with his black-toothed pirate grin, skin more charred than when we set sail from Constantinople.

'Look everyone, the mist's rising – keep looking. See her pink walls, like a fortress. These old sea legs go weak every time I see The Temple.' The aging sea dog will be flogging tourist tickets after he's whet their interest.

Kelso bounces on the balls of his feet. The mist raises its white skirts like teasing maidens, ever so slow, as the ship glides past the Lighthouse.

'Keep looking, Kelso, you'll see it soon.'

'Serapeum. Starboard,' bellows the Captain.

'Ahhh!' A collective sigh as passengers' heads turn in unison to their right.

The Serapeum, elevated on its hill above the city, glows bold pink in the morning sun: now I'm home. A deep line of blue tapers into the canal that weaves around the Serapeum and the city walls, then into Lake Mareotis and out to the Nile that snakes into Egypt, green shores and the barren desert beyond.

'It's a temple for giants!'

I tousle Kelso's hair. The nights would have been longer without him … but only one man can quell my loneliness. Can I see Biblos from here?

'What is that?' Kelso's finger points to the sandy dunes outside the city walls, beyond the Western Necropolis.

'Looks like a plague of locust swarming down the dunes, but they can't be insects …' the distance is making whatever that moving herd is appear smaller. Even from the city, the sand dunes of the Western desert are a long way off. If the approaching herd is making any noise, we're too far away to hear it. The slop of waves against the hull and the yells of the deckhands are all we can hear out here in the harbour. They don't move like animals. My gut clenches. 'Captain, what is that?'

Kelso leans further over the side and squints. So do the other passengers.

The Captain frowns and yells up at the lookout, 'What do you see, boy?'

'MONKS!' The panicked yell of the watch competes with the screams of seagulls high above our heads.

'Monks, sir, they are.' The Captain's gruff voice is full of disdain. 'Religious revolution's no good for the tourist trade.'

My breath's caught in my chest. Feels like I'm wearing heavy stones, not sandals, when I try to shuffle down the deck.

'Just like Athens. That's how it started there.' The Captain clears his throat and spits. 'The bishops calls 'em in from their monasteries and the swine come running in their black rags.'

'It's against the law for monks to enter cities.'

The man next to me has been with us from Constantinople. Round his neck hangs a cross. 'Who's going to remind that ignorant horde of the law? There'll be blood on Alexandria's streets tonight, Captain, mark my words. Best stay away from the temples.' Even Christians are repulsed by monks.

'That's difficult in Alexandria: there's a temple on every corner.' My tone is sharp.

'They won't touch the Serapeum.' The Captain spits again, oblivious to the sympathies of his cross-wearing passenger. 'Not even the monks would dare mess with the jewel of Egypt.'

'I have to get to the city, Captain, before that black army arrives.'

'That mob will reach the city before noon.'

'Fire! Fire! East. Fire!' The lookout's voice sends panic across deck. Heads turn away from the army of monks. Over the tiled rooftops of the ghetto a thin flute of black smoke rises into the hazy-blue sky. From this distance it looks harmless like the exhalation of a pipe-smoker.

Get your bearings, Aeson. Where's the Temple of Dionysus in relation to the smoke?

'What's burning?' My voice is trembling.

The Captain nods, black teeth clench, his attention is on the lookout.

'What do you see, lad?'

'Temple of Dionysus on fire,' shouts the lookout.

'NO!'

The Captain catches my urgency.

'And the buildings nearby? Can you see, lad?'

'Just the temple.'

'That's the pattern we've witnessed in other cities, sir: the monks target the old religions first.'

A passenger chips in. 'Same as Athens.'

'It is, sir, indeed it is. Safer at sea than on land these days. When they've destroyed the pagan temples, they'll move on to the small fry: their own kind, the heretic churches.'

I can't take anymore of this gruff old sea dog's complacency.

'Captain, can't this boat move any faster?' My voice trembles with impatience.

'Calm, sir. That smoke's no fire. It's a mere smouldering, a bonfire.'

Henite and Kiya don't burn their rubbish – it goes to the tips, to avoid drawing attention to themselves.

Passengers look alarmed – heads dart from the smoke to the approaching monks.

'Stay calm everyone; no need to let a little religious fervour spoil your trip. Serapis is untouchable. The Serapeum is safe to visit. We'll dock here tonight.'

He's thinking profit.

'Get the *Artemis* docked, Captain!' It's an order. I learnt that sharp tone from Rufius. I rarely use it. 'Back downstairs, Kelso. I need your help.'

* * *

'Egypt.' The Captain bellows our arrival and frowns as I rush down the gangway before he's given the signal to disembark, pirate grin set stiff in his face like comic graffiti scribbled on the wall of a public toilet.

'Sail on the *Artemis* again. Avoid the temples tonight,' shouts a deckhand.

The wooden walkway lunges sideways to the mooring as I grab the rope.

'Tickets for the Museum, Pharos and Temple of Serapis – buy at a discount from your cabin slaves. Disembark for Alexandria.'

The deckhand delivers his stock line to the group behind me. 'Pleasure to sail with you, sirs. Don't forget to buy your tickets for the wonders of Alexandria.'

Business goes on as usual in the tourist trade!

Solid ground feels strange. My legs sway with the rhythm of the sea. The hum of the docks waking up comes into earshot: deckhands shout orders, cargoes lugged here and there, roars of wild animals in cages that swing from pulleys. Incense … sandalwood and frankincense … and camel shit: the smell of home.

Library slaves at the customs desk look more like regal concubines. Rufius has certainly made his mark as Director of the Scriptorium.

'Copy and return service. Declare your books for the Great Library of Alexandria.'

For Serapis' sake! Rufius has upped security. Every boat moored has a desk at the end of it. I could push past the guards and make a dash for it up Neptune Street … but what if they catch me and lock me up? My priority is to reach my friends to warn them about the monks … if I'm not too late. I'll have to declare *The Book of Wisdom.* Rufius will have to help me get it back. I want Kiya to have this one, penned on the best quality parchment in Tyrian ink. It took me ages to copy, hunched over the Library of Constantinople's version.

'Any books to declare, sir? Bag for searching, please.' The slave looks at my bag in anticipation. It was never this strict before. They always searched the boats, but not a passengers' personal hand luggage.

I look towards the Temple of Neptune. Or shall I make a run for it? Soldiers stand shoulder to shoulder with armed Library Guards along the exits from the harbour. Why all the security?

Passengers from the *Artemis* shove past me. The two library slaves in pristine white tunics with plaited leather belts both look up at me impatiently. The rope between me and the streets that lead into the city makes my heart leap at the thought of being detained. I need to get to the Temple of Dionysus.

'Sir, your bag, please … if you could give your papers to my colleague.'

'Just this book.' I take the leather bound codex from my bag and put it on the desk.

'Name?'

'Aeson Biblus Catamitus.' Curiosity lights up the official's face. My cheeks heat under his gaze. These are Rufius' staff. Everyone at The Library knows the name Biblus and the gossip about the scandalous *cinaedus* who adopted his lover.

'Papers, master Biblus.' Extra polite. This is Alexandria. They don't care. Rufius is his boss: end of story.

The slave takes my identity papers and copies the description onto his parchment on the large desk. I'd forgotten how beautifully Alexandrian scribes write.

'Skin: honey-coloured.' He looks up.

'Distinguishing marks: none.'

'Eyes: blue.' His dark Egyptian gaze meets mine for an instant. Slaves know better than to hold a stare, even Library slaves.

I don't have time for the bureaucracy.

'I'm late for an appointment.' Careful, don't sound too impolite. This is the only bit of power they have.

'Welcome home, sir. The new process takes a little longer. Your residence in Alexandria?'

'Villa Biblos.'

'First two words of the book?'

'Aoi, aoi.'

'What's that? Spell it please, sir.'

The Library official leans forward to listen to our conversation. Have they been asked to listen out for heretical books entering the city? Officials were confiscating books in Athens. No, Alexandria is not Athens and Rufius is always on the look out for heretical books. It's his business. I'm being paranoid.

'Alpha, Omicron, Iota.'

'Here's your book collection ticket. It will be ready to collect in one month. There's a fast service for a fee if you need it sooner?'

My hand shakes as I snatch the small square of parchment.

'One month is fine.' Rufius will get it back sooner than that.

'Thank you, sir.'

At last! His colleague lifts the rope from its bronze post.

Now, let's get out of here. I duck into a familiar street just before the Temple of Neptune, drop the folds of my toga on the ground and step out of it. Stomach muscles and thighs clench: time to run.

The image of hundreds of monks in black robes racing into the city fires my limbs to a speed I've forgotten I had since being chased through these same streets in my youth. Good job I kept up my exercise regime on board ship. The ground beneath me feels as though it's still swaying with the waves as I speed past familiar buildings. My legs remember the short cuts to Dionysus Street without thinking about the way. Serapis, keep my friends safe.

34

RUFIUS

—The Agora—

Half the city's in the Agora. There's a tension in the air like something's about to kick off. I could do with a dose of entertainment. Let's see what going on?

'Cassius, dear, stop the litter over there.'

Silk curtains sway and jerk as the boys slow to a halt.

'No, no, not here. Closer to the Magistrate's podium. I want to hear what's going on up there.'

Theophilus. What tyranny is he conducting today? He's morphed into a bloody Damasus ... without the frilly frocks. The Archbishop looks more like a monk in that drab black cloak. At least he shaves. At thirty-six he was an irritation; at forty-six he makes my chins wobble. He has the height foreigners talk about when stereotyping Egyptians, a head taller than the inspectors and the Magistrate – Fatty's father must have bribed every voter to secure Aeson's fat little school chum that post. Theophilus dwarfs them all.

'Bring up the heretic.' That's a voice people won't mess with: the hard arrogance of a lawyer with a gentleness that wins hearts.

A man ... a Greek ... is dragged onto the podium. Theophilus' lictors have had their fun: arms, legs and face swollen and bloody. I do believe it's that Ophite Aeson was arrested with ten years ago … Seth, that was his name. Thank Bacchus Aeson's in Constantinople.

Theophilus clutches Seth's jaw in his long fingers. 'This man …' Theophilus looks startled as he turns Seth's head to the side and peers closely at his ear. 'A serpent? This man wears Satan's seal!'

O the drama, dear!

'This odious Ophite …' Theophilus surveys the crowd. His pause creates a soft murmur from the audience. 'The followers of Satan are still among us, citizens!'

The audience looks startled, as if Satan himself might creep up and throttle them.

'The monstrous worshipper of the Serpent will be tried this afternoon. If found guilty, in the eyes of the one and only Sublime God, he will have a public execution. Take him away.'

What a dull lot this is! Not one heckle as the lictors drag the Greek off the podium. Perhaps the crowd will liven up when the laws are read out. How I despise the way the people hang on distant orders from the Emperor.

Theophilus waves his hand at the Magistrate. Poor Fatty looks like a scared sheep.

'The h-heretics, namely the M-manicheans, the Apollonians, the Encratites, the Apotactites, the H-hydroparastatae, the Saccophori …' Fatty's tone's changed; he's adopted the metallic hardness of a university-trained voice, but he never lost the stutter. He's more nervous today than usual.

Theophilus raises his voice above Fatty and points at Seth, '… and the monstrous followers of the serpent, the odious Ophites.'

Supporters mumble their agreement.

'O-o-ophites are not listed in the edict.'

Theophilus ignores Fatty's objection.

'Carry on, Magistrate.'

'N-no heretic shall establish a church, tomb or perform their feral rites in small towns or in renowned cities.'

Fatty's flushed face clashes against the thick red stripes of his toga, he looks up from the scroll, as if offering the hecklers a chance to speak. Fatty's no heretic basher.

I've never witnessed a large crowd remain so quiet.

'I-if this right be rashly p-presumed by any p-person, the aforesaid house, wherever such forbidden constructions have been made, shall immediately be vindicated to the resources of Our fisc. All p-places which have received either the abode or the ministers of this sacrilegious doctrine shall immediately become fiscal p-property.'

'Confiscate property?'

'They can't do that.'

That got a murmur at least.

'If any heretic should f-flee the company of the good under the false p-pretence of the solitary life and assemble the secret gatherings of the lowest classes, he shall be subjected to the law as a p-profaner and corrupter of the C-catholic discipline, which we all revere. Thus he shall be outlawed during his lifetime.'

No one will object to that. Most city people think hermits are troublemakers.

'It is a crime to leave inheritance to hermit communities that subscribe to the heresies, namely the A-apollinarians, the V-valentinians ...'

Theophilus leans over to whisper in Fatty's ear. He shakes his head, then looks at the Archbishop's lictors and adds,

'And the O-ophites.'

Women prisoners lined up at the bottom of the podium steps pull their scarves tight round their heads. I recognise that old woman. She was at the Law Court the day Aeson was arrested too.

Fatty's level voice hardens. He's not comfortable with the administration of this law with Theophilus breathing down his neck.

'Investigators will be appointed by the b-bishops of every province.'

The audience looks at the black-cloaked Investigators on the podium. Motionless, lined up like soldiers ready for their orders.

'Informers will be well r-received and no crime will go unheard, r-regardless of the period of time since it was c-committed.'

Lawyers mumble, gathered in groups at the front.

Theophilus' long face is non-negotiable.

'All p-persons will convene on the same day for Easter in line with the C-catholic discipline.'

Heretics mutter and shush each other. One of the investigators shifts; his heavy shoes scratch against the wooden podium like gladiator sandals in the sand of the arena.

And the sentence? The question on everyone's closed lips.

'The supreme p-penalty applies.'

Lawyers mutter and rearrange the white folds of their togas. Only the young ones, without a reputation to lose, will risk defending a heretic after this.

Theophilus surveys the response with a look of satisfaction. Perhaps it's the harshness of the sentence, or the threat of the inspectors that's clamped the hecklers' mouths.

'The sentence is death.'

Oh, you just love the sound of your own voice, don't you, Arch-bloody-bishop. Let's pull these curtains apart.

'And the sentence for farting, dear?' Diana stops fanning me, Cassius looks startled, and Fatty's eyes widen. Theophilus isn't amused.

'Seize any man who dares to make a mockery of the Emperor's laws, of God's sublime jurisdiction.' His dark gaze fixes on me.

Let's have a swig of wine … and raise my beaker to him.

Nervous sniggers and coughs snort from the crowd. Children giggle. Everyone needs a little light-relief.

'Ah, the *cinaedus* thinks the death penalty is amusing. I wouldn't laugh, *cinaedus*, the same penalty applies to your kind. Magistrate, I suggest the law updated last year which condemns *cinaedi* to death by public burning is displayed in the Agora. The party's over, Rufius.'

A lump's stuck in my throat only laughter will dislodge … and laughter has no place on Theophilus' podium. Fatty looks over at me apologetically; he's weaker than his father.

'Ignore Rufius. He's on the drink again.' That was Olympus' boom of a voice. Has he finally discovered a sense of humour?

Seagulls screech overhead. Those gulls know that Ophite will be fresh quarry before today's over. Theophilus looks set on revenge.

'Inspectors, show the people the heretical relics found in the Temple of Dionysus.'

Two black-robed inspectors display an enormous silver goblet and some old bones above their heads.

'It's sacrilege,' mutters a woman.

Boos and hisses gain in volume from the pagan mob. An argument's started at the back of the Agora. People look round nervous; some hide weapons beneath their tunics. The tension's at breaking point. This crowd's going to riot.

It's time to leave.

'Cassius, take me home. To Biblos, fast as your legs will run, boys.'

'Bloody bumpy ride. I thought this litter was supposed to be more comfortable on my old bones than the carriage.'

Winding up Diana is one way to get her arms to work faster. 'You told Cassius run to avoid arrest by Archbishop.'

'Don't be ridiculous, Diana. Theophilus won't arrest the Director of the Scriptorium. Heckling in the Agora is standard practice. You know that, dear.'

That's it, fan those peacock feathers like you're trying to fly this litter.

Biblos' high walls appear to jig up and down as we bounce past. Home sweet home.

'Diana dear, what's that?' It looks like large black letters scrawled on the wall near the gate. Graffiti! Bloody kids. The paint is still shiny and wet. It's blurred. Damn these old eyes.

Diana looks out of the litter's silk curtains, then back at me. Her gold bangles jingle as she speeds up her fanning. Is she being thick on purpose? My girl has the eye of a hawk.

'Diana, what's that graffiti on the wall?'

Insolent girl! She doesn't want to tell me.

'Stop with the fan, Diana. Apollinos didn't teach you to read for nothing, dear. What does it say? You know my eyes aren't what they used to be.'

'Nothing.'

My neck's too stiff to crane out through the curtains.

'Stop!'

The bumpy dash towards the gate continues. What's wrong with these slaves today?

'STOP I SAID.'

I crane out of the curtain at Cassius. He's hurrying them past the graffiti.

'Cassius, stop this litter immediately, or I'll have you all flogged.'

The litter stops at the gates. Both polished pink sandstone walls either side of the great gates are covered with large ugly letters. I can read that myself it's so big.

C I N A E D U S

The word smacks me round the face. Surely I'm numb to the sting of ridicule? But this isn't kids having a laugh; this isn't the plebs joking in the Agora. The brush that painted this graffiti was thick with malice.

'Cassius, help me down.' He doesn't look me in the eye.

All eight slaves stand with their eyes fixed on the ground. A numbness floods my body and mind. None of us has moved; we all just stare at the huge, ugly letters.

Apollinos' snorts as he opens the gates to let us in.

'I'll call painters, master.' His voice sounds distant.

My face is hot with tears. The last time I cried was when Aeson left for Constantinople ten years ago. Diana's small hand, bangles jingling, finds its way into mine.

That bastard Theophilus is behind this.

'Come, master, come.' Diana gently tugs my hand, directing me through the gardens. Slaves stop clipping and pruning and drop their gazes.

Tears quietly fall and I stumble on the folds of my toga.

She clicks her fingers when we reach the atrium. 'Prepare a bath.' Her small hand squeezes mine. 'You feel like new man after bath.'

Sweet girl. A new man! Her dark mane of hair glistens in the sunlight. We both look at the statue of Aeson's coming of age in the atrium fountain. Maybe it's time to leave? Alexandria has changed; it's getting as intolerant as the West … and I want to see my boy again.

I reach up to touch Aeson's face.

'Come, master.'

Outside the walls of Biblos, Apollinos shouts orders at slaves to clean the walls … to wash away the shame that I have worn with pride all my adult life. The thought makes my cheeks flush in anger.

'Fuck you, Theophilus.' Enough of these tears. I'll show you which one of us is the fop. Every heretical book in The Library will be copied, despite your ignorant laws and policies. I'll flood the market with books. Rufius the *Cinaedus* will have the last laugh.

AESON

Must catch my breath. Blue veins rise on the backs of my sweaty hands rested on my knees. This corner used to reek of incense, bellowed out from the Temple of Mithras; all I can smell is piss in this deserted doorway. That flute of smoke has thinned, but I need to keep running. Trouble's on its way.

The streets of my childhood are the same ... even the dogs congregate in the same shady alcoves, but on my sprint across the city I felt disorientated. Streets that are usually busy day and night were deserted. I saw no violence, but the streets perspire a silent threat. Women rushed into alleys, quietening crying children, fear in their eyes. They know an army of monks is descending on the city. I need to warn my friends, check they're safe ... then I'll tackle Rufius. He won't be happy I'm back against his will.

The Canopic Way. I stop and gawp at the width of it, the colonnades stretching ahead of me. It must be the widest road in any city in the Empire. Why's it empty? That pounding ... the heavy shoes of soldiers. Here they come. Eight men to each row march in my direction. I need to get out of their way.

At last: the Temple of Dionysus. Fear whips and tosses in my gut at the smell of burning. Why are the great wooden doors ajar? They're always shut tight. I fling them open and rush into the courtyard. I'm too late. The huge incense braziers have been thrown on to a fire in the centre of the courtyard. Tables, chairs and beds are piled up, charred black they crack and hiss. A thin line of smoke reaches into the morning sky. My heart pounds in my ears. Where is everyone?

Fragments of pages with blackened edges stick to the sides of one of the braziers. No one in Alexandria would burn parchment even if they were desperate for fuel.

Fear sends my legs sprinting inside the kitchen. That bucket's been dropped in a panic. Spilt water stains the floor. What happened here? The echo of my feet thudding upstairs in the emptiness makes me nervous. My throat tightens at the thought of what I'll find inside.

'Kiya? Henite?'

There's no one here.

Why am I going to Kiya's bedroom? The temple's deserted. Her room is empty … except Sophia's basket. That will be empty too. Kiya doesn't go anywhere without her snake.

I kick off the lid. Ah! Sophia! She rears up her head and opens her hood. What a size she's grown to. What's she doing here? Panic paints horrific images in my mind in my rush from room to room. The frenzy mounts … if they're not here, where are they? Seth, Henite, Kiya … Croc. Venus Street. Turk will know where Croc is.

I stop in the courtyard. The letters scrawled across the courtyard wall where Croc, Kiya and I used to line up for Seth to measure our heights make me want to puke.

HERETICS

My fingers trace the faded names on the wall below the graffiti: Croc, Kiya, Aeson. The lines that marked our heights are still visible below our names. We were so small.

The graffiti paint's still tacky; they can't be far. The roof. I might be able to see something from up there. I run into Kiya's room and pull myself up onto the roof … I lifted Kiya up here countless times.

I pace in circles on the flat roof. No sign of them in the deserted streets of the ghetto. Black smoke rises from temples all over the city, blown inland by a sea wind. The Khamaseen's coming.

Sun's hot on my back and a sharp pain shoots through my temples. This can't be happening ... but somehow this feels like it was always going to happen, that I was always going to stand here on the roof and watch Alexandria burn.

The monks are still a long way off, a plague moving down the dunes. The army has done this.

Is that a voice? A girl's voice. 'Kiya?'

Like a child who's lost his mother, my movements are uncoordinated – I bang into the stairwell walls in my rush to follow her voice.

'Kiya?' I turn in a circle in the courtyard. Absentmindedly, I pick up a basket and put it upright. A snake! Half a snake, cut by a sword. My gut pinches.

There it is again. A whimper. It's coming from outside the temple.

Opposite, on the steps of the Temple of Aphrodite, a young priestess sobs and chants to her goddess as she covers her face in the wet ash from the braziers with mournful strokes.

Let's crouch next to her, try to get her attention. Glazed eyes stare through me: the empty look of grief.

'Child, what happened here?'

She's bewildered.

'They took them all.' She raises an arm and points in the direction of the Agora. Her hand trembles, teeth chatter.

'Who? Who took them?'

'Soldiers. They took them all.'

Other children peer out from the doorway of the temple and watch us.

'Where are the adults?'

'They took them all.' Still she points towards the end of the street, her long sleeve in eerie profile, eyes suddenly wide as if she has seen a ghost, or a monster behind me.

I turn to where she is pointing, but there's nothing there.

An older girl tiptoes in quick silent steps, takes her hand and leads the child away.

There is nothing I can do to help these children crouched in the shadow of a temple raped of its sacred purpose like street urchins in the Necropolis. Doom thickens around me. I have arrived at the destiny Dera warned me of … but I feel strong, like for the first time in my whole life I have a purpose, like this is my cue to fulfil some fated task. How strange. I feel more confident than I've ever felt in my life.

Serapis, keep my friends safe until I find them.

RUFIUS

Good, the folds of my toga are perfect today, and I've kept Theophilus waiting just long enough to let him know who's the master of this house. How dare he barge in here and demand to search Biblos.

'In we go, Apollinos.'

'Perhaps, the cameo is too, er, audacious for a meeting with the Archbishop, master. Why don't you give it to me?'

This brooch is just the right accessory for the occasion: my favourite cameo: me as a young buck. I'll not have him think those bigoted laws have riled me. The death sentence. Indeed! The law condemning *cinaedi* has been echoing round and round in my poor head since this morning … *atone for a crime of this kind in avenging flames.* Erase the thought, Rufius. He wouldn't dare.

'The brooch stays, Apollinos.' I'll not have Theophilus think he's frightened Rufius Biblus Catamitus!

'But, master, the Archbishop knows about your library. You need to tone down …'

'That self-righteous prat doesn't know anything, Apollinos. Why would he be here talking and not burning my books as we speak? He suspects, but suspicions have no weight in court, dear.'

What in Bacchus' name is that squeak? The slaves who pulled open the tall doors to the ground floor parlour look mortified.

'How can I make a serious entrance accompanied by squeaking doors, dears!'

Apollinos is still fussing behind me. 'They will be oiled, master.'

'Don't bother me with the method, Apollinos.'

How disappointing – no slave head bobbing between Theophilus' legs! Biblos hospitality not good enough for him? Where does he find his pleasure? In the darkness of the shame he preaches with church orphans, or does he obey that pleasure-hating god of his and abstain?

The dark cloaks of the Archbishop and his inspector strike a harsh contrast to the sunlight steaming in from the terrace. Antinous' sweet voice and the strum of the harp are at odds with Theophilus' sour face: dark eyes framed by bushy black eyebrows –they've never seen a pair of tweezers.

My stomach is a tight knot. This is the first time Biblos has failed to seduce her guests. The slaves look insulted. Cassius and Antinous aren't used to being rejected. Even the centaurs and satyrs look like they want to leap from the frescos and run out of the room.

Straight-backed on the couch, Theophilus' dark eyes meet mine. This will be an entertaining battle.

'Theophilus! What a pleasant surprise.' Not bothering to rise to your host? To Hades with etiquette.

Let's flash a plucked leg as I recline, to irritate him.

'Wine.'

Let's fiddle with my brooch as Cassius pours. Oh, the disgust on the Archbishop's face. Superb!

'Thank you, Cassius.' My wine's well-watered. The slaves want me to keep my wits: they're afraid of him. 'A beauty isn't he, Bishop?' I flick up Cassius' tunic and his muscular buttocks tense.

Not rags you're wearing are they, Theophilus. Now I'm closer to you, I can see the quality of the fine linen mix. Possibly open to a little bribery then?

'I see your walls have been painted, *cinaedus.*' So he did order the graffiti. Pathetic! What an intellectual disappointment. Well if it's cheap insults he wants …

'Apollinos will put you in better humour, Bishop. I keep him for guests with unusual tastes.'

They both look like they want to kill me. Theophilus' furry brows furrow to a hard black line.

'I'll be brief, Rufius.'

'Excellent! Your little speech this morning must have exhausted your oratory repertoire.' My smile is wide and sarcastic.

His temper flushes his cheeks pink.

'You're not above the law, Rufius. You would be wise to co-operate with me.'

'Bah! Enough of this nonsense. That law is nothing new. The death sentence has been in place since the forties, and not a single case has reached trial. And as for books, you'll find nothing even mildly heretical at Biblos.'

'Your kind is an embarrassment to the Empire and an insult to God.' His deep growl of a voice is level, his gaze moves in disgust from my brooch to my hair.

'Didn't my hairdresser do a splendid job today.' I twirl a ringlet. I do like a good hair day! Ha! That riled him.

'Guards!' Theophilus' voice rings across the house.

A metallic clatter from the Atrium and two centurions appear in the doorway, both sheepish. Good Romans: they didn't turn their noses up at Biblos' pleasures.

'My dear centurions, I'm pleased to see Villa Biblos' hospitality is appreciated.'

'ENOUGH!' Theophilus stands, drinks tray clatters to the floor. The soldiers' backs straighten, hands move to hilts, but they're ready for nothing.

'Enough, Rufius! You mock the Church, you mock the Empire, you mock mankind.'

'That's better, dear. You needed a little colour in your cheeks.'

Theophilus glares at me. I do believe his eyebrows are as black as my kohl.

'Where is it, Rufius?'

Ha! I win today, Theophilus! I lift the folds of my toga and pretend to search for my under-exercised penis. 'It's been dormant for years, dear.'

Apollinos' gaze heats the back of my neck and Theophilus' dark robed silhouette casts a shadow over me as he blocks the sun from the terrace. The size of him towering a head above me is disturbing.

'Do not underestimate me, Rufius. Tell me the location of your secret library.'

I drop my toga. He's knocked the play out of me. At least Damasus could banter.

My fingers twist my curls faster.

'Secret library? Oh, you must mean my private collection.' An almost imperceptible movement of my index finger has Apollinos behind my couch in an instant. 'Apollinos, dear, fetch my collection of pornography for the Bishop.'

Theophilus is seething. 'The privilege of your birth has dimmed your senses. This is not the Empire you were born into. The Emperor has a vision and minor details such as trials will not stop us stamping out heresy. Your heretic collection is well known to the Church of Alexandria.'

That's the same look on Theophilus's face as when I left the Law Court ten years ago with Aeson. He's not forgotten how I belittled him. This is about his personal revenge.

'What! Hear that, Apollinos. The Bishop's not interested in my pornography! Look around you, dear.' My arm waves at the statues and frescos. 'I'm a collector of art … or do you call this heresy too?'

'Harbouring heretical books is the reason I am here. Your motivation does not interest me. Nor will my Inspectors be interested in the protests of a *cinaedus*. I can pin you down with heresy or infamy.

There are enough young boys who can make declarations in the courts about that.'

'Oooo! Pin me down!' A swing of my hips is in order. 'Bring on your inspectors, Bishop. This old Roman could do with a little fun.'

Theophilus' thin top lip curls in disgust, his smooth steely voice deepens. 'Give me the information I want, and I will show you mercy. Fail to disclose vital information regarding the pollution of heresy in this city and I'll see you burn.'

'Come now, Bishop, this is very dull. You've been sucked in by idle gossip. What interest would an old *cinaedus* have in heretical books?' I do enjoy demoting archbishops.

KIYA

Dera kneels and ties my scarf round my head to hide my earlobes.

'Give *The Book of Wisdom* to the Librarian, sister. He will protect it. Now dry your eyes. Sophia tests us all. That's his house across the street, the one surrounded by the high pink wall.'

We touch foreheads the way Snake People do. His energy field pulsates around me like he's wrapping me in his strength.

Off he runs back in the direction of the Agora, huge in his rough hermit cloak. Will I see him again? Will I see my family again? I feel naked without Sophia round my neck.

Sweet Sophia, why are slaves painting walls in the midday heat? It's baking. Those young beauties all look like Aeson – how he used to look anyway with that curly black hair.

Sophia, give me courage, I must get this book to the Librarian. The Library is the only safe place now. That's what Dera said. My head spins at the memory of the soldiers and inspectors, the confusion. *Go girlie, do what Dera tells you.* Sophia, keep Henite safe. My heart aches at leaving my snake. Some terrible foreboding makes me think I won't kiss her scaly skin again. Stop it, Kiya. It's up to me to save *The Book of Wisdom* now.

The bump of the scroll against my hip feels wrong under my dress, like it's just a recipe book. The slaves will hear the knock of my crutch ... yes, that's right, Beautiful, ignore me, back to your painting. To them I just look like an old woman hunched over her stick.

What's the Librarian trying to cover up? Graffiti! It's all over the city. The atmosphere's thick like after a funeral: quiet, but not peaceful.

This must be the entrance. Grand like the gates to Cleopatra's palace Poseidon sent a wave to swallow. Will they let me in?

'Oi, where do you think you're going?'

What a silly short tunic he's wearing. Gym-pumped thighs, but his chest and legs are not plucked. *Young, but manly, hard and hairy: that's how he likes me,* Aeson had told me when I asked him why he didn't shave his chest like other boys his age. This slave might look like Aeson, but he doesn't make me think sinful thoughts like Aeson did.

The slave looks at my crutch.

'Beggars go round the trade entrance.' He points down the palm-lined road. The wall looks like it goes on forever. 'All the way to the end.'

There's fear in his eyes. What terror are you expecting?

'Thank you.' I'd like to rap him over the head with my stick.

Sweet Sophia, the heat. This dress is damp with sweat. My armpit will be chaffed raw by the time I reach the back entrance. A throb of urgency quivers in my gut. I can't have passed the trade entrance. There's been no gate, no door in the high wall. Seagulls perched in palm trees move their necks at the knock of my crutch on the pavement. Even they are silenced by the heat. The trade entrance must be round the next corner, at the back of the house.

Thank Sophia, Aeson's far away. Remember that day, sweet Aeson, when you gave me a piggy-back after Lanky broke my crutch? The memory of running through the Necropolis makes me smile. We will have you in common at least, the Librarian and me. My stomach groans with nerves at the thought of meeting him. *He's harmless, a soft-hearted old Roman when you get to know him* ... but Aeson, you were a beautiful boy and I'm a cripple. What if he won't receive me? What will I do with *The Book of Wisdom* then?

It's slipping round the back of my left hip. Dera tied the linen too loose on my right shoulder. Let's hitch it up. That's better. It won't bounce now.

What's that sound? Heavy, measured footsteps. They're getting closer. A black-cloaked man turns the corner. For a moment he's as alarmed as I am. Sweet Sophia, an inspector like the ones in the Agora this morning, large wooden cross round his neck. My heart squeezes tight, my good leg's solid from fear.

'What do we have here?' He speaks like a ventriloquist, through clenched, broken teeth.

'Just a beggar, sir.' My voice is loud and angry.

A strong hand grips my arm.

'Let me go!' Quick, think.

His other hand grabs my shoulder. My crutch hits the ground. Sweet Sophia, keep the book safe.

'Not *just* a beggar. Ah! The mark of the serpent. The Archbishop warned us there would be more of you.'

'Get off me.'

He yanks me up; my feet lift off the ground.

'Stop, you're hurting me.' The linen sheath feels light on my shoulder like the scroll's been dislodged. Don't fall out. Sophia, keep the book safe.

'What are you doing here, heretic?' Yuk, Spittle. Better shut my eyes, or his gob might blind me. 'WHAT ARE YOU DOING HERE?' Oh shut up! And stop spraying me through the gaps in your nasty chipped teeth.

'Begging, sir. Hungry, is all.' Blessed Sophia, please don't let *The Book of Wisdom* fall out. I must stay as still as possible, not struggle.

The book's slipping free. Sweet Sophia, no! Panic makes me light-headed. A gull gives out an unnatural cry from the palm tree above my head.

We both look down as the discoloured, yellow papyrus bounces on the pavement. His face is so close I can smell wine on his stale breath. Teeth grind together, menace in his demon eyes like he's working some evil magic.

'Let me go.'

His hands release my shoulders.

'Ahh!' A sharp pain stabs my hip as I land on the pavement. The book! My nails scratch the dust, desperate to pull myself towards the ancient scroll. His big hairy hand snatches it. Sacrilege: an ape hand embracing a goddess!

'What do we have here then?'

'Give it to me.' My eyes are hot with tears.

'Shut your mouth, Heretic.'

He unrolls the papyrus. His face is hideous, his sharp chipped teeth grind with an evil fervour. 'Heretic magic. This is going to the Archbishop, and so are you. Get up.'

He picks up my crutch and swings it high in the air as if he intends to thrash me with it.

'Give me the Book.' Whatever the demon was thinking about doing with my crutch, he's changed his mind.

'Get up, Snake Bitch.' He throws the crutch on my gammy leg. Numb. You can't hurt a lame leg, Demon. 'You've got some explaining to do.' His fingers pinch my arm, drag me after him faster than my crutch will move. I'll have to hop.

'Slaves, open the gates.'

Two guards open the gates onto great gardens full of exotic plants and pale slaves from the Northern provinces. He pushes me inside.

'Follow me, Snake Bitch.'

'No! I curse you. Aoi-aoi-aoi. I came into this world like mice from the rubbish tips. No father, no mother. Aoi-Aoi-AOI- AOI …'

Ouch! He slaps my face so hard my head swings back.

'Shut your heretic mouth, or I'll shut it for you.'

The Inspector's other hairy hand has *The Book of Wisdom* tight in his grip.

Sweet Sophia, keep the book safe. Kiya, we must keep quiet, chant silently, for the book's sake.

What are the slaves staring at … have they never seen a cripple beaten?

Gates squeal as they close behind us.

What beautiful flowers. The Librarian must be a good man to grow such a sweet-smelling garden. Keep your focus on the book, Kiya.

'You two, lazy good for nothings.' Two centurions reclining in the atrium rearrange their tunics. 'While you've been tempted by the devil, I've been doing God's work capturing heretics.'

Fear, not a soldier's honour, makes them scramble to their feet.

The demon brandishes *The Book of Wisdom* in the air like an eagle on a battlefield.

'If there's one heretic book, there's more to be found somewhere in this house.' He looks up at the terraces, room after room. It's enormous.

'Now make sure this Snake Bitch doesn't try any magic on you. Don't let her out of your sight. She's as sly as the serpent god she worships.'

'We don't worship a serpent god.'

'Quiet, Bitch.'

Are those centurions looking at him as if he's mad, or looking at me as if I might bite them? Both.

This atrium's grander than the Law Court, all clean white marble.

Aeson! It's only a statue of my old friend posing like the god Antinous, but it's so lifelike I yearn to reach across the fountain and hold his perfect marble hand. Will I ever see you again, sweet friend? Did you find another copy of the sacred book in the great libraries of the Empire? Or did you forget?

The centurions on either side of me poke a finger into my shoulder to hurry me.

'Tut. You try walking with a crutch.'

The inspector stomps ahead. I must keep up with him, mustn't lose sight of *The Book of Wisdom.*

38

Rufius

'What, in bloody Hades, do you think you're up to, bringing beggars into the house?' Has the whole world gone mad?

'Sweet Sophia, Let me go!'

What a couple of gormless centurions – they release her armpits and she finds her balance on the old crutch she's carrying.

Theophilus, Apollinos, the slaves and I all stare at the cripple. She gawps at the painting of Dionysus cavorting with nymphs and satyrs by a lake like she's never seen a fresco before. Her deformed figure looks like some strange creature stepped out of the scene. That smell of stale sweat must come from her.

'Apollinos, take the poor wretch outside and feed her.'

Theophilus' toothy inspector waves a papyrus scroll in the air. 'Not so fast.'

'Well, have you found the heretical library, inspector?'

The inspector yanks the cripple by the ear.

'Get off me!'

'No, Archbishop. But I caught the heretic delivering this – look, Archbishop, the mark of the snake, on her lobes.' Toothy hands the scroll over to Theophilus like he's showing his mother his exam results. Now what? I've had enough drama for one morning.

'Give that back to me.' She's a feisty little monster. I like her. She didn't bat an eyelid at the Archbishop and she must recognise him.

We watch Theophilus roll open the papyrus and hold it under his long nose like he's holding a toilet sponge from some public latrine.

'"*Aoi-aoi-aoi*" … magic words … Jesus said, "I led Sophia out of the chaos …"'

The cripple gasps to hear the sacred words of her people.

'The same heresy you bribed a Magistrate to return to The Library ten years ago I believe, Rufius?'

That bloody book again! It's like a lingering fart. Theophilus will try to frame me for this. The Snake People's heretic book in my house does not look good. Why was she bringing it here? Turk wouldn't have sent her. He's learnt prudence.

'Where's the rest of your books, Rufius?'

Theophilus looks from her to me, triumph in his eyes. The smack of the scroll in his hand makes us all jump.

Cassius quivers and drops his flute. 'The inspector found her outside the gates of Biblos, master.' Clever boy.

Think you have me, don't you, dear? We'll see about that.

'What were you doing creeping around my house, girl? Cassius, tell us what you saw.'

Apollinos nods for him to speak up.

'I was by the gate with Antinous. The inspector found the cripple outside the house.'

'Is this right, Antinous? The cripple was not intercepted on the grounds of Biblos?'

Poor Antinous, he can barely manage a nod.

The inspector takes a step closer to Theophilus. 'She was on her way here to add that book to the Librarian's heretic library, Archbishop.' Does he have to accompany each syllable with a spray of spittle?

'You can't prove a jot, dear.'

'I will have evidence, Rufius. With the cripple's testimony, I'll bring your heretic black market business to its knees.' His thick eyebrows crease like he's giving a naughty boy a telling off. 'Inspector, we need a confession from her.'

'I will have the truth from her before the day is out, Archbishop.'

Keep your venom in that gob of yours, Toothy.

'I've never seen this girl before in my life.' I dart the girl a swift look. There is intelligence in her dark eyes. I hope you follow my drift, dear … for both our sakes. 'Come here, girl.'

The click of her crutch and drag of her shrivelled child-sized foot along the mosaic is foreign to Biblos. Even my latrine slaves are perfect. Get over the stench, Rufius. I need her on side. If they take her, they'll torture her until she will confess to anything. 'Do not be afraid to speak, dear.'

Straightening as much as her crooked back allows, she takes a breath like a young Library student about to deliver his first public oration. But with a difference – I detect no nerves, no twitching or fidgeting. The girl is stillness itself. There is beauty in that.

'I'm not scared of that demon.' What a little fireball. With the resolve of a judge, she continues in her level tone, a voice trained to sing, to hold a steady note. Balancing on her good leg, she raises her crutch and uses it to point at the inspector. 'He's the heretic.'

Like a great black crow diving for its prey, the inspector raises his arms to swipe at the girl. 'You, Snake Bitch …'

'STOP! Only I administer punishment in this house.' Well … and Apollinos.

That's it man, you and your rank, toothy grin can just back off.

'That's better, Inspector, remember your place, dear.'

'Let her speak, Inspector.' Theophilus needs to check he has a reliable witness. He needs to know she'll crack. I think not.

'You weren't on your way here, were you, dear?'

'No, sir.' Good girl. 'I was on my way to the Kingdom of God – that's the only confession you'll get out of me.' Her face is defiant.

Ha! The cripple has a sense of humour.

The inspector's teeth clench. 'I'll wring the truth from your godless lungs.'

Oh my dears, the boys are trembling. It's getting far too serious in here. Let's see what fun we can have with these badly dressed Christians.

'Music!' Apollinos just stares at me. 'Something jolly. That tune they play when the *cinaedus* comes on stage in Petronius' *Satyricon.*' Even if it is at my expense, I'll hear laughter in Biblos today.

Cassius makes a squeak on the flute and Antinous raps the tambour.

'Excellent. Now Inspector, take a drum.' Don't just look at it, you ill-humoured idiot. 'Here.' His face is a masterpiece of confusion as I shove it in his hand.

'I'll play the tambourine. That's it. Now, you must have seen the play. The dance goes like this, two steps to the left, then a jump to the right.' Better tuck my toga under my left arm, or I'll lose it.

They all stare at me as if I've lost my mind. Maybe I have.

'DANCE, I SAID!' At least that got a jump out of the dull Philistine.

Even a shimmy of these old hips failed to illicit a titter. Alright, Apollinos, you can stop shaking your head at me. And you, you dull Christian oafs can stop glaring.

'ENOUGH!' Theophilus' face is red with fury.

The tiny drum catapults from the inspector's hand and skittles across the room towards the terrace.

'Yes, enough cavorting, dear, I'm the only dancing queen in this house.'

Theophilus' irritation is reaching fever pitch. This is almost fun. He turns on the centurions. 'You two useless hounds.'

The centurions straighten in unison, with a click of their army issue heels. 'Yes, sir!'

'Take the heretic to the Agora prison.'

'Yes, sir!'

Theophilus looks ready to explode with the irritation of leaving Biblos empty-handed. His black robe swishes as he storms towards the door.

'Watch your step, Rufius.'

Toothy follows him out. At the door, the inspector turns to me, 'I'll get a confession from her, *cinaedus*.'

'Enough of these insults! Get out of my house! Out, out, out.'

Stomping my feet like a child scaring pigeons feels good. The inspector eyes me warily.

'OUTTTTT!'

That's it, off you run.

Where does the cripple think she's going? No point you hobbling after him, girl. The centurions take an armpit each. She's so slight their fingers meet at her shoulder.

'You're coming with us,' they say in unison.

Her crutch, smooth and dark where her armpit rests on it, clatters to the floor.

'Why the rush, my dear centurions?'

'We got our orders, sir.'

One of them lets go of her arm. 'Ah, you little minx! She bit me.'

'Ha! Just a scratch, centurion. You've seen worse than that in battle surely?'

'Cassius dear, go and check the horrid old crows leave Biblos.'

'Orders is orders, sir.'

They're not comfortable with this work. Killing barbarians is one thing, torturing a harmless cripple … there's no honour in that.

Cassius returns short-breathed. 'The Archbishop has left Biblos, master.'

'Apollinos, close the parlour door.'

That bloody squeak had better be fixed.

'Let the girl go, centurions.' They stop, but do not release her.

'Stop struggling, dear.'

'But *The Book of Wisdom!*' Her face is wet with tears. If her will was matched by her body she'd floor these two oafs.

'Apollinos, bring me two purses and a generous handful of gold coins.'

'We're not open to bribes, sir.'

'Come now, are you not Mithras' men? All legionaries worship that mighty god. Look here, even an old *cinaedus* like me respects his might in war.' I point to my new mosaic floor. The image of the bull being overpowered by Mithras was Apollinos' idea. I wasn't sure at the time, but it will serve its purpose now – create an affinity between us.

Both men mutter under their breath. Dear gods, what have those bishops done to our men? They're afraid of praying aloud.

'Mighty Mithras is your protector in battle, is he not?'

The bolder one turns over his wrist and looks at it. The bull, the mark of Mithras is obvious from here, even with my old eyes.

'I am no Christian, sir, but we are sworn by oath to our legion.'

The other one touches his wrist to cover a scar, white like a sunburst, as if he's cut out his mark. He's hidden his faith. At least I wear my shame: I finger my cameo brooch.

'These are strange times, and we must all do what we think is right.' They'll not be able to refuse the gold, enough to take themselves and their families away from this warring city.

Coins clink as they pour from my right hand, then drop like water into my left palm.

'More than the meagre pension the Legion will give you in twenty years when you retire … if you live that long.'

Yes, that's it. They're mesmerised by the sound of money falling through my fingers.

'Buy a few hectares somewhere, watch your children grow and marry.'

Gold winks in the sunlight from the terrace, a blurred waterfall, as I let it drop into two leather purses. 'Men of property, with country villas.'

They're both won over, faces full of the future I've painted for them. At least money's not lost its power.

* * *

Only when the hard slap of centurion shoes can no longer be heard in the distance does Diana slink back into the parlour. She curls up at my feet and hisses at the Snake Girl. 'What's she doing here?'

The cripple gazes at the bust of Aeson.

Diana looks ready to pounce. 'Fancy him, do you?'

The cripple's mouth moves in silent dialogue with Aeson's bust.

'Stupid cripple.'

'Diana, stop that hissing.' The soft light of love in the Ophite's eyes stirs something within me. 'Do you know this boy, dear?'

'Aeson was my friend.' Her speech is measured and spacious.

A friend of Aeson? Her back is wet with sweat. She walked here in the midday heat. She could do with a bath, but there is no time for that. I'll pour her a cup of water myself.

'Drink this … and tell me your name, dear.'

'Kiya.'

'Why did you come here, Kiya?'

'To ask you to protect *The Book of Wisdom,* keep it safe in your secret library.'

How does everyone know about my bloody library?

Her glazed stare fixes on something invisible in the distance. 'To save our secret mysteries from the Archbishop's bonfires.'

'I'm no Christian, dear.'

'You're a librarian, protector of books.'

She looks at me in a way nobody has ever looked at me … as if she is looking at a brave man.

'I'm just an old fool, dear.'

Her eyes lock into mine again. She may have a crutch but I do not pity her. She's sexless, but somehow mesmerising.

'Sir?' The intensity of her gaze makes me feel read, absorbed by her.

'Yes, dear?'

'You do have a library, don't you? It's not just city gossip?'

Apollinos shakes his head.

'Yes, dear, but I don't have a copy of *The Book of Wisdom.* It was returned to your people ten years ago on Aeson's request.

Apollinos' lips tighten in disapproval.

'Then the Archbishop took the only copy.' She hunches further over her crutch, defeated.

A rare rush of kindness makes my heart do a nosedive. Or is it a need to make amends for separating Aeson from his friends, from his home? A kindness to Kiya is a kindness to my boy.

'Kiya, there is one other copy of *The Book of Wisdom.*'

What a trusting smile.

We don't have much time. Those inspectors will be back here as soon as they realise the centurions have defected. 'Apollinos, ready my litter.'

39

AESON

The Arch of Venus: this is the very spot I first met Rufius. How strange. In that moment I never imagined I'd stand here desperate for Turk's help. Venus Street was always quiet before sunset, but today the silence is eerie. Only the lustiest pleasure-seekers scuttle into brothels – nobody will dare loiter outside taverns today. Sensible Alexandrians are locked safe inside their homes.

By Serapis, Turk's prospered by the look of The Honeypot! Marble clad entrance … and not all this stone's been pinched from the Necropolis. The door boys are in better condition than we were. No scars or bruises.

'Can I interest you in Desert Honey, our house speciality, sir?'

'I'm looking for the boss.'

They look at each other and one runs inside without saying anything.

Luxurious for a brothel. Even the furniture looks new, not random pieces stolen from the rich. Incense mingles with the sweaty smell of sex. The Honeypot lacks the sophistication of Constantinople's brothels, but the boys look more fun.

Is that Croc on the couch? Thank Serapis!

'Croc!'

'Eh?' His head rolls back on the cushioned couch, eyes try to focus then close. Skin as flaky as ever. He looks like a leper. The only other customer lolls on a couch the other side of the room, a head bobbing up and down in his lap.

'Oi! Croc, wake up.' I need to know what's happened at the church. Let's chuck that jug of water in his face.

'Man, what yer go and do that for?' Croc's eyes clamp open in alarm. 'Aeson?'

His face completely changes when he grins: generous and gappy as ever. By Serapis, I'm pleased to see him.

'Mate?' He blinks like he's seen a ghost and rubs the water from his face. 'Aeson, man, is that you?'

Judging by the trouble he's having pulling himself off the couch, uncoordinated as an excited pup, I'd say he's mashed on Desert Honey.

'Aeson, man!' Arms bigger and stronger than they were when we said goodbye fling round my neck. The old feeling swells inside me. Memories of nights curled up together return. This is living, not the cold accumulation of knowledge. Living is belonging.

He can't have any idea about what happened at the church.

'Croc, where's Kiya?'

'Still squatting in the old Temple of Dionysus. The religious life wasn't for me, man.'

'Croc, the temple's been looted – everyone's gone.'

'Gone?'

Confusion changes to alarm as he looks upstairs. No need to turn round: I know why.

'Long time, no see, eh, Pretty?' The sting in Turk's voice tells me he's not forgotten our old feud. He strides down the stairs like an emperor in his palace. His scar's not faded. Age has deepened the deep gorge that travels from cheek to eye.

Croc reaches for his knife. A blue tattooed hand grabs his wrist. Druid!

'That won't be necessary.' My voice reverberates in the small room – how different to the mouse of a voice I used to have.

'You've changed, Pretty. Not as soft as you used to be.'

Turk lunges at my scabbard. No you don't. My knife's out and at his throat before he reaches it. Who's fastest on the draw now?

Trained by gladiators in the university gymnasium, I've worked my body as well as my intellect these past ten years. From the look of his gut, Turk's been spooning Desert Honey for exercise.

'Slower than you used to be, Turk.' My knife hovers at his neck, his arm twisted back to his spine. A single slice of his throat and I'd never have to watch my back in Alexandria again.

He laughs, like it's just a game. 'Yer old honey-daddy wouldn't be too happy if yer slit his partner's throat, eh, Pretty?'

I lower the knife. He's got the message: Pretty's no pushover.

'Turk, it's been ten years. Why don't we call it quits? You've done well for yourself here.' Heretic books paid for that emerald fit for a Pharaoh's finger.

'I am a rich man, but that's no thanks to you, eh, Pretty?' Turk juts his chin. 'S'pose you come here looking fer your heretic friends, eh? Well, by sunset, they'll all be dead, the lot of 'em, and that dandy Greek will burn alive for being a soothsayer, performing magic rites in a temple, a whole bunch of crim-in-al offences they pinned on him.' He says it as if he's an upright citizen.

'Where are they, Turk?'

'Man, whatcha talking about? I was at the church yesterday. Went to give Kiya some Desert Honey … helps the pain in her leg. They was all fine.'

Turk's enjoying this.

'Inspectors looted the Temple of Dionysus this morning, eh. The Snake People were rounded up and thrown in the Agora prison. The Archbishop kicked off a riot when his inspectors paraded the sacred relics of Dionysus in the Agora. Prefect's sent the army in to sort it.'

Croc's eyes, glazed from the plant, fix in a wide stare on Turk. 'Even the children?'

Turk's face is serious. Even he doesn't like kids punished for nothing. 'The Archbishop's inspectors took them all. Soldiers are herding heretics all over the city. Trial's this afternoon. Public burning of the ringleaders at sunset. The rest will hand over their possessions to the powers that be – if they're lucky they'll just lose their heads.'

Think, brain, think. Under the 383 law some heresies can receive the death sentence, but Ophites don't appear in any of the Emperor's rescripts. What difference does it make? When they failed to pin heresy on a man in Athens, he was tried and executed for being a soothsayer instead.

'Who's the Magistrate?'

'It's not the Magistrate they got to worry about – he's the Archbishop's puppet.'

'Man, shit! Man! The Archbishop's an evil bastard.'

'Croc, calm down, we'll get them out.'

Turk's dark eyes meet mine. He wants me dead. Come on, Aeson, what did those years of rhetoric teach you? Turk values money more than revenge.

'Turk, I have a proposal for you.'

'What can you give me I ain't got, eh, Pretty?'

'My inheritance.'

His eyes narrow, scar creases. That hooked his interest.

'I will have papers drawn up and sign over the money I received on my twentieth birthday to you, every last solidus of it.'

Croc rolls his eyes in disbelief. 'Man, are you mad?'

Turk licks his lips and grins.

'Pretty's not mad. He needs a gang to storm the Law Court. The two of yers got no chance of getting your friends back without my help, right, Pretty?'

'How do I know you'll keep your word?'

'You don't. But you've cursed me every morning for ten years when you looked in the mirror at your shave. You'd love an excuse to default on whatever agreement you made with Rufius – or have the ammunition to bribe him for a larger cut of the profits, wouldn't you?'

Turk throws his head back and laughs. 'A honey-nose inheritance for old Turk. You got a deal, Pretty.'

It's ten years since I clasped wrists like a gladiator. Turk's emerald throws a green light on my hand and my mind flashes back to the first time Croc introduced us. History repeats itself: shaking my life away feels familiar.

Turk slaps my back, just like he did when he welcomed me to the gang. 'It'll be just like old times, Pretty.'

'My name's Aeson, until we free my people.' My people . . . yes, the Snake People are my people, my friends. My friends are my family.

'Who'd a thought you'd come running to me, eh, Pretty? I was hoping for a chase at least, or have you lost your running legs? Never mind, you've still got a face on yer. Squealing like a *cinaedus* you'll be if you screw me over.'

He eyeballs me and strokes his scar. 'Druid, bring Pretty something to eat.'

Turk and I will always be enemies, but I'm relieved to face up to him. There's a cold respect between us.

It's Patch! He's huge. The eye patch makes him look more like a pirate than an unfortunate street urchin now. 'Patch!'

'Aeson. Our little spies said you were back.' His hand is large round my wrist. My second gladiator welcome home.

'Man, Henite and Kiya can't hardly walk. We'd need a small army to take on the Archbishop's inspectors. I vote we wait 'til they're released, then we jump the soldiers and . . .' Sober now, Croc?

'No, Croc, that won't work. We need to get them out before they're tried.'

Patch butts in. 'Aeson's right.'

Turk waves his emerald-ringed hand in the air.

'Listen up lads, 'ere's the plan. Trust uncle Turk. He's a strategist now. How do you think I've been shifting tonnes of her-et-ical books for your honey-daddy right under the bishops' noses for ten years without getting caught, eh?'

Kiya

Sweet Sophia, what a way to travel! I never dreamed I'd be carried through Alexandria's streets in a litter! It's bumpier than I imagined. I wish Sophia was here. I miss her scaly skin round my neck.

The Librarian's not how I imagined either. He's funny and kind. The only time he stops cursing is when he's knocking back the wine or sucking on his silver pipe. Whiffs of Desert Honey that Croc brings me. Didn't know you could smoke it. I could do with a lug – to numb the pain in my leg.

What's the Librarian pointing at through the curtain of the litter?

'What, in the name of Bacchus, is that on the hillside?' He coughs on pipe smoke and swigs from his wine jug.

Rufius, me and the two slaves jogging along side the litter all squint at the high dunes beyond the city.

'It looks like something's moving on the surface. Unnatural. Apollinos, what is that?'

My heart twangs. I know what.

'A demon army.' My voice is level, but the mass of black bodies charging towards the city makes me gulp.

'Demons? Ha! You're not far wrong, dear. They will be Theophilus' reinforcements. Wily bastard.'

The Librarian looks angry ... or maybe it's the wine he's been knocking back since we left the house that's made the veins in his cheeks turn purple.

'Apollinos, tell them to hurry up! The Museum. We must be quick.'

We bump and jerk, curtains swing as the slaves speed up.

'I thought we were going to the Serapeum?'

'My most valuable books are hidden in the Serapeum, but *The Book of Wisdom* is in the Museum. It will be the first place that ignorant swarm loot.'

'What books?'

'Of no interest to you, dear. Joke books, cookery books, the ancient *Karma Sutra* … odd bunch, the Indians, obsessed with sex with women. Perhaps that's where Emperor Claudius got the idea …'

'Romans and their pleasures. What value are those books to mankind?'

'… and the comedies, there are hundreds of Greek plays in the copying queues. They might be the only versions left in the Empire.' He looks like a eunuch the way his kohl eyebrows rise when he shouts. 'Hurry, I said.'

Goose bumps creep up my arms. My heart bangs fast as we jerk along. That sea breeze is not a good omen. Summer storm brewing.

'Give me a drag on that pipe please, sir. The Desert Honey will help me stay open to Sophia's guidance. We might need it.'

'No need to make up excuses to indulge, dear. Here you are, don't inhale too deep.'

We're nearly there. Here's the road that runs between the high brightly painted walls of the Soma and the Museum. Museum Street crosses Soma Street at the far end and runs parallel with The Canopic Way. A dash of chariots speed straight across both streets.

'Put your head in, girl. You're not on a donkey.'

'There's something not right about those chariots.'

'What's that, dear?'

'Sweet Sophia, what's that noise?' Angry voices come from inside the walls of the Museum. A curdled shriek of human pain makes my spine stiffen. The Librarian's chins wobble.

Chariots speed past us.

'The chariots are all going one way, all heading for Sun Gate!'

He's not listening to me. There's danger up ahead. I feel it in my spine.

41

RUFIUS

'Master, run!' Antinous' small legs are pumping towards us, fast with terror as the bonfires spread, merging one into another. Red flames roar up the white marble pillars into the great golden domed roof. The Museum looks like an enormous brazier.

Sacrilege! They're burning books.

Theophilus' inspectors flee like bats, from every alcove. Scribes run from the burning building. Librarians in togas carrying armfuls of books are thrown or pushed into the pyres by the inspectors, who chant their war-cry,

'Burn the heresies – '

'Burn the heresies – '

Book after book is thrown onto pyres. Soldiers help Theophilus' bat-like army of inspectors. The fire will spread quickly now. Come on, Antinous.

What's that soldier doing? He's after my boy.

'Run, Antinous. Run, my boy.'

The soldier's sword swings and slices straight through his legs. Small knees hit the paving slab. A knife stabs his tiny chest. Still looking at me, still aiming to reach me, his gaze fades.

'No!'

Apollinos unravels my toga. 'Quickly master, step out of your toga. Master, quick. It's too late.' He drags me by the arm back towards the gates.

'We must retrieve his body.' What will I tell his brother, Cassius?

'There is no time, master. Come.'

My feet are practically carried off the ground by Apollinos' strong arms.

'Master, what are you doing?'

Pulling away, I stumble to pick up a few scrolls scattered on the grass. 'But the books! Apollinos, we must save the books.' The Museum stored the classics and the only surviving copies of books in languages of ancient cultures. Authors' names jumble in my mind … yellow rose petals falling in the Lateran Basilica … Damasus knew it would come to this.

'Quick, master.'

A cohort of soldiers charge out towards the gate as the domed roof collapses into the roaring brazier of the building. That's the most horrible noise I've ever heard: the groan of the Museum roof falling inwards smothering a building packed full of books.

'The Serapeum, master. Please hurry.'

My chest is a heaving mass of phlegm. My legs are so heavy, I can barely run. Poor little Antinous. At least it was instant when the knife entered his tiny chest.

At the far end of Soma Street, Cassius waits with Kiya. How will I tell him?

'We can't cross the Canopic Way, master. We'll take the streets parallel to the docks.'

Nearly there. Kiya's watching us from the end of Soma Street. Her lips are moving, chanting her snake prayers. Cassius' gaze searches behind us for his little brother. He's seen the tears in my eyes and hides his face in his hands. Oh, how I've failed you, my dear, dear boys.

Kiya's chant is a full-blown chorus. 'Aoi-aoi-aoi …'

'Please, stop that racket, dear.'

'These words will guide the young slave's soul to the Kingdom of God.'

'Shut up, dear.'

Cassius' muscular arms fling around my shoulders.

'Cassius, it was quick, dear. Young Antinous did not suffer.'

He looks at the ground and nods.

'Master, which way?'

'We take the back streets behind the Agora.'

Apollinos orders the four litter slaves. 'You boys run back to Biblos, alert the household to lock up and stay inside, then meet us at the Serapeum.'

Apollinos looks at me. He's right: only the slaves are safe at Biblos now. 'We will be faster on foot, master.'

As we turn left round the back of the Museum walls, the army and monks turn right towards the Canopic Way, now a seething mass of black robes and soldiers. Alexandria will be a battleground by sunset.

I cannot bear the crying. I think I might break into a million pieces if Cassius continues. He's nearly Aeson's age. It's unmanly.

'Cassius, shush, dear, your brother was a Biblus and he died a Biblus.'

Kiya chips in, 'He was a protector of books. His death was not meaningless.'

Cassius snivels, wipes his snot on the back of his wrist and nods.

That salty gust has the power of Neptune behind it. The Khamaseen's coming.

'Your scarf, Kiya, dear.' Too late. The wind takes the orange cotton. The snakes on her long earlobes are dangerous marks to show.

'Aeson gave me that.'

'I'll buy you a new one, dear.'

Make sense of this madness, Rufius. My temples thump. Surely the Emperor does not support this anarchy?

AESON

'Wind's whipping up.' Even my mouth tastes of salt, the gritty taste of home. I'd forgotten how unpleasant sand grating against my teeth is when the Khamaseen pelts the city with dust. Mouth's so dry there's hardly enough saliva to spit.

That's it: my gob hits the pavement. Croc's tatty old sandal stamps on it as he dodges a chariot. My nostrils are filled with the stench of fish; reminds me of fishing with Dad. Funny, how memory works, even in the middle of a crisis.

Ten years, but not much has changed running with the old gang. Turk's gathered a paunch. Look at the state of you, Turk, gut weighing you down, more waddle than sprint. Alexandrian pickpockets don't get paunches. A thief needs the agility of a goat in a city. It's obvious who's been doing the real work. Patch is up front, herding feral young recruits. At twelve we ran as fast as these wild winds too.

'Patch's legs are as muscle-bound as Saracen's. Remember him?' My voice jerks as my feet hit the ground. I might be fit, but my lungs aren't used to running and talking. The gymnasium track's a solitary sprint.

'The champion of Alexandria.' Croc's voice is smooth as he runs. 'Man, what a gladiator he was. Don't let Patch hear you. Head's big enough, ain't it, now he's second in command.'

We had to talk and run to avoid getting caught: *take that street, climb this roof.* Serapis knows, our lives went in different directions, but here we both are again as if time in the gang was just preparation for running through Alexandria's streets today. Hang in there, Kiya, Seth, Henite. We'll get you out.

'Croc, what's with all the rubbish?' The riot must have passed through Museum Street. Abandoned baskets of fruit and vegetables are strewn across pavements, melons crushed to pulp by chariot wheels like they've been discarded in a panic. That orange scarf's heading for the sewage duct; it twists, phantom-like in the wind before landing in the muck. Water flowing down the gutter drags it into its stream. I gave Kiya a scarf that shade once.

'Trouble ahead, man. Just how we like it!'

Croc's shaggy hair whips in his face – still avoiding the barber – as his head darts left and right. Gang life taught us to keep spirits high before a job. We've a way to go before we reach the end of Museum Street, and the east entrance to the Agora. Laughter will take our minds off the nerves, but this isn't just another job.

'Brought the weather with you, man.' That good-humoured grin; I've missed it. I've missed this: Croc bobbing along next to me like we're sprinters on the track. We fell back into the competitive spirit of our youth straight off.

'Poseidon's bin eating lentils.' Still laughing at your own jokes, Croc?

'Shit man, look at the sea!' Croc's finger points down Pharos Street as we run past. 'The Lighthouse is getting a right spanking.' Huge rollers spray as their white caps break and boom beyond the harbour. The roar blasts right through me.

'Summer storm coming.' I can still predict the weather like a city boy. Am I still the same to Croc, or have my years perfecting Latin sibilants and rounding Greek vowels changed me? 'Or Poseidon's sending another Day of Horror!'

Where's Croc's grin gone? We grew up with the stories of storms that sent houses out to sea and beached whales and ships.

'Don't take the piss, man. You know my ma was eaten by a sea monster.'

'I thought Poseidon kidnapped your mother?'

'Poseidon, sea monster. Same thing, ain't it, man?'

No answer to that.

'Race yer! Last one to the obelisk's a *cinaedus*.'

'Watch your mouth, Croc.' Racing will slice through these nerves. Our legs kick up dust. I'm glad of the wind now, cooling my skin. Those chariots are all tearing in the same direction … towards Sun Gate, out of the city … the only sensible direction.

The beat and flare of dust under foot feels good. So does winning. No need to reach for the marble of the obelisk, rising up, high above the walls of the arcades. Croc's a good few paces behind me. Alexander plonked so many of the monuments all over Alexandria the city must look like a pin pad from the sky. It was odd seeing its twin in Rome. Caligula pinched it.

'Who's the *cinaedus*, Croc? You're panting like a dog.' Serapis knows, I'm still a hybrid Alexandrian boy, even if I speak Greek like a well-bred Roman. Although … the roundness of my Greek vowels is sliding away now I'm back with Croc, my old gutter accent's trying to surface. All that contorting of my gob never felt natural.

'Have you seen him, yer old honey-nose?' Rufius was just another deep purse, a generous arsehole to Croc.

'Not for ten years. Went straight to the church when I got off the boat. Have you?'

'See his litter at the end of Venus Street now and then. His slave, the tall Greek … he delivers books to Turk sometimes. Deal's done behind closed doors.'

'Apollinos.' So, Rufius never freed him. Apollinos would never leave Rufius anyway.

Croc shrugs. 'Whatever his name is. I'm not in the inner circle.' That shrug was resignation.

Slowing down to a jog are you, Croc? 'Sure you don't need a rest, to catch your breath?'

That squint and scowl means shut it, or I'll shut it for you.

'Croc, come on, Turk's nearly at Harbour Street.'

'Aeson, man, you can still run even now you're a honey-nose.'

He'll drop the *cinaedi* jokes now I won the race. 'Get a move on Croc, we've got locks to pick.'

'Turk was right: skirting round the back of the Agora is a better route.' A gang of forty odd youths is suspicious.

'Strategic, Turk calls it.' Turk's precision in planning a job still makes Croc roll his eyes.

'Keep up, Croc! Pump those lovely legs of yours.' Running against this wind is tough. Up side is it cools the sweat.

'He's still a tosser, man.'

'And the rest.'

What's that chant? More like a battle cry. It's coming from the other side of the arcade wall. 'What … the fuck's … going on … in the Agora?' My voice jerks as I speed up.

Citizens run towards us down Museum Street. Men's togas whip up in the wind and women's long dresses twist against their bodies as they hold wailing babies against their chests.

'Man, this lot all look like Pan's been making mischief under their tunics.' I've missed that to-Hades-with-it look.

'Something's panicked them. They look petrified.' I witnessed that same expression in Athens. Urgency pumps my thighs faster.

'Watch it, old man.' Croc pulls a man fumbling with his toga out of the path of a chariot. The scrolls under his arms bounce into the muck in the road.

'Oh Apuleius, my only copy, ruined!'

'Here, sir. Just horse shit, sir, is all.' Trembling hands take the books from Croc. He'll laugh when I tell him it's a story about an ass.

'What's happening in the Agora?' My voice is gritty, throat scratchy from the dust.

What are you looking up at sky for, old man? Fury contorts his face.

'Soldiers. They've set the Museum on fire. Gods, piss on their graves.'

Olympus is closed. The gods prop up the masonry of churches now, old man.

We look down Museum Street towards the Museum. Black smoke billows upwards into grey clouds. Rufius, I hope you had the cowardly sense to stay at home today. Picturing Rufius safe at Biblos doesn't relax the tug in my gut. We have to free Kiya and Henite and Seth.

'Take my advice, take refuge in the Serapeum until sanity returns.' The Librarian hurries off towards Serapis Street clutching his soiled books, his curses swallowed by the wind. Croc and I stare after him. I never thought I'd see a librarian on the run, like a street kid with his purse-pickings.

Urgency grabs me like a great fist by the throat.

'We don't' have much time, Croc.'

'The Magistrate won't try them until late afternoon. They never do in the summer. Too hot for honey-noses.'

If it's anything like Athens, it will happen fast. The Prefect must be in cahoots with the Archbishop if the soldiers are looting. Monks are banned from the cities, but once they arrive there'll be real trouble.

Turk's words are lost on the wind as he stands at the crossroads of Museum Street and Harbour Street shouting orders at the gang.

'What's Turk saying?'

'Look's like he's telling us to back up.'

Turk's left arm rises to halt us. He peers round the corner of Harbour Street, head darts left to the harbour then right. His hand shoos us back. What's he seen?

Without a word, the gang backs up, heads and shoulders against the arcade wall, necks stretched as far right as they'll go; forty pairs of eyes strain to see the danger down the street, muscles tense and ready, hands feel for the hilts of daggers.

That chant again. Heretics what?

'HERETICS BURN, HERETICS BURN, HERETICS BURN.'

The mob, the Christian mob. They're inside the Agora.

Soldiers surge towards the Agora, swords bloodied to their hilts. They must have come from the Museum. The Archbishop of Alexandria is behind this – I've heard the dark rumours. They say he's a fanatic. And now he has the support of the army … my gut churns … I have to rescue my friends.

Turk juts his chin up: the silent order to climb the arcade wall.

Another signal, for Croc and me: *keep watch at ground level.* You would order me over to the opposite side of the street, wouldn't you Turk? Always did put me in harm's way.

Dagger out … the hilt's warm from being pressed close to my skin. Croc clocks it and grins. He recognises the knife, a gift from his stash the night he fleeced Rufius. Let them come; this corner is defended. My gut tenses; I'm ready for whatever marches round that corner.

Sandals round necks, forty youths between the ages of twelve and twenty-five pull themselves up onto the long flat roof of the arcades. Patch orders the gang with the old hand signals. Surefooted they creep, knees bent, backs low to take up their positions. This is a well-practised drill. What scraps does Turk throw you, Patch, for your loyalty?

That chinking noise … where's it coming from?

Turk's gladiator chest plate knocks against the wall as he climbs, covering pects he never had. He's dressed for the occasion!

Patch's head hangs over the roof, slicing his neck with the flat of his hand. Croc waves me over from the far side of the street.

My shrug and frown asks, *what does that signal mean?*

'Trouble.'

'Let's get up there then.'

We both run at the wall. Croc's hands and feet are less confident than mine. Still hate heights, don't you Croc?

43

RUFIUS

Kiya and I sway like we're riding bloody camels across the desert – being carried across the city on the backs of slaves is even less dignified. Apollinos' back is wet with sweat. Ha! Kiya's face couldn't get any redder; she made such a fuss about Cassius carrying her.

'Comfortable up there, dear?'

'Sweet Sophia, make the slave put me down.'

Cassius has held his breath all the way from the Museum. Kiya smells like the rubbish tips. At least it's stopped him sobbing, taken his mind off his younger brother … memory plays the scene of Antinous' legs being sliced off yet again: the boy collapsing on his kneecaps … crushed yellow rose petals falling from Damasus' fingers … block it out! I must block the memory.

What in Bacchus' name is going on in the Agora?

'Halt, everyone! Apollinos put me down.' Apollinos releases his grip on my arse and I slide off his back. I don't believe my eyes. Hundreds, no thousands of black-cloaked monks chant and pump their staffs in the Agora. 'What's that pyre for?'

'Sweet Sophia, pyres are built for one reason: funerals.'

Cassius looks up, blonde curls lash his face in the wind. 'The heavens are angry.'

Kiya nods. 'This weather is an omen.'

Rain clouds drift over the Agora and the sun casts a sickly glow through the grey.

I must have a closer look; an invisible cord of curiosity pulls me to the Agora entrance.

'Master, get on my back. We need to get to the Serapeum.'

'Get off me, Apollinos.'

The old slave's right – we should move on before the monks spot us – 'Where did they all come from?' My voice sounds confused.

Kiya leans over Cassius' shoulder to get a better view down the street. 'Sweet Sophia, the demon army has descended from the desert. The End of the World has come.'

We stare, jaws loose with amazement, through the arch at the arcade entrance. The spectacle is too fantastic. 'That can't be Phallus!'

It is Phallus! The horny old god's being paraded on the shoulders of the monks. Their wild dance, black robes swish as they hoist the god on their shoulders. By Bacchus, they're trying to bash off his knob!

We watch their sadistic ritual: they queue, to give the god's enormous cock a mighty whack with their staffs. My hand moves to my groin; I wince as Phallus' cock droops. My heart does a nosedive as if a heavy weight is dropping through me, heart to stomach. It's off …

Like a great fist has punched us in the guts, we gasp in unison as the god's huge cock is flung into the fire.

'Phallus, a eunuch!' The shock cracks in my voice.

'Sweet Sophia! Where's the army?'

'The army's in the Archbishop's purse, dear.' Disgust makes me spit out the words.

A cheer goes up; the monk that laid the final blow is raised up on shoulders and paraded around the Agora, arms punching the air in victory.

We stare dumbfounded. Even Apollinos is rooted to the spot. This cannot be happening.

44

AESON

Chins to the roof, like birds on a branch, lined up, we watch. Eyes dart along the line, alert for orders. The same question puzzles all of us: how are we going to get past that mob?

We can't reach the prison down the side of the Law Court as planned: too many soldiers. I've never seen the Agora like this: full and tense like an enormous lung holding its breath underwater. Clouds throw fast-moving shadows over the seething mass of bodies below. Monks in black brandish desert staffs – hundreds more flood the Agora as we watch. They outnumber the pagan mob gripping hammers, kitchen knives and curtain poles. They're not fighting, yet …

The pyre in front of the Magistrate's podium outside the Law Court makes my gut churn. Monks are using it as a bonfire to destroy the sacred relics of the temples. The mob jeer, but nobody wants to be the first to strike a blow.

Kiya, Seth, Henite: so close, but how to reach them? Arcade walkways flank the Agora on two sides. On the far side, the Temple of Isis' tall black granite walls; the Temple of Phallus reaches nearly as high. Between them is the Law Court. The prison is behind it.

Croc's mouth is a tight line: your thoughts are mine too, old friend.

'Croc. We'll get them out.'

'Man, these tiles are sharp.'

They're piercing the flat of my stomach too. We shift … no difference.

'Turk's gut might burst on these tiles. You seen the size of it? It's like dough, man.' Croc puffs out his cheeks.

Neither of us can force a grin.

'Shush!' An arm's length away, on my other side, Turk scans the Agora. What's he scheming? For once I'm glad to have his cunning on side.

'Better get comfortable, Croc. We're in for a long wait by the look of things.'

Even the Commander of the Army – bullish and dressed for battle – is down there on his horse by the podium as his men loot the temples. Soldiers hold back temple priests who cry like children as more book chests are emptied into the flames. The pyre licks higher as sacred books are used as kindle; fragments of burnt paper spin up into the wind.

That pyre's way too close to the Magistrate's podium.

'Man, they gonna fry the Magistrate, or what?'

This is how it always was with us. We think in unison.

'Croc, are those a pair of tits in the pyre?' Charred black tits … a headless torso … the suckling baby Horus has been prised from her breast.

'Tits … must be a goddess … no way, man … Isis' tits!' Croc's eyes stare like a corpse. Mute disbelief travels down the line of gawping faces. I felt the same astonishment when I witnessed the destruction of the temples at Athens.

Temple priests rally anyone who will listen and point to the sky; shop owners cower under the arches of the arcades. Despite the frenzy, no blood's been spilt … but it's going to kick off. Alexandrians won't stand by and watch their gods hacked to pieces on the steps of their temples.

Is that my bowels? A rumble of apprehension rolls in my gut. I need a shit. Never would have gone on a job without having a shit ten years ago.

Even Turk's amazed. 'Eh? Not Isis?'

Only one black marble statue remains in the portico of the forty-foot entrance to the Temple of Isis. Ropes hang loose around her regal neck. What's drawn the soldiers' attention?

'Shit, man, look!' Croc's nod is manic. The blue-robed priests of Isis are being marched through the crowds to the podium by the soldiers like bounty for a military triumph. If hatred were a sound, this is it: the growl of the pagan mob as their priests are shoved up the wooden steps and into a queue on the Magistrate's podium.

'Blood's gonna flow, man. Look at their faces ... the old bloke with the broom, look ... and that woman with the hammer. Man, it's gonna kick off.'

The mob waves domestic weapons at the podium, their fury focused on a tall man in the black cloak of the monks ... but he's no monk. His air of authority dwarfs the inspectors who've formed a line at the back of the podium. There's something familiar about his slender features, his heavy brow ...

'Who's that?'

Croc flicks his hair from his face as he turns towards me. 'Archbishop.'

Turk chews and spits. 'Theophilus. His scumbags bin snooping around Villa Biblos for months. Rufius laughs it off, but Theophilus, he's a hard man.'

Theophilus, Theophilus ...

Turk spits out some Desert Honey he's been sucking on. 'What's the Archbishop up to on the Magistrate's podium, eh?'

'Search me?' A gormless Croc shrug.

'I'm getting closer so I can hear better.'

We crawl along. Patch points to a few lads to follow us.

What's Turk frowning about? 'Eh, careful you two ... we need a strategy.'

'We have a deal, Turk.'

'To break into the prison – not risk our lives against an army of monks, eh?'

Serapis knows, Turk has the integrity of a woman.

'Just think of my inheritance, Turk.'

'Eh, what's happening there?' Turk's chin juts at a group of disorientated prisoners being pushed and shoved by inspectors towards the queue for the podium. His scar furrows as he squints. Eyesight failing you, Turk?

'Looks like the Archbishop intends to start the trial before the Magistrate arrives, Pretty.'

'He can't do that.' My guts! I need a shit.

'I was here this morning. Theophilus might be out of line, but he's got the army behind him and he's got it in for yer Snake Mates.'

Theophilus … I know that name, and the face … those dark eyebrows, that long nose. It's the priest from the Law Court. Rufius warned me he'd make Archbishop one day.

We strain to make out the faces in the queue of prisoners. Kiya, where are you? Where's your lurch?

'How's Kiya's leg?'

Croc's searching for her too. 'Tongue as sharp as ever, but she's more hunched than she was.'

He nudges me and nods to the back of the queue. Henite! She must have been born old. Now she's ancient. Supported by a child on each side, her long white plaits swing as she shuffles.

No! An inspector raises his whip and lashes her back.

Henite, hold your ground. If she falls, they'll drag her through the dirt.

Good, the man in front of her caught her weight before she toppled forwards. By Serapis, he's a Priest of Isis … and in front of him are the Priests of Phallus, gold phallic diadems on their heads.

That inspector's preparing to lash the whip again? 'Fucker.' A rush of anger pumps me to my feet. I'm not watching this.

'Easy, man.' Croc's hand's on my arm, pulling me down.

Theophilus steps to the front of the podium. The mob hush. I've seen bishops raise their arms like that all over the Empire.

'Hear me.' That's him: stern, hard metallic consonants ring round the Agora. Monks nearest the pyre push forwards.

'Hear me! The heretics will be tried here today in God's eyes.' Since when did the Archbishop run legal proceedings?

'Where's the Magistrate?' The mob won't stand for this. Pagans won't watch their priests tried by a Christian.

'A-Archbishop! Archbishop. L-let me th-through.' That can't be Fatty's stutter?

'FATTY!' What a surprise. Fatty's nearly as tall as Theophilus but twice as wide. His toga has the imposing thick purple stripe of a patrician. Shame he still has the stutter.

'Croc, why didn't you tell me Fatty's the Magistrate?'

'Don't make no difference. He's shit scared of the Archbishop.'

Turk juts his chin towards Fatty. 'That's what an inheritance buys you, eh? Where's your purple stripes then, Pretty?'

Fatty and Theophilus look like they're arguing at the back of the podium. Theophilus shakes several documents at the Magistrate. Fatty looks angry. He won't want to try the Priests of Isis. Theophilus forces the parchment into Fatty's hands. If that's an Imperial rescript, Fatty has no choice. He has to read it.

'The h-heretics, namely the M-manicheans, the Apollinarians, the Encratites, the Apotactites, the H-hydroparastatae, the S-saccophori ...'

Theophilus steps forward, black cloak raised like bat wings as he lifts his arms, '... AND THE MONSTROUS FOLLOWERS OF THE SERPENT: THE ODIOUS OPHITES.' He bellows it.

'What bullshit! Theophilus added that on his own authority. As far as the Emperor is concerned, Ophites were flushed out over a century ago.'

Not a single heckle. The pagan mob couldn't care less about a heretic Christian.

Fatty steps forward, his round body wrapped in the folds of his toga eclipses Theophilus.

'B-bring out the heretic ringleader. The Ophite will be tried first, then the P-priests of I-Isis will be tried for the crime of sacrifice.'

The mob roar like a stadium audience hungry for a fight. Jeers, hoots, hisses from the pagan mob. My ears thump with their hate. They will riot if their priests are sentenced. Fatty looks worried; he knows it too.

Seth! What have they done to you? Shackled like a slave, long hair lank over his face. An inspector jabs Seth's back up the wooden steps and on to the platform. We may not share a god, but friendship binds us. For an orphan friendship's as strong as blood.

'This man.' Theophilus clutches Seth's face in his fingers, forcing Seth to look at him. 'This odious Ophite is not only a heretic of the most monstrous order, but a soothsayer. He was caught charming snakes from baskets and divining the future.'

Theophilus surveys the crowd as if he owns them. That pause is well practised. Citizens look startled, the monks disgusted. Nobody moves. It's as if their position were fixed, from the moment he first spoke.

'This monstrous worshipper of the serpent will be tried before God. If found guilty, in the eyes of the one and only Sublime God, he will meet his death in avenging flames, burned alive for heresy and magic.'

'What the fuck, Aeson. Sit your arse back down.' Croc's at my ankles, yanking me down by my tunic.

'But the death penalty only applies to the Encratites, Saccophori, and the Hydroparastatae.'

'Don't be a fucking martyr, Pretty.'

'Shut it, Turk.'

'That's it, man.'

Stomach flat to the tiles again, my gut tenses for a fight.

'Croc, is that old rope still there?'

Don't give me that look like I'm a mad fucker, Croc. You never managed the jump – the drop made you lose your bottle.

'What, the one we hooked on the Temple of Isis? Don't get any stupid ideas, man. Say you make the jump without breaking your bloody neck? Then what? They'll tear you to pieces before you get up onto the platform. But let's say you made it, what's your plan? Kill the Archbishop, carry Henite to safety? You and me, we're street kids, not heroes.'

Fatty raises both arms for silence. The obedient hush from the monks is punctured by pagan catcalls.

'Th-this man is accused of being a magician and a p-procurator for the rites of heresy in the Roman Province of Egypt in the city of Alexandria.'

The monks' jeers drown Fatty's voice.

'S-SILENCE. The law s-states, as promulgated by the Emperor Th-theodosius …' – so, it's Imperial parchment – 'All p-persons who resort to their own h-heretical rites, who assemble in public to present the false appearance of m-mysteries, to the outrage of the t-true religion, We order to be afflicted with the supreme p-penalty.'

Poor Fatty looks like he's surrounded by a bunch of school bullies up on that podium, with the lines of dark-cloaked inspectors and soldiers and Theophilus towering above him.

'W-who will defend this m-man?'

Lawyers mutter from the safety of the arcades and rearrange the white folds of their togas. No one will defend him today.

'I will …' Seth's voice is thin from lack of water.

Theophilus swishes his cloak in front of Fatty's white toga. Did the arsehole smile at Seth?

'Present the Magistrate with the evidence, inspectors.'

Four inspectors climb the podium with bundles of scrolls and baskets of snakes. A toothy one with a skeleton grin steps forward. 'This scroll contains evil spells used by the Ophites, those despicable heretics who worship the snake, for all manner of heretic rites. And in those baskets are the snakes several of my men witnessed being charmed and kissed by this man during his magical rites.'

'Aeson, sit down.'

'No Croc.' You're right to be afraid, old friend. So am I. 'I'm not going to lie here and watch my friends prosecuted without Justice having a hand in it.' The streets gave me my wits, but I'm now part of another world and I know the law.

Patch grabs my ankle, Croc my tunic.

'Lads, please.'

They release me. The leather tie holding the eye patch has engraved his skin between eye and ear, like a wedding ring grown tight on a fat finger.

'We've got your back, Aeson.' Patch's grip is strong on my shoulder.

Turk spits. 'We don't have his fucking back.' By the look of Patch's glare, there's no love lost between those two over the years. 'If you want to risk your life for that bunch of fanatics, you're on your own, Pretty. The deal's off.'

'Is your word nothing, Turk?'

'You know the rule of the streets: save your own arse.'

'He's right, man. If you go down there you're dead.' Croc, your voice is so gentle. How many nights did I fall asleep with your breath in my ear?

'Will no one defend this man?' Theophilus' voice is slow. Every word is accentuated, provoking, threatening.

'Go, before I sit on you, man.'

First, feel how I love you, my old friend … you always kept your eyes open when we kissed. Your long hair's as greasy as ever. Lips dry from the wind, but generous as I remember them. It feels like kissing a brother now.

'How sweet, a parting kiss.' We ignore Turk's sarcasm.

'If I'm going to watch you die, I expect a good show.' Patch's comment is for Turk's sake.

'Patch.' I nod him a salute.

Must keep my legs bent so no one in the Agora notices me. Crouching low as I run back along the arcade roof, several heads nod. The eyes of the young ones follow me. What stories have Patch and Croc filled their heads with? *He could jump through the skies. He took on the leader. He's the reason for Turk's scar?* Or am I just *Pretty, the cinaedus' boy?* Whatever, I don't expect them to risk their lives. This is not their battle.

Here's where we climbed up, good a place as any to slip back down.

45

RUFIUS

What's Theophilus doing on the Magistrate's podium again? Fatty looks lost.

'Does that bishop think he's the bloody city Magistrate, Apollinos?'

Kiya is in a panic. 'Sweet Sophia! They have Seth! And there's Henite too … oh, no, and the children. They're going to burn him alive.'

She must know the Ophite they arrested this morning. In front of the line of soldiers and inspectors, the heretics are shoved up onto the platform with the Priests of Isis and Phallus, their robes blown about in the wind.

'W-will someone d-defend this man?' Fatty's not as eloquent as his father was.

'*I* will defend him.'

That voice. It is like milk and honey over broken skin. It cannot be …

'My boy?'

'Aeson! I see him.' Kiya's finger stretches towards the opposite end of the Agora over Cassius' head. Cassius cranes to see too.

'Apollinos, hoist me up onto your back so I can see him. That's it, dear: over you bend, quickly.'

Where is he?

'*I* will defend him.' Even from this corner of the arcade, Aeson's voice projects with clarity.

I let out a groan: my money paid for that university accent. Where is he? I can hear him but I can't see him.

Apollinos cranes his sweaty neck too. 'There, master, heading for the podium.'

The crowd part, as if Aeson's voice has sliced a pathway through the mob. Their gaze follows him. That is how it always was: mesmerised eyes stalked him. Boy no longer, a confident, muscular stride. Fashionable tunic, short Roman haircut, a glint of the gold necklace I gave him for his *toga virilis* around a neck strengthened in the gymnasium. My money drips off him. They will listen to that voice. That's one thing a *cinaedus* knows: the people love a drama. This mob will demand his defence is heard. What say you to that, Theophilus?

'Sweet Sophia, Aeson's walking into the demon's lair.' The priestess' head dips into the nook of Cassius' neck, tense with anticipation.

'My fearless boy, have you lost your senses? Leave the heretic to his fate.' My fatherly pride is deflated by fear for my son.

'He's doing the goddess' bidding. Seth is an Aberamentho!' Kiya's head swivels like a meerkat from Aeson to the heretic waiting to be tried. Why does my boy love these foolish Snake People?

'Yes, dear.' I pat her coarse mop of hair, but my eyes do not leave Aeson: a real man … but then he always was the manly one of the two of us.

'Will they kill Seth?' The priestess' voice rasps with fear.

'Theophilus is acting beyond the Emperor's rescript. There is no telling what he will do, dear.' There's no point lying to her; the answer will unravel before our eyes. Swallowing is becoming difficult: calm yourself, Rufius.

Aeson coughs as he climbs the podium steps. A seagull circles, then swoops away from the black smoke billowing off the pyre.

'I, Aeson Biblus Catamitus, will defend this man and represent all the accused.' He faces the crowd and waves his arm to indicate the line of prisoners on the podium, poor Christian heretics shoulder to shoulder with Priests of the temples adorned in gold diadems.

A cheer goes up from the mob, hammers and brooms punch the air. Clever boy, he has the pagan mob on side.

'Look at Seth: the joy of seeing Aeson has brought the power of the serpent into his spine!'

What nonsense is she blathering about now? 'Save your tears, dear. Win or lose, Aeson's made himself a target.'

'He's brave like you – like when you took on the Archbishop this morning.'

'I was just entertaining myself, dear. Aeson's nothing like me.'

Aeson's a head shorter than the Theophilus, but beauty swats all other qualities like flies. We hold our breath: us, the mob, the soldiers: who will speak first – archbishop or lawyer? The two men face each other. Silently, I sense their minds circle each other.

'On what authority do you defend this man?' Theophilus hides his surprise. He did not expect a defence, and less from a Biblus Catamitus; he'll be seething. A swell of pride stings my eyes. Don't get sentimental, Rufius.

'I have trained and practised in the Law Courts of the Empire: Constantinople, Athens, Carthage, Antioch. I am familiar with the Emperor's rescript … and the Ophites are not mentioned. The Magistrate will verify this.'

'Th-that is correct.' Fatty looks so confused his fat face wobbles.

'Furthermore, charming snakes from baskets can be seen everyday in the Emporium, and there are no laws sentencing snake charmers to death.'

The pagan mob laugh; some hoot. My boy's on a roll.

'I put it to you, Archbishop: on whose authority do you speak? For it is not the Emperor's.'

Direct as ever. The Archbishop stiffens. The noise from the crowd is deafening. They couldn't care less about the Ophites. Most are too young to have heard of the sect. They holler for Priests of Isis, for their gods burning on the pyre.

Fatty raises his arms to hush the mob. Everyone in the Agora waits for Theophilus' reply. Aeson looks out across the crowded Agora. You have the stage, my boy: what will you do with it?

'Sweet Sophia, there's the inspector from this morning. What evil is he whispering into the Archbishop's ear?'

'What is that book Toothy has in his hand?'

'I have a bad feeling about that book, master.'

Theophilus takes the leather-bound codex from the inspector and opens it. His smile makes me gulp. He passes it to Fatty and turns to the mob.

'Aeson Biblus Catamitus, you are unable to defend the aforesaid persons due to being found in possession of heretical books. This morning you deposited this book full of magic and evil spells with Library Customs. Inspector, arrest this man. He is suspected of being part of an Empire-wide heretical smuggling ring.'

A gasp from the mob.

'What in the name of Bacchus possessed Aeson to register a heretical book?'

What's Kiya so excited about jigging up and down on Cassius' back? 'I knew he'd keep his promise. It's *The Book of Wisdom,* I know it.'

'What evidence do you have?' The sturdiness of Aeson's voice doesn't give away the twitch I sense in him, slight bend of the knee, clench of his calf. He's contemplating his next move.

'Here is the ticket.' The inspector waves a strip of parchment in the air. 'It reads: Aeson Biblus Catamitus.'

Oh, the fool! Why did he register it? Theophilus' spies are everywhere.

'Until you charge me, I can put forward a defence.'

That's it, my boy. Who'd have thought you would grow up to take on the Archbishop of Alexandria.

'Then we will try your case first.'

Fatty looks like he has something to say about that. 'I d-decide the order of the cases.'

Good old Fatty! What's my boy doing, itching his ear like that? Now the other ear: what's he up to?

'Cassius, what's excited you, dear?'

'Look, master, look.' We follow the direction Cassius' finger is pointing – behind the podium to the Temple of Isis. Men and boys swing, one after the other, from the temple roof to the Law Court to the ground and scatter into the crowd. So that's what the ear thing was: a signal.

There's the blue Briton … and there's Aeson's friend with the flaky skin. Crocodile. Well I never!

'Croc! He hates heights. Sweet Sophia, cushion his fall.' Her eyes are scrunched up, not daring to watch Crocodile make his jump.

'Calm down, Kiya. They're like monkeys, those street boys.'

'You can open your eyes now,' Cassius murmurs to her.

'He did it, he did it.' She's like a child, poise gone.

Now what's he doing? Aeson points into the crowd, then back to the podium; then to another head whose face is hidden from us. He's giving orders.

Toothy makes a dive for Aeson.

'Move Aeson. That's it my boy! Ha, they'll need to be faster than that if they want to catch him.' He's not lost his speed. Apollinos could never catch him. 'Now get off that podium, Aeson.'

Street kids stream on to the podium. Ten, twenty, more … inspectors lunge at them. The mob won't watch for long … there's no spectators at an orgy … here they go!

The crowd surges forward in a thrash of metal. Hammers and kitchen utensils hack desert staffs. The Commander of the Army shouts from his horse to soldiers. Swords are drawn. There's no space for battle formation – the Agora's too frenzied for military order. Soldiers and monks crowd onto the podium to protect the Archbishop. What does the Priest of Isis think he's doing barging up the stairs? He should be running away … he's going for the Archbishop. He won't get very far. Monks jump him like a pack of wolves. His white robe flutters in the wind as a tall, hooded monk hoists him onto his shoulders. Another monk throws his diadem into the pyre.

'HERETIC BURN, HERETIC BURN.' The mob demands his blood.

Our mouths slack, necks strain forward, eyes wide in disbelief.

'By Bacchus, they're not going to throw a Priest of Isis onto the pyre? Surely not!' He's not been tried …

Fatty flaps an arm and tries to stop them. His mouth opens and closes but we can't hear him. The hooded monk slings the priest like a sack of rubbish into the pyre. The blue robe of Isis flutters … flames swallow him.

A roar reverberates around the Agora: a battle cry, visceral and furious. Theophilus surveys the mob with a look of smug satisfaction. How many supporters did you plant in the Agora today, Theophilus?

Fatty gives up trying to call order, hugs *The Book of Wisdom* to his chest like a baby and runs off the podium.

'Master, we must get to the Serapeum.' Apollinos starts to turn.

'Sweat Sophia! Noooooo!' What's Kiya doing?

'Don't kick poor Cassius. He's not a horse, dear.'

Cassius' face disappears behind her wild hair; the two of them resemble a strange creature: a hermaphrodite centaur or some Egyptian god as she writhes about trying to get him to enter the Agora. 'Relax, please lady.'

'Save Seth and Henite! Please.'

The tall hooded monk who helped throw the priest is heading towards Seth.

Aeson's seen him. He swoops towards the monk. Who does he think he is, Aeneas?

The monk pushes his way across the podium. That's a knife, not a staff in his hand.

We bellow, 'Aeson, look out! Behind you,'

He can't hear us. Leave the heretic. He's been tortured half to death anyway, dear.

The wind catches the monk's hood and throws it back. He's lost an eye. The cloaked Cyclops and Aeson run at each other like gladiators in the arena.

'Sweet Sophia, it's Lanky!'

46

AESON

'Lanky, it's you and me, Lanky.'

What's he doing? Why's he stopped? He grins and turns towards Seth and Henite lined up with the rest of the prisoners, at the edge of the podium, ankles chained, and dangerously close to the pyre.

Serapis, no! Lanky means to throw them into the pyre like the Priest of Isis. I've got to get to Seth and Henite before he does. Gut and heart pound as one. Out of my way. An inspector tries to block me. Take that, you mongrel. He slides forward into my knife, close as a lover he grabs my neck as if to kiss me. 'Serapis, forgive me.' My knife whines as I pull it free and he rolls towards the pyre.

'Lad, get down, Aeson.' That's Dera's voice. Where is he?

So much blood, so many tortured cries. It's impossible to pinpoint anyone over the mass of seething, fighting bodies: the Agora's a battlefield. And the stench … burning flesh, it's making me dizzy. Hold on, Henite. I'm coming.

A soldier. He's slashing his sword at me; his stomach's open to my attack: metal slips too easily through human flesh. In sinks my knife.

I've got to get to Henite before Lanky does. She's hunched over, muttering, praying. Lanky's going to push that young priest off the podium. Desperate, he flings himself into the pyre rather than be pushed by Lanky. An acrid stench of burning flesh makes me swallow. Henite, I'm coming.

'Aeson, I'll get Henite.' Dera's voice. It's calm, even when he shouts … but where is he? He must be close.

Another sword swipes past my arm. It belongs to a soldier. A knife spikes the soldier's neck like a piece of chicken; blood squirts in my face and he crumples at my feet. Croc pulls the knife out and grins. 'Twenty.' That was close.

'Aeson, down here!' Follow Dera's voice … there he is, pushing his way up the stairs towards Henite. As tall and strong as I remember him, skin an onyx gleam. Lanky's spotted him.

Another inspector, the kill in his eyes, sword coming at me. Shit, he's bashed my knife from my hand, the bastard! Where did it land? His sword's at my neck; can't move. He's got me in an arm lock. The inspector spins me round so I face the Archbishop. Theophilus, surrounded by bodyguards, sits safe on horseback. He nods.

'Goodbye, Aeson Biblus Catamitus,' growls the inspector in my ear … 'Arhhh!' A yelp of pain and his arm goes limp. Croc got him. Thank Serapis!

'Man, you're out of practice.'

'Thanks, Croc. Serapis, No!'

Dera's nearly up the stairs. Hurry up! Lanky's too close to Seth. I can't get past this mass of bodies.

'Aeson, duck.' That's Patch's voice.

I'm ducking, I'm ducking. And again: that soldier's going to lob my head off if I don't find a weapon. Feet shuffle around bodies, dead or dying, but no sword.

'Pretty, catch!' There's Patch. Thank Serapis! The metal blade glints as it spins through the air: got it … and got you. The soldier's face freezes in shock as he slips to the ground, eyes wide with surprise.

More soldiers force their way up the crowded steps. We're outnumbered.

'Patch, help Dera.' I point towards the stairs. He's nearly at the top.

Patch lunges his knife into the chest of another monk, hilt to heart.

What's that? An earthquake? Wood creaks, the podium groans: it was not built to hold so many.

'What?' Patch shouts above the roar, arms outstretched to balance himself as the podium moves, tilts downwards. Henite sways.

Oh no! The stairs have collapsed. Dera's gone! Monks, soldiers and prisoners look down at their feet in confusion. The podium sways under the excess weight.

'Lads, JUMP.' Patch herds the boys. They stab at monks and soldiers in their rush to jump off the collapsing platform.

'Aeson, JUMP: it's gonna collapse.' Patch's urgency is drowned out by the groan of wood. The podium legs splinter and crack … one's leg gone. A thick shard of wood breaks away at an angle. The podium wobbles, the side nearest the pyre slopes downwards. Need to widen my stance to keep my balance, lean forward into the tilt of the platform: that's it.

Henite, I've got to get to Henite. I'm too close to the pyre. It's hot on my legs. 'Henite!'

She turns, she knows my voice. Her ancient eyes meet mine.

Lanky's seen me coming; he knows my mind. He lunges at Henite and shoves her thin body into the pyre.

'Die, heretic.'

'HENITE!'

She smiles as she falls into the flames. Her plaits whip up, spark and disappear. I look away, cheeks hot as the red glowing cinders that spin up from the flames. The hiss of spitting flesh makes me wrench.

Got to hold it together. Seth needs me. Where's Seth? Serapis, No! Monks follow Lanky's lead – the black-cloaked swine push the shackled prisoners into the pyre.

'NOOOO!'

Seth's head jerks back as he's shoved into the flames. He heard me. Too late.

'Aeson, get yer arse off there!' Patch's voice cracks with panic.

'Behind yer, mate.' Patch's knife whizzes past me, into the shoulder of another inspector. They're still coming at me.

Wood splits … another groan, a steep tilt. The other podium leg's given way.

Where's Lanky? I'll kill him.

His one eye looks my way and he jumps off the podium.

I'll slide into the pyre if I'm not quick. That back will do. Calf muscles tense, left foot on that dead man's rump and I'm off.

Serapis, keep that spot clear.

Feet thud the ground. Failure is heavy in my chest as I land.

Henite's dead.

Seth's dead.

'Aeson, get away from the fire.' Sparks spit and sting my skin. That was Dera's smooth voice. Where is he?

There, fighting his way towards me, both eyes swollen like he's been kicked in the face.

'Dera …' my voice cracks.

'She's with her god, lad.' His hand's on my shoulder, but I can't feel it. I'm numb.

'Where's Kiya?'

'She's with your father.'

'My father?' Does he mean she's dead too? I stare at the hissing pyre in disbelief.

'With Rufius.' Dera yanks a sword from a dead man's chest and passes it to me. 'We need to get out of here, lad.'

What's Kiya doing with Rufius? No time for questions – that monk's aiming straight for us. Out of the way, Dera … in goes the blade … the monk slips off my sword, agony in his young face. That thrust, into the black cloak of the boy, went through his middle like skewering a piece of chicken. So skinny, these desert monks, and so young. Where's Lanky?

'Man, come on, let's get the fuck out of here.' Croc darts past, slaps my back. Patch is behind him. Dera and I forge forward into the knot of bodies. Croc swipes at a monk. Instant death. 'Twenty-three down.' Croc can even grin in the middle of a kill. That's my Croc.

'Where's the others?' Croc spins his head, hair whipping around.

'I see them, behind us.' Patch and the boys dodge their way towards the exit nearest to Serapis Street.

'Did you see where Lanky went?'

'Lanky's a deadman if I see him again.' Croc loved the Snake People too.

'Now what?'

'The Serapeum.'

Dera's strong face shines like polished jet; as a child I imagined he was made of a precious stone, not flesh. His gaze locks into me. 'No, Aeson, lad. You must not go to the Serapeum. Please lad, come with me.'

'Dera, we have to get the children to safety.'

'The Serapeum is not safe.'

'Dera, I know the prophecy, and I'm living it. If this is my destiny, I'm not hiding from it.'

Where's Fatty? He has *The Book of Wisdom.* At least I can get that to Kiya like I promised. There he is, hugging the book to his chest on the Law Court steps.

'Croc, get the children. Head for the Serapeum. I'm going to get Fatty.' My throat's sore from shouting above the blare of battle.

Where did Turk go?

'Watch out! The Archbishop's inspectors have spotted us.' Croc points to the Temple of Phallus. An inspector points back at us, calls to some soldiers nearby and sends them towards us.

'Shit, man. The legions are after us now.' Croc, wide-eyed, darts me a look: *time to run, man.*

I take a last look at the pyre. Faceless, black-charred corpses flop on top of the statues of Isis and Phallus.

'This is not the time to grieve.' Dera slaps my back, grabs a child in each arm and runs.

'Run.' Patch and about ten lads sprint past.

'Faster.' They're gaining on us.

'When we're clear of the Agora, take the alley by Venus Street ... we'll loose them, man?' Croc's hair flaps round his face as he runs.

My gut feels like it's on fire. My legs don't need cajoling; running will keep back the tears.

Are we all here? Patch and the gang check out the corner that leads to Serapis Street up front. Dera's coming up my rear with the children.

'Run, boys.' Croc herds the kids, their nimble limbs giving it all they've got. The fear and grief on their dirty faces; they know this isn't a game. They've just watched the woman they called mother murdered.

'Aeson, lad. Head for the Necropolis. It's safer.'

'I'm going back for Fatty. You run on ahead with Croc.' The Archbishop won't dare attack the Serapeum.

47

KIYA

This must be the prophesied Apocalypse! The Khamaseen screeches through the arcades. That sky is a sign: red-scarred horizon bleeds through dark clouds. Lanky, I should have plucked out both your eyes. Pain and hate make it hard to breathe.

Cassius sways beneath me, then regains his footing. We're helpless as children on the backs of these slaves: a cripple and an old man. All we can do is watch. The scene is slow, like in a dream. Henite and Seth martyred. My fate is to witness.

The Librarian throws his arms over Apollinos' head.

'Apollinos, Cassius, where's Aeson gone?'

'Master, we must go. Once the monks have had their fill here, they'll hit the streets again.'

Rufius is in a panic. 'We cannot desert Aeson.'

I can't see him either. He jumped off the podium before it collapsed into the pyre, but it's impossible to see anything beyond the carnage: soldiers, monks, the pagan mob, the priests of the temples all stabbing and bashing and killing each other. Another desperate yelp of pain. The sound of men and women dying vibrates in my ears; my whole body is shaking.

'BURN, BURN, BURN.' Monks chant with lust.

If only I could salvage their bodies from the pyre. Sweet Sophia how it rages now, full of bodies, flames feed on the flesh of martyrs, the black smoke thick with the smell of cooking meat. I must retrieve their bones. I must have something of them: Seth and Henite were father and mother to me. I know what they would say: the body is only a temporary home for the soul … but I want something solid to hold, something …

'Sweet Sophia! There's Aeson on the steps of the Law Court with Fatty … and there's Lanky … our side of the podium, but the demon's seen him … I must save Aeson … Cassius, take me in there.'

'Cassius, hold your ground,' Apollinos orders.

'Aeson! The demon will kill him. Please, we must do something.'

Lanky hates me more than he hates Aeson: I took his eye. I have an idea.

'Over here. Lanky! You demon! LANNNKKKKYYYY!'

'What, in the name of Bacchus, are you doing, girl?'

'Aeson's doomed. The prophecy said he will perish in flames. Aeson's doomed. We must divert the demon's attention.'

Lanky grins as he charges towards Aeson. That puckered face sends a hot stabbing sensation through my chest as if the Demiurge himself is prodding me with his trident. How I've tried to forget that face. It's haunted my dreams for ten years. How I wish I'd gorged out both his evil eyes. That night, the push of thumbs into liquid flesh like thrusting into a scallop, the shriek of pain before Lanky dropped me. Pyre-hot, my cheeks flush at the memory. The nights I would wake, my thumbs in his eye socket, his curses whipping around my ears.

I knew we would meet again, knew you would seek out your revenge. I've felt your hate across the years, growing, hunting me. 'Aoi, aoi, aoi.'

'Aeson, my boy! Careful! That one-eyed Cyclops is after him.'

Aeson can't hear us from over there, but Lanky can.

'LANKYYYY!'

Red robes and white tunics block our view. Temple priests and slaves, they're making a run at the monks. A mad surge of monks like a black wave pushes them back towards to the pyre.

'HERETICS BURN, HERETICS BURN.'

Lanky's long scrawny face contorts, socket puckered where he's missing an eye. He can't get past the monks. He licks his lips; he's enjoying this, a monster thirsty for blood. He laughs as another priest joins the flames. I must catch his attention before he's out of earshot.

'LAAANNNKKKYYY. Over here.'

'Shout, dears.'

'LANNNNKKKKYYY.' We scream ourselves hoarse.

'I will kill you, Lanky.' My throat is a swollen knot. I will meet my mortal enemy. 'Cassius, take me to that demon.' I point my crutch at Lanky.

As if he felt the evil eye on his back, he turns.

'Sweet Sophia, Lanky's seen me.'

He raises his knife, points the tip towards our corner of the arcades, aiming right at me. The gaze of the demon is on me now.

Whatever he's shouting at me is drowned out by the monks' chant. 'HERETICS. HERETICS. HERETICS.'

Terrified citizens flee the madness. Monks swarm past in pursuit – out of the alleys leading from the Agora as if the demons are running out of Hades.

'He's seen us! Lanky's seen us!'

'By Bacchus, that Cyclops is coming after us!'

'We must stand and fight. Sweet Sophia, give me another chance. I will not fail you this time. I too am a warrior of Christ. This time I will kill him.' Hate has made me strong. 'Aoi-aoi-aoi.'

Apollinos turns. 'That's it, master. We're leaving.'

The Librarian's neck twists to keep Aeson in sight. His old eyes squint. So do mine. What's wrong with Fatty?

'Take me back, Apollinos. I will not leave Aeson. I am the master.'

'Sorry, master. You'll have to whip me later. Cassius, follow me. We can't help Aeson now.'

Monks run towards us, Lanky with them, mouth wide open in a raging battle cry. Cassius turns away from the Agora towards Serapis Street.

The Librarian bellows out abuse and curses at the monks surging down the street. 'Bastard butt-fuckers, bishop-whores.'

'Cassius, put me down.' I screech it, but his legs pump faster after his master. The Librarian's still cursing at monks from Apollinos' back.

RUFIUS

This cursed sea wind's whipped my hair into a frenzy of knots. For the first time in my life, I couldn't care less. From up here the mob looks like a swarm of insects. Monks flit like flies in the Agora in their black cloaks where the battle continues; others chase pagans down Serapis Street towards the gates of the Serapeum. On its manmade mount, two hundred steps from ground level, the battlements are lined with anxious faces, all smarting with the hot lust of hate, knuckles clenched to the bone. The frowns of important men: librarians in togas, Priests of Serapis, seven-starred gold diadems on their heads. Revenge rages in all of us.

We squint down the length of Serapis Street. Sphinxes line the road all the way to the harbour, trunks of palm trees bend in the Khamaseen.

'Cassius, Apollinos – any sign of Aeson?'

'I'm looking, master.'

'Dear Bacchus, this riot's out of control.'

What a sight! Pyres send black smoke up into the storm clouds above the marble city. The mob's set the roof of the Temple of Isis on fire; the Museum, and hundreds of other temples, smoulder in the distance. Has the world gone mad?

'Sweet Sophia! They died in a swarm of sinners!' Kiya stares like a woman possessed. She's not taken her eyes off the black column of smoke coming off the Agora pyre.

Cassius, the poor dear boy's clutching his spear like he's got a hard-on. 'Cassius, use your bloody eyes. Is Aeson on Serapis Street?' Surely he would have the sense to seek refuge here.

'I can't tell, master.'

Curse these old eyes; I can't make out a single face in the blur of people on Serapis Street.

'It's Dera! Look, he's reached the steps.' There's hope in Kiya's voice.

'It's the giant!' Cassius looks petrified.

'It's Dera!' She points her crutch at the colossal hulk of a man. I know that African. It's the hermit. My promise slides into my mind, *If Aeson tries to return, I will stop him.* Gods, keep my boy safe.

'Who's that on his back?'

'It's the Magistrate, master. The giant's carrying the Magistrate on his back.'

'He must have the strength of bloody Hercules to lift Fatty!'

What's wrong with Kiya? 'Calm down, dear!' She looks murderous.

'Come, my mortal enemy, I will have your life this time.'

'Apollinos, what's she ranting about now?'

'It's that tall, skinny monk who martyred her people, master. He's climbed that sphinx half-way up the Serapeum steps.'

'Lanky didn't catch me so he's looking for Aeson.'

A blur of black and steel-grey armour, a surge of horses and men enter Serapis Street from the Canopic Way, the harbour end. Bacchus, where's my boy? 'Cassius, fetch a jug of wine, dear.' My nerves are stretched tight as a lyre.

'No, Cassius, go down there and kill the demon.'

How dare she order my slave about? Poor Cassius lost his little brother today. Grief's selfish.

'Cassius, wine, dear.'

Her rage smoulders to frustration. She wants to run down there and take her revenge. Being a cripple must be like being old. We're able-bodied for a sliver of time.

'Off, off! Stop tugging on my tunic, girl.'

'Librarian, is the gate open?'

'Yes, yes, the gate's still open.' But Aeson had better hurry up; it won't be for long.

Apollinos frowns. 'They'll close the gates before the army get here. He doesn't have long.'

The army charge down Serapis Street: half-way here. Horses' hooves pound louder as they close in.

'Shut up, Apollinos!' Bloody idiot slave, stating the obvious!

Ah, here comes Theon. Kiya's tugging on my tunic again. Don't turn on the waterworks, dear.

'Kiya, be quiet, or I'll have Apollinos here take you inside, is that clear?'

'Rufius, here you are. Thank Serapis you're safe.' His voice booms with bravado.

'Theon, my dear, thank the gods. And Hypatia?'

Theon places a hand on each of my shoulders. I'd forgotten this sense of comradeship, hazy memories of my military service. Don't get sentimental, Rufius – remember what they called you in the army? *Rufius the Cinaedus.* Theon's bravado is dread disguised as team spirit.

'My daughter's tending the wounded. What a political cock up this is.'

'More like political manoeuvre. The Archbishop, the Commander and the Prefect: a suspicious triumvirate. Theophilus must have called in the monks to do their dirty work.'

'What makes you think the monks were summoned, Rufius?'

'Theon, dear man. Have you had your nose so tightly tucked in your books that you've missed the wave of destruction blowing across the Empire? Alexandria may feel like an island …'

'Rufius is right, Theon.'

We hadn't noticed Olympus approach. Even at his age Olympus' arms are hard. What's he wearing a breastplate for?

Theon turns to Olympus. 'So you have been voted in as our Commander Olympus. Congratulations! I would have supported that action of course if I had been here.'

'I'm surprised the Priests of Serapis gave you dominion over their sacred precinct, dear.'

'It's only until this blows over. My military background put me in the best position. Not that there will be any action – it's impossible to scale these walls, but we're ready for them if they try.'

'Bah, you've got as much military experience as I have, Olympus.' That wiped the smile off his smarmy face.

'At least he's not soft as a mollusc.' Whose cheeky young voice was that?

'Which one of you little runts said that?' The insolent faces of young students smirk behind Olympus.

'Rufius, my dear friend, since when haven't you taken that age-old jibe on the chin? Ignore them. Their spirits are ready for battle; their manners can be forgiven after what we've witnessed today.'

Here comes Cassius with the wine jug. 'Give me that here, dear.'

Ah! That's better. Humour regained, thanks to Bacchus … Theon's right. My sense of humour failure started this morning when I saw the graffiti on my wall.

'Forever the peacekeeper, Theon. Thank the gods they didn't vote you in as commander of this pathetic army of priests and librarians.'

'Yes, Olympus is the right man for this job.'

Olympus clears his throat at Theon's sarcastic compliment.

'Rufius, I heard your boy Aeson in the Agora. You must be proud of him. It's a wonder he turned out such a fine figure of a man.'

Ah, yes, Olympus taught him his *Grammatica.*

'Well, men,' Olympus thumps us both on the shoulder: ridiculous gesture from a librarian, even with those aging muscles! 'Looks like those stragglers are the last of the citizens. We'll need to get the gates closed after we get this lot inside.'

'But, Aeson. He's still out there.'

'What do you expect me to do, Rufius? Let the army in?' Olympus strides away, shouting orders to the Serapeum guards stationed along the fortress wall.

'Who in bloody Hades does he think he is? Give a man a title ...'

Theon looks tired; his age has caught up with him. 'Rufius, you shouldn't taunt Olympus.'

Cassius' spear knocks wildly on the wall. 'Master, master, it's Aeson!'

'Where Cassius?'

'Just shot out of an alley near the Serapeum steps.'

'Sweet Sophia. It is Aeson. But where's *The Book of Wisdom*?'

Theon heard her. 'Well if he has *The Book of Wisdom* then it's the only copy left in Alexandria. Books salvaged from the Museum have been coming in all afternoon. We've run out of shelf space. It's times like these one puts one's hope in those book smugglers the Archbishop was complaining about.'

Theon's gaze makes my face heat up. Did he know about my book business all along? It doesn't matter now. Nothing matters anymore apart from my boy keeping his speed up.

'Cassius how far is Aeson behind the giant and Fatty?'

'Not too far. He's reached the Serapeum steps.'

'Will he make it before they close the gates?' You're my eyes, Cassius, now Apollinos' sight is failing him too.

'Yes, master. The citizens who've just entered Serapis Street won't, but Aeson will. He's racing up the steps.'

Come on my boy, run.

Theon's voice is a low whisper when he finally decides to ask. 'Tell me you saved the comedies, Rufius?'

My eyebrows rise in surprise from the habit of acting, then drop: what's the point of the pretence now? 'So you know about my little venture, Theon?'

'I had my suspicions since the inspectors began snooping about.'

'You turned a blind eye. Why?'

Theon's bookish squint is on the tendril of smoke above the Museum in the distance. 'My love of literature surpasses my duty to Library policy. You may have saved more books than the Muses this afternoon, Rufius.'

'CLOSE THE GATES.' Olympus' voice is crisp above the noise. Fear snaps in my gut.

'Cassius, is Aeson nearly at the gate? Will he make it?'

'He's near the top of the Serapeum steps, master.'

If only these old eyes could distinguish him from the rest of the rabble. 'Point him out to me, Cassius.'

'There, taking the marble steps two at a time. Look for the black giant. Aeson's right behind him.'

'My boy, yes, I see him. He'll make it.'

'Close the gates,' echo the slaves as the order is passed on.

'Lanky's seen Aeson. He's jumping off that Sphinx. Look!'

Cassius looks at Kiya confused.

'Kill the demon. Cassius, your spear, stop him!'

'What?'

'That one-eyed monk – in front of Aeson – kill him, or give me your spear if you lack the balls to use it.'

By Bacchus, the Cyclops monk has his knife out. Cassius adjusts his feet to take aim.

'Throw it, Cassius, dear. This isn't a bloody tournament in the gym'

'This wind, master.' The spear judders in the strong sea wind. 'Argh! Take that.'

We all hold our breath and watch the spear spiral through the air. It's a good throw, direct and fast. We will it to spear Lanky, to stop him, cloak flapping about his feet, charging at Aeson.

'No!' A sharp gust of wind twitches the long spear from its course. Our gasps are a unison of disappointment.

'Sweet Sophia, grant me revenge!'

Come on, my boy, faster. Just a few more steps and you'll reach the gates.

Aeson and the one-eyed monk look up at the Serapeum gates. The great creak of them, iron grates on stone as the two huge doors move on their ancient hinges. Faster, Aeson.

Lanky lunges at Aeson's feet. Back they topple and roll down the marble steps.

The huge hermit's on the top step now, Fatty on his back. He ushers the children in through the doors, then looks back to Aeson.

'DERA, GO!' We all heard that. My heart trots. Aeson's going to fight.

We jump at the thud of metal bolts being put in place. Citizens outside the walls bang on the gates. Soldiers and monks run at the steps, slaughtering pagans in their path.

'Oh, Apollinos, I cannot watch! So much blood.'

Cassius is as frantic as Kiya. 'Lanky's throttling Aeson, master!'

Kiya knocks her stick against the wall. 'Aeson, get up. Kill him.'

'Aeson, get up, my boy.'

'Take aim.' Olympus gives orders to start an attack on the monks outside the walls. The army pound up Serapis Street towards the steps.

'Theon, you must persuade Olympus not to attack. Please, imagine if it were Hypatia out there.'

'I'll try, Rufius.' He sounds defeated.

'I'm the wealthiest man in Alexandria. Offer him whatever he wants: land, money, slaves. Theon, please.'

'The giant, master.'

The huge hermit strides towards us. Men move aside for him to pass. He kisses Kiya on the forehead and hands her the leather-bound book. She hugs it to her chest like a new born.

'Thank you, Dera.'

'Fuck that bloody book. How could you leave my boy out there to die?'

Dera leans over the wall. 'They closed the gates before I could get back out, brother.'

'Oh, my boy!' Lanky has Aeson pinned down by his wrists.

That's it, Aeson – reach for Cassius' fallen spear.

He's got it!

'Kill him, Aeson!' Apollinos pinches my shoulder.

Aeson stabs Lanky's right foot with the spear then runs up the steps. The Cyclops howls like of a wolf shot by an arrow.

Lanky pulls the spear out, then stumbles after Aeson.

What's the hermit up to with that rope? What use is that? No one can climb this wall. It's smooth as glass … and it's too windy to pull Aeson up. He'll be smashed against the wall like a fly.

'Save him, dear, and you'll live like a king for the rest of your life, but harm a hair on my boy's head and you'll regret it.'

The hermit ignores me and ties one end of the rope round his waist, the other he flings over the wall. 'Everyone, catch Aeson's attention.'

'Aeson, up here,' we shout. Biblos slaves wave and yell; Kiya screams like a Siren. Our voices are lost on the wind.

'Keep shouting, brothers.'

'Aeson's seen us.' My boy, he's a blur but close enough at the foot of the Serapeum wall to know it's him.

'Aeson, lad. The rope.'

Lanky stumbles up the marble stairs, bloody footsteps trail behind him.

The rope's too short. He'll never reach it. My stomach's in my mouth.

49

AESON

This Khamaseen's strong. It whines like a siren and bends the trunks of the palm trees lining Serapis Street so they look ready to uproot and join the soldiers and monks charging towards me … I don't believe it, Lanky's still after me, limping up the steps.

The wind catches his black cloak, topples him sideways.

Curse it, he's up again.

'Careful Lanky – don't trip on your dress.'

'Will you laugh when I cut off your lips and make you eat them, Pretty? You little fucker, you *cinaedus-lover.*' He looks demented with his one eye fixed on me. 'You butt-boy, you chicken-liver *cinaedus.*'

Still gabbles like street scum. He's nearly within reach of my knife. Patience, Aeson: I have a better chance of knifing him if I keep my ground, wait for him to come to me.

'I'll take out the cripple's eyes when I find that heretic witch.'

Has he seen Kiya? My gut jerks.

'Come and get it, Lanky. Monasteries will take anyone, even scum like you.' Saliva splatters my chin. Why bother goading him, palms up, drawing his hatred towards me? Revenge. We both want it.

The army and the Christian mob rage up Serapis Street; makes my insides churn. Focus on Lanky. Serapis, let me avenge my friends before I die.

'I'm going to kill you, Pretty.' Lanky's single eye bulges as he limps closer, struggling to keep his balance in the wind.

Come and get it, you swine.

'Aeson!'

Dera' voice? Where is he?

'Aeson, up here.'

The Serapeum wall's so high, my neck wrenches right back. Ah, that's sore where Lanky tried to strangle me. Dera's up there on the battlements. What's he yelling? The storm's taken his words. Looks like he's pointing down here.

Is that the tail end of a rope swinging against the wall? Hard to tell in this light.

'Aeson, … dear boy …' Is that Rufius? Where are you, Rufius? … There he is, the other side of Dera. Oh, Rufius! My heart wants to run up the wall and kiss him. The roar behind me drowns out his voice.

I don't have long … the mob's closing in fast, a seething mass of soldiers and monks tear up the two hundred steps. There's not a hope in Hades the Priests of Serapis will open the gates to the sacred precinct now. I must see Rufius. Fight Lanky, and I die here on the Serapeum steps … I can't leave Rufius with that memory. Revenge can wait.

'Running away again, Pretty?' Lanky's teeth grit like a jackal thrown into a fighting pit.

'I'll kill you another time, Lanky. Careful now, or you'll trip!'

'Come back here, you …'

Time to dash for the wall.

Shit, this rope's short by the height of two men. Come on, Dera – give me some more slack.

Can't he see it's short? Miming pulling on a rope isn't producing any slack from Dera.

'What?'

Looks like he's mouthing *jump.*

Jump? No chance of that. I need a leg up to reach the end of it.

Lanky stabs a finger in my direction and mouths at his cronies: *kill him!* His words are inaudible but the monks understand. Black cloaks flap as they speed up –they're after me! They'll swat me like a fly against this wall.

Think, Aeson, think.

The wall's the only way … the pink polished surface must have one or two notches to get a foothold. The cool, ancient stone is puckered with tiny cracks where black veins run through the pink … hardly large enough for a child's foot let alone my big feet. Let's get these sandals off. I don't scale a wall barefoot for ten years, then twice in one day.

Come on wall give me a hole, just one nook to get me started. There's one for my left foot … and a handhold above it … and there's another. That raises me off the ground at least.

Kill him! Lanky mouths the words and points at me. Monks bolt past him up the steps.

Shit, come on, just one more crevice and I'll be out of their reach. Come on, wall.

There! Shallow, but it will take my big toe.

Come on, come on; just one more foothold and I'll reach the rope.

Fuck, a spear! Missed. Chucking spears now are we, Lanky? He never was much of a shot.

Hold tight, Aeson. Keep your grip. My palm strokes above my head, fingers like antennae. Shit, the wall's smooth here. What about over to the left?

Oh great, that was a raindrop that hit the back of my calf. And another.

Come on.

Come on. Ignore the pain in your clenched fingers and toes. Stomach strong, hold the position. That's it. No rushing. This wall will lose what little grip it has in the rain. Just one more nook, that's all I need.

Arrows? Where did they come from? Above my head. What in the name of Serapis? … more arrows clatter and bounce off the steps … that one pierced a monk in the neck. Shit, I'm caught in the crossfire!

'Take aim!' Who's instructing them? I recognise that voice; it makes me feel like a naughty schoolboy.

Hundreds of arrows slide back above my head as bows are set. I'm out of range … if I'm lucky they'll fly right over my head.

'FIRE!' A military voice – Olympus. I bet my old school master's loving this. A flurry of arrows shower down on monks and soldiers. The wounded fall back on the steps. Shrieks of pain make my head spin. This is no riot in the Agora. It's full on war. Come on wall: get me the fuck out of here!

Yes, a nook big enough for three fingers. If I can get a solid grip, I'll be able to push off with my left leg and use the inertia to thrust my body up to the rope in one movement. Deep breath in … and out …

Chink of metal on marble. Fuck, where did that arrow come from? Misaimed from the battlements. Don't tell me they've armed the Priests of Serapis!

Concentrate. Let the noise recede: the wind, the rain, the battle; it's just me and the rope. I can do this. I did jumps like this a million times as a boy.

Now, jump …

… Made it!

A cheer from the battlements – so I have an audience.

And Lanky?

Still on the steps, wringing your fists at me. Your men won't reach me with their spears now.

Ouch! By Serapis, this wind is strong. Even with my weight, it's swinging the rope. Dera will have a hard job pulling me up all that way safely. I'll have to climb.

Oh, Alexandria, what a mess you are! Temples burn despite rain pelting in briny sheets off the sea, carnage everywhere.

The rope swings and twists violently. Keep your grip, hands. Just climb. That's it, one hand over the other. Now I've got enough rope below me, let's get my legs round it. No use walking up the wall against the rope in this rain – I'll slip all over the place. Come on arms, find your rhythm.

How much further? Rain runs down my neck as I look up at the faces hanging over the wall, willing me upwards. There's Rufius. I'm coming. My fingers speed up urged on by my heart. I've missed him most of all.

That was a clap of thunder out at sea: white horses froth high and fast. Sea rain's the wettest, coats everything in oily brine. It's not just the wind howling as it shuttles up Serapis Street from the sea. What's going on down there now? It's hard work to spin the rope so I can look down over my shoulder.

By Serapis! So many, packed into Serapis Street, the mob undulates and writhes up the wide avenue like a great snake. That's blood, washing down the steps with the rain. Only moments ago I was down there; my feet are clean. So many dead, so soon. All those limp bodies at the bottom of the steps. Centurions step on corpses as if they're ramps. How did this happen?

'Aeson, get a move on.' Dera's voice … I can't look up without the rain pelting my face. This rope's getting way too slippy. Dera's thick neck strains. Come on, hands, faster … focus on the rope. It's losing grip.

Fuck, the pain's pulling at my armpits from every angle now: feels like my shoulder muscles are tearing. Muscles wobble like fig syrup. Come on, arms, don't fail me now. This is the highest wall I've ever climbed. I must move more gently, conserve my strength.

'Aeson!' Dera's voice. I must be close – I hear him clearly now.

The ledge. At last!

By Serapis, the men's eyes: right up close. I can see the colour of them as they look down over the enemy, hatred in their gargoyle-faces.

Biblos slaves in white tunics stretch their arms over the ledge. Rufius must be up with them, but I can't see him. Come on, arms, just two more hands up the rope and then they'll pull me over, just two lunges away from Rufius.

There's Cassius' mess of blonde hair, wild in the wind. His hands reach towards me. 'Master, throw up your hand.'

Where's Rufius?

Dera's thick neck strains from my weight. 'I've got you, lad. That's it, leg up, lad.' His firm grip's round my wrist. Skin squeaks against wet skin … and slips free. It's too wet.

'Get his legs.' Dera's order to the Biblos slaves is pointless. Three of them reach for my legs but it's no good, the strength's gone from my kick. All I feel is the slip of smooth granite as I slide from Dera's grip.

'Aeson. Don't let go.'

Serapis, give me the strength to kick. This kick's for Rufius.

Four Biblos slaves grab my ankles. Dera holds his position.

'Over you come, that's it.' Dera's huge hands lift me under my armpits.

My feet slap the wet stone of the battlements. The ground feels good and solid.

Dera's face is blacker than I remember, eye sockets darker, eyes sunk deep into their hollows. His skin has that leathery look of hermits, but he still has a builder's body.

'Dera! I've never been more relieved to see a rope!' It feels good to rest my hands on his shoulders, broad and strong as ever.

Cassius and Apollinos. How I've missed them all. Biblos slaves crowd in around me, but I need to find Rufius …

'Your fate is tied to the fate of the Temple, lad. We must get you out of here. There's still time, before the army completely surrounds the walls.'

'Forget the prophecy, old friend. I'm not running from my destiny anymore.'

Dera's bare chest heaves and drops – even his sigh is bigger than most men's. His gaze has that faraway look, like he's having a vision.

'Dera, can you hear me … where's Rufius?'

There's Kiya. Thank Serapis she's alive. Croc was right, Kiya's smile's still the same, but her wet dress clings to the bones jutting out in the wrong places. Her small frame's so contorted she has to twist her neck sideways to look up at me. It wasn't just Rufius I returned for. I wanted to deliver on my promise in person.

'The book, do you have it, Dera?'

'I gave it to Kiya.'

'Does she know Henite and Seth are dead?'

Dera's nod is slow and sad.

'Our brother has returned!' She's learnt to project her voice like the Aberamenthos. She leans against the wall, crutch raised in one hand like a wand, and there it is, *The Book of Wisdom* in its leather binding in the other. She wants to give me a grand welcome. How I've missed her big, determined love. If she'd let me I'd pick her up and squeeze her like a puppy.

'Sweet Saviour, you kept your promise. I knew you would … but Lanky is back. We must kill him.' There is something unhinged in her speech – she's gabbling, her teeth chatter.

'Don't worry about Lanky, Kiya.'

'Your Librarian, he's a saviour of books too.'

'Rufius, saviour of books!' That copy would have gone to the highest bidder. If I wasn't welling up, I'd laugh. Where is Rufius … to share the joke? Why didn't he call me back from Constantinople? My gut churns in anticipation. Some new boy in his life I expect: a fresh young project.

Biblos slaves fuss and try to towel me down.

'Stop that. Where's Rufius?'

50

AESON

Everything's a blur, a wet mirage in this rain. Where are you Rufius? Impatience throbs fast in my heart. How will it be, now I'm a man?

My friends – Dera, Kiya, Apollinos – crowd in around me, but I'm not home until I find Rufius, not properly.

No Rufius here . . . just drenched archers, hair pasted to foreheads and shaved heads of Temple guards. Poor excuse for soldiers: shiny swords hanging from belts are for display not battle. One of those old bookworms is responsible for misfiring at me I expect. They wipe the rain from their eyes like children. No match for Egypt's legions. He's taller than most men, so why can't I see him?

'Apollinos, where's Rufius? I heard his voice just now.'

Apollinos nods towards the porticos and smiles.

The porticos – that's more like Rufius – he wouldn't want to get his hair wet.

There he is standing with the other librarians, Cassius beside him. My heart leaps to sob. Catch it, hold in my tears. Rufius doesn't like me blubbing.

How Rufius' face has bloated, cheeks and nose red from too much wine. His height doesn't disguise his weight anymore. Even Cassius, who's shot up, is still a head shorter than him.

Has he seen me? He's squinting in my direction. I have to get to him. The longing makes me push past my friends; the urge to touch him, to feel his solid, grounded weight in my arms again drives me to the portico.

'Rufius, I'm – ' my voice cracks, interrupted by his shift in focus. What's he looking at?

Rufius' frown shoots to Kiya.

'Librarian, saviour of books!'

'Oh do shut up, dear, for Bacchus' sake!' That's my Rufius! Insensitive as ever. I mustn't let my amusement show.

Kiya continues to mutter to herself, teeth chattering. She must be in shock.

'Take her inside, Cassius, and dry her off.' My authority surprises me. That tone was spontaneous. Well, I'm still a Biblus heir, but what should I call my guardian now? Not father – too domestic for Rufius.

Rufius shuffles to the front of the portico. His gaze is on me. I feel the hotness of it. How I've missed being watched by him. We're trying to reach each other, like there's an invisible cord connecting us.

Kiya hobbles over and plants herself between us. 'Saviours of books, Sophia thanks you.'

Dera's face is creased in concern; his age shows now. 'Sister, if you will not let go of the book permit me to carry you.'

Kiya doesn't put up a fight as Dera lifts her crumpled frame into his arms. She let me carry her once, the night she took Lanky's eye out. She saved my life.

Was that a swift pulse of affection on Rufius' face? 'Show them to my rooms, Cassius dear.'

Cassius gracefully indicates the way through the porticos to the corridor that leads to the librarians' chambers. Dera follows, Kiya in his arms, then turns and looks at me, grief-stricken. He's thinking of the prophecy.

I love him, I love them all, but I just want them gone so I can give Rufius all my attention.

The old man's been slowly making his way to me, shouldering librarians and slaves. This is a first – people move to Rufius, not the other way round.

Khamaseen wind blasts sheets of rain inside the porticos forcing the librarians to the back wall to stay dry. Not Rufius. He shuffles to the edge of the portico, jug of wine in hand.

I can't move, like my feet are in cement. The over-flowing gutter on the roof of the portico showers me in a steady waterfall.

Rufius clasps a portico column for support. He's just an arm's length away from me. He hugs the red granite column. Keep that sob down, Aeson.

'I'm here.' My voice is a whisper. 'Take my shoulder, Rufius.' Yes, Rufius, that's what I'll call him. Man to man now.

Why doesn't he take my shoulder? He's unbalanced. I'm kissing distance from him. If he falls I'll catch him. He's still squinting at me, even this close. Are those tears on his face? Impossible to tell in this rain. His thin hair's wet, probably white under the yellow hair dye, and plastered to his scalp – so he did watch me climb? Why does that please me, that he saw me? Close up his age is sharper. His tunic sags over his belly like the dress of a pregnant woman.

'Still the hedonist I see, Rufius.'

'Ever the man, my boy.' He surveys me as he would a repainted room, checks me for flaws.

'Polished enough for you, Rufius?' Why am I searching his eyes for approval?

His head jerks, surprised. This is Rufius without the act. I have such an urge to rub away the smudged kohl where his eyebrows have run down his face.

'Still climbing like a monkey, dear?' What is that expression on his face? Disappointment?

'Well, Rufius, are you pleased to see me?'

It is my own disappointment, that he no longer sees a boy he desires. I didn't expect this … those years, yawning at the thought of performing my after-dinner duties, gagging at the sight of his saggy arse … and now I miss his lust …

He's never held my stare so long. His eyes were brown, but the steel-blue film of age has clouded them, the whites of his eyes now the colour of yolks. His face has not sagged, but filled – makes him look almost jolly. Better not tell him that.

'What do your young eyes see? An old *cinaedus* gagging for a blow-job?'

He still reads a face like he sucks meaning from a book.

'An old friend is all.'

Rufius' free arm reaches to me, at last, jug in hand.

'Come here my boy, my heir … if you can bear to embrace a doting old fool.'

We both jump at the smash of pottery – red wine splashes our feet.

Is that joy folded in the creases of his eyes? It's hard to tell. I've seen him satisfied, amused, pleased with a recent purchase, self-congratulatory at my progress, but simply happy? My chest heaves as I scoop his bulk into my arms and kiss into his ear. 'Why didn't you reply to my letters, Rufius?' My arms barely reach all the way round his middle.

He lets go of the marble column. Lean on me, Rufius. His soft cheek slides against mine, wet and warm with our tears. Relief trembles through our arms as we hold on to each other.

I didn't picture our reunion like this. Everything I've achieved in the Empire has been under his gaze; his scrutiny followed me everywhere. When I won my first oratory competition, delivered my first defence – when I fucked it was under Rufius' omniscient surveillance.

'Why didn't you visit me, Rufius?' My sob puffs into his ear.

'Who's the *cinaedus* here, dear?' I've never heard such tenderness in his voice before. There's no edge to it, just the lightness of the joke.

'Hold your fire.' That was Olympus' voice. Archers shuffle backwards away from the wall in response to the order, pushing us into the shelter of the portico.

'I've got you, Rufius. Hold on to me.'

My feet balance for both of us; his weight in my arms, his smell near me again is the thing that was missing in my life. This closeness is what I needed to feel whole.

'Who put Olympus in charge?'

'Can you believe it, dear? Olympus was in the mil-it-tary, don't you know. Terrifying thought isn't it, dear?' Rufius lifts his tunic for effect. Our laughter breaks our embrace.

I'll have to take a step back from Rufius to get a view of the arcades on the level above the porticos. There he is, my old teacher, dressed for battle, skin sagging over bony knees.

'Let's get out of this bloody rain. You look like a drowned rat, dear.'

My bent arm extends for Rufius to rest his hand, as if he were a young maiden on her wedding day. Will he take it?

'Shall we?'

'I'm not your young wench, dear. You can lead my funeral procession but until then, this *cinaedus* does the leading.'

'I wouldn't have it any other way, Rufius.' My grin is ear to ear and our laughter is filled with the relief that we have negotiated a way to cope with my age without compromising Rufius' reputation.

'Appearances, dear, are everything. Have you forgotten what I taught you?'

He may be a *cinaedus*, but he's more man than most.

'Pagans, hear me!' Theophilus! His voice projects from below the battlements. Rufius and I look at each other.

'Surely you remember the Archbishop's dulcet tones from the podium, dear?' Rufius chuckles and whistles to himself.

He saw me? 'You were there, Rufius?' What did he think of my delivery?

That wink tells me I didn't let him down. 'He looked ready to murder you, dear. Didn't I warn you he'd be trouble?' He chuckles between wheezes. His tired eyes turn serious and he nods towards to the wall. I take his weight and we walk into the rain and find a place along the battlements.

'What nonsense is Theophilus spouting now?'

'Pagans, is there someone in charge, or are you an anonymous collective hiding behind your false god?'

A roar of anger goes up from our men; spears and bows punch the wind.

Theophilus stands at the front of the mob, a head taller than the two men dressed in their official garb either side of him.

'That's the Prefect, Evagrius, on his left. Look at the thickness of his purple stripe dear. I bet there's no blood spilt on that toga.'

Romanus stands on the other side of Theophilus, chainmail belted at the waist, long sword at his hip and ridge helmet; the copper strip the length of his nose is too thin to cover his broken hooter, splayed flat from too many battles. The commander of Egypt's legions mutters something to Theophilus and spits on the bloody steps.

'Now there's a man, dear.' Rufius gives my hard muscle a playful pinch, but frowns as he watches the scene below us.

Olympus steps out of the arcades on the floor above us, arms raised, palms flat, patting the air for quiet.

'You address Olympus. I represent the Priests of Serapis and the people. This is a matter for the law, not the church.' I keep expecting him to pull out his whip and tell them to bend over Memory's bench. If Fatty's watching, he'll be thinking the same thing.

Evagrius holds up his arm.

'Olympus, you address Evagrius, Prefect of the city of Alexandria. I do not have to remind the Priests of Serapis that they are breaking several laws by barricading the Serapeum. Now, open the gates, release the prisoners and let the law deal with the guilty.' His voice struggles against the howl of the wind.

Bowmen's heads on the battlements tilt upwards and wait for Olympus' response. Olympus looks uncertain of himself, a far cry from the tyrant who whipped me for getting my Latin wrong. The Priests of Serapis whisper in his ears.

'The Temple is fortified to protect it from sacrilege. Blood cannot be spilt in the sacred precinct.'

The Head Priest of Serapis steps in front of Olympus. The seven pointed star on his diadem glints in the rain. 'Evagrius, the Nile will not flood if the precinct is not protected. In just a few weeks we must perform our duties to Serapis or Egypt's crops will fail. These doors will remain closed until you call off the legions and send those swine back to the desert. Serapis will protect us – '

Only someone who had been at the receiving end of Olympus' whip would sense his struggle not to whack the Head Priest for stealing his thunder.

Evagrius raises an arm again. 'If you refuse us entry, we have no option but to inform the Emperor and let him decide.'

A hush falls over both sides at the mention of the Emperor. More muttering between the Head Priest and Olympus, inaudible from down here … here we go: Olympus has his arms up in the air again.

'You have our agreement that the only course of action is to inform the Emperor.'

We look at each other. The following year's taxes are estimated based on the readings of the Nilometers, positioned strategically along the river and gathered by the Priests of Serapis.

'Too many chiefs, dear. They want control of the Nilometers – taxes are what Theophilus gets out of this. He's no fool. Whoever controls the Nilometers controls Egypt …'

'If Theophilus takes the Serapeum, he takes Egypt, but surely the Emperor won't allow that, Rufius?'

'We'll see, dear. The Emperor's ear's been bent by bishops before.'

We look down Serapis Street. The sacred avenue is packed all the way from the temple steps to the harbour with the peaks of copper helmets, the black hoods of monks and the Christian mob. A drawn out peel of thunder beyond the harbour turns their heads to the sky. Both sides wait for the thunderbolt in silence.

What a bright bolt! Rufius and I gasp with the men on the battlements. A jagged scar cuts through the sky. Thousands of helmets glint in the white shock.

An old librarian screams, shaking in a sodden toga. 'We're all doomed!'

'Oh will you shut up! It's a summer storm and yes, it's bloody likely we will all die here. Now, Aeson, dear. Toddle off and tell Apollinos to collect my stash of best Egyptian wine from the cellar and some of Turk's Desert Honey.'

He's not changed one bit.

PART IV

THREE WEEKS LATER

While the Serapeum swelters and stinks under siege, festering in the heat that followed the summer storms, watched night and day by the Egyptian legions and hordes of desert monks, messengers whip their horses into a gallop along the Nile. One carries Emperor Theodosius' reply in his saddlebag sealed with Imperial wax.

At the top of the two hundred marble steps cut into the hill, behind the enormous gates of the Serapeum, Aeson paces the western battlements that overlook the Necropolis. Did Croc and the gang take refuge in the Necropolis? he worries. He can't sharpen one more sword, throw another dice with Fatty, or stare beyond the city for sign of horses kicking up dust another day. The ocean, flat as a mirror to his right, teases him, the way the smell of cut grass teased him cooped up in the schoolroom with Apollinos as a boy. He kicks the red Aswan granite wall – the Serapeum's become his prison.

Steam pumps into the hot blue sky above the bath complex on the far side of the temple buildings. At least the Prefect hasn't cut off the water supply … yet. The Nile still flows into the cisterns under the temple where the Nilometer measures the river level, but Evagrius' tolerance hinges on the Emperor's reply. The Prefect's not as cock-sure of the Imperial response as Theophilus.

The wait makes Aeson's gut groan with anxiety. Is this how Seth and Henite felt, queuing up on the Magistrate's podium for their trial? He just wants it over with. The bruises where Lanky and countless soldiers and monks attacked him have faded, but Lanky's stalked his dreams for three weeks. Aeson runs down the battlement steps, nine floors below to the sacred precinct. He wants to find Dera. He never believed the prophecy, but fear has taken hold of him, and now he has a burning need to know how he will die.

The heat's more oppressive in the sacred precinct than up on the battlements. It's unnatural, even for summer. Aeson flaps his tunic to cool his sweaty skin and sniffs the stagnant air in the large courtyard dominated by the colossal statue of Serapis. That's a sharp stink! The back of Aeson's throat heats up like he's eaten too much pepper. The first time he smelt rotting flesh was when he took Dera to have his wounds dressed. He remembers how it hit them both, how their necks jerked backwards with the shock of it as they entered the room where the doctors had set up a makeshift hospital. It's a smell that lingers in your memory, reaches all the way down your throat, strangling from the inside.

Delirious moans come from a makeshift surgery as he passes. Flies and wasps hover around the door. Aeson clamps his mouth shut to avoid swallowing them and sweeps semicircles with his arms as he walks through the swarm. The hum makes his shoulders tense.

Dera crouches under a palm tree near the statue of Serapis built into the spacious columned sanctuary that only the Priests of Serapis can enter. The statue looms above him, its head with the basket of grain level with the fourth floor. It's rumoured the inside is gold, overlaid with the less precious metals – silver and bronze. The statue's so large its right hand touches one side of the sanctuary and its left hand the other.

Dera looks up. His face is still bruised where Lanky and the monks attacked him in his cave.

'Still a devotee of Serapis, lad?'

'I don't know what I believe anymore. Perhaps Rufius' hedonism is the only sensible faith.'

'How is the Librarian?'

'Rufius? He's been locked away in his rooms, petrified he'll catch a disease.' Aeson's laugh is hollow.

'That's wise. The Serapeum's full of fever, tiny invisible demons hover in the air.'

'The death toll reached eighty this morning.'

'Sit down, lad. Pacing won't speed up time.' His voice is calm, patient as Aeson crouches beside him.

'What will become of us, Dera? First the rain won't stop, now the sun burns hotter than a furnace. The bread's mouldy, the people are sick – look at the state of everyone.'

They look over at the tables under the arcades that skirt the sacred precinct. A queue of wounded women and children shuffle forward, gazes fixed on the ladles of slop being handed out in bowls by temple slaves.

'I suppose this is luxury after your years in the desert.' Panic quivers in Aeson's voice.

'This siege is tougher than the desert, lad. Harsh as it was, I chose that life. In here we're prisoners.'

'I should have followed medicine instead of a public life. At least then I could help. What good is the law at times like this?'

'Stop taking the responsibility of the world on your shoulders, Aeson lad. There are more qualified doctors in the Serapeum than in the whole of Alexandria.'

'Cursed flies.' Aeson waves his arm around his head. 'A battle I can deal with, but this waiting's driving me mad.'

Dera rests a hand gently on Aeson's knee. 'Save your anger for the final battle, lad.'

'Will there be one?'

Dera's eyes focus on an invisible point above the large rectangular pool of water. He's having a vision, thinks Aeson.

'Yes.'

'Will I die here, Dera? I was never clear on the exact details of the prophecy.'

Dera claps his palms loud in front of his face, as if to wake himself from the vision.

'Our fate depends on our wits. Look, the temple slaves know to keep themselves occupied. Take up a mop and join them. This must be the cleanest fortress that's ever been under siege.'

Dera's focus shifts to a procession of priests wearing the seven pointed star diadems of Serapis. They enter the sacred precinct to perform the daily rites. Frankincense wafts from hand-held burners they swing from side to side.

'Or comfort Kiya, lad.'

'She's busy with Rufius. They've put the scribes to work copying books.'

'Excellent use of time. Sophia works in mysterious ways. Talking of which ...'

What's caught Dera's eye? He's looking at the balcony two floors up.

Kiya lurches along, hunched over in an expensive blue dress. Rufius must have given her that.

'The Librarian's charity has always impressed me.'

'The city's waifs and strays entertain him.'

Dera shoots Aeson a look, dark eyes soft with compassion. 'Does an act of love have to be serious, Aeson?'

'I'm just disappointed Rufius didn't visit me in Constantinople, that's all.' Aeson's index finger traces the black lines in the pink marble floor. He knows he's being childish.

'Perhaps that was an act of love too ... perhaps the Librarian worried you might be ashamed if he turned up in the capital with painted eyebrows and jewellery?' Dera's voice is soft.

Kiya is almost graceful as she passes the food queue. Children, crouched under the arcades woofing down their rations, look up when they hear the click of her stick on marble.

Dera stands and bends over to greet Kiya, forehead to forehead the way Snake People always do. Aeson wonders what secrets pass between Aberamenthos when their brows meet.

'Aberamentho.'

Dera nods with the same reverence.

'Aberamentho.'

Kiya's contorted right shoulder rises with pride.

Aeson's happy she's achieved her goal. What have I achieved? he thinks. I've met Rufius' goal, but did I ever really want to be a lawyer? It wasn't my idea to learn to write either. How pointless my years of study seem now. The only useful thing I learnt was how to climb ropes. My life's been composed by other people … until now. I chose to return.

Kiya's stick clicks as she shifts position to look down at him. She doesn't have time for self-pity. 'Aeson, what are you doing hanging around nattering? We need your help.'

Dera slaps his shoulder. 'Go with Kiya; help with the copying. Write, lad.'

A commotion draws their attention. The sacred geese clack and flap out of the way of a slave running towards the Priests of Serapis.

'Your Holiness, the Nilometer,' shouts the slave in a panic.

The Head Priest of Serapis appears from the inner sanctuary. The slave bows and jabbers at him, 'If we have no water we'll all die in here, your Holiness …'

'Guard the cisterns until I have assessed the situation.'

'But the baths need a constant flow, and the lavatories use 200 cubits to maintain a ceaseless flush of fresh water. We have to block the pipes to the baths and lavatories in order to ration the drinking water supply.'

The Head Priest notices Dera, Aeson and Kiya listening.

'Shush, slave. Keep your voice down. You'll cause a panic.'

Kiya knocks Aeson's shin with her stick and hisses at him. 'Aeson, come on. We can't do anything about the water supply. There's books to copy.'

Σ

AESON

How can Rufius stuff his face when everyone else is on rations? His rooms have been completely redecorated since the last time I was here. And now he has not just his office and a room leading off that for relaxation with couches, but two additional rooms beyond those. Looks like they've turned it into a makeshift scriptorium – scribes sit hunched over desks scratching reed pens across parchment as fast as they can.

Kiya's crutch clicks as she hobbles round desks and checks their work.

'How do you manage it, Rufius?'

Rufius looks up from the couch by the terrace. I know that bitter smell: Desert Honey.

'Manage what, dear?'

'All this?' I wave my arm over the tables in front of him – pastries, fresh figs and exotic delicacies on enormous gold plates.

Rufius' kohl eyebrows crease in disapproval as he takes my drift. 'I didn't see you complaining during your ten year jaunt around the Empire. Wrapped in rags were you, dear?'

A click of his fingers above his head and Apollinos, grey now, passes him the other half of a fig.

'Where did you get those from? The fig trees in the Serapeum courtyard are bare.'

'Oh, do stop dishing out the judgment, dear. Go and play Magistrates with your friend Fatty.'

Rufius' nerves are as frazzled as mine.

Apollinos points over to the terrace. 'There are four fig trees on the terrace, master Aeson.'

'If I need a defence, Apollinos, I'll pay a lawyer, dear. I don't owe anyone an explanation.'

Kiya clicks back into the office. 'There you are, Apollinos. Get to work. All who can write must copy – we don't have much time.'

'Ha, do what you're told, Apollinos!'

It's funny to hear Kiya boss Biblos slaves about. Rufius has that indulgent look on his face he saves for Diana. It amuses him that orphans and slaves – especially women – can be bold.

A sigh rolls up inside my chest and I plomp down next to him on the couch. At least some things are constant: Rufius is still Rufius.

'Any word of Diana, any messages getting through?'

Kohl eyebrows crease in concern. 'None, dear.'

'Serapis, keep her safe.'

'Still committed to your old god, dear? You do humankind a disservice. Diana will survive on her wits, my boy, on her wits.' His speech slurs.

'That's rich coming from you. I still can't believe you suggested to Damasus that I convert.'

'What are you complaining about? You refused, didn't you? Always wilful. It was for your own good, dear. Christians advance in this new world.'

I still can't work Rufius out. He's full of paradoxes. He chooses infamy, but insists I conform.

What mischief swirls in his cloudy old eyes? He raises an eyebrow. 'What dirt do you have on Damasus? Not that it matters now he's dead – and good riddance – but I always thought he was playing around with the novices.'

'How can you gossip as Alexandria burns?' I look over the balcony. Thin tendrils of smoke make patterns in the blue sky. Those pyres have been kept alight for three weeks.

'Well, what do you suggest? Here, have a spoonful of Desert Honey – it might cheer you up, dear? I'm sure it's got weaker over the years.'

The initial joy of being reunited soon thawed – Rufius is more infuriating than ever.

Kiya stamps her good foot on the ground and twists her contorted back to face us. 'Either you two stop bickering, or pick up a pen and start copying.'

'Ha! That told us, dear.'

That made us laugh too – the topsy-turvy absurdity of it: little Kiya ordering about the Director of the Scriptorium. It's made Rufius wheeze he's laughing so much.

'That's better. I was worried you might have gone soft. And that wouldn't do for the fine Roman you've grown into. You're too old for me now, so I do hope you're not jealous, dear?'

Rufius' gaze rests on his young body slave's thighs.

He's being ironic, but what perverse twist of emotion is this? Resentment? Disgust, that the old man still lusts after boys … am I jealous? I'm jealous! But why? As a boy I was relieved when he bent over for a Biblos slave instead of me. I don't want to fuck him, but I still want him to desire me.

The boy giggles. His skin's the same honey tone as mine, his eyes a paler blue. Rufius squints at the plates of food.

'You're going blind aren't you, Rufius?' The blue film over your eyes, the way you pat the table around objects before you find them. I couldn't sleep with a man who can hardly see me, couldn't admire me. Some of my lovers were as ugly as Gorgons but that heightened my own pleasure, fed my narcissism. I imagined their lust more lascivious on account of their ugliness. After all these years of calling Rufius shallow, I realise that's exactly what excites me.

'Not so blind that I can't see you're still my little Antinous beneath all that brawn, Aeson dear.'

He knows how I feel – he was someone's ephebe once. I'm solidified in his memory. It pains him too, that I'm no longer his beautiful boy. Better change the subject.

'Alright then, Rufius, here's the gossip – I don't usually speak ill of the dead but the Archbishop of Rome was a fat old crook.'

'Ha! Was he fatter than me? Tell me he was, dear.'

'That hippopotamus Damasus and his yapping widows – skinny as rakes – '

My pause allows Rufius to finish wheezing. Apollinos offers him a glass of water. Rufius shoos it away and points at the wine.

'That's better. Carry on, dear.'

'The year Damasus died, the flabby old Archbishop fleeced an old matron called ...'

A bang at the bolted door makes us all jump.

'What in Hades is that racket?'

'Master, it's Cassius. Let me in.' Cassius' muffled shouts increase in volume as a young Biblos slave lifts the iron bolt and opens the door. He stands in the doorway, eyes round with fright, and gasps for breath. 'Master, they're letting them inside. They're opening the gates, master. The Emperor – '

'What, the Emperor here? Impossible.'

'Slow down, Cassius.'

Cassius gabbles on without taking a breath. 'Master, master.' He addresses us both. 'The Emperor's reply arrived. They have agreed a short-term truce so the Prefect and the Archbishop can enter the Serapeum and read it out.'

We look at each other. The scribes in the adjoining rooms have put down their pens and lean over their desks to listen. The only sound is the click of Kiya's stick. 'Keep writing. Keep writing.' She whacks her crutch on the desk nearest to her.

'Ha, I'm convinced she's got a pair of balls under her dress.'

Rufius and I walk out to the terrace – those fig trees are sinfully heavy with fruit. Monks, soldiers and citizens congregate outside the Serapeum walls and jitter with expectation. Beyond the harbour the Pharos reflects the midday sun. The sky is a brighter turquoise than I've ever seen it. A perfect day for fishing Dad would have said. What an odd thought, with the army stretched like a silver snake down Serapis Street.

Rufius looks at me – he doubts the wisdom of a truce as much as I do. He turns to the Biblos slaves gathered around the terrace. 'Arm yourselves, my boys. This may not go as that old fool Olympus expects.'

Trunks are opened, scabbards and swords strapped to waists.

At last, something's happening. My heart beats strong and steady in my chest. My limbs move towards the door as light as if walking through a dream. The stench of decay is hot in my nostrils. I am here. I've never felt so wholly in my body, so fully in the present moment.

From the balcony we watch temple slaves run across the courtyard to the Serapeum doors. The huge hinges crunch and scrape as they're pulled open for the first time in three weeks.

Helmets of the soldiers form a line at the top of the Serapeum steps to prevent the mob from entering the temple.

Bring on my destiny. Whatever it is. Serapis, bring it on.

52

RUFIUS

We crowd the third floor balcony. Even Biblos slaves shove for a view of the sacred precinct three floors below. Why, in the name of Bacchus, Apollinos made the slaves polish the thick granite balcony ledge is beyond me. Now what's he doing?

'Apollinos, leave the door to my office open, dear.'

Olympus looks ridiculous with that breastplate over his toga. Bloody idiot! What is he thinking letting Theophilus and his pawn Evagrius and that hairy centurion Romanus into the sacred precinct? They could have read the Imperial response from outside the temple walls. Typical, typical!

'Did Olympus consult the Director of the Scriptorium? No! Even if the Museum Library's been burnt to a cinder, I'm still in charge of the Serapeum's collection. At least if Olympus and the Head Priest of Serapis didn't consult the old *cinaedus* they could have warned me, given me some time. Are they really so confident the Emperor will favour us? Bloody fools the lot of them, fools!' Anger's made me as sober as Hades.

'Shush, master.'

Olympus and the Head Priest of Serapis look nervous as they wait for the party to approach the steps of the inner sanctuary.

Serapis stares ahead as if the god is waiting for them too. The sacred precinct gleams from the sunbeams that fall into the courtyard open to a turquoise sky and reflect off the bronze statue. We're only at neck height. Serapis' head looms above us at the level of the fourth floor. I could touch the god's left earlobe if my arms weren't so old and stiff.

'How many slaves fell from the scaffolding building the statue?' Aeson's voice is morbid.

'You should know, dear, being a builder's son.' That poke wasn't necessary.

'You're my father too, Rufius.' Aeson's sapphire gaze is sincere. He might be hard and hairy, but there's still nothing to match looking into those eyes – they calm me.

'What are you muttering, Rufius?'

Aeson's furious I didn't visit him in Constantinople. But I did it for him. Everything's been for him. 'Nothing. Ignore me, dear.'

That stupid slave's closed the office door again.

'Apollinos, I said leave the bloody door open. Take the boys to the Serapeum Library and gather as many books as you can – you know which – the ones we can sell.'

'Yes, master.'

Apollinos points to four Biblos slaves. Where's he going?

'Apollinos, take the slave stairs. You won't be seen that way. If you can get into the inner sanctuary, take the books from the chests.'

'But, master … that's forbidden.'

'Fuck the rules, Apollinos.' By Bacchus, does he expect a happy ending? 'What are you waiting for, a whipping? Bring the books to my office – and hurry up about it.'

Bare feet slap marble as they run.

What's that clicking? Wretched cripple: I told her to stay put. Will no one do as they're told?

'Saviour of Books, you will be rewarded in The Kingdom of God.'

Aeson spins round, a frown on his face. He usually has a smile for her. 'Kiya, get back inside. Rufius flogs books to the highest bidder. He's a trader, a smuggler not a saviour. And Rufius, this isn't an opportunity to profit. How, in the name of Serapis, do you intend to smuggle those books past the mob? If this goes the way we think, we'll be lucky to get out of here alive.'

What's eating him? I follow his gaze ... he's staring at the hermit in the sacred precinct ... he's thinking about the prophecy. That's fear, not anger. 'Keep your tunic on, dear! You should go inside yourself. If Theophilus sees you he'll want revenge for humiliating him in the Agora. He'll pin the blame for inciting the bloodiest riot Alexandria's ever seen on you. He's probably already commissioned that hack of a historian, Rufinus. Ha! That's a fine epitaph: riot-starter. Personally I'd prefer to be remembered as a *cinaedus*, dear.'

The veins in my neck throb. Aeson still drives me mad. Ha! I've not felt this alive for ten years.

Kiya shoos Biblos slaves back into my office and sets them to work. The rest of us, Cassius, Aeson and Kiya – she's as wilful as him – lean over the polished ledge.

'Here comes the entertainment, dears.'

Evagrius marches into the main courtyard with Theophilus.

'Oooo, dressed for the occasion!'

The purple stripe on the Prefect's toga's thick enough to put him under suspicion of treason. Theophilus kicks up his ankle-length black robe – at the head of the pack by a stride. That black hat makes him look even taller and meaner.

'Perhaps I should try black? It's very slimming.'

'Shush, Rufius.'

Romanus cuts a stocky figure in comparison. The commander leads twenty men in chainmail and helmets, faces red from the heat. Centurions are unarmed at the gates by temple slaves. Swords clatter, thrown in a heap. Ten or so monks in black cloaks file in, shouldering for a position as near to the Archbishop as possible. Flies to shit.

Olympus and the Head Priest of Serapis stand between the bronze feet of Serapis, seated on his throne. Behind them are three rows of priests, gold seven-pointed star diadems on their heads.

Now what's happening? Looks like a mothers' meeting on the steps of the inner sanctuary between the scheming triumvirate.

'What are they saying, dear? Can you hear them?'

'Rufius, shush. They're whispering.'

Aeson's right hand moves to the hilt of his knife, white knuckles clench.

'No playing the hero, dear.'

He taps my hand to pacify me. His palm's sticky with sweat.

Evagrius takes up his position on the steps leading to the inner sanctum.

My gut churns: too many figs. Don't let me get the runs now.

Serapis shines behind him. The god's sapphire eyes wink in the sunlight; his massive arms and hands out-stretched either side of the sanctuary make the men beneath him look like toy gladiators.

Evagrius holds up the letter in his right hand. We hold our breath. Even the hum of flies has stopped. 'Citizens, the Imperial letter has arrived.'

Evagrius' fingers fumble as he breaks the seal. He's as anxious as we are. Whoops, the letter nearly slipped out of his hand. The Prefect wipes his brow with the back of his hand and casts his eyes down the page. Evagrius' shoulders roll back, he straightens with confidence.

Aeson whispers something to Kiya.

'No, I'm staying here.'

Aeson's sensed the Prefect's confidence too.

Evagrius clears his throat. 'Emperor Theodosius to Evagrius, Augustal Prefect, and Romanus, Count of Egypt.' Evagrius' voice booms around the sacred precinct, engineered along the lines of a theatre to bounce sound off walls and into the central courtyard.

The Prefect clears his throat again and raises his chest as if preparing for the performance of a lifetime. Maybe it is.

'Spit it out, dear.'

Shaved heads and helmets turn upwards in our direction. Aeson kicks my shin.

'Ouch, what was that for, dear?'

'Keep quiet, Rufius. Don't draw attention to yourself.'

Theophilus looks up, searching the balconies on every floor … he's spotted me. Under his dark gaze I feel as if I'm falling, plummeting down into the crowd beneath us. Me and my mouth. That wasn't so clever … but someone had to heckle.

Theophilus' focus returns to the Prefect – Evagrius' voice booms with authority.

'All persons shall recognise that they are excluded from profane entrance into temples by the opposition of Our law, so that if any person should attempt to do anything with reference to the gods or the sacred rites, contrary to Our prohibition, he shall learn that he will not be exempted from punishment by any special grants of imperial favour – '

Monks in the courtyard cheer. Although the army outside the gates can't hear the words, they join in.

Theophilus raises his arms for silence but it's no use. That is the cry of victory.

Our men exchange desperate and confused glances as the courtyard fills with monks. Olympus raises an arm to order the gate slaves to shut the Serapeum doors. Watch out, Olympus. Too late, that hooded monk's got him, pulled down from his perch on the top step of the inner sanctuary. It's such a scramble of bodies I can't make out what's happening … the hooded monk looks up, his face splattered with Olympus' blood. His eyes lock onto Aeson and Kiya.

'Lanky!' they gasp together.

Kiya twists, contorts her back to look up at Aeson. 'This time he must die.'

Cassius looks petrified. 'It's going to kick-off, master.'

No it's not, dear. Our people are running. Look at them slip and hide themselves among the mob, ducking under the arcades and into concealed passageways leading off the courtyard.

Cassius tries to take my arm. 'Master, come.'

'Off me, Cassius.' My fist pounds the air. 'Cowards, stay and fight, you cowards.'

The courtyard's filling up with monks. Black-hooded scoundrels keep their gaze fixed to Theophilus like dogs to their master. What's he saying, index finger pointing up to Serapis?

'... God's work ... heresy ... destroy Serapis.'

A silent shock wave skims across the sacred precinct and monks and pagans stop in their tracks. Muttering flitters from every tongue:

'Destroy Serapis?'

'No human hand can touch him – '

'The earth will split open – '

'Crumble into the abyss – '

'The Nile will not flood – '

'Egypt will starve – '

'The sky will crash down – '

'Ha!' Nobody will dare touch the statue.

Theophilus doesn't believe a word of that nonsense – the people's superstition doesn't serve his purpose, does it?

Romanus struts up the steps, double-headed axe in hand. His soldiers stand straight and still at the sight of their commander.

'Legions of Egypt, there is more wealth in this temple than the Emperor has locked away in the Imperial Treasury. This statue is made of gold, laid over with silver and bronze to disguise it. Who will take up this axe? The man who takes the first strike earns his weight in gold for his pension. Who will take my axe?'

He waves the axe like a gladiator in the arena goading his opponent.

'Clever bastard.' That's the same carrot I held under the noses of those two centurions at Biblos: gold. Romans can't resist it. My gut groans.

'Apollinos, where's Apollinos and my boys?'

We can't shift our gaze from the spectacle below. Romanus holds the axe above his head and bellows again.

Centurions push and shove through the gates into the sacred precinct. Word's got out there's profit to be made. They look to Romanus. Here goes again, muscular arm raised, axe high above his head.

'I said, who will take up this axe?'

'These old knees will buckle in a swoon if that hairy commander does that again.'

Not even Cassius pays any attention to my attempt at lechery. Humour died when Evagrius read out the Emperor's letter.

'Who will take this axe?' Romanus barks it like an order this time.

53

KIYA

Sweet Sophia, what blasphemy! This can't be happening? Surely that centurion's not going to hack off Serapis' head with the axe he snatched from the Commander? He's no god of mine, but Serapis is as old as Alexandria.

The centurion's nearly reached Serapis' shoulder, nearly at our level: neck level. We stare gormless as fools. Aeson, the Librarian and his slave, all of us clench the balcony ledge for support. They're gobsmacked. My jaw's slack too.

The centurion looks up from the ladder with greed for the promised gold – then looks down at the upturned faces and waves the axe. There's no cheer of support. Everyone's petrified. Will the skies fall? Will the ground swallow us up?

My breath catches high in my chest. What would Dera do now? Should I pray? Yes, I'll pray. 'Aoi-aoi-aoi …'

'Stop that, dear.'

Where is Dera? It's impossible to single him out in the squash of bodies packed into the sacred precinct below.

'Aeson, can you see Dera?'

He leans over the balcony, muscles in his forearms tense as he swings forward on the wide ledge to peer under the arcades of the courtyard.

Rufius is wheezing with worry. 'Can you see my boys? Apollinos, where are you?'

We should have stayed together.

Aeson? His mouth gapes open in shock. 'Sacrilege. This is sacrilege. That centurion, he can't … Serapis, stop him!' Aeson's words blurt out in a panic.

Turn neck, turn: I must face Aeson to know he hears my words. He must snap out of it. Aeson must keep his wits. Twisting my neck hurts more everyday.

'Aeson, we are watching Dera's prophecy unfold. Dera's teacher, Antoninus, dead and buried now, saw it before him. I have seen it too. Serapis will die today.' My voice sounds far away from me.

I can't hold this position: my neck's seizing-up. Sweet Sophia, keep me supple, at least until Aeson is safe, keep me mobile. Henite would massage my spine when the tightness set in. A tear splats the pink granite ledge. It's mine but I can't feel my face.

This scene below, this was in my vision: black-hooded monks, helmets glinting in the sun, the centurion on the ladder climbing in our direction, the tall evil Archbishop, all fade in and out of focus, their edges brushed out like we're in a desert haze. Rubbing my eyes doesn't help solidify the scene. My vision is happening now. The marble ledge feels solid but this moment has collided with prophecy.

What's Aeson saying?

The sound's gone.

What's he looking at? Why's he pointing?

My head turns slowly, movement is thick; everything is slowing down. What's Aeson shouting about? Why's he climbing onto the edge? Rufius is trying to stop him. He's shouting too. They're looking at the ladder, but it's not the centurion Aeson's climbed on to the ledge to meet.

Sweet Sophia, it's Lanky! He's on the ladder, close behind the centurion. He's coming for Aeson.

Come on neck, bend. I know what happens next, but I must witness it, like a compulsion. I have to watch the events for real, for them to be real. That's it, an awkward angle but if I can hold this contorted body, one arm on the ledge, and lean my weight into my stick, I'll be able to see the demon coming. Come on, demon. I'm ready for you.

Lanky looks up at the centurion. So do we.

The centurion's at chin height now, level with the fourth floor. His mouth is wide open, ferocious like a lion roaring before a kill. Serapis waits, bushel of grain on his head – the grain he makes grow when he floods the Nile. The centurion swings the axe in circles to build up inertia, sunbeams flash white off the double-headed blade.

We hold our breath.

The axe swings into his jaw.

His attack gains force. There's a dent in the metal of Serapis' jaw. Hollow? The god is hollow! Splinters of wood chip and fly out at every bash of the axe. It's speeding up now, faster, faster he swings.

Sweet Sophia, the noise! My ears are working again. The mob is wild in the sacred precinct below … no thunder, no earthquake … only the sound of metal bashing metal again, and again, and again. Sobs choke up into my throat with each strike.

'Fake. Fake. Fake. Fake,' chant the monks.

Victory and relief heckles from the mob: they're jubilant.

'The sky's still there – '

'The sun's still shining – '

'The old gods are dead – '

Theophilus raises his arms, his black cloak spread out like bat's wings. 'In God's name, bring the false god to his knees. You see what tricks your priests have played with you. Hollow! The idol is hollow …'

The Archbishop rages on, but my gaze is fixed on Lanky. Sweet Sophia he's jumped on the ledge where Aeson waits for him. The one-eyed devil grins. They fly at each other like gladiators in the arena. Like dogs set on each other in a pit, they bare their teeth and lash their knives at each other. Hate makes men ugly. Their feet shuffle near the edge of the ledge, but they don't care if they fall …

Sweet Sophia! Aeson's down. Lanky throws himself on top of him, black cloak shrouds them both …

… Lanky's up. He grabs a fist full of Aeson's hair and yanks him up.

'Prepare to die, Pretty.' Lanky's knife is at Aeson's throat.

'Cassius, do something!' Rufius and Cassius try to grab Lanky's legs. The demon kicks back, sending Rufius flying.

I can't save him from down here. I need to get up on the ledge.

Sophia, give me the strength. Bless me with mobility, just this once. My arms are strong: I can pull my body up onto the ledge.

'Cassius, leave me – get Kiya off that ledge, dear.'

Now, crawl, crawl to him. His ankle. If I get his ankle I can topple him.

'I'll kill you Lanky.'

Got it.

Lanky lets out a yelp. 'Snake Bitch!'

Kick as much as you like, Demon. I won't let go. His free foot kicks me in the face. That hurt. My blood tastes metallic. I'm not letting go.

'Leave her ALONE!' Aeson punches him. The demon's head swivels as if it will turn right round on his neck. He's losing his balance; now's my chance … I don't have the strength to push you, but this broken body can pull you … I'm going to kill you demon. Shift my legs to the edge, that's it. Now, reach for his ankle with my other hand. Got it. You won't kick me off like a dog this time. Ready to fly, Lanky?

Aeson runs at us, lands stomach down on the ledge arms out stretched.

'KIYAAAAA!'

… Oh, Sweet Sophia, what have I done? My heart stabs in shock, my hand releases his ankle; Lanky's falling faster – he'll die before me … alarmed faces in the sacred precinct look up, fighting bodies part … we'll land by the foot of Serapis … the lightness of falling … Sophia will have eaten all the dormice by now. Keep her safe, Sweet Sophia …

54

RUFIUS

By Bacchus, she's thrown herself off. I knew she had balls under that dress.

'KIYAAAAAA!' Aeson stands frozen on the ledge, staring down at the sacred precinct in shock.

Lanky lands first, face down, black cloak on pink marble. Kiya floats down above him – her blue dress blown up like a pavilion. She lands on top of him and shrouds both of them in silk. Their bodies must be smashed – thank Bacchus we can't see the mess.

Aeson jumps down from the ledge and runs towards the main staircase. Dark stubble casts a shadow on his usually perfect, clean Roman shave.

'My boy – no one could survive that fall.'

'I'm not leaving her down there. She landed on Lanky – he might have broken her fall. I have to check. Go inside, Rufius. Bolt the doors. I'll be back for you.'

'Aeson, it's suicide to go down there, Aeson – '

Sweat hits my cheek as he spins to face me. Hope quivers in eyes that might have been painted by some Etruscan artist: tightly packed lashes frame sapphire ink-wells. They still turn me to pap.

'Rufius, go into your office and bolt the door.'

I can't stop him. He flies downstairs two steps at a time, the back of his tunic wet with sweat. If Theophilus spots him, he'll have him killed.

'My boy … Aeson, come back.' My words wheeze into a cough, smoke fills my lungs. Where's it coming from?

The books! They're burning the books. Below hooded monks throw armfuls of books onto pyres. Four, no five pyres burn. Trapped high in my chest, my breath halts. From up here the monks look like beetles. Librarians and temple slaves try to stop them. That monk, he's going to knife that young librarian … right through the chest. The boy looks down at the knife in surprise – I can't believe this is happening either. The others drop their weapons; they realise we've lost. That's it, run for your lives. Temple slaves and priests flee towards the entrance as more monks and soldiers squeeze into the sacred precinct. This is a greedy mob. The Archbishop's unleashed a merciless bacchae … *The Bacchae*! Not Euripides! His play will be on the Archbishop's heretical hit list. Athens had a copy, or did we pinch it? But what's left of the Athenian Library since the looting?

'Cassius, can your young eyes see Apollinos?'

'No, master. We should do as Aeson says and go inside, master.'

'Cassius, will you stop pulling on my toga … I must blow my nose.' I'm as snotty as a street kid. Cassius passes me a cloth. 'Thank you, Cassius. I'm too old for all this excitement, dear.'

Cassius sighs loudly and flings his arms around me. He's overwhelmed the poor thing. 'She had spirit, Kiya did, master.'

'She did indeed, my boy.' I pry him off me. At least I can save her bloody book. 'Cassius, we have work to do. Go into my office, find *The Book of Wisdom,* and the copy the scribe was in the middle of, and pack them into book bags – pack as many books as you can carry. Off you go.'

'Yes, master.'

'And don't forget to pack the originals – ' Scribes always miss things out or add their own bits. The task will hold his wits together. Mine too.

Kiya's stick. It looks sad without her on the marble floor. These knees haven't crouched down for years but if I hold on to the ledge

I can bend to reach it. Got it. I would have liked to buy her a new one. The cloth wrapped round the armpit rest is filthy. Oh, these old legs. My weight rests on it. Vanity prevented me using a stick. Who needs one when you have slaves?

What's that almighty groan?

'By Bacchus!' Serapis' head is breaking away. His enormous chin balances at the front of his neck, now a hinge of precious metals, bent and torn. The god's eyes are gone – the centurion has prised out the enormous sapphires and pearls. His neck is a yawning hollow. Screams yelp up from the courtyard as the great head creaks and topples forward in a deep bow. The mob scatters for cover under the arcades.

Biblos slaves join me on the balcony.

'Boys, back inside, back to work.'

They ignore me, rooted to the spot in amazement as Serapis' head spins and falls. We jump at the thud, the balcony trembles: the head's hit the floor.

'Serapis has sent an earthquake – '

The air is thick with silence, as if the temple is holding its breath. Biblos slaves brace themselves for the god's revenge. It's not Serapis they should fear now.

Theophilus steps up on to the steps of Serapis' inner sanctuary. 'The old gods are dead. Serapis was rotten wood and trickery. The gods are dead.'

A cheer goes up and travels outside on a wave of victory.

What a forlorn sight: the twisted scene of greed below us. Serapis' head smashed on impact, the huge skull cracked open on the marble floor. Serapis has lost his basket of grain. His nose is gone. The plates of metals are yanked loose at his neck like thousands of severed arteries. Precious beads and gems roll in all directions; soldiers chase them like children after marbles. Monks smash the statue with new confidence. Soldiers, intent on their plunder now nothing is sacred in the temple, yank off the silver, frantic for the layers of gold beneath.

This reminds me of the time I witnessed a pack of hyenas wrench apart a gazelle in Libya; the animal was transformed from grace to slivers of red flesh in moments.

Take that you scum. My spit dribbles down my chin. Panic wobbles in my gut. This must be what a slave feels like in the stadium: my death will be mere entertainment. Panic flicks its snakelike tail.

What's that scurrying? Mice! Mice peer over the neck's jagged edge and scuttle down the length of Serapis' arms – thousands of them scramble down to the god's hands and into the sacred precinct. They run for their lives like the few remaining priests and pagans.

A musty reek of dry rot and incense wafts out of the gaping hole at the neck of Serapis' body.

'Master, master – '

Thank Bacchus, it's Apollinos. The skinny old Greek limps behind Biblos slaves laden with books, ancient yellow scrolls tucked under armpits. There's a red gash in his leg.

'Apollinos, quickly Apollinos.'

One, two, three, four. Good, all here.

'That's it, boys, quick as you can, into my office. Pack those into book bags, as many as you can strap across you. Hurry, boys. Does someone have Apicius' *On the Art of Cooking?*

Saviour of Books she called me. I'll show you, priestess. I still have a few tricks tucked up my toga.

'Apollinos, keep an eye out for Aeson. He's gone after Kiya.'

'We saw Kiya fall, master. It would take a miracle to survive it.'

My old slave looks at my hand on the pit-rest of her stick. He's grief-stricken. So she got under your skin too did she? What's he muttering?

'What god are you praying to, Apollinos?'

'Serapis, master.'

'He can't help her now, dear.' I never thought to ask what god he prayed to before. 'The gods are dead. Men built this temple and it's up to us to salvage what we can of civilisation.'

Why's Cassius hovering in the doorway looking lost? 'Cassius, did you find *The Book of Wisdom?*'

He pulls the leather-bound codex from his bag. 'Here, master.'

I flick through the pages: new parchment and Tyrian ink. He loved her. Aeson's handwriting's certainly improved …

'*Cinaedus!*' The insult pricks like quills down my spine. That's Theophilus' steel voice.

Where is he? On the top step of the inner sanctuary, Theophilus surveys the spoils of battle in Hades' black cloak.

'Yes, dear?'

'Shush, master.'

He points up at me. Monks closest to him look in my direction.

'Heretic! You won't get out of here with those books, Rufius. You'll have to pass me first, Director of the Scriptorium.' He pronounces my title as if that too is an insult.

I chuckle and whisper for Apollinos' benefit. 'Ha! That's what he thinks, Apollinos.'

'*Cinaedus!* Bring down the heresies. Order your slaves to throw them on the fires or we will pry them from your sinful grip.'

'Apollinos, can you see Aeson down there with Kiya?' All I can make out is the blue dress I made Diana give her.

'Aeson's kneeling beside her body, master.'

'There's no time for mourning. Go and get him.'

Idiot! He can't take the main stairway without running into Theophilus. 'How many times do I have to tell you, take the slave stairs, Apollinos.'

'Yes, master.'

'Do you hear me? *Cin-ae-dus!* Bring down the books.'

Theophilus is furious. I can just about hear him above the cheers each time another piece of Serapis is thrown on the fires.

'Don't order me about, you jumped up bishop.'

He can't hear me. My voice won't project like it used to. Bloody smoke. My lungs can't take it. Now out with the offending mucus.

Can't get enough air to spit. Out with it! Yellow-brown gunk splats on the floor polished just yesterday by diligent temple slaves.

'Bah! That's what I think of …' Throw the insult Rufius, project your voice above the noise … 'you plebby Christian scum.'

The cheek of it! Monks just laugh at me. For once I'm being serious.

'*Cinaedus*, you are a stain …'

Theophilus' words are lost in the chanting of his monks.

'Cinaedus – '

'Cinaedus – '

Make yourself comfortable, Theophilus. You'll have a long wait.

Theophilus shouts orders at monks and points at the main staircase. Here they come. My heart drums in my ears, in sync with the pounding feet on the staircase. What air I can draw in makes me cough. The smoke's getting thicker. The whole machinery of my body totters. My feet can no longer feel the floor, or the soft leather sandals they're strapped into. I've never been this afraid before in my life.

Theophilus raises his staff and points it at me. Monks run ahead of him.

'Cassius get the boys inside. We're running out of time.'

'Master, you must come inside too. We have to bolt the door.' Cassius drags me away from the balcony. His nails pinch into my arm as he forces me inside my office.

'Boys, back inside. We have work to do.'

My office is a rush of activity: tables piled high with books; stray pages cover the floor dropped in the rush and confusion. My boys sob and mutter to themselves as they pass books to each other from the makeshift scriptorium to my main office. They must all be devotees of Serapis. Why didn't I realise that before? Why should I?

'Stop sniffling. Those scrolls are hundreds of years old. You'll damage the papyrus.' Let's get some order into this process. 'Right, boys, we don't have much time. What do we have in this pile here?'

We stare at the stacks of books and ancient papyri: all those words, sentences great men have angst over, contemplated, poured love and drained out their lives into. Defenceless books: many of them the only copies in existence, over a millennium of knowledge. Athens, Pergamum, Antioch, Rome, Carthage – the Great Library of Alexandria has begged, borrowed and stolen from them all. And for what?

Cassius' face is slack with despair. 'There's too many books to take in one go, master.'

'Take what you can, boys.'

A cough chokes up from my smoke-filled guts. My tongue's sticky on my lips. Licking them makes no difference.

'Wine, Cassius pour me a drink … no, guard the door. Just give me the bloody jug.'

That's better. I'm glugging like a vagrant.

'Keep at it, boys. That's it, get the bags strapped to your chests. Quickly.'

Poor Cassius looks ready to faint at the door of my office. The sword shaking in his hand is making me more nervous than I already am. His head darts from side to side – from the grand staircase to slave stairs. 'Master we must bolt the door. The monks have reached the second floor.'

'No! Wait for Aeson and Apollinos.'

'But, master the monks, they're nearly here.' His voice is a high-pitched panic.

Let's get this great mound of flesh I call my body onto the landing. Kiya's stick means I can move faster. My knees click and twinge; it doesn't look like I'll be having my massage today.

By Bacchus! What a bunch of savages: monks stop to bash the heads off the statues of the philosophers lining the stairs. Those old bores will slow them down at least.

I lean over the balcony and squint. There's her blue dress ... and there's the hermit lifting her body into his great black arms. What a sorrowful sight. Kiya's head hangs loose like a chicken that's just had its neck wrung. She's dead.

But where's Aeson?

55

RUFIUS

'Shut the door. Apollinos. Hurry!'

Thank Bacchus they made it! My old slave slams the door and throws down the iron bolt. Smash of stone and murderous shrieks is muffled now the office door's shut. The boys are terrified.

Aeson's hair is caked in blood. Where's it coming from ... is that a cut on his hairline?

'You're hurt my boy.' A coughing fit doubles me over. The smoke's getting thicker.

'Have you lost your mind, Rufius? We can't stay here. The Archbishop will be up the stairs in moments. We need to get to the slave staircase before that's overrun by monks too.'

Cassius opens his book bag for me to pass him the book I'm still clutching.

'Hold it open, Cassius. Apollinos, you should see Aeson's handwriting now, dear.'

Cassius takes *The Book of Wisdom,* and squashes it into the leather bag thrown across his chest.

'Are you mad, Rufius? Forget the books. Cassius – give me your sword. We won't get out of here without a fight. Rufius, you go first with Apollinos.'

I haven't seen that determined look on Aeson's face since the night I caught him in my library trying to pinch the very same book.

'No madder than usual, dear. There's another way. Shift those shelves back from the wall, boys.'

The boys are scared, but do as they're told. Apollinos puts his weight behind the bookshelves as the boys push. The bookcase shudders stacked with ancient scrolls, tube upon papyrus tube.

What's that? The room trembles. That must have been Serapis' torso. The thud is followed by butcherous screeches.

Aeson grabs me tight on the shoulders. It is a desperate grip.

'This is no time for interior decoration, Rufius.'

'Trust me, dear. Help the boys. Such brave boys. Push.'

The bookshelf scrapes as it drags on the marble, papyri bounce and scatter on the floor.

'Watch this.'

The wall's smooth. Where is it, where is it? My hand fumbles for the catch.

Here's the little lever.

Stone scuffs stone and separates to reveal a narrow vertical slash of darkness. The entrance to the hidden limestone passage slowly widens, grates and groans as the ancient mechanism opens onto a narrow passageway.

'In you go, boys. And you, Aeson.'

Aeson's face scrunches from grief to anger.

'You could have saved her! You could have made her go – ' His voice cracks.

Apollinos puts a hand on Aeson's shoulder to console him.

The pound and scrape of an army of disorderly feet makes the floor shudder. They're on this floor. We all look at the bolted door on the other side of the room.

'Blame me later. We need to get the boys to safety. 'Here, take this torch, Apollinos. I'll be right behind you.'

Apollinos shakes his head. 'No, master, I will not leave you.'

He guesses my intention.

'Apollinos, get – ' His eyes fill with tears. My hand lifts to stroke his cheek. That will make him worse. A slap across the face: that should do it.

'Take the boys, Apollinos. Keep them safe … my old friend.' My voice is soft.

He nods, takes the torch, stoops and bends his head to fit under the low doorway.

A thud on my office door lifts the iron bolt. It clanks free.

Aeson's strong legs stride past me across the room. He clicks the bolt into place. Oh the yearning to clean the cuts and grazes disappearing up his thighs under his short tunic, like I once did when he came home from school bullied by Library brats. He never cried.

'*Cinaedus* – '

'*Cinaedus* – '

'*Sinner* – '

'*Cinaedus* – '

'Fuck off! Filthy swine.' They terrify me but hearing my own voice gives me spirit for what I must do.

Aeson strides back across the office towards me. Anger replaced by urgency.

'Rufius, get inside the passage.'

'No, dear. This door needs to be closed or none of you will have a chance of escape. You must go now, Aeson.'

His bare shoulder, the smell of his skin calms me. We stare into the darkness: a low doorway roughly carved in the days of the Pharaohs. A cool briny dampness travels up from the entrance.

The mob's ransacking the room below us. Thuds, cheers, the educated voice of a librarian begging for his life … his last pained scream makes me want to piss. This is no longer my office, but my impatient grave.

'Go! Before I lose my nerve.'

Strong hands rest on my shoulders, turn me gently to face him. My breathing slows down in his grasp. The fury of the mob, the choking smoke, the fear falls away as I return his gaze. There are only his eyes, flickering as if a golden light is illuminating them from their depths. Drink them in, Rufius. Let this be the image I recall in my final moment. What is he searching for in my eyes? Some stolen treasure? 'I have nothing left to give, my darling boy.' Sobs stutter up from my stomach. 'W-was I ever more to you than an old fool?'

A faint smile begins in his eyes, but does not reach his lips. 'You made me, Rufius.'

The thump of hatred on the wooden door throws the bolt free again from its iron latch. Aeson dives on it; shining muscles force it back.

'Go, now.' The panic's gone from my voice. My belly is a bag of smoke, but my heart gives me courage. The foreign sensation propels me towards him, pushing his hard chest into the passageway. He looks disorientated as he shuffles backwards through stray papyrus. It's elating, the strength I have in my body from this new bravery. 'Mind your head.'

He ducks, bends his knees to fit under the low ceiling of the passageway.

'It will take you to the Necropolis.'

He looks shocked. At the change in me? I want to laugh from the lightness I feel.

'Now GO!'

The wooden door buckles, cracks and spits under the weight of the monks. They're working together now.

'Go on.' I push him further into the passage.

'You're coming with me, Rufius.'

'No chance of out-running them with my old legs. Go, my darling. Run.'

I understand for the first time why the Greeks put lovers into battle together. I would rather die than live without honour in his memory.

He leans forward and pulls me to him in an embrace. His smell, sea-salt and leather, coupled with a foreign sensation. So this is what it feels like to love from my heart, rather than my loins. This whole wretched life of mine was worth this one moment.

'You must go now, Aeson.'

He's frozen, hunched bent-kneed in the damp mouth of the passage. No matter, as long as I can get this bloody door back in place. No one can see the joins when it's closed. Now, let's push the door back in position. As long as Theophilus gets what he wants he'll be satisfied. And the Archbishop wants this old *cinaedus'* arse nailed to a crucifix. Don't think about it, keep pushing. They'll knock the door bolt free any moment. Every thrust hurts my old knees.

Wood splits. An axe winks maliciously through the splintered gash in the door. A hot fear burns my skin from the inside. The roar of the mob makes my stomach jerk. No time to vomit, Rufius.

The gap's narrowing.

What's he doing in there?

'There's a torch in the wall bracket. Pick it up and RUN!'

Nearly there … one more heave and I'll have the secret stone back in place. This will be my final act. Oh no! Accompanied by incontinence it seems from the warm wetness trickling between my legs. Skidding in my own urine is not the way to do it.

Right, let's regain my footing, that's it. Now, heave.

Another hack: a metal axe head glints through the wood.

Push, Rufius, Push.

Sweat drips from my hair onto my dry lips. Salty. I miss the dinner I'll never eat. The wine jug's still on my desk where I left it.

No time. I cry and push, grunt and push.

The old stone grates. The black gap narrows. I have the chance to do my duty before I die: a father's duty … one more push, Rufius … on an empty stomach, incontinent and bloody sober. Well Bacchus, it seems the only god I ever really worshipped will have the last laugh.

56

AESON

What's Rufius trying to do, close the door to the passageway? His old legs slip and slide on the wet marble; he's pissed himself.

'Run, my boy, RUN!' His voice is fast and shrill like an ibis protecting her nest.

'Rufius, leave the door. Get in here.' My voice echoes in the low passageway hacked into rough granite. Looks like it slopes downwards. It's dark in here. One torch doesn't throw enough light. Biblos slaves must have taken the rest from their brackets.

Rufius pants and pushes.

'Dear boy, you won't outrun them with me. GO!'

Stone grates and another inch of yellow light is shut out from his office. He's nearly got it closed.

'Rufius, for Serapis sake, get in here.' My voice cracks. 'I know you love me.'

'Stop bloody gibbering. RUN.' His face is red with tears; he grunts against the will of the ancient stone, wet sandalled feet skid.

'You'll do yourself an injury, Rufius.'

'I beg you, dear, go.'

The stubborn old fool intends dying in his office. I'll have to go and get him.

Thuds at the door make the room shudder. The monks have given up with the axe – they're battering it down. We don't have long before the mob break through.

Phew! If he watered his wine his urine wouldn't reek. If I turn to the side, I'll get back through the slit.

'No, no, Aeson do as you're told. I'm your father …'

His legs give way as I gather his flesh into my arms.

'Put me down, dear.'

I'll struggle to carry him through the narrow slit between the ancient granite and the wall.

'You're coming with me. Now, get in there before I push you in … '

By Serapis! That thud dislodged the door from the top hinge.

'Get inside, Rufius. Sideways, go in sideways.'

'I'm too fat, dear. What … what, I'm not a cow to be pushed and … '

Another thud and the top bracket chinks on the marble floor. A hand gripping an axe reaches through.

'*Cinaedus,* we'll roast your fat arse.'

'That's it, dear. Push!' Fear got the better of him. 'That's it, now in you come, my boy.'

He's in. Now let's squeeze back through myself.

Just in time. The door flies inwards. Monks rush into the room.

'Let me pass, brothers.'

That's Theophilus' voice. Rufius' face is furious in the torchlight.

'Rufius, take the torch. Go now.'

Feet pound into the office.

'They're gone!'

'What?' The Archbishop's fury makes his usually steel voice judder.

'There's nobody here.'

'Impossible. Search the place. Find him.'

Bookcases bang as they're pushed over, and book trunks hacked to pieces.

'Wait. Brothers! The walls. Check the walls. This temple's full of secret chambers, hidden rooms. I know you're here, *Cinaedus,* crouched in some hole!'

A monk points at the gap.

'Your Holiness, look: a hole in the wall.'

Monks run towards the slit, push each other to get through. It's too narrow; only one man can enter sideways. Daylight's blocked as monks gather around the narrow entrance. Wild sun-scorched desert faces flicker in the torchlight.

My feet are planted firmly on the floor, cool granite either side of me. Cassius' sword in my right hand, my faithful gold knife in my left. I'm ready for them.

'Rufius, go.' My voice is a rough whisper.

A monk, wide-eyed and deranged, glares at me through the gap. He tries to squeeze through sideways. One thrust of my sword slices right through his neck. Got you! He falls, half his body inside, half outside the passage.

The monk behind him steps on his chest, sideways to the wall.

'Got you too.'

Blood explodes into my face as the arteries in the monk's neck spurt their contents.

The next launches from the head of the second dead monk, and throws himself sideways through the narrow gap.

'In the name of Christ!'

My knife: up and under his stomach. That's it. His hands fumble to hold in his guts as they empty, hot and stinking onto my feet.

'Arh!' Sharp pain; that's a knife through my thigh. How?

Bastard monk the size of a dwarf's crawled in over the dead bodies. Keep your balance, Aeson. Ignore the pain.

Rufius stabs the monk through the back before he's on his feet. 'Take that, dear!'

He grabs the monk's axe.

'Rufius! What are you doing?'

'Giving you a hand, dear.'

'The heretics are in that secret room, Archbishop.' The monk's sycophantic pant makes me want to kill them all.

'Kill them, brothers.' We can hear Theophilus, but we can't see him. All we can see are the angry faces of the monks.

'Rufius, stand back.'

A skinny monk swipes at me as he throws himself through the gap. 'Pagan pigs.'

His throat throbs under my left arm as I slit his throat. His head falls back slack from his body where he's fallen in the doorway. If their bodies pile up high enough, that will create a temporary barrier.

'Kill them, I said.' Theophilus is impatient.

'Rufius, I'll hold them off. Take the torch and go. Now!'

Take that! Madly I stab at each one that tries his luck. Their numbers work to my advantage. In their crazed hurry to kill us, they've blocked the small gap in the doorway.

One by one they fall.

Rufius kicks at heads. The cluck of a crushed skull makes him puke. It's a different thing to whipping a disobedient slave.

Here's the next red-faced desert madman climbing over the fallen bodies. Rufius thrusts the torch as I follow up with the blade. The mad monk falls back against the monks behind him and the gap gives me a brief view of the office.

My bladder slumps. The room's full.

New arrivals pull bodies away from the entrance.

'Kill the pagans.' They scream their war cry.

How long can we keep this up? My thigh's a wooden ache where I was stabbed.

'Brothers, empty the books into the room and torch it.' Theophilus' orders halt the frenzy to enter the passageway. The Archbishop must think we're trapped in a room. That may work to our advantage.

'Theophilus, the fool!' Rufius whispers.

Books, scrolls, a chair leg catapult through the gap and force us further back down the passage.

'Burn in Hell, pagan pigs.'

Torches fly through the gap.

Rufius' hand is on my back.

'Oh my books, my books! You ignorant bastards.' Rage makes his voice squeak.

Monks snigger at his girly lisp.

'Burn, *Cinaedus.* Burn with your books.'

'Burn *cinaedus* – '

'Burn heretics – '

Oil! They're throwing on oil. More torches. This thing's going to go up. Books ignite and flare, bodies of monks hiss like snakes as the flames burn through cloaks to their flesh.

Rufius drops the torch in a coughing fit.

I must get him out of here before he chokes. The fire's eating the air. I'll have to carry him.

Flames lick the walls around the low entrance.

'That hermit … he said …'

'I thought you'd know better than to listen to prophecy, Rufius.' I've never once seen him consult a soothsayer.

'Hold this.'

He takes my torch. His wheezing is sharp, dangerously quick.

'Let's get you … in my arms … that's it. Got you.'

'How far is it?'

'Too far to carry my old blubber, dear.'

Bent-legged, shuffling down the low passage with Rufius in my arms is killing my leg. Small mercies we're travelling downhill to the Necropolis, but the staleness of the air worries me more than the heat on my back. Once I've put enough distance between us and the fire we'll be safe from the flames but the smoke only has one way to go if they close that door …

'Rufius, how far into the Necropolis does this go?'

An unintelligible groan is all he can manage.

'Rufius?'

He's losing his strength. The torch he's holding waves around and knocks against the tunnel wall.

'Keep hold of that torch, Rufius.'

'Shit, fucking ceiling.' It's getting lower.

Come on legs, keep going. I can't see more than a foot's pace in front of me.

What's that rumble? The door. They're closing the door to the secret passage. The heat, smoke and sickly smell of burning monk flesh makes me retch. The final thud of stone into its groove shuts out the murderous chants of the monks.

It's getting harder to breathe. That doorway was the only ventilation. The ceiling's jagged surface forces me to bend nearly double over Rufius.

'Rufius, don't give up. Rufius.'

The torch swings and drops from his hand.

There's no way I can hold Rufius and the torch. Let it go. There's only one way out – I don't need my eyes. I limp into the blackness.

Must keep going. At least it's downhill. We must be beneath ground level now. It's cooler, but the smoke followed us. My lungs are tight.

Rufius' feet hit the walls. Careful, don't break his legs. The passage is narrowing. What if I adjust my angle to the side, like this. That's better.

Breathe.

Can't breathe.

Have to breathe.

The air's putrid down here. It's thick, hard to suck in a breath at all. Shit.

Don't panic.

Rufius' limbs loll heavy and slip in my sweaty grasp.

'Rufius, hold on, Rufius.' Stay with me old man. Don't leave me now. Not now.

Endless blackness, more jutting ceilings, no sign of an end to this stifling heat.

Keep going, Aeson. The exit can't be too far now. We must be passing directly under the Serapeum. The ground's levelled. If it's level that means we'll have to head upwards to exit. Don't think about it. Keep going.

Curse you to Hades, Theophilus.

My sandalled feet shuffle, back edges against the limestone wall. Mind his legs.

Need to clean my nostrils. Too much filth and dust up them to breathe. Every tiny inhale makes me cough.

We could lie down, folded in each other's arms just for a moment.

Mustn't crumble to that image, mustn't imagine stopping.

'I refuse to die in the way you've ordained, Theophilus.'

The tunnel echoes with my voice …

A violent cough. I gag, desperate for air. The lack of air will kill us if we don't get out of here, and fast. Focus, Aeson. Forward, legs. I can do this. Ignore the pain.

Rufius, a dead-weight now, pulls my arms low to the ground. He's stopped wheezing.

'Rufius?'

No sound. I strain my neck to reach my cheek to his mouth: a faint snuffle. He's alive.

I push on, readjusting Rufius' limp body in my grip at every step. Jaw clenched and defiant I struggle uphill. Don't give up, Rufius.

I refuse to die down here.

Every step is a great achievement now. Am I moving at all? I'm not certain. My body is foreign to me, like that first attempt to propel my pen across a page. I want to give up, but I won't.

The rooftops of Alexandria tease me. I wish I could be running to my death along red tiles under a turquoise sky. To see its skyline once more, the Great Harbour, the Pharos. The thought gives my legs some strength.

I will see Alexandria one last time.

Keep going, just keep going.

We've travelled in a straight line the whole way. The exit must come out somewhere in the centre of the Necropolis. I can see the rough-hewn tunnel walls.

Or is my tired mind playing tricks on me?

Yes, I can see the edges of the tunnel.

'Rufius, we're nearly there … Rufius?'

Rufius

By Bacchus, I must have been out for the count. Where am I? Is this the Underworld? The sky's dusk blue. Why do I feel like I'm riding a camel?

'Rufius, we made it.' Aeson's voice. I'm in his arms; the familiar briny-leather smell of his sweat is a comfort. He's limping, that's why it's such a jerky ride.

'Rufius?' His voice is faint … the Serapeum, we were in the secret passage, fighting monks. That's the last thing I remember. I must have passed out. Never had the stomach for blood. The poor boy, he must have carried me the whole way.

'Put me down, dear.'

'Ouch!' My arse. No need to drop me.

Aeson?

Has he collapsed? His eyes are closed.

Come on, elbows: lift and pull. If my gut didn't get in the way, I might be able to push myself onto my knees a little easier than this. That's it.

'Aeson? What's wrong, dear?' Panic throbs fast in my chest. His tunic's covered with blood. Not his – monk blood. Does he have a heartbeat? Need to check. Let's get my ear closer. Yes, there's a distant thump in his chest. Thank Bacchus! Perhaps he's just exhausted from carrying my fat rump.

'Please, dear. Wake up.' Shaking his arm does no good. At least he's breathing.

Where's my boys? They left ahead of us. This ancient tomb's deserted. Tall columns stretch up into the twilight, row upon row of loculi cut neatly into limestone. It's still hot, but the air has the salty freshness of the ocean in it. The stars are out. White underbellies of seagulls fly overhead: are they the only living thing here?

Something's happened. Biblos slaves would not have deserted us … Apollinos needs me.

'Aeson, dear boy. Wake up.' Out cold. His leg's caked in dry blood.

What's that shuffling?

Probably the surf scuffing the shore in the distance. Calm yourself, Rufius. Apollinos must be close by; he wouldn't desert me … and Cassius, and where's my new young body slave?

I want to call out to them, but something's made me afraid to raise my voice.

There it is again: a shuffle: feet … above us … at ground level.

'Apollinos, is that you?' I sound like a timid virgin. 'Apollinos, come down here and help me.' That was an order.

'I'm sorry, master.' His voice came from up there, above the tomb.

'Apollinos, where are you, boy?'

More shuffling feet, dirt kicked over the edge. There he is. I can just about make out his gangly shape in the twilight. The old slave's being pushed forward, pelvis out, torso bent backwards, awkward and contorted … and what's that … a blade at his neck? My throat dries.

More Biblos slaves, all with knives at their throats, are pushed forward, necks pulled back. Dark figures hold the row of slaves at the edge of the tomb. My poor boys! Their captors hide behind them.

'Rufius! So you made it out then, eh?'

Turk! I know that cheeky street-sharp voice anywhere.

There he is. He strolls along the line of prisoners. The rogue's dressed as a soldier … more like an actor with that old-fashioned breastplate he's wearing. His face is a ghoulish blur under his torch. I've never liked being looked down on. It irritates me.

'Turk, what in Hades do you think you're playing at ...?'

Oh, I see, that pimp's changed sides. Those knives at my boys' necks belong to monks. I can just make out their hooded cloaks. The scoundrel!

Aeson's still breathing. If I whisper they won't hear me from up there.

'Aeson, stay here. Play dead. I'll deal with Turk.' Can he hear me?

'Kissing Pretty goodnight, are yer? How sweet!'

Come on, knees, up you push ... on to my feet. That's it. If I walk to the middle of the tomb things will look less of a blur up there. What's that brightness behind me? The Serapeum burns on its mount. Fires rage on its terraces, the canal below it, and Lake Mareotis beyond glows orange.

Turk follows my gaze.

'Shame! That put an end to our little book business, eh?' He juts his chin up, teeth glint in the torch.

'Trading with swine now, Turk?'

The monks growl and curse. Spit as much as you like, dears.

'Pagan scum, I'll slit your neck.' That was a monk's snarl. Cassius whimpers and falls to his knees. The monk with a knife to the poor boy's throat kicks the backs of Cassius' legs again. How dare they manhandle my boys.

'These slaves have committed no crime. I'm the one you want.'

'Oh, yes. The Archbishop – my new mate Theophilus – he'll be well pleased when I deliver the *cinaedus'* secret her-eti-cal library, won't he, eh?' Should earn a fortune for that lot of books, eh!'

What's he pointing at? The books bags are in a pile near the exit to the tunnel.

'Ha! And I thought you had brains, Turk. You disappoint me. You won't get a single copper piece for those books. They'll burn, every last one of them.'

'You're right there, *cinaedus*. We'll burn your enormous arsehole along with the books.'

'Oooo! And I'll stoke the flames with my enormous farts, dear.'

The monk pushes Cassius aside. Oh shit, humourless monk coming at me … now what? Aeson's knife, where is it?

'Arhh – ' That shrill shriek of pain and then the silence is horribly familiar. Who's been killed?

'Leave my boys alone.'

White tunics of Biblos slaves flash as Turk waves his torch to see who's been knifed.

A monk falls forwards from behind Apollinos. That's it shove him over the edge. The thud on the ground as the monk falls on the far side of the tomb floor makes me jump. A silver hilt sticks out from his back.

More monks fall forward from behind Biblos slaves. My boys look as surprised as I am.

Hands reach down, pull knives from the monks' backs or slit throats to finish them off.

Who's up there?

'Turk, man, you double-crossing bastard.'

Crocodile! That flaky-skinned street urchin … and there's more of Turk's gang. The one with the eye-patch, the tattooed Druid and three or four more wipe their knives clean on monks' cloaks. Ha! They didn't even see them coming. Ha! Ha! It's a mutiny.

Crocodile lunges at Turk. Ha! I could fight better than that; waving his torch about won't save him.

'Turk. Fight me, man, you coward.'

Oh why couldn't Crocodile just stab him in the back and be done with it? Why the display of brawn?

'Come on, Crocodile, give it to him. Ha! Outwitted by one of your own, Turk, dear.'

Turk juts his chin and pulls a short sword from his scabbard.

They circle each other; the gang watch. What's Cassius shaking his finger at?

'Master, look out – '

A monk jumps off the bottom step. He's got a knife. Oh shit. My stomach flips. Back to the tunnel …

He's got me by my tunic.

'Help!'

'Not so fast, *cinaedus!*' He's jumped me. My knees won't hold his weight and mine … down I go. Off, get off me … he's on my back, pushing my face into the dirt. Not the hair. A cold blade's at my neck … he means to slit my throat …

Aeson! Those are my boy's sandalled feet – left foot dark with his own blood.

'Get your filthy hands off him.' My boy's voice is raspy. 'Drop the knife, monk.'

The monk's raised his weight off me, his arm jerks backwards, elbow into Aeson's groin.

'Arh!' Aeson's gasp. My boy stumbles backwards on to his heels. He's over, in the dust. Get up, Aeson …

'Leave him to me, brother.' It's the hermit. He appears like a bloody genie. The African's huge legs tense as he grips the monk by the neck and gives it a sharp twist. Snap of breaking bones makes me shiver. That's the end of him.

'Turk, man, I should have slit your throat years ago.'

We look up at the edge. Croc has Turk in an arm lock, knife at his throat.

'Well boys, what shall I do with him?'

'He'd make a perfect latrine slave, dear.'

Ha! Turk looks ridiculous: flabby gut fallen out under his breastplate.

'Tuck yourself in, dear! Your gut puts mine to shame!'

That got a laugh from what's left of his gang.

'Cut off a hand.'

'A leg – '

'Cut off both legs – '

'I wouldn't want to be on the wrong side of you, dear boys.'

'Aeson, you decide, man. What's the punishment for betrayal?'

Biblos slaves run down the steps to me. There's no time for fussing. The urgent throb in my gut's telling me we have to get out of the city.

'Apollinos, go to Biblos. Find Diana. We're leaving Alexandria. Theophilus may think I'm dead, but he'll send his hounds to loot Biblos. We take the next ship to Rome.'

Will my Alexandrian boy stay here in Alexandria with his friends? He's a man now. I have to let him go. Look where control got us.

Cassius and my young body slave help Aeson to his feet, weight on his good leg.

'You're gang leader now, Croc. It's up to you.' My boy's weary.

Croc pushes Turk over to the man with the eye-patch. 'I'll decide your fate later, Turk.'

'I'm going with Rufius.' Aeson's voice is a mixture of regret and resolve.

He's coming with me? My heart calms. I feel like I've been holding my breath since he left ten years ago and now I can breathe again.

The hermit rests a hand on Aeson's shoulder. 'I buried Kiya, lad. Her soul is at peace.'

Aeson puts his hand on the African's and nods.

The hermit picks up a torch and raises it in the air so we can see each other. He looks down to face me. 'Brother, the Great Harbour is overrun with soldiers and the Prefect has enforced a curfew on the city. Any man without his authority on the streets at night will be arrested.'

'Well, I won't abandon my household … my family …'

'The safest route out of Alexandria is by river or over land.'

'Go, Apollinos. Fetch Diana.'

'You can't travel with an entourage of slaves. You must be inconspicuous.'

'And what do you mean by that, dear?'

Aeson limps forward. 'Apollinos, we will travel separately.' Aeson's voice has my authority in it. By Bacchus, he's my son. 'At Biblos change into rough cloaks – you'll find a guide on Venus Street to take you across the desert. Meet us at Aswan. We'll regroup there and find a tribesman to take us out of Egypt.'

'Yes, master.' He clicks his fingers for the slaves to follow.

My poor boys look afraid to leave me. 'Don't worry, dears. Apollinos will take care of you.'

Croc jumps down from the ledge, runs over to Aeson and plants a boisterous slobber on his lips. They laugh their old we-got-away-with-it laugh. I've heard it before; it used to make me jealous.

'Man, you crazy fucker! Only you could climb the Serapeum wall!'

'What's that noise?'

Dera and Croc run to the top of the steps. They don't say anything, they just stand there looking east towards the city. Aeson and I climb the steps up to ground level to see what they're staring at.

It looks like a funeral procession winding up Serapis Street, a twinkling line of torches. Instead of turning left towards the Necropolis, the lights snake down the Canopic Way.

Patch pokes the air with his finger. 'Heading for the Theatre, I reckon. Look there's a pyre burning in the Theatre, see.'

'Serapis knows what poor bastards they're burning.'

'I imagine, dear, that Theophilus is roasting something far more impressive than a bunch of heretics.'

'Serapis.' Aeson's tone is bitter.

'That's the Archbishop's style dear … in full view, so the whole city can watch the cremation.'

The hermit turns to Aeson and I. 'We must go. Alexandria won't be safe tonight. Those monks have a taste for blood. Tonight they will do unspeakable things.'

58

RUFIUS

Does the hermit seriously think I can pass for a fisherman with my dyed hair?

'I'm not getting in that thing, dear. I'll sink it.'

The hermit steadies the boat, checking both sides of the canal for people. Water laps against the wooden hulls of colourful fishing boats as they bob in the torchlight by the bridge.

Aeson takes my hand to help me in. Thank Bacchus my Biblos slaves went with Apollinos. They would never have forgiven me for such demeaning transportation. What a life fishermen must have, paddling down these mosquito-infested canals, back and forth to the lake everyday. Doesn't bear thinking about. These reed sacks the hermit made us throw round our shoulders reek of fish.

'Not even a cushion, dear. It stinks worse than a smokery. Bah! We're doing the owner a favour pinching his boat.'

Aeson pulls the oars back slowly in time with the hermit. I can't see his face, but I know he's nervous. 'Shush, Rufius. Keep your voice down.'

There's the city wall, coming into view ahead of us. I can't see any guards on the bridge. Why are Aeson and Dera being so cautious?

'Every last city guard will be in the Agora looting the temples, dear. What – '

'Rufius, shush! Alexandria's under curfew.'

It's such a squash in here. We should have taken a bigger boat.

'Who goes there?' The bridge guard's voice makes me bounce on the hard wood. Give a pleb an iota of power and they act like the bloody Emperor. The bridge is almost above our heads … so where's the bossy guard?

The hermit stands and speaks in his slow, level voice. At least he pronounces all his consonants.

'We are just fishermen, sir. We request permission to pass under the wall to fish in Lake Mareotis.'

The guard peers over the bridge, his torch held out in front of him. Well, that's a first: a bridge guard dressed in full armour.

'Oooo, isn't he grand!'

'Shush!' Aeson turns to face me. It's impossible to make out his features but I know he's frowning.

'Why's there three of you fishing together? You lot usually fish alone.'

'Safety in numbers, sir.'

He sucks the night air in through his teeth, coughs and spits. Delightful manners, dear! His gob plops somewhere in the black water near the boat.

'Gutless fishermen,' he mutters loud enough for us to hear him.

Dera stands, huge black legs spread wide on the curved sides of the hull, and sways with the movement of the boat to retain his balance. What a man. He wouldn't look out of place in the arena. Aeson holds his breath in anticipation.

'Why should I let you pass?'

Oh, I've had enough of this. Since when does a bloody bridge guard pose a threat?

'Because a gold coin might put a smile on that ugly face of yours, dear.'

Aeson groans.

'Who's calling me ugly?'

'Never you mind, dear. You'll feel like a beauty after a night on Venus Street. Whores will tell you anything if you pay them well enough.'

He disappears from the bridge. That's the clank of the gate bolt being released, the slap of his sandals on the bridge steps … here he is, the surly oaf. He must have outgrown his old armour years ago.

'Show us yer money, old man.'

He leers over us, one hand gripping the hilt of his sword, the other outstretched towards us.

Come on, purse, let's have you. Here it is, tied inside my fishy tunic. What I'd give for a bath.

'Hand it to him, Aeson, will you, dear.'

The bridge guard holds the coin up to his torch, bites it between his teeth and grunts. What's he going to do, eat it?

'Where did a bunch of poor fishermen get a gold coin, that's what I want to know … an' you don't talk like a fisherman talks.'

I'm bored of this oaf.

'The Serapeum. Where else, dear man? What are you doing here when the rest of the city guard is looting the temple? I do hope your colleagues give you your fair share of the profits.'

'What, no one told me …' His breastplate clanks as he stuffs the coin under his tunic.

That's it: back up the steps you go, dear. His sandals slap along the wall and out of earshot.

'Ha! Off we go, dears. Put your backs into it. I want off this stinking excuse for a boat as soon as possible.'

'Rufius, will you keep your mouth shut. He might alert the army.'

How can a beauty travel the Empire and retain his innocence?

'You still have a thing or two to learn about people, dear. We'll finish your education when we reach Italy.'

My gut's tight and I'm sweating so much my tunic's stuck to my skin under this fish sack. The relief of being outside the city walls has turned to apprehension. The sight of so many boats on fire in Lake Mareotis harbour makes me queasy.

Dera and Aeson stop rowing and look at the lake port. Dera exhales with a low whistle. 'Deserted as the streets of the Necropolis. The looters have been and gone.'

Taverns and shops along the port are shut up, some have had their windows smashed in, and furniture and rubbish litter the street that runs parallel to the lake. The torches have not been lit tonight and the flames from burning boats nearest to the port don't throw much light out here. We're swamped by the blackness of the lake. It feels like we're being swallowed up by the dark.

I feel a tantrum coming on. I've not eaten since midday – even this fish sack's starting to smell appealing.

'If those looters have burnt Biblos, I'll, I'll . . .' My shoulders slump forward. I don't have the energy to throw a temper fit. Aeson's hand on my shoulder is a comfort at least.

A great blast of noise – like an avalanche of rocks falling – comes from the city. We turn towards Moon Gate. Can't see a thing from here.

There it is again. It's coming from the Serapeum. Aeson stands up in the boat to get a better view.

'They must be pulling down the great columns that support the temple.'

And I thought I would get old and die here in Alexandria. It was home for a while. Where in the world will an old *cinaedus* rest his fat old knees now?

'Aeson, sit down, dear. Exile isn't so bad.' I fell in love.

'He's right, lad. We must go, there's a long journey ahead of us.'

Lake Mareotis stretches out into infinite blackness; it will take us to the Nile, then up river into Upper Egypt. Perhaps we can charter a decent boat and crew further up river. This is going to be an uncomfortable journey. By Bacchus, I hate boats.

The oars slosh in the water. Despair hangs in the silence between us.

* * *

We'll find no rest in any town along the Nile tonight. Pyres rage high from of the Temple of Antinous; their flames light up the riverbank. What a sad sight.

'Looks like the destruction has spread down river, brothers. Every Temple of Antinous we've passed has been in flames.'

Does that giant hermit have to state the obvious?

'The Emperor Hadrian would turn in his grave, dear.'

'You're shivering, Rufius.' Aeson offers me his fish sack.

'Don't be soft, Aeson. It's boiling, dear. I'm shaking with rage.'

Perhaps Rome's not the best destination. What if this new law condemning *cinaedi* is actually enforced … *in avenging flames in the sight of the people*? Bloody intolerant Emperor this one, and now his head's stuck up the church's arse it's only going to get worse. At least the lawyers who drafted it made some concession for a final show of exhibitionism.

'Here, Rufius, I pinched a pot of Turk's Desert Honey.'

Ha! That's my boy. What did Apollinos say? – *once a thief, always a thief.*

'Shall we retire to my villa on the Naples coast? It's near Baia.' I was joking, but why not? Retirement has never occurred to me. But look where being Director of the Scriptorium got me: on a stinking fishing boat dressed in a sack!

'What do you think, Aeson?' Please say you'll come. My heart pounds with longing. Bacchus, do not part us again.

'Really, Rufius! Would you retire to the coast?' Is that hope in his voice? 'It might be an idea to keep a low profile …' He's worried about the laws too, about a *cinaedus* who refuses to hide his tasselled tunics and jewels in the closet.

'We could copy a few more versions of *The Book of Wisdom* in honour of little Kiya, dear.'

'Thank you for saving Kiya's book, Rufius.'

'Ha! We gave the Archbishop the run around, didn't we?'

The hermit clears his throat. 'I will make a copy of *The Book of Wisdom* in Henite's native tongue. Coptic is the language of her people. She would like that.'

'Of course, Dera. You take the book.'

Aeson is pensive … I know when he's thinking. His rowing has fallen out of time with Dera's strong strokes. My boy never was able to multitask.

'Rufius, you know, I felt a little cheated when you sent me off to Apollinos to learn to write. I mean, Apollinos was a brilliant teacher, but … '

'But you wanted to learn the ropes from an old *cinaedus*, is that it? Ha!'

'You must stop calling yourself that now, Rufius.'

'What, at my age, dear? I'm too old to jig to the beat of a different drum …' My voice is shrill in the night … like the stars are listening to us. '… now I've lost my eyebrows, you mean?' With all this sweating they must be halfway down my face.

Aeson's laughter echoes up into the night sky. It lifts me; I want to laugh long and hard, until the laughter turns to tears and back to laughter again.

The hermit chuckles. 'You are blessed with a lightness of spirit, Master Librarian. It is a gift, to see life's comedy, even on a night like this.'

'Oh, it's no joke, dear. A *cinaedus* without his eyebrows is a very serious matter.'

Σ

HISTORICAL NOTE

Cinaedus comes from *kinaidos,* the Greek word for an effeminate buggeree. A *cinaedus* was an adult male who dressed effeminately, wore make up and the Latin insult implied that he was the receptive partner. The Ancient Romans defined their sexuality not on a spectrum with gay at one end and straight at the other, but whether you conquer, or submit. Gender was not the issue. For the Romans, if you were a rich adult man, you were expected to conquer and penetrate. It was a social outrage to deviate from the hard ideal of Roman masculinity, wear make-up and bend over for your pleasure. On the other hand, it was perfectly acceptable for boys to submit to older men as long as the boys had sprouted soft down on their faces and were showing the signs of manhood. Once a youth had grown a full beard, he was expected to take the 'active' role. Julius Caesar, for example, was accused of being a *cinaedus* by his political opponents due to a rumoured interlude with King Nicomedes when he was a young soldier – and too old to play the receptive role. The laws which condemned the *cinaedi* became harsher under the Christian Emperors. In 390 AD, a law was passed which sentenced *cinaedi* to death by public burning.

There are several sentences or phrases in the manuscript commonly referred to as *Pistis Sophia* (called *The Book of Wisdom* in the novel) that are a mystery even to scholars. The manuscript was bought by the British Museum in 1785 from the heirs of Dr. Askew, and is catalogued as Askew Codex MS.Add.5114 in the British Library. It is possible the book was hidden at some point in fourth century Egypt, when non-canonical texts were condemned as heretical, a copy of an earlier Greek original. The book contains Jesus' secret teachings to his disciples after his resurrection on the Mount of Olives and the story of Holy Sophia's, or Faith Wisdom's fall into matter, and her journey back to the Father.

Alexandria had been under Roman rule for three hundred years by this point. Although it is a Hellenic city, I assume a fair amount of Latin would have entered the language and so refer to gods and temples with both their Greek and Roman names. Certainly there is evidence of both Greek and Roman temples in the city at this time.

Several conflicting accounts of the events leading up to and including the destruction of the Serapeum in 391 A.D. have survived. The two contemporary accounts are from the Christian historian Rufinus' *Ecclesiastical History* and the pagan historian Eunapius' *Lives of the Philosophers.* Neither of them were eyewitnesses. There are other historians (Socrates, Sozomen and Theodoret) who wrote about the destruction of the Serapeum, but were not contemporary to the events. It is probable that the Christian accounts are as hyperbolic in their exaggeration of bloodshed as is Eunapius' conflicting insistence that the soldiers met with no pagan resistance when they attacked the statues in the Serapeum. My only firm conclusion of the historical sources is that the contemporary accounts are so starkly in opposition that none of them present the actual events and so I have taken the liberty of assuming, rightly or wrongly, that the truth resides somewhere between the two. I've cherry-picked elements from Socrates and Sozomen's later accounts to add some pagan spice.

Please note that any apparent departure from history is to be blamed entirely on Rufius Biblus Catamitus.

ACKNOWLEDGEMENTS

I am deeply grateful for the guidance of so many historical experts that it would be exhaustive to list them here, but I would especially like to thank Dr David Bagchi, not only for his historical wizardry, but also his literary suggestions; Dr Kelly Olsen, fashionista of the Ancient Roman World; Dr Craig Williams for a fascinating interview; Dr. Jennifer Inglehart for allowing me to not only gatecrash, but present at Durham University's *Romosexuality* Conference; Dr Alexander Petrov, Director of the Moscow Library for Foreign Literature who oversaw the most recent translation of the Askew Codex and his kind invitation to deliver a paper for the International Russia and Gnosis Conference, and Dr Nersessian, curator of the Askew Codex for giving me permission to view the manuscript in 2004 – and for his patience and enthusiasm while I picked his brains. It was during those long days in the Oriental Reading Room at the British Library poring over the manuscript that Rufius first spoke to me.

A warm thank you to the novelists who so generously shared their creative process for writing the ancient world – Steven Saylor, Bernadine Evaristo OBE, Allan Massie CBE and José Luis de Juan. I'm grateful for creative feedback from D.D. Johnston, Dr Bethan Jones, Allan Massie and José Luis – as well as tea in Deià in view of Robert Graves' house.

Amicus means friend in Latin, and I owe so much to all those friends who came on the journey with me, and some I met along the way. Thank you to Martin for believing in Rufius and James for his sharp editorial eye – and to Barbican Press for taking a punt on a novel partly inspired by an obscure Latin insult. Also for Christina and Emilio's cartography help, Jude's proofing; Miles and Patricia Walton, Phoebs, Amanda, Angela, Richard, Frode, Fizz, Geoff and Kat's firm faith. Eternal love to both Davids for letting me bore them for years with Ancient Roman law and the everyday clutter of Roman life. You're all fabulous, by Bacchus!

A special thank you to cartoonist Mariana de Oliveira for her artistic impression of Rufius, which can be found at: www.sarahwalton.org.